PRAISE FOR ROBERT DUGONI

"I would follow Robert Dugoni anywhere."

—Lisa Gardner, #1 *New York Times* bestselling author

"Dugoni is a superb storyteller."

—*Boston Globe*

"A writer at the top of his game."

—Authorlink

"An author who seems like he hasn't met a genre he can't conquer."

—Bookreporter

"Dugoni's writing is compellingly quick, simple, and evocative."

—Seattle Book Review

HOLD
STRONG

ALSO BY ROBERT DUGONI

A Killing on the Hill

The World Played Chess

The Extraordinary Life of Sam Hell

The 7th Canon

Damage Control

The Keera Duggan Series

Her Deadly Game

Beyond Reasonable Doubt

The Charles Jenkins Series

The Eighth Sister

The Last Agent

The Silent Sisters

The Tracy Crosswhite Series

My Sister's Grave

Her Final Breath

In the Clearing

The Trapped Girl

Close to Home

A Steep Price

A Cold Trail

In Her Tracks

What She Found

One Last Kill

"The Last Line" (a short story)

"The Academy" (a short story)

"Third Watch" (a short story)

The David Sloane Series

The Jury Master

Wrongful Death

Bodily Harm

Murder One

The Conviction

Nonfiction
with Joseph Hilldorfer

The Cyanide Canary

HOLD STRONG

A NOVEL

ROBERT DUGONI

JEFF LANGHOLZ
and CHRIS CRABTREE

LAKE UNION
PUBLISHING

Published by Lake Union Publishing, Seattle

www.apub.com

Amazon, the Amazon logo, and Lake Union Publishing are trademarks of Amazon.com, Inc., or its affiliates.

ISBN-13: 9781662516313 (hardcover)
ISBN-13: 9781662516306 (paperback)
ISBN-13: 9781662516320 (digital)

Cover design by Jarrod Taylor
Cover image: ©Trevor Penfold / Alamy; ©simonkr, ©Solskin, ©Giordano Cipriani, ©diatrezor / Getty; ©r.classen / Shutterstock
Interior image: Photo courtesy of the National Archives, Record Group 111-SCA, Book 3769, Photo 184798

Printed in the United States of America

First edition

To all the men and women who served in World War II.
May we always honor the sacrifices they made and protect the
freedoms for which they fought.

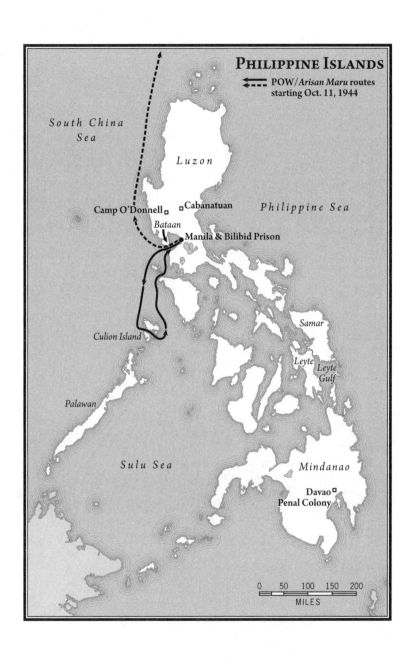

PHILIPPINE ISLANDS

◄▬▬▬ POW/*Arisan Maru* routes
starting Oct. 11, 1944

South China Sea

Luzon

Philippine Sea

□ Cabanatuan

Camp O'Donnell □

Bataan

● Manila & Bilibid Prison

Samar

Leyte
Leyte Gulf

Culion Island

Palawan

Sulu Sea

Mindanao

Davao □
Penal Colony

0   50   100   150   200
MILES

PROLOGUE

The Arisan Maru
Pier 7, Manila Harbor, Philippines
October 11, 1944

Sam Carlson stepped from the gangplank, following the single-file line of haggard prisoners of war onto the 420-foot gray Japanese freighter, the *Arisan Maru*. The human chain behind him stretched from the ship's deck, down the fifteen-foot gangplank, then bent right for another four hundred feet along Pier 7. Eighteen hundred men—walking skeletons who had managed, somehow, to survive years rotting in Japanese POW camps in the Philippines—would be boarding. Where this ship was headed, they did not know.

Throughout September, Japanese guards had transferred POWs from Camp Cabanatuan to the Bilibid Prison, fueling rumors the US had negotiated a prisoner exchange. Early this morning, their captors had ordered the POWs to this transport without providing any information on their destination, though daily sightings of American warplanes over their prison camp, and later over the prison, as well as the sound of Allied bombs exploding nearby, indicated the war neared its final days. It was something unthinkable when General Douglas MacArthur had abandoned the Philippines on March 11, 1942, and the men had been ordered to surrender. The Japanese military machine had seemed unstoppable then, and MacArthur's vow to return just far-fetched propaganda.

Two and a half years later, MacArthur had returned and the POWs' freedom seemed imminent.

Japan was losing the war.

Sam and his fellow POWs were, mercifully, going home.

Maybe.

The clang of a bell high atop the ship's superstructure announced its imminent departure. The bell reminded Sam of a poem Father Thomas Scecina, Sam's close friend, had often recited during the hell they endured in the POW camps—torture, starvation, beatings, and executions. The poem was about turning darkness into bell towers. POWs becoming like bells. And as they ring, what pummels them becomes their strength.

"We're probably going to Japan or Korea," Pete Chavez said from directly behind Sam. "Someplace cold." The twenty-one-year-old private first class tugged on the tattered clothing they'd been issued before their transfer from Cabanatuan. "Why else would they provide us this fine clothing straight from Marshall Field's?" Sam didn't know about that, but he did know he didn't trust his captors. Still, he figured anywhere would be better than the Philippines' oppressive heat and humidity, and unrelenting mosquitos.

Father Tom, directly ahead, turned and said, "There's a rumor spreading that the Red Cross negotiated a prisoner exchange."

"I heard Formosa or Japan," another POW said. "Heard they're going to work us in the mines."

Father Tom stopped and stared up at the ship's superstructure. He looked concerned.

"What is it, Padre?" Sam asked.

Father Tom nodded to the ship's masts. "No Red Cross markings."

The Geneva Convention mandated a freighter fly a Red Cross flag or pennant to signal nonmilitary cargo.

Chavez grunted. "Bastards told us the Geneva Convention didn't apply to them or to us. What makes you think they'd start following those rules now?"

Father Tom looked as if he was about to answer, but a commotion in the line ahead of them drew the men's attention. Five armed Japanese guards roughly searched each prisoner, ostensibly for weapons or contraband, but they were also stealing the POWs' last few treasures.

One took a wedding ring. Another took a POW's watch, then slapped him hard across the face.

"Here we go again," Chavez said. "Gotta tip the bellhops."

Sam pinched the hem of the ragged vest he'd fashioned from a green Army blanket and felt Sarah's high school class ring, which he'd sewn into the vest's lining along with a small pocketknife. The guards would take Sarah's ring if they found it.

They'd kill Sam if they found his pocketknife.

Father Tom, aware of Sam's hidden items and the consequences if found, gave him a grave look as they neared the inspection point. The guards hardly searched the priest before waving him on. When Father Tom stepped forward, he glanced back at Sam and made the sign of the cross. Nothing else the priest *could* do but throw it upstairs, Sam thought.

"Speedo. Speedo! Hands. Hands. Raise hands!" a guard shouted.

Sam stepped forward, hands raised, but Chavez cut in front of him, smiling at their tormentors and raising his shirt, offering his stomach and chest like a cat seeking a belly scratch. "Have at it, boys. Don't be shy," he said as the guards ran their hands over his emaciated body. "That's the ticket. Oh yeah. A little lower, if you wouldn't mind."

"You done," an embarrassed guard said. He shoved Chavez, nearly knocking him down.

They turned to Sam, their hands moving over his body. Sam held his breath.

Chavez again stepped to the guards with a goofy grin. "Excuse me, fellas, but I heard this luxury liner has got shuffleboard on deck. Tell me it's so!"

The guards couldn't have understood more than a word or two of what Chavez was saying, but they knew he was needling them. They surged toward him. One swung a bamboo cane, striking Chavez across the shoulder, though without any real force behind the blow.

Chavez spun, and in doing so, he shoved Sam in front of him, away from the guards. He used his emaciated arms to block the blows. "No shuffleboard! Sheesh. Got it," Chavez said, before falling back in line.

"Thanks, Pete," Sam said under his breath.

"Don't mention it," he said. Then he shouted to the others in the line, which continued to surge forward. "Once we check into our cabins, let's belly up to the bar, boys. Who's with me in raising a pint of ale to our kind and generous hosts?"

The line's momentum stalled. POWs whispered and pointed at the upper deck. Katsuo Yoshida, their tormentor—and Sam's, above all—leaned over the metal railing and leered down at them beneath his Civil War kepi–style cap.

3

"Faster, please," Yoshida called out. The former English professor had been educated in America and worked at the University of Tokyo. "Move faster. We are behind schedule."

"If I get the chance, I'll kill that bastard," Sam said.

Father Tom, who had waited for Sam and Chavez, said softly, "We're close now. You're so close to going home."

"Padre's right," Chavez said, looking up at Yoshida. "I'd kill the son of a bitch myself. He's given us all a good taste of hell, and I'd like to send him there for eternity, but"—Chavez swiveled his hips—"I got a date with a certain hula dancer in Hawaii."

The line moved again, and Sam dutifully shuffled forward.

Moments later, Chavez halted. "Whoa. End of the line, amigos."

They'd reached a six-foot-square opening in the freighter's deck. Weakened POWs descended a steep, narrow wooden staircase into darkness, the first indication they would travel inside the freighter's hold rather than on deck. Sam looked back at the line behind him. "How can we all fit?" he said to no one in particular. "Must be a thousand men down there already and at least that many behind us."

"We can't," Scecina said.

As if in answer to Sam's question, the POWs already in the hold passed an unconscious soldier up the staircase. Others laid him on the deck. Chavez knelt, fanning fresh air on the man's face. "Wake up, buddy," he said. If he didn't, the Japanese would kill him.

"No. No," Yoshida screamed. "Only down. Only down. Faster, faster."

"Speedo. Speedo," the guards repeated, using bamboo sticks and bayonets to prod the POWs forward.

Chavez took a deep breath, then bleated loudly, like a herded sheep. "Baa, baa."

Dozens joined him as they trudged toward the hatchway. A guard cracked Chavez across the face with a bamboo pole. Chavez winced, smiled, and spat a bloody wad near the guard's boot. He gave Sam a wink. "Just pulling the wool over their eyes."

"Go," Sam said.

But Chavez wasn't finished. He perched on the hatchway's edge, puffed out his bony chest, raised both arms to the men behind him, and boomed in his best General MacArthur voice, "People of the Philippines. I shall return!" He gave a dramatic salute, quickly ducked under another bamboo strike, and descended the staircase, keeping up his running monologue. "Don't forget, boys, I get the king-size bed and the window cabin."

Sam followed Chavez down into muggy, stifling heat and the familiar, horrific stench of sweating bodies, excrement, soiled clothes, puke, and diesel fumes from the ship's engines. He choked back vomit and waved at swarms of flies. Beneath him men moaned in agony, cried out for water, and pleaded for air. Chavez stopped on the stairs, which halted Sam's descent, but the guards, becoming more agitated by Yoshida's insistent orders, kept forcing POWs down the staircase.

"Stop pushing," Sam yelled back above him. "It's blocked. Wait till the line moves."

He fought to hold his position, but the weight of the POWs pressed down, becoming heavier. He stuck out his left foot to find a perch but found only air and tumbled off the narrow staircase.

He thought he'd been to hell inside the POW camps, but as he fell into the darkness and stench, he sensed a depth of madness he never could have conceived.

PART 1

1

OPTIONS AND OPPORTUNITIES

Eagle Grove, Minnesota
May 26, 1938

Sarah Haber stared at her reflection in the compact case's round mirror, her little sister, Nora, watching closely from Sarah's bed in their second-story room. Sarah grabbed a tissue and wiped off the red Max Factor lipstick, and the rouge, then tossed the tissue into the trash can. A light breeze caused the thin curtain across the narrow window to flutter, indicating the temperature in Eagle Grove was finally starting to cool with the fading light of day.

"You wiped it off? Why?" Nora asked. She lay on her stomach, chin propped on her hands.

Sarah shrugged. "It isn't me underneath all this stuff."

Nora sat. "Can you make me up?"

"And have Mom pitch a hissy? I don't think so."

Her mother had given Sarah the compact and other makeup as a high school graduation present, telling her, "Now that you'll be going off to college, you'll have some need to look your best."

Whatever that meant.

Her mother hadn't allowed Sarah to wear makeup while attending Eagle Grove High, though the other nineteen girls in Sarah's senior class had. It had been another subject of their teasing, along with Sarah not being the least bit interested in cheerleading at the football or basketball games, and Sarah not getting all worked up or waiting breathlessly to be asked to the school dances. Like with makeup, Sarah really hadn't cared about the dances or any of the boys with whom she'd ultimately gone. An equal number of boys and girls in her class had assured her a date.

"Do you have a date with Sam?" Nora asked.

"I do."

Sarah should've just ignored her. Now Nora's questions would fall on her in waves. "Have you and Sam kissed?" "What's it like kissing a boy?" When those elicited no answers, Nora heaved an exasperated sigh and withdrew to safer ground. "Why are you wearing *that* sweater?"

"Because it's comfortable."

"Comfortable?" As if this were the most ludicrous consideration imaginable. "'Baggy,' you mean."

"Because it's baggy, then," Sarah said.

"It's a *mom* sweater."

"Mom has some lovely sweaters."

Nora could only moan at this. Then, after a freighted pause, she asked, "Can I go with you?"

"You'd be the only ten-year-old there. You'd be too lonely."

"I could sit in the projection booth with you and Sam."

"I don't think so."

"Why not? Are you going to be smooching?"

Sarah only smiled.

"Ooooh," Nora cooed.

Sarah and Sam seemed an odd pairing on the surface. Sam excelled in sports, and just about every girl in their class had practically swooned when he'd passed in the halls. He was over six feet, with blonde hair and blue eyes. The girls said he looked like the actor Dick Powell. Sarah had never looked that closely, and she hadn't been trying to get a boyfriend, but Sam had started showing up at the school library, trying to get her to close her books and go into town. When she hadn't, he'd sat across the table from her and opened his books, then walked her home. Turned out, despite all his accomplishments on the athletic fields, Sam wasn't the brash, full-of-himself athlete Sarah had thought him to be. He had a tender and caring side. School hadn't come as naturally to him as sports, but he wanted to go to college. That was no longer on the table, however. The Depression had hit his family hard. College was not a luxury the Carlsons could afford.

"When you go off to college," Nora said, "can I sleep in your bed?"

Sarah heard a catch in her little sister's voice and turned to see a tear roll down her cheek. "Hey, why are you crying?"

"I'm going to miss you."

Sarah closed the compact and went to her bed. She stroked Nora's hair. "You'll still have Tommy." Tommy was their eight-year-old brother.

"Ugh. Don't remind me."

"And I'm not leaving forever," Sarah said. "I'll be home for Christmas. You won't even miss me."

"I will so," Nora said, rolling onto her back. "I wish I could go to college."

"Someday, you will," Sarah said. At least she hoped that would be the case. Sarah would be the first woman from Eagle Grove High School to attend college, just like she'd been the school's first female valedictorian. There were other bright girls, she knew, but unlike them, Sarah hadn't sat in class pretending to be a dumb bunny. When she'd known the answer to a question, she'd given it. The other girls had called her "bookworm" and other unflattering nicknames, but that, too, had never stopped Sarah. She'd earned a full academic scholarship to Mankato State Teachers College in Minnesota, where she planned to study mathematics, then return to teach at Eagle Grove. She wanted her little sister to also look beyond classes such as home economics, typing, shorthand dictation, and bookkeeping, as she had, and instead take math—a subject Sarah had a special affinity for—science, English, history, and Latin.

Their mother knocked on their bedroom door and pushed it open. Their father stood behind her in the narrow hall. "Nora," their mother said, "go down and play with your little brother a minute."

"I don't want to play with him. He picks his nose and eats it."

"He doesn't," their mother said.

"He does so. He picks it to annoy me."

"Go down and watch your brother pick his nose, then," their father said. "We'd like to talk to Sarah."

"About Sam?" Nora said, practically singing the name.

"I'll give you until the count of three," their father said. "One . . ."

"I'm going. I'm going," Nora said, climbing off the bed and moving to the doorway. "Sarah and Sam sitting in a tree," she sang. "K-I-S-S . . ."

"Go." Their father grabbed her by the head and pointed her in the direction of the staircase.

When Nora had left, their mother stepped in close to Sarah. "You're not wearing any makeup."

Sarah felt guilty. She knew her mother had gotten the compact from her father's pharmacy downtown, a luxury most people in Eagle Grove couldn't afford these days.

"I think I'm going to need you to show me," Sarah said, knowing the answer would please her mom.

Her mother and father sat on the edge of Nora's bed. This would be a serious conversation.

"You're going to the picture show with Sam?" her mother asked.

Sarah nodded.

"Your father and I wanted to talk with you for a moment about that," her mother said. Then she elbowed her father, who sat with his head down, gazing at the floor.

He lifted his head. "That's right, honey. We . . . uh . . . we like Sam. We do. But . . ."

Sarah waited, uncertain. "But . . . ?"

"But you're going off to college," her mother said with a smile that looked pained.

"You're going to be meeting lots of new people," her father added.

"Girls," her mother said, "and boys."

"What are you saying?" Sarah said.

"What your mother—" her father started, then, after a stern look from his wife, amended to "What *we're* trying to say is there are going to be a lot of college men you will meet. Men studying engineering and medicine and law."

"And business," her mother chimed in. "You've worked so hard, Sarah, and you've earned this opportunity."

"To do what?"

"To meet all these people. Your father and I are just concerned that you're going to forsake some of these opportunities because, well, because of Sam."

"Sam's my boyfriend," Sarah said. "He's kind and caring. He's not like other boys."

"Of course he is," her father said. "Kind and caring, I mean. And we're not saying we don't like Sam and his family. We just don't want you to pass up opportunities at Mankato. We think maybe it would be best if you and Sam were to put your relationship on hold . . . until you finish college. That way you won't be holding each other back."

"I love Sam."

"You think you do," her mother said. "But love . . . changes."

"It didn't for you. You married Dad." Her mother and father had been high school sweethearts.

"Yes. But I didn't have the opportunities back then that you have now, Sarah."

"Are you saying you wouldn't have married Dad?"

"Are you saying that?" her father said.

"No, of course not," her mother said, jabbing him with another elbow.

"Of course not," her father agreed.

"I'm just saying with the Depression and all . . . Well, wouldn't it be exciting to marry a doctor? Or someone running his own company? You're so good in math, you could be his bookkeeper."

"I don't want to be anyone's bookkeeper. I want to come back here and teach at Eagle Grove."

"You think you do," her mother said. "We both know that."

"But dreams change, Sarah," her father said. "As you get older, you may find you want different things in life. We just want what's best for you, that's all. As our daughter. Because we love you. We just want you to be well cared for, especially with this Depression going on and no end in sight."

"What about happiness?"

"What about it?" her mother asked.

"Don't you want me to be happy?"

"Of course we do, sweetheart," her father said.

"But don't you think you'd be happy married to a doctor?" her mother asked.

"Sam makes me happy. He loves me for who I am. I don't have to pretend with Sam."

"All we're saying," her father said, looking to Sarah's mother and then giving Sarah that furrowed brow he pulled into service when he wanted to bring a subject to a close, "is that we don't want you to pass up opportunities that you'd like to pursue at Mankato. Can you promise us that you'll at least keep an open mind to whatever opportunities come your way?"

2

DREAMS; NOT YET

Eagle Grove, Minnesota
May 26, 1938

Seventeen-year-old Sam Carlson walked Main Street on an unseasonably warm evening, doing his best to ignore the newspapers covering the windows of so many shops, and the dark mood that gripped those Eagle Grove residents who remained. The Great Depression that began in 1929 had ripped through the town like a tornado, cutting a path of economic destruction and despair. Eagle Grove's two thousand remaining residents had fought hard to survive, but nine years of economic blight had closed their businesses, emptied their bank accounts, and left many homeless. Successive droughts had withered farmers' crops to dust and killed what livestock they did not sell. Desperate families left town in overloaded jalopies in search of work.

Sam had listened on the radio to President Franklin Delano Roosevelt's 1936 speech to the Democratic National Convention, promising Americans better economic times, what he called their "rendezvous with destiny." But two years after FDR's speech, economic recovery seemed further away than ever, especially in Eagle Grove.

Sam's focus this night was the Paradise Theater's marquee. The two-story brick building had become his and other residents' refuge, drawing the townspeople the way a lighthouse guided ships through a storm. The theater was the only air-conditioned building in town, and it played uplifting movies. For ten cents a ticket, Eagle Grove's down-and-out could escape the heat, the Depression, and their misery, if only for ninety minutes. The films carried moviegoers miles from their desolate hometown to exotic locations filled with joy and laughter, music and dance, romance, and happy endings. They could glimpse better lives and better places—where FDR's promise of a "rendezvous with destiny" had seemingly already arrived.

Sam worked multiple jobs—selling newspapers, sacking groceries, and often doing grueling farm labor—but he liked working in the projection room best.

The films allowed him to dream.

And, when he had a date with Sarah, to neck a little.

Outside the theater's entrance, he paused to admire the poster of dapper Fred Astaire and stunning Ginger Rogers. Tonight's movie, *Shall We Dance*, was the couple's seventh film in just five years. Sam had seen all seven films so many times from the projection booth, he knew each plot and could recite—and often did—every line along with the actors.

Sam's reflection in the large glass window was a sharp contrast to Fred's glamorous clothing. He'd worn his thin cotton shirt to its threads, and his pants had holes in the knees his mother had yet to patch. He walked barefoot, wearing shoes only to and from school, to church, and while playing sports.

Despite his circumstances, Sam couldn't help but dream of a life as glorious as a Hollywood actor's—not on screen, but maybe a life that others might read about, or even be inspired by.

But then he'd catch himself. Who was he kidding? He'd been a decent enough student at Eagle Grove High, and though he'd entered high school hoping to move on to college, that was no longer in the cards. What actually remained in the cards he didn't know. His plan B, to work the dairy farm, was gone too. Ever since he could walk, he'd followed his father around their ninety-acre dairy farm. Twice a day he had helped milk their seventy-five Holsteins. The milk, cream, and butter they produced had earned the family a decent income and a pleasant life—until the Great Depression hit and the drought forced his father to sell their cows one by one. When he could no longer make loan payments on the house and the land, the bank had foreclosed. His father had moved Sam and his mom, two sisters, and cousin to a rental closer to town.

They had no place else to go. Unable to find work and desperate to feed his family, Sam's father ultimately accepted public assistance through the government's Works Progress Administration. Taking the handout had devastated him. Sam vowed he'd someday buy back his family's farm and restock the cows. At the moment, however, making good on that vow felt as far off as achieving his dream to have a life like the actors in the films he watched.

Sam stepped into the theater lobby and savored the cool air. The Paradise's air-conditioning might have been an even bigger draw than Fred and Ginger. During the scorching summer weekends, unemployed residents would watch the same movie three times in a single day just to escape the heat.

"Two cups?" Mr. Larsen asked Sam from behind the long wooden counter. He adjusted his wire-rimmed glasses and smoothed the tufts of white hair on the sides of his otherwise bald head. His red suspenders held up gray trousers and stretched across his blue collared shirt. A Great War veteran, Mr. Larsen had nearly died in France, and had come home with a body too broken to farm. He and his wife had opened the town's only movie theater, and though the expense of a show was now a luxury most residents could hardly afford, the Paradise, like Mr. Larsen, soldiered on.

"Yes, sir," Sam said. "Thank you, Mr. Larsen."

"Coming right up." Mr. Larsen stepped to the popcorn machine and filled a paper bag for Sam while Mrs. Larsen poured Sam a Coke from the fountain.

"How's your family, Sam?" she asked.

"We're doing well," he said. His family was anything but well, but his mother and father had told him everyone had their own problems and didn't want to hear theirs.

Mr. Larsen handed him a generous bag of fresh, buttery popcorn, and Mrs. Larsen gave him the Coke and an extra paper cup.

"Thanks," Sam said. They all knew the popcorn and Coke would be Sam's dinner.

Just past the counter, Sam climbed a curved staircase to the upper balcony, then the steps between the rows of balcony seats to the very top. There, he kneed open the door to the small projection room, flipped on the light switch with an elbow, and carefully set his drink, popcorn, and extra cup on a small table beside one of the two mounted projectors.

He removed the lid from the film canister on the first of the two short cartoons that would precede the movie, and extracted the reel, then threaded the film through the projector, clicked on the machine's power, and confirmed it hummed to life. The projector's arc light cast the film's image through the rectangular opening in the projection room to the massive screen ninety feet away, and the sound roared from six speakers mounted along the theater's side walls.

Satisfied everything was as it should be, Sam shut off the projector, switched on a small desk fan, and grabbed the arm of a second tall chair, sliding it across the floor beside his own. He looked through the rectangular opening, peering down to watch Mrs. Larsen usher customers to their seats.

After several minutes, he smiled when he glimpsed Sarah entering the theater. She stopped to chat with Mrs. Larsen, as she did each visit, but this time they no doubt discussed the *Minneapolis Star*'s article on the class of 1938's graduation, and its mention of Sarah's scholarship to attend Mankato State Teachers College in Mankato, Minnesota, in the fall.

Sam was happy for Sarah, but he also couldn't help but be envious of her college plans. He also worried that the college boys at Mankato would be more what Sarah wanted, well educated and worldly, that they could offer her things Sam couldn't.

The house lights lowered—the Larsens' signal to Sam to begin. He moved back from the window, flipped the projector switches, and ran the first of the two cartoons, Mickey Mouse. When finished, he switched on the second projector for the second cartoon, which he'd already loaded, Donald Duck. And while it ran, he rewound Mickey Mouse, removed it, and loaded the first of the reels to *Shall We Dance*. Opening credits flashed on the screen, set to the Gershwin brothers' lively music, and those in attendance cheered and applauded when Fred Astaire entered.

The projection room door slid quietly open. Sarah stepped in.

Sam stood, gave a deep, exaggerated bow, then made a sweeping motion toward her chair like Fred and said, "Ginger, your chair awaits. Best seat in the house."

"Fred," Sarah whispered. She kissed him lightly as she passed, but he pulled her back, needing more. He kissed her harder, until Sarah pushed him away with a giggle and eased onto the wooden chair. "I want to watch the movie," she said.

"I've seen it a dozen times already," Sam said.

"Well, I haven't."

Sam had hoped to neck, and maybe a little more. Sarah's reputation at school had been as a bookworm, given her grades. Other boys in his class hadn't seen her the way Sam did. She wasn't loud, the way some other girls were just to get attention. She hadn't tried to hide her intelligence in class; when she'd known the answer to a question, and she usually had, she'd said it. Her smile was genuine, not intended to flirt, and her blonde hair and sparkling hazel eyes gave her a natural beauty, though she wore no makeup. Sam's mom said Sarah also had "gumption."

Sarah slid the empty paper cup toward Sam, and he poured her half his Coke, careful not to spill. They raised the cups and tapped the edges like the clinking of champagne glasses, then Sarah settled back to watch the movie from their private suite while Sam rewound the Donald Duck cartoon reel and loaded the second film canister to *Shall We Dance* on the second projector. In between, they sipped their drinks and shared the bag of popcorn. Part of tonight's film took place on a luxury ocean liner, a floating palace. Sam remained patient because he knew Sarah hadn't seen the film, but his mind was still on her leaving for college at the end of summer. At times she already seemed to be pulling away. Maybe she thought it would make their separation easier, or maybe she was already just growing apart from him.

In the film, Fred proposed marriage to Ginger, but she refused.

Sam shifted in his seat, relating to Fred's pain.

Sarah's gaze darted from the film to Sam. "Are you all right?"

"Fine." He forced a smile.

"You're so quiet tonight."

"Just things on my mind."

"Such as?"

"You," he said. And leaned in for a kiss.

She smiled. "Charmer." She gave him what felt like an obligatory peck. When Sam tried to tickle her waist, she squirmed and said, "Stop. I want to see what happens."

So did Sam, but not what happened in the movie. In the end, Ginger professed her love for Fred and the movie ended happily.

"Wasn't that good?" Sarah said.

"Yeah," Sam said, removing the last reel after rewinding it, and putting it back in its canister. "But not exactly like real life here in Eagle Grove."

"You have to see things as half-full, not half-empty."

"I see things as they are. Happy endings are rare." He stopped himself, realizing he was sabotaging his carefully thought-out plans. "I liked the ending, especially when he finally gets the girl." He thought it sounded genuine.

"You're a romantic, Sam Carlson."

"I guess so," he said. He quickly cleaned the projection room before they descended into the lobby. Most who'd attended had already departed. Mr. and Mrs. Larsen cleaned up behind the counter.

"Hopefully a good night. They could sure use it," Sam said to Sarah.

"Sixteen dollars and fifty cents," she said. "Based on the number of people in the theater and figuring those people spent a total of six dollars or so for candy, popcorn, and fountain drinks," Sarah said. "Give or take."

"I thought you wanted to watch the movie."

"I could do both."

"Brilliant," Sam said, but he worried Sarah's preoccupation was further evidence she was moving beyond him.

"Not so brilliant, really," she said, feigning modesty. "Just simple math."

"For you," he said. "Not for anyone else."

Outside, the sweltering day had at last cooled, and a chorus of crickets and cicadas serenaded Sam and Sarah as they strolled hand in hand down Main Street. Lightning bugs blinked in the sultry air, and Sarah's perfume smelled like spring flowers. When they passed the town's only department store, Sam paused before the three female mannequins in the window. Part of his plan.

"That one is my favorite." Sam pointed to the mannequin dressed in a long wedding gown made of white silk and satin. A white veil adorned her head.

"A hopeless romantic," Sarah teased.

"Guilty as charged."

"She's very pretty," she said. "But not much personality."

Sam didn't care that each mannequin had worn the same dress for years. He didn't care if the Fred and Ginger movies were a reality he would never live. He wore torn and patched clothes and stood in bare feet, and he had never ventured beyond the state's borders.

But he still had a chance to get the girl.

Sarah tugged Sam's elbow and steered him down Main to Maple Street, leafy trees lining the avenue leading to Sarah's home. Sam slowed their pace and pointed to Polaris, the North Star; the only star he knew by name. "Star light, star bright . . . ," he began.

Sarah turned to face the North Star and together they said, "I wish I may, I wish I might, have the wish I wish tonight."

Sam had a special wish this night. He shut his eyes tight, but Sarah tugged his hand and arm and they walked on.

A block later, Sam pointed to the tall steeple atop the white clapboard church. "The miracle of Eagle Grove," he said with a chuckle.

On a pitch-black night the previous autumn, just past midnight, the cast-iron church bell had rung, seemingly on its own. Dozens of confused residents had stumbled from their beds and their homes and stared as the bell clanged. The minister had rushed from his home to the church and unlocked it, expecting to find pranksters, but instead finding no one. He'd declared the spontaneous ringing bell "a miracle."

The prank had been Sarah's idea—a chance to supply a harmless glimmer of hope to a town that had about run out of it. Sam had taken a ninety-foot strand of wire scrounged from his family's abandoned dairy farm, scaled the church roof, and connected the wire to the bell, then unspooled it to their hiding spot in a nearby tree. When finished, Sam unthreaded the line and removed the only evidence of their prank.

Sam had dreamed of someday marrying Sarah in that church, she in the white silk dress from the store window, he in a tuxedo like Fred Astaire's.

No time like the present.

As Sarah turned from the church, Sam dropped to a knee on the sidewalk, lifted a closed palm toward her, and opened it. She clasped her hands in a steeple over her mouth, her eyes wide.

"It was my grandmother's ring," he said. The diamond sparkled in the ambient light. "Please marry me, Sarah Haber." He nodded to the white wooden church. "Right there."

"Oh, Sam," Sarah said softly, then closed her eyes.

Long seconds passed without a response. Then Sarah gently folded Sam's fingers back around the ring and guided him to his feet. Sam's heart sank. He didn't know what to say. They walked the final three blocks to Sarah's home in silence.

At her front gate, Sam said, "Is that a no?"

"It's a 'not yet,'" she said.

3

Rendezvous with Destiny

Eagle Grove, Minnesota
May 26, 1938

After walking Sarah home, Sam returned to the tiny rented house at the town's edge. He refused to call it home. He considered it temporary, despite the reality of his family's circumstances. He stepped onto the front porch and eyed the house's cracked walls and busted screen door. His English teacher would call the broken house a metaphor for Sam's life. And he wouldn't be wrong.

Sam wanted to feel sorry for himself, but he knew Sarah's "not yet" had been the right answer. She was being who she was, pragmatic. They were both still teenagers. They had their futures ahead of them, though Sarah's future seemed a lot brighter and more interesting. Still, Sam knew they shouldn't get engaged just because he feared losing her. His mother had told him that was no way to build a relationship, let alone a marriage, when he'd asked her about his grandmother's ring and told her his plans. He wished he'd listened to her. Now he looked desperate.

His mother, perhaps having anticipated Sarah's answer, had also said Sarah had her own dreams, worthy dreams. After college Sarah wanted to teach, not just cook, clean, and have babies. She'd said in the newspaper article that she wanted young women to dream bigger, especially in these hard economic times, where every nickel and dime counted. Sam's mother had reminded him that Sarah had gumption, and of the time in their senior year, before they'd begun dating, when their history teacher, Mr. Pembroke, had made the mistake of saying, "Women must understand their proper role in society. After all, women have never produced anything of value to the world."

Sarah, of all people, had stood, and although usually quiet and respectful, she'd said, "And your existence certainly proves that proposition." Then, she'd gathered her books and walked to the classroom door. About to leave, she'd turned back to her shocked instructor and classmates and added, "The chief 'product' of women, in case you hadn't noticed, is men. I'll leave you all to decide if that 'product' holds any value to the world."

It wasn't the moment Sam fell in love with Sarah, but it was the moment he'd noticed her as much more than the smartest person in the class. Sarah had not been afraid to speak her mind, and what she'd had to say was profound. Sam didn't think he'd ever admired anyone more, so much so that he, too, had hurried from the classroom, while Mr. Pembroke and everyone else remained in a state of stunned silence. He searched the hallway but didn't see Sarah. Ordinarily if you wanted to find her, the place to look was the school library, but Sam didn't think she'd gone there. He hurriedly dodged students as they exited their classrooms for their lockers. Outside the school's front door, he looked about. Sarah walked quickly across the lawn. He shuffled down the steps and hurried after her, calling her name.

"Sarah! Hey, Sarah Haber!"

When he got close, he reached out and touched her elbow, but she pulled it away and walked on.

"Hey," he said, realizing she was crying.

"What do you want?"

"Are you all right?"

"What do you care?"

"I just . . . It seems like you're upset."

"Of course I'm upset."

"Why? I think you had every right to say what you said back there."

She stopped and stared at him. "You do?"

"Sure. I mean . . ."

"Then why didn't you say something? Why didn't anyone say anything? You all just sat there like a bunch of zombies." She started off again.

Sam followed. "You're right. I should have said something. At least I shouldn't have agreed with him. I mean, I don't agree with him. If my mom had heard him say what he said, she would have done the same thing you did."

"Fat lot of good that will do me now. I'm sure he's down at Principal Dean's office and I'll be suspended. How is that going to look on my college applications? Not to mention what my mother is going to say. She'll tell me I should have just held my tongue."

"Is there anything I can do?"

"There's nothing *anyone* can do."

"I'm sorry," he said. "Could I at least walk you home?"

"Why? I'm not some pity case, Sam Carlson."

"I didn't say you were."

"Then why do you want to walk me home?"

"Well, they've been having problems with aliens here in Eagle Grove. I don't know if you know that."

She rolled her eyes and kept walking, but he thought he might've seen the start of a smile lift the corner of her pretty mouth.

"I'm serious. I heard they send down a beam of light and people just disappear in an instant."

"People are disappearing because of the Depression," she said.

"No," he said. "That's what we all think, but really, it's aliens with these ray guns."

She sighed. "What would little green men with ray guns want with us?"

"Well, it seems that they're from the planet Mongo and have this evil ruler Ming who's trying to destroy planet Earth."

"That's Flash Gordon. I took my little brother and sister to see *Topper* and *Flash Gordon* was the short."

"You were at the Paradise?"

"It's the only building in Eagle Grove with air-conditioning. Everyone was there."

"Would you like to go again this Saturday?"

"I told you I already saw the movie."

"Yeah, but not from the best seat in the house."

She looked at him, warily.

"I work in the projection room. The sound is better in there, and nobody's head is in your way. Besides, they'll be showing a different movie, *A Star Is Born* with Janet Gaynor and Fredric March."

"I don't have the money."

"That's the beauty of working the projectors. I get in for free, and I can bring a guest. Come on. It will be fun. Mr. and Mrs. Larsen give me a Coke and a popcorn."

Sarah stopped walking again. She seemed to be searching for words, then said, "Why are you asking me? Seems you could ask any girl in the class."

"Yeah, but you're the one who told off Pembroke."

Sarah smiled.

After walking Sarah home, and securing a date for Saturday night, Sam went to the house his parents were renting. His mother was in the kitchen, and he told her what had happened in class. "Sarah's afraid she's going to get in trouble, maybe suspended, that it will hurt her chances of getting into college."

His mother seemed to digest what he'd said, which had been purposeful. Sam knew it would make her angry. "Watch your sisters and cousin for me."

"Where are you going?"

"To let Mr. Pembroke and Mr. Dean know a woman's purpose."

Sarah didn't receive any disciplinary action, which surprised others in their class, but not Sam. When he told his mother the next day, she said, "He wouldn't have dared."

———

Sam slapped at a mosquito feasting on his forearm, leaving a red blotch of blood, then flicked the insect away. If he could change anything about Eagle Grove it would be the hot, humid summers, and the blood-sucking mosquitos.

He pulled open the screen door and entered the kitchen. His mom dried her hands on her stained apron, then hugged him. "How was the show?"

"Good," he said. "You should come, Mom. Mr. Larsen said you could sit in the projection booth with me."

She smiled and put a hand to his cheek. "I won't take charity from others who can hardly afford it, Sam. And Sarah. How is Sarah?" Which he knew was the real topic she wished to discuss.

"She's fine."

"Looking forward to college, I'd imagine."

"Very much," he said.

"You okay?"

He smiled. "Not much choice, Mom."

"I know," she whispered. "I assume you asked her?"

"I did."

"And her answer?"

"Practical Sarah," he said, opening his hand and giving back the ring. He kept it light. God knew his mother had enough troubles of her own. "She said, 'Not yet.'"

"That is Sarah; isn't it?" she said, matching his tone. "It makes sense."

His mother had done her best to keep her spirits up when around Sam and his younger siblings, but the Depression years had taken a toll on her and his father. They were just thirty-six, but each year the Depression had etched deeper crow's-feet around their eyes and worry lines around their mouths, and his mother's blue eyes had lost more of their luster. Gray strands twisted through her blonde hair.

"How was work?" she asked, changing the subject. She sounded tired.

"Not much today." Sam pulled a few coins from his pants pocket—money he had earned running the projectors—and handed them to her. Then he slumped into a wobbly metal chair at the kitchen table.

She kissed him on the forehead. "Are you sure you are okay?"

"I'm fine," he said. "Just worn out from this heat."

"It certainly saps your strength." She stepped across the worn linoleum floor to a cupboard and put the coins in a tin can.

Sam's two little sisters entered the kitchen then, dressed in their pajamas, their smiles wide and bright in anticipation. He opened a crumpled paper bag, and poured a dozen or so fluffy white popcorn kernels into their cupped hands. Mr. Larsen gave him any remaining popcorn at the end of the night.

The girls beamed, which always made Sam sad, a reminder of how little they had.

The popcorn-sharing ritual, like the church bell prank, had been Sarah's idea. Rays of hope were her specialty.

Sam's five-year-old cousin, Jacob, also wandered into the kitchen, half-asleep and dragging his worn blanket. Jacob had joined their household a year earlier, when Sam's uncle had become a Depression statistic and taken his own life and his aunt had had a nervous breakdown. The Carlsons could barely feed themselves, but his mother and father had warmly accepted Jacob.

"Here you go," Sam said. "I didn't forget you, Jacob." He handed the boy the bag containing the last dozen fluffy pieces.

His father entered the now crowded kitchen, but Sam had nothing left for him. "Hey, Dad."

"Hey, son." His father pulled out a chair and sat. "How was work?"

His father's broad shoulders sagged. His brown hair was turning gray, and his face was furrowed, though not from farming, Sam knew. From worry.

Sam's father made quick eye contact with his wife, and she put her apron on the counter.

"Shoo now. Off to bed," she said to his sisters and cousin, and ushered them from the room.

His father lumbered to the small refrigerator in the corner. He had bought the boxy white appliance when times were good. Its humming motor had affirmed their solidly middle-class station. "I got you something." His father pulled a small metal bowl from the refrigerator, then grabbed a spoon from a drawer. He set the bowl on the kitchen table and sat across from Sam. When Sam didn't eat right away, his father said, "Strawberry. Your favorite." His calloused hand slid the bowl and spoon toward Sam.

Sam wasn't ungrateful. He hadn't tasted ice cream in years. He just knew it wasn't a luxury his father could afford. "You didn't have to do that, Dad."

His father smiled, wistful.

Sam dipped the spoon into the bowl and raised a slightly melted mound to his mouth, but when tears pooled in his father's eyes, Sam's hand froze. He lowered the spoon.

"You've graduated," his father said. "The first member of our family to finish high school." His voice cracked a bit. "And I have nothing for you."

Sam eased the spoon back into the bowl.

"I'm broke," his father said. "I can't help you pay for college. I wish I could, but I can't." A tear slipped down his father's cheek. He quickly wiped it away.

Sam had never seen his father cry, not when he lost the crops, the cattle, the farm, or the house. He felt paralyzed, uncertain what to do or say. He rose from his chair and put an arm around his father's shoulders. His dad lost his last bit of composure, sobbing.

"It's okay, Dad; don't worry about me," Sam said. "You taught me to be a fighter, didn't you? Never give up; remember? I'll make it, Dad, and when I do, I'll help you to get back on your feet and get things back to the way they used to be. We'll be happy again, Dad. You'll see."

At the moment, happy seemed a long way off for all of them.

———

A half hour later, Sam slid onto his thin mattress. His cousin lay in the bed next to him, sleeping peacefully, clutching his popcorn bag. Sam wished he were five again. He wished something as simple as a few popcorn kernels or a bowl of ice cream could make the world right. He rolled onto his back and stared at the ceiling. His words to his father had been hollow. He had no idea how he'd save his family, and he knew their completely, utterly hopeless situation had been the reason for his father's tears. This time Sam ignored Sarah's admonition. "Half-full my ass," he said. "We don't even have a glass."

A mosquito buzzed Sam's head, as if taunting him, then landed on his forearm. Rather than swat it, he let it prick his skin, then balled his hand into a tight fist and squeezed, trapping the mosquito's stinger. The mosquito feasted on his blood, wings beating, body getting fatter, gorging itself.

He raised his hand and smashed the insect, blood marking his arm. Then he wiped it away and rolled onto his side, his grief giving way to anger. He silently cursed the drought. The Depression. The banker who now owned their farm. President Roosevelt's "rendezvous with destiny" speech was crap. It certainly didn't help end the Depression or get his family back on their feet. They didn't need words, they needed help. They didn't want handouts. His father wanted to work. When was that gonna happen? Seemed like never.

"I can't wait around for your rendezvous," Sam said. "I'm going to make my own destiny."

4

Committed

For a week after graduation, Sam had tried to find work, but no one within half a day's drive of home was hiring, even if he'd had a car to drive. He didn't. He moved to his next plan, plan C, and hitched a ride to Brainerd, Minnesota—ninety miles from home—to talk to a recruiter at the National Guard. Guys he knew in the high school class ahead of him had joined the National Guard. With the money they received, they planned to pay for college. Sam hadn't given his decision a great deal of thought, but he figured there was no time like the present to get started, and beggars couldn't be choosy. He didn't want to be like FDR—all words with no action.

Sam stepped into the National Guard office and nodded to the recruiter behind the desk, who stood. He didn't look much older than Sam, but he wore a pair of freshly pressed khaki pants and a shirt, and a dark-green jacket and tie. Ribbons and pins hung above his left breast pocket. His neat appearance made Sam self-conscious about his own dress, though he'd picked the best of his few clothes. He still looked ragged.

"Good afternoon," the recruiter said. "I'm Sergeant Tom Walker. Welcome."

"Hey," Sam said, extending his hand. "I'm Sam Carlson from Eagle Grove."

"Eagle Grove. That's what, a couple hours from here?"

"About," Sam said.

"You took the Northern Pacific here then?"

"No, sir."

"Ah, the bus then."

"No, sir. Hitched."

"Well then, you must mean business. Take a seat." Walker gestured to a metal chair across from his desk. Behind him were half a dozen flags, including the American flag, the Minnesota state flag, and a flag depicting a blue soldier outlined by the state boundaries and the words "Minnesota National Guard. Always Ready." A golden eagle sat atop each flagpole. "Let me give you some information I have here about the National Guard." Sergeant Walker collected several pamphlets and handed them across the desk one at a time. For the next twenty minutes, Sam listened attentively, but he only had a few questions.

After the last pamphlet, Walker sat back and said, "So what more can I tell you, Sam?"

"You're taking recruits now?"

"We sure are."

"And you pay a salary?"

"It's right there in the brochure. It's a sliding scale. As you move up in rank, the National Guard rewards your successes with pay increases. We'll also teach you a skill, for when you get out into the workforce. What are you thinking you'd like to do, Sam?"

"I thought about maybe becoming a pilot, or a medic, or maybe an engineer or mechanic. I'm not sure yet. First, I want to go to college."

"Well, certainly the National Guard can help you save up to get there."

"You said the commitment was three years?"

"That's right. In three years, you will have saved enough to pay your four years of college, or if you change your mind, you will have perfected a skill that will make you a valuable part of the workforce."

"Any chance of being sent overseas?" His mother was worried about Hitler and what she called "all the shenanigans" he was pulling in Europe.

"The National Guard's history dates back to 1636, with its primary job to protect the homeland. National Guard members served throughout the

American Revolution, as well as the War of 1812, the Mexican-American War, the Civil War—"

It sounded like a canned speech Walker gave each recruit. Sam wanted to get back to the present. "I promised my mother I wouldn't have to fight overseas. She's worried about Hitler and the Nazis stirring up trouble. She thinks we're likely to get dragged into another world war."

Walker rested his hands on his desk. "Well, no one has a crystal ball, but President Roosevelt has said many times the United States would not be dragged into another world war. What's going on in Europe isn't America's business."

"Where would I be sent to train and serve my time?"

"Right here in Brainerd. You'd serve weekdays and have weekends free. You got a sweetheart in Eagle Grove, Sam?"

"I do. And I'm planning to marry her when my commitment is finished. She's going off to college on a scholarship."

"Sounds like a solid plan, Sam. You'll finish your commitment before she graduates and have some money in the bank for your education. You'll be able to buy a ring and maybe put down a deposit on a home. You seem like a bright, enterprising young man."

"My mother and father are going through a hard time, with the Depression and all."

"You too, huh?"

"Your parents going through hard times?"

"Whose parents aren't? My first plan was college also, but when the Depression hit, I had to make my own way."

"That's why I'm here."

"I'm going to tell you the truth, Sam. The National Guard isn't for everyone. We take only the brightest and the most industrious young men who want to make something of themselves. Your days will be regimented and disciplined. But you fulfill your commitment, and there isn't a job in the workplace you won't be able to handle. In the interim, you'll get three square meals a day, clothing, and a place to live. You'll grow stronger and become more mature. That's more than most can say in these hard economic times, even those fortunate enough to go to college right away."

It was, Sam knew.

"What do you say, Sam Carlson? Can your country depend on you?"

—

Each week that summer, Sam hitchhiked from Eagle Grove to Brainerd. He learned that Brainerd had a booming forestry industry and shipped logs by the Northern Pacific Railway and on barges down the Mississippi River. Its twelve thousand residents gave it a big-city feel that tiny Eagle Grove never had. Walking the city streets, Sam counted three movie theaters.

During basic training Sam got new boots, warm clothing, and three square meals a day, as promised, and his father had one less mouth to feed. He learned discipline and close order drills—marching, formations, and how to handle arms while standing shoulder to shoulder with others. The company commander drilled them to perfection, then made them do it again. Given Sam's athletic talents, he flourished in basic training, and by eating regular meals of pork and beans, boiled potatoes, bread and butter, cabbage salad, and apple pie, he put on weight and even grew another inch. When he returned to Eagle Grove wearing his uniform on weekends, people walking the streets smiled, which made him puff out his chest an extra inch or two.

It also seemed to impress Sarah. She told him she missed him during the week and how much she liked seeing him in his uniform. They had some romantic evenings together when they could get away. Sam even agreed to work in the projection booth when home to have a little privacy. The Larsens were playing mostly reruns that neither he nor Sarah were interested in seeing again. It made for good necking time, though it didn't completely erase Sam's gloom, knowing Sarah would soon be leaving and they wouldn't see each other for months. That hung over him like a large boulder threatening to crush him.

At Brainerd, Sam completed basic training and was assigned to the National Guard's 34th Tank Company. His officers said he was learning leadership skills. He thought that was a bunch of bull. The Guard stuffed him into a cramped, mobile metal box. This made Sam a "tanker," as the men called themselves. The 34th had long depended on leftover six-ton M1917 tanks, but shortly before Sam arrived in Brainerd, his company had received two modern M2A2 tanks. Considered a "light" tank, the M2A2 had strong armor and .30- and .50-caliber machine guns. It could hit a top speed of forty-five miles per hour on a paved road, which made it at least fun to drive. Sam and his fellow tankers dubbed it "Mae West" for its twin turrets.

Sam gave one-third of his pay to his parents to help care for his sisters and his cousin and socked another third away for college and for his and Sarah's future. After three years, he might even save enough to walk into that bank in Eagle Grove and slap down a wad of cash on that banker's desk to get back his parents' farm.

At summer's end Sam took the train home to ensure he and Sarah had as much time as possible before she departed for Mankato, which was two hours from Eagle Grove and just about four hours from Brainerd. His train, however, was delayed nearly three hours due to a derailment. By the time he arrived at the train station, it was dark. Sam stepped from the train, carrying his duffle bag and flowers, and ran to his house. He quickly said his hellos, dropped off his bag, and hightailed it to Sarah's, only to find she wasn't home.

"She's at the Paradise Theater," Mrs. Haber said. "She waited several hours but heard there'd been a derailment."

Sam checked his watch. He was really late. He ran from the Habers' to downtown Eagle Grove. Mrs. Larsen was in the lobby, peeking through the doors to the theater to watch the film. She turned. "Sam?"

"I'm late. I'm meeting Sarah?" he said, out of breath.

"She's not in there," Mrs. Larsen said.

Sam deflated. "She's not?"

"She's upstairs, running the projectors."

"Running the projectors?"

"I've been doing it since you've been away, but Sarah volunteered."

Sam hurried up the curved staircase to the balcony, which was nearly vacant. He pulled open the door to the projection room. Sarah stood beside one of the two projectors in a pleated skirt and light blue sweater, her hair pulled back and tied in a matching blue ribbon.

"Fred," she said. "You're late."

"Sarah. I'm sorry. The train—"

"Not Sarah. Not tonight," she said and wrapped her arms around his neck. "Ginger. And I'll wait forever for you, Fred."

—

Sunday afternoon, Sam returned to the Northern Pacific platform for his ninety-minute train ride north to Brainerd, and the Habers helped Sarah with her luggage for her ride south to Mankato. It made for an awkward goodbye, with Mr. and Mrs. Haber and Sarah's siblings present. Sarah was teary eyed, which made Sam teary. Black smoke spewed from the engine's stack and created a haze in the still air. When the conductor called out "Last call for Mankato," Sarah looked to Sam. Problem was, Sam really didn't know what to say. They stepped away to have a little privacy, what there was to have.

"I'll come to Mankato first chance I get," he managed, then felt uncomfortable with Mr. and Mrs. Haber still standing so close by. "I mean, we can both come back to Eagle Grove." They both knew the Northern Pacific had no direct trains from Brainerd to Mankato, because Sam had looked it up, and the cost would have been prohibitive even if it did, with Sam helping out his parents and trying to save for his and Sarah's future. And while Sarah was on scholarship, that only covered her tuition and room and board. Her family, better off than most in Eagle Grove, still couldn't afford the expense of train fare for her to return before Christmas.

"Write to me," she said, holding back more tears.

"Yeah, I will," Sam said.

"You be careful, Sam Carlson, handling all those weapons. Don't shoot off a foot or a finger or something."

"I won't," he said, managing a chuckle.

"I have to go."

"I know." He walked her to the step beneath her car's open door. The conductor stood close by in his navy-blue uniform, waiting. So did Sarah's parents.

"Last call, young lady."

Sarah hugged and kissed her parents, then she turned to Sam. "Bye, Sam."

"Bye, Sarah."

He thought that was it, but Sarah took one step up, turned back, and wrapped her arms tight around his neck, kissing him and holding him tight. When the embrace ended, Sarah quickly turned and stepped onto the train. Sam gave Mr. and Mrs. Haber a polite smile. Both were crying.

Sarah appeared again at the train window, which was lowered, and did her best to smile and wave to Sam and to her family as the train jerked, black smoke again spewing, and rattled from the station.

Sam watched the train until a bend in the track prevented him from seeing Sarah at the window.

He wondered if he was just fooling himself, and this really was goodbye.

———

Sarah's first letter arrived at Brainerd one week later. Sam waited until after dinner to read it, when the men had settled on their bunks to read mail, write letters home, read books, or just listen to music piped through a speaker in the barracks. The music was a mixed blessing. Sam would find himself loving numbers like "Cheek to Cheek" and "The Way You Look To-night," both of which Fred Astaire had sung to Ginger Rogers, but then he'd have to block them out, keep himself busy, since they only reminded him of how much he missed Sarah.

> *Dearest Sam,*
>
> *Though it has only been a week since our teary goodbye at the train station in Eagle Grove, I feel like I haven't seen you in ages. Life here has been an adjustment. My roommate, Maryanne Dimple (no kidding!), is from Minneapolis and has never even heard of Eagle Grove. Her father is a lawyer and her mother a nurse and she has so many new outfits I gave her some extra space in my closet, since I only brought a few. Despite the differences in our circumstances, we also seem to have much in common. For one, we're women, and there aren't many here, at least not in our department. She's also a math major and finished at the top of her high school class.*

Sarah went on to tell him about school, her classes, and how much work she had each day. It sounded like she was keeping herself busy.

Of course he wanted to hear it all, but it wasn't until near the end of the letter that she moved into more personal things and his heart quickened.

> *Maryanne doesn't have a boyfriend, and I get the impression she never has. She asks a lot of questions about you, and us, some personal (like whether you're a good kisser. I told her you are).*

37

Maryanne is excited because she says finding dates will be like shooting fish in a barrel since there are so few women in our major. We tend to be the only two in our math classes.

Sam felt his stomach lurch at that—Sarah, surrounded by college men. How could he hope to compete with those guys?

But I only have eyes for you, Sam Carlson, and I'm saving up all my dates until we see each other again.

Just that quickly, the planet tilted back onto its axis.

Maryanne has invited me to meet her family in Minneapolis. She says her father will pick us up and bring us back in his car, so I don't have to worry about the cost of the train. I'd like to see Minneapolis. I've never seen a big city. Maryanne says I'd love the Institute of Art, and the Basilica of St. Mary, and Minnehaha Park (that sounds like a miniature joke; doesn't it? Ha-ha).

I'm meeting a lot of other nice students here, Sam. Everyone seems to have finished first in their class and is serious about their education. Given the cost, especially these days, you have to be. I haven't told anyone I'm on scholarship. I don't want them to judge me.

Well, it's getting late, and Maryanne has early classes, so I had better shut off the light.

I miss you, Sam, and I'm counting the days until I see you again. Write me back when you can.

I love you with all my heart, Fred.

Sarah (Ginger)

Sam tried not to reread her letter too closely and let his paranoia run wild. He envied her getting to see Minneapolis, but wondered again if all her experiences might drive them apart. He reread where she wrote about meeting so many "nice students" and the part about her and Maryanne being the only two girls in the math program. He had no defenses against the images that rose up in his mind—college men climbing all over themselves to ask Sarah out.

No. He set her letter down on his bunk. He'd only make himself sick worrying. He picked it up and reread the last line of the letter again. *I love you with all my heart, Fred.*

He would focus on those words. That, and his regimented schedule, made the time pass a little easier.

5

Not a Hero

Brainerd, Minnesota
November 8, 1940

Sam and the others in his unit had taken warm showers after working in the cold, and the barracks smelled of liberal amounts of pomade hair tonic and Old Spice cologne. Sam caught a glimpse of Captain Oscar Kristiansen, their company commander, in his locker mirror as Kristiansen entered the barracks and the men dressed or busied themselves packing a bag for weekend leave. Kristiansen was much older than the rest of them, having served in the Great War, and Sam sensed he liked giving them orders. Tonight his expression was grim. Sam had seen it before. The men were about to lose their weekend pass because some officer decided the tanks needed maintenance, or some other crap work needed to be performed.

"Don't say it, Kristiansen," John Anderson said. "Don't even think to say it. I've got a date set and I'm told this gal is easy, so don't say it."

"You dating your mother now, Anderson?" someone yelled.

"You want a mouth full of teeth, chump?" Anderson shot back. Just five foot six, the guy should've had his picture in the encyclopedia's entry for "Napoleon complex." He had a chip on his shoulder as big as a house.

"Stand down, everyone," Captain Kristiansen said. "I don't like this any more than you do, but orders are orders and I'm stuck."

"Shit, Oscar," Sam said, amid loud grumbling and profanity.

"The good news is, they don't need both units, just one," Kristiansen said. "So this doesn't have to affect everybody . . . if we can work this out. If not, then nobody takes leave."

"Good. I nominate Carlson's unit to stay," Anderson said.

"Screw you, Anderson," Sam said. "You can have the honor."

"No way. Ain't happening. I told you. I got a date waiting for me."

"In your dreams," cracked Bill Meyers, a member of Sam's unit. "You couldn't find a girl ugly enough to go out with you."

"Not planning on going *out*," Anderson said. "That's my point, knucklehead."

"All right, I said everybody stand down," Kristiansen said. "It is what it is. Since we'll never get a consensus, we'll flip a coin. That's the only fair way."

"Why don't we have a little competition?" Anderson called out. "What do you say, Carlson? Your unit against mine. You game?" Sam put his comb in his locker and turned to face Anderson, who stood grinning at him. "Unless you're chicken."

"What did you have in mind?"

"I don't know. Something quick and easy. Just me and you. How about basketball? One on one."

Sam smiled inside. He'd led Eagle Grove in scoring and rebounding both his junior and senior years, plus, at six foot one, he had half a foot on Anderson. What was the little man thinking?

Meyers walked up and leaned close, turned his back to Anderson, and whispered, "Don't do it, Sam. Yeah, he's a shrimp, but word is Anderson played here in Brainerd, and he would have played in college but didn't have the grades."

Sam considered Anderson with his silly grin. He looked like a redheaded leprechaun. "I've played a little myself," he assured Meyers. "We'll all get leave."

"We'd be better off flipping a coin," Meyers said. "You lose and we all pay the price. And the guys'll tear you a new one."

Anderson started clucking. "If you're too chicken, Carlson, or if your unit doesn't have faith in you . . ."

Sam turned to Meyers. "Yeah, but when I win, they'll all think I'm a hero."

"No, we won't. All we'll get is what we were already entitled to."

"Relax," he said. "I got this." He stepped clear of Meyers and nodded to Anderson. "All right. Let's do it."

The men cheered and hurried outside into the cold. No rain or snow fell, but that just kept the temperature low, in the teens, a bone-jarring cold so deep your joints hurt. The two units moved to the asphalt basketball court, white puffs of breath hanging in the air. A gray had settled over the area, the sky so low you could almost reach out and touch it.

The court was only half a court. The rounded wooden backboard was worn and chipped along the edges, the rim and metal chain rusted red. Anderson tossed Sam a basketball. Sam removed his jacket and handed it to Meyers.

"I'll get this back after I beat your butt," he said to Anderson.

"Big words from a little man," Anderson said.

"That doesn't make a lot of sense," Sam said. "Got you by six inches."

"Should be easy for you to beat me, then."

The two of them warmed up, with the men from both units standing under the basket and in a half circle around the top of the key, shifting from one leg to the other and swinging their arms to keep warm.

Sam proceeded to swish his first five practice shots. Anderson clanked the rim three times in a row. The men in Sam's unit looked at one another with nods and grins.

"Let's get started," Anderson said. "It's too cold to be horsing around."

"You're not having second thoughts, are you?" Sam said. His breath burst from his mouth in white wisps from the exertion.

"Loser's out," Anderson said. "And you're the loser. First guy to make five baskets wins. The loser and his unit spend the weekend as the grease monkeys. Deal?"

"We'll be sure to let you boys know all about our time off . . . in detail."

The men in Sam's unit hooted and hollered, confident.

"Let's go, Carlson."

"Make it quick, Sam," one of his guys called, "so we can get out of here."

"I'll even let you take it first," Anderson said. He tossed the ball hard, hitting Sam in the chest.

Sam dribbled the ball to the top of the key and faced the basket, grinning. He'd cross Anderson over, bust to the hoop, and hit a layup before Anderson had time to recover.

Sam faked left and Anderson shifted. Sam crossed from his left hand to his right, but Anderson stuck a hand down, stole the ball, then spun quickly and hit a layup, leaving Sam flatfooted.

The men in Anderson's unit cheered. Sam heard a few "uh-ohs" from his unit.

Anderson returned with the ball and again hit Sam in the chest with it. "You use that move in Eagle Grove, pretty boy?"

Sam smiled, but now he'd be more cautious. This time he rocked the ball right, left, right, then drove to the basket. He rose up, but Anderson's quick hand slapped the ball as Sam brought it up, knocking it from his hands. Anderson took it and sped away, smiling. Sam recovered and moved quickly to defend, but Anderson blew past him. Sam recovered. As Anderson rose, the ball in his right hand, he threw an elbow with his left arm, and smacked Sam in the nose, knocking him down. Anderson easily made the shot.

"Foul!" guys under the hoop yelled. "Foul!"

Sam winced from the pain, which also made his eyes water. He glared at Anderson from the ground, gravel embedded in his palms. Anderson stood over him, grinning. "I don't see no referees, Carlson. You want maybe to call your mommy?"

Sam stood. "So that's how it's going to be. Let's go."

Anderson again shot the ball at Sam's chest, but this time Sam caught it. He busted to his left and lowered his shoulder to knock Anderson down. Anderson, however, stepped back quickly, and Sam fell forward, off balance, losing the ball on his way to the ground. His shoulder hit the pavement hard, as did his knee, tearing a hole in his best khaki pants.

Anderson stood over him, holding the ball. "I'm going to wait for you to get back up, Carlson. Just to be fair, give you a sporting chance."

Sam rose from the ground and squatted to defend the smaller man. Anderson jabbed a foot forward, and when Sam rocked back, Anderson rose and sank a fifteen-foot shot. The metal chain on the rim rattled and the ball hit the ground.

"Three to nothing," one of Anderson's men crowed.

The men in Sam's unit stood with eyes down and grim expressions.

Sam now realized Anderson had missed his warmup shots on purpose.

"Going to go to a nice dinner," Anderson announced. "Take my gal dancing, maybe a picture show. How about you, Carlson?"

"Give me the ball," Sam said. Anderson did. At the top of the key, Sam jabbed as if to drive to the hoop, then stepped back and rose to shoot. Anderson rose with him, only a little faster and, impossibly, a little higher, and blocked Sam's shot. Did the guy have springs in his shoes?

Anderson recovered the loose ball, spun, and quickly shot. The net again rattled.

"Four to nothing," he said. "I haven't even broken a sweat. I've guarded girls better than you, Carl-son. Or maybe that should be Carl-daughter."

"You're a fool," Sam said.

"Ooh. Big words from the guy losing four to nothing." He tossed Sam the ball. Then he stepped back. "Shoot it, Carlson. You're wide open."

Sam needed a bucket, and a fifteen-footer wasn't the best percentage shot to take. He turned his back to protect the ball and backed the smaller Anderson down inside the key, the two of them heaving their bodies against each other. Anderson was short, but surprisingly stout. When Sam had at last worked them below the basket, he spun to shoot over the smaller man, but again Anderson rose with and then above him, raising a knee as he did and driving it square into Sam's groin. He crumpled and dropped to the ground in pain, curled in a fetal position.

"That's five," Anderson said, the basket's chain again rattling. "Geez, Carlson, I thought you'd at least make it interesting." He knelt at Sam's side and put the ball by Sam's head. Then he leaned in close and whispered. "News flash, pretty boy. This ain't little Eagle Grove, and you ain't anybody's star no more. This is the real world and you're a grunt, like the rest of us. Here, we play for keeps." He laughed and stood. "Looks like we got the weekend free, boys," he said, arms spread, but the men in his unit didn't yell with the same enthusiasm. They also didn't decline to take the weekend passes from Kristiansen.

As Sam got to his feet, Meyers and the other members of Sam's unit approached. "I told you it was a sucker's bet, Sam," Meyers said. "You gambled, but we *all* lost. You let your swelled head and your grudge against Anderson hurt the rest of us. I told you this wouldn't go well. You should have just flipped a damn coin. At least then we would have had a chance."

The men shuffled off back to the barracks, leaving Sam out in the cold.

6

A Change of Plans

Time passed in a flurry of activity for both Sam and Sarah, based on the letters she wrote and the frequency she wrote them, which was less and less. They saw each other every Christmas and then again on weekends, at least during Sarah's first summer. Sarah had done so well in her classes, one of her teachers had encouraged her to get an advanced degree in mathematics, which meant she spent her second-year summer in Mankato taking additional classes and would spend her third-year summer there too.

It wasn't ideal, and though Sam sensed they were both changing, she told him her feelings for him hadn't changed. She still loved him.

And he still loved her.

Everything was somehow both different and going as he'd planned.

—

The Thursday before Sam's weekend leave—he was planning to meet Sarah back in Eagle Grove to celebrate Valentine's Day and spend the weekend together—he returned to the barracks from afternoon tank drills. His unit was roughhousing in the barracks, trying to get warm after drilling in subzero temperatures. The Andrews Sisters sang "Boogie Woogie Bugle Boy" through the barracks speakers as Sam and others sat on their bunks and pulled off their boots. As needles of pain shot from Sam's toes up his legs, guys on all sides of him moaned in similar discomfort.

"Boots are worthless," one of them said, and he tossed his boot against the wall. It hit with a thud.

"Anyone know what frostbite looks like?" Anderson asked.

"Like your balls: cold and blue," Meyers said. "They may have to amputate."

Sam laughed in between grimaces of pain. He was flexing his hands and rubbing his toes and feet—all of which was excruciating—to restore circulation, when Oscar Kristiansen entered their barracks.

"Listen up," Kristiansen called out.

The men did their best to snap to attention at their bunks, standing lopsided, favoring one frozen foot over the other. Neither the company in general, nor Kristiansen in particular, was a stickler for military formality.

"At ease," Kristiansen said, and the men gladly dropped back onto their bunks. "I just got some news that affects us all. So, I need you to pay attention and listen up."

Something in Kristiansen's voice gave Sam a bad feeling. "What now, Oscar?" he asked.

"President Roosevelt just federalized our unit."

"Federalized?" Sam said. Kristiansen now had the attention of every man in the unit. "Captain, what the hell does that mean?"

He and Sarah, and his family, had been worried when, on September 16, 1940, Roosevelt signed into law the first peacetime draft in the nation's history, ordering all able-bodied men to serve one year in the armed forces. The president had assured the nation that service would be restricted to the continental United States. Moreover, during FDR's campaign for a third term in office, he had again reiterated America would not become embroiled in another foreign war.

Despite the president's assurances, the National Guard had seen a surge in commitments, young men who did not want to be sent overseas to fight. If it came to that.

"It means with a stroke of his pen, FDR just converted every one of us into the property of the United States Army, extending our commitment," Kristiansen said.

Kristiansen's news elicited uncertain grumbling and a lot of profanity.

"My three-year commitment ends in four months," Sam said. "I'm going home."

"I got two months," someone else said.

"Not anymore," said Anderson.

"What's it mean, Oscar?" Sam pressed. "US Army property?"

"It means we don't fart unless the Army tells us to," Anderson said.

Kristiansen said, "It means we've been ordered to Fort Lewis for advanced tank training."

"Where the hell is Fort Lewis?" someone shouted.

"Washington."

"DC?" Sam said.

"Washington State," Kristiansen said.

More grumblings of disbelief and more profanity. The only thing Sam knew about Washington State was it was clear on the other side of the country.

"For how long?" Sam asked.

"I don't know, but FDR said when he implemented the draft it would be just a one-year commitment."

"Yeah, and I heard it never rains in Washington either," Anderson cracked, then broke into a recent hit song about a man being drafted into the Army and hoping to return in a year.

"Shut up, Anderson," someone barked.

"Why don't you make me?"

"When are we leaving?" Sam asked, thinking it would be months before they departed.

"We ship out by train February twentieth. Plans are already being made to ship the tanks and other equipment before us."

"But I'm headed home to see my sweetheart."

"Well, I'm sure if you just *explain* that to the president—" Anderson started.

"Shut the fuck *up*, Anderson!" Sam glowered at him.

Anderson took a step forward. "Or what, princess?"

"I said stand down. Everyone," Kristiansen said, stepping between them. "Anderson, go back to your bunk and don't move an inch or I'll write you up."

Anderson stepped back but his eyes simmered.

"I don't make the orders," Kristiansen said to everyone. "I just deliver them. I suggest you all go home, get your affairs in order, and get your asses back here Monday. There's a lot to do before we ship out. I'll provide more information as it's received."

"Why now?" someone asked.

"Yeah. What's going on, Oscar?" someone else shouted.

"I don't know," Kristiansen said, his tone reflecting his own frustration. "I'm telling you what I know."

"It's because of all the shit happening in Europe," Anderson said. "The damn krauts are stirring the pot and are going to pull us into another world war."

"America's neutral," someone else said. "FDR said we'd stay neutral, that what happens in Europe is none of our business."

"Yeah, and I got oceanfront property in Kansas I'm looking to sell. Will you buy that too?" Anderson said, always needling.

"I don't know anything about any of that," Kristiansen added. "I know as much as you do at this point. I'm sorry." Then he turned and departed.

Sam sat on his bunk in a room of stunned silence.

"Look at the bright side," Anderson said.

"What bright side?" Sam asked.

"At least we all won't get blue balls from marching in subfreezing temperatures and have to get castrated."

———

February 20, Sam and eighty-one khaki-clad men gathered on the Northern Pacific Railway station's snowy platform for a warm send-off from friends and family, despite a freak snowstorm and frigid temperatures that had plunged to twenty degrees below zero. Dark clouds hung over the platform, reflecting the mood of the men in his National Guard unit. They shifted and swung their limbs while standing in place, doing what they could to keep warm. Their breaths and the breaths of their family members clouded the platform like fog, and they dabbed beneath their runny noses with tissue and handkerchiefs.

Sam's parents had come to see him off, as had the Larsens from the Paradise Theater, and Sarah and her parents. The Habers had picked up their daughter from Mankato State Teachers College so she could say goodbye. The train was scheduled to leave at 12:19 a.m. but was fifteen minutes late, and everyone waited on the platform, teary eyed, while the Brainerd Ladies' Drum and Bugle Corps struggled in the cold to play patriotic music to keep the mood upbeat. It wasn't working. The music sounded flat, and the corps missed notes, their fingers not flexing well.

Sam had told his parents, and Sarah, this was just a temporary rotation, but that was for them. He didn't for a minute believe it. They could have rotated his unit without federalizing it. Anderson was right. This had to do with the Nazis stirring up trouble in Europe.

Sam and Sarah stepped away for a moment to themselves, though given the crowd and all the luggage, that wasn't really feasible.

"I'm not sure when I'll see you again," Sam said, being honest.

"It's only temporary," Sarah said. "You'll be home before you know it. Besides, my math classes have really picked up this semester. I'll study better if I'm not always thinking about you."

Sam smiled and pulled her close, hands around her waist. "You always think about me?"

"Every moment of every day, Sam Carlson. And will you be thinking about me?"

"I'll count the days until I see you again."

When the train arrived, Kristiansen walked down the platform shouting, his arms folded across his body. "Let's go. Get a move on and get on the train. I just got word we're moving out."

Sam nodded then locked eyes with Sarah. "Don't cry. Your tears will freeze."

"Let's go, Carlson. Move your butt and stow your gear. The train isn't going to wait for you. You miss it and the Army will throw your butt in the stockade for desertion."

"I got to go."

"I know," Sarah said. "I want you to have something." She removed her thick gloves.

"What are you doing? Your hands are going to get frostbite."

Sarah set to work rotating her class ring on her finger, finally pulling it off. "Here," she said. "I want you to have this while you're away."

"Your class ring?"

"Not anymore. Now it's a promise. Until the day you ask me again."

"Does this mean yes?"

"It means I'm promising myself to you and only you, until the time when we can be together forever."

"Are you serious? I mean, this isn't just because, you know . . . I'm shipping out."

"I'm serious. And you had better come home to me, Sam Carlson."

"I will. That's a promise. I don't have a ring to give you, but . . . you have my word. I'm coming home to you, Sarah Haber."

7

Rain, Rain, and More Rain

Fort Lewis, Washington
February 22, 1941

When the train stopped in Tacoma, Washington, the men climbed into trucks that drove them from the station to Fort Lewis. Entering the base, they passed row after row of newly constructed barracks and two-story recreational and supply houses—as noted on posted signs—all built among the fir trees, as if the base was preparing for a significant surge in personnel. *Not good,* Sam thought, but didn't say.

"At least we have a view." Anderson pointed to Mount Rainier, the majestic snowcapped mountain looming on the southeastern horizon.

"Yeah, always wanted a volcano looming over me," someone else said.

"Don't forget about the earthquakes," Anderson said.

Sam's Minnesota unit consisted of two tanks, one reconnaissance car, and six trucks. It merged with other tank units from California and Missouri to form A Company, 194th Tank Battalion. That was all well and good, but no one knew why they were in Fort Lewis, or what their orders would be. Their commanding officers would only say they were drilling.

Washington's warmer weather appealed to Sam, though the rain did not. Many caught colds and were sent to the base hospital to keep the sickness from spreading in the barracks.

Sam's day began at 06:00, when a bugler blasted reveille. He jumped from bed, shaved, dressed, made his cot, swept the floor, and cleaned outside the barracks, all before breakfast at 06:30. He drilled on foot and inside tanks until 11:30, then cleaned up, ate lunch, and drilled again until 16:30. Dinner was at 17:00 sharp. The remainder of the day he stood around waiting and wondering. They all did.

His evenings free, except when he had all-night guard duty, Sam read in his barracks, or enjoyed bull sessions with fellow tankers until lights-out at 21:00 hours. On weekends, Sam and the men were bused to Tacoma or Olympia, or played football, basketball, and softball on base. They visited the canteen near their barracks or went to the theater to watch an epic saga of romance and war called *Gone with the Wind*. And, as promised, he wrote letters to Sarah and devoured the ones she sent. Sarah's letters detailed her final months at the university, which included a student teacher position in Rochester, Minnesota.

Sarah always started her letters with some bland observations, this time about the students in her classroom being future doctors, engineers, and business leaders. Maybe even president.

Wouldn't that be something, Sam, if I taught a president?

That was fine—she could read him the telephone book and he'd love it—but before long, she would transition to more intimate subjects, describing the things she loved and missed about Sam. He saved each letter, but he carried one with him in his uniform, one that served as a reminder of why he needed to get home to her.

I think about our last kiss on the platform before you left. Do you? I felt it all throughout my body, like you were kissing me with every ounce of yourself, like those nights in the projection room. I know you haven't forgotten them. You'd better not have. It makes me think about when we can finally marry, and I can give myself to you completely. Do you think of that also, what our wedding night will be like? I do.

Tell me they're sending you home to me, Sam. Tell me all the terrible things happening in this world won't prevent us from beginning our life together.

I pray it is so.

With all my heart, I love you, Sarah

That was more like it.

When three months came to an end, Sam's gut-tweaking premonitions of bad things to come returned. Sure enough, rather than ship him and his unit back to Minnesota where he could finish his commitment, the Army ordered his unit to Fort Knox, Kentucky, and the dark prospect of his Guard unit being sent overseas seemed more and more a real possibility.

"It's okay," Sam told Sarah by phone when he finally had the chance to call, trying to sound upbeat. "Kentucky is closer to Minnesota than Washington, and the Army promoted me to sergeant, meaning higher pay. We can use the extra money when I get out."

What he didn't tell Sarah was that at Fort Knox, his unit was drilled on how to use machine guns, pistols, and M1 rifles. He learned to use a gas mask to survive poison gas attacks. He could take weapons apart and put them back together blindfolded. Afternoons, their unit worked on tank-driving tactics and radio operations. They honed their map-reading skills and practiced firing the M2A4's 37-millimeter cannon and the M2A2's mounted .30- and .50-caliber machine guns. This wasn't just for kicks and giggles. They were preparing to go to war, if needed. Seemed like someone thought they might be. If that was the case, then Sam would take every training exercise seriously, because he had every intention of surviving whatever was to come.

His diligence did not go unnoticed. The Army promoted Sam again, this time to staff sergeant, in charge of an entire platoon. Sam loved the recognition, but if he were being honest, it scared the hell out of him. At twenty-one years of age, he would no longer just be looking out for himself. He'd be leading others. He'd be responsible for them. Hell, he was hardly capable of taking care of himself. Now if he screwed up in the field, he could be liable for others' deaths.

He wasn't sure he wanted to live with that kind of responsibility, or that he could cope with those kinds of consequences.

At Fort Knox, Sam's platoon added four more tanks, all of them new M3s, bringing the total to six. The day after his promotion, Sam stood in a sea of red mud overlooking the Ohio River and wondered how the tanks would handle it.

"What do sheep do after playing in the mud?"

Sam turned. A private first class stood at his side, also staring at the mud. He looked young enough to be fresh out of high school, with a wiry build, jet black hair, and mischievous brown eyes. He also sported a pencil-thin mustache, the kind Clark Gable had in *Gone with the Wind*, along with a better than passable imitation of Gable's brash confidence, right down to the cocked head and raised eyebrow, as if daring Sam to answer his riddle. Sam figured he'd play along. "I don't know, Private. What do sheep do after playing in the mud?"

The private cleared his throat. "Well, Staff Sergeant, they take a baaaaaath."

Sam groaned. "What's your name, Private?"

"Pete Chavez," the young man said. "And who might you be?"

It was Sam's turn to cock his head and arch his eyebrow. "I might be your staff sergeant, Sam Carlson."

Chavez's eyes widened and he grinned. "No kidding. Well then, Staff Sergeant, I am your new tank driver."

"Is that so?"

"I've got the orders to prove it."

"Lucky me. Tell me, Private Chavez, can you drive a tank better than you tell jokes?"

"I'm working on both, sir."

"Then we have a long way to go." Sam smiled. "You know anything about sheep, Private?"

"No, sir. I'm from Salinas. My family farms vegetables. No sheep."

"Where is Salinas?"

"Middle of California. Family has farmed there since the land was still part of Mexico. Can tell you a lot about sugar beets if you're interested. My family used to pick sugar beets alongside a local guy named John Steinbeck."

"*The Grapes of Wrath* guy?" Sam wondered if the private was pulling his leg.

"That's the one. He picked beets until he came out with *Tortilla Flat*. Never saw him again. Did you hear what happened when Steinbeck stopped eating vegetables?"

"No. What happened?"

"His heart missed a beet."

"Better, but still needs more work," Sam said. "Tell me, Private, how would you handle crossing this muck?"

"Me? I'd handle it the way two freight trains barreling down the same track from opposite directions would handle it. Head on."

"You a comedian, Private Chavez?"

"That depends."

"On what?"

"Whether you think I'm funny, Sergeant. My father always told me to be the headliner of my own life."

"Looks like you're getting a good start on the comedy. Now let's see what you can do in this mud."

—

On June 16, 1941, Sam, his new tank driver, Pete Chavez, and the rest of their detachment drove their twenty tanks and various support vehicles through the Kentucky countryside for what Sam's superiors would only refer to as a three-day training exercise. The men considered the reprieve from the incessant drilling in the scorching Kentucky summer a vacation, but Sam now thought of everything as further preparation for war, and that scared the hell out of him.

Thirty miles from Fort Knox, they set up camp at the Harrodsburg fairgrounds. The following day, the armored battalion drove to Herrington Lake, east of Danville. Finding no Nazis, the men passed the day swimming, boating, and fishing. They returned to Fort Knox the following afternoon through Lebanon, New Haven, and Hodgenville, Kentucky.

Sam believed the mobilization a success and thought that was the reason his commanding officer had called him into a meeting with battalion inspectors.

"We have a problem," his commanding officer said.

"A problem, sir?"

The officer looked to a battalion inspector, who said, "As you know, Sergeant, your company's four tank platoons each carry identical equipment identified by serial numbers."

"Yes, I'm aware, and I'm confident all the equipment we left with arrived back here."

"It came back," the inspector said. "But somebody switched dozens of items between the platoons. We discovered the problem while checking inventory. It's going to take nearly an entire day to return the mixed items to their proper units."

"Do you have any idea how this could have happened, Staff Sergeant?" Sam's commanding officer asked.

Sam suspected Chavez, who had told Sam, with a touch of pride, that a high school teacher called him "the most dedicated class clown" she'd ever taught. Switching the platoon items meant the men in the company got another day off from drilling while those checking inventory sorted out and returned each item to its proper unit.

"No, sir," Sam said. "But I'll be sure to try and find out." He didn't. He believed the men had drilled enough. They all could use an off day relaxing in the barracks.

Sam's training in Kentucky would not wind down until late August, and Sarah would be taking summer classes toward her master's degree. They didn't know when they would see each other next.

They didn't talk about the Nazis having taken over multiple countries, including France, or that Hitler didn't seem inclined to stop there. In fact, Germany had signed a military pact with Japan, an indication, according to Sam's superiors, that they intended to rule not just Europe, but the world.

What did not make the newspaper headlines, but which became well known at Fort Knox, was that an American pilot, flying a routine mission from the US base at Clark Field in the Philippines, had spotted an odd line of flagged buoys floating in the ocean, which extended thirty miles north from Manila to a Japanese-controlled island, as if to guide an invading fleet.

On August 13, 1941, Sam and his unit received more, but no longer unexpected, bad news: Congress had extended the federalized National Guard's commitment another eighteen months.

Just about one month later, it seemed all the rumors came to fruition. On September 4, 1941, Sam and the 194th were sent by train to Fort Mason, north of San Francisco. From there they were ferried on the USAT *General Frank M. Coxe* to Fort McDowell on Angel Island, where they were inoculated and given physicals. Men over twenty-nine years of age or with medical conditions were excused. Their replacements had never trained in tanks, adding to Sam's concern that he would be responsible for their lives.

Sam was going to war.

———

On Monday afternoon, September 8, 1941, the battalion's tanks had their turrets removed so they would fit in the hold of the USAT *President Coolidge*, which was an American luxury ocean liner put into service as a troopship. At 20:45, Sam and other soldiers stood at pay phones on a pier in San Francisco, California, during a freak summer rainstorm, hastily calling loved ones to tell them they were shipping overseas.

Sam called Sarah's dorm at Mankato but had a bad connection. "Hello? Hello? It's Sam Carlson. Sam Carlson." He put a finger in the ear not pressed to the receiver. "Is Sarah Haber there? Sarah Haber. Yes, I'll wait, but I don't have much time. I'm on a pay—Hello?"

The girl had put the phone down. "Dammit," Sam said.

Sam glanced at the massive ocean liner moored at the pier. Soldiers were swarming up the *President Coolidge*'s gangplank like ants and disappearing into the hold.

Next to Sam, Pete Chavez finished his call and slammed down the receiver on his pay phone. *"Vámonos, mi amigo. El* President Coolidge *no espera a nadie,"* he shouted to Sam and took off running through the rain, his coat pulled over his head.

Sam checked the second hand on his watch. *Fifty seconds.*

"Sam?"

"Hi, sweetheart."

"I'm so glad you called. There's something I need to tell you."

"Me too," Sam said, unsure how to break such unsettling news to her. "I only have a min—"

The horn blast announcing the ship's imminent departure drowned out Sam's words.

"What was that?" Sarah said.

"Part of what I have to tell you."

"Let me go first," she said. "I'm finally ready, Sam."

"What?"

"I'll graduate with a master's degree, and I'll return to Eagle Grove to teach. There's only one thing missing, Sam. You."

"Are you saying yes?"

The ship's horn blasted again, the final warning to passengers to be on board or get left behind.

"I'm ready to get married," Sarah said. Sam's head swam. Was he really hearing this? "Let's pick a date," she went on. "How about two weeks from Saturday, September twenty-seventh? You'll be home then. We can get married in the Presbyterian church, like we've always dreamed."

Sarah's words jolted him like an electric charge. Her "not yet" three years earlier had just become two weeks from Saturday.

The operator interrupted the call and requested additional change for three minutes.

Sam patted his pockets, desperate, but unable to find coins to buy more time.

"Are you there, Sam?"

Sam checked his watch. *Ten seconds.*

"Listen, Sarah, I don't have much time," he said. "I've received new orders."

"What? I can't hear you."

"I have new orders." He was nearly shouting into the receiver.

"New orders?"

"I won't be home in two weeks. They're sending me overseas."

"Who are you overseeing?"

"Not who. Where. I'm getting on a ship. They're sending me to the Philippines."

Click.

The line cut off.

The ship gave one final blast of its horn.

Sam had run out of time.

8

Fred, Ocean Liners, but No Ginger

USAT President Coolidge
September 8, 1941

The USAT *President Coolidge* set sail at 21:00 for the Philippine Islands. Sam had never been on a military ship or a luxury liner. He'd only seen ships like this in the Fred and Ginger movies. A member of the ship's crew told Sam the ship had been built for affluent vacationers traveling to the Far East. Sam took a quick tour and learned the ship stretched almost six hundred feet, had nine decks, and was even more grand than the ship in *Shall We Dance*. The interior included spacious staterooms, posh lounges, a gymnasium, a beauty parlor, and two swimming pools. Its grand salon had a sweeping, majestic staircase said to be even bigger than the one on the *Titanic*.

But the grandeur did not impress. His Ginger Rogers was back in Eagle Grove, had finally agreed to marry him, and Sam had shipped out without giving her an answer.

He should be going home.

He'd more than served his three-year commitment.

He should not be on a ship filled with soldiers headed to Manila.

The Army had kicked Sam's dreams down the road, yet again.

The soldiers' first days on ship consisted of a strict routine of drills, cleaning the ship, kitchen duty, and other mundane tasks intended to keep them busy. Sam did the work with little enthusiasm, then lay in his bunk bed below deck to avoid the scores of happy young men who'd gotten engaged or married before departing. Their smiles, wedding bands, and wedding photos rubbed salt in Sam's wound, but it also worried him. He knew many had taken the plunge because they feared they would not be returning home.

While Sam grieved, Pete Chavez flipped the situation into something positive, as was his way. If Chavez had a sad moment, Sam never saw it. The private rolled with each punch and every abrasive personality the military threw at him and kept Sam's and the other men's spirits up with a string of jokes, most corny, some amusing, but all, Sam realized, intended to distract their attention from what awaited them.

When word spread that the ship's chaplain needed an assistant—someone to organize entertainment—Chavez nabbed the job. He distributed equipment for badminton, shuffleboard, and other games for the soldiers to enjoy when off duty. He also ran contests like egg-and-spoon races and tug-of-war.

Sam, depressed, sat out and instead read in his three-tiered bunk bed in the ship's hold.

One afternoon, Chavez came to his rack and said, "Get up."

"What for?"

"I want to show you something."

"What?"

"I said, 'show you,' not 'tell you.' On your feet, soldier."

"That's Staff Sergeant, and I outrank you, not the other way around."

Chavez snapped to rigid attention and fired off a stiff salute. "Aye, aye, Staff Sergeant. Now get your ass up off that bed, stop moping, and follow me."

Chavez led Sam up to the top deck. They walked along wide, carpeted corridors with expensive lighting. Chavez stopped at a door and twirled a key on a ring around a raised finger.

"Whatever you're thinking, I want no part of it." Sam turned to leave.

Chavez grabbed his shoulder and pulled him back, then opened the door. Sam hesitated, then followed Chavez inside a deluxe, private two-room suite. The first room contained a large bed and a sitting area, the second a desk and two chairs. Both had wood paneling, exquisite furniture, and round windows overlooking the Pacific Ocean, like Fred and Ginger's rooms on ship.

"I don't know whose room this is," Sam said, "but I suggest we get out of here and fast."

"You're looking at the person whose room this is."

"You? No way."

Chavez just grinned and spread his arms wide.

"Who did you scam to get it?"

"No scam. The room came with the position of chaplain's assistant. Why do you think I took the job?"

"Wow," Sam said, walking about. He didn't know the job came with plush accommodations, but that was Chavez, seemingly always one step ahead of everyone else.

"Not bad for a guy from Salinas who grew up sharing a bed with his two brothers, huh, Staff Sergeant? What do you call a man with a private room on a ship full of soldiers?"

"I don't know. What do you call him?"

"Private," Chavez said with a shrug.

Sam groaned. He should have known.

—

Over the next five days, Chavez's positive attitude gradually infected Sam. It helped that Chavez refused to let Sam alone. He recruited him to be the projectionist for the comedies shown in the ship's theater each night. Back in his sweet spot in the projection booth, missing only Sarah beside him, Sam laughed along with the men in the theater below him. His gloom at last lifted, and he tried to see the positive in this latest twist in his life. In three short years he'd been promoted, moved from rags to fresh clothes, eaten three square meals a day, and stashed some money in his pocket and in the bank. He'd also improved life for his family with extra cash. He'd traveled across the entire United States, and now he was on this luxurious ship he never could have otherwise afforded, on his way to an exotic country considered the Pearl of the Orient. Most important, Sarah's "not yet" had become a firm commitment to marry him.

Things certainly could be worse.

The ship docked to refuel at 07:00 on September 13 in Hawaii, another place Sam had never dreamed of visiting. Soldiers received four-hour shore passes to Honolulu. As Sam and Chavez hurried to depart, a senior officer pulled Chavez aside and handed him cash.

"Buy more games to keep the men entertained for the remainder of the voyage," the officer ordered. Then he turned to Sam. "You go with him, Staff Sergeant. Keep him out of trouble."

Sam kept Chavez away from Honolulu's bars and two-dollars-a-throw cathouses and confined him to the manicured lawn and white sand beach behind the Royal Hawaiian Hotel, where Hawaiian women swayed to island music in grass skirts and flower headbands. Behind them, palm trees and a turquoise ocean served as a gloriously cinematic backdrop.

Chavez seemed awestruck by the dancers, but not like the rest of the men, who were just grateful to see the female sex after long days at sea with nothing but men. "Look at the one on the far right," Chavez said to Sam without taking his eyes off the young woman.

"They're all pretty," Sam said. "We might have a hard time getting the men back on ship."

"She's radiant," Chavez said. "I think she's smiling at me."

"It's just a show, Pete. She's smiling at everyone."

"Not the same way she's smiling at me."

Sam had to admit, the young woman did seem to be sneaking peeks at Chavez.

"Don't go falling in love," Sam said. "We still have to pick up the extra games."

"Too late," Chavez said.

When the hula dancers sought a few audience members to dance, Chavez was first to volunteer. Sam and the other soldiers howled and hurled catcalls at Chavez's awkward attempts to sway his hips and wave his hands, but the nineteen-year-old Salinas Valley vegetable farmer clearly didn't care. He didn't take his eyes off the young woman, a big, goofy grin on his face. And Sam had to admit, the young woman looked just as interested.

Minutes later, at Chavez's urging, a hula dancer draped a flowered lei around Sam's neck and pulled him into the dance. The men in Sam's tank platoon let him have it good. Sam, a demonstrably worse hula dancer than Chavez, gave in and served the men a lot to cheer about. For a few precious minutes, Sam's worries evaporated along with everyone else's. He set the past and the future aside and made peace with his present—but when he sat again, the twinge in the pit of his stomach dragged him from the moment. Things were not as they seemed. The hula dancers weren't real. Their affection wasn't real. The women were entertainers in costume. The backdrop—an island paradise—was too perfect. It wasn't reality. Sam, too, was just a character in a show. Entertainment. Like Chavez, he'd been pressed into service as a tool to buoy the other men's spirits.

When the show ended, Chavez remained engaged with his hula dancer. Sam attempted to interrupt, without success. Finally, he said, "Pete, we still have to pick up supplies and get back to the ship."

Chavez handed Sam the wad of cash from his pocket and turned his back to his hula dancer. "You go. Please. Do this one thing for me and I'll meet you on board."

"I don't know what to buy."

"Use your imagination. Anything to keep the men occupied. Come on, Sam. Don't deny me this."

Sam wanted to tell him the hula dancer wasn't real, was just an actress, but he didn't want to bring Chavez down. What purpose would it serve? Besides, the young woman had stayed on stage. She hadn't run off like the others to prepare for the next show.

"All right," he said. "But you owe me. And remember, I'm responsible. So don't screw up and be late."

———

Sam returned to the ship loaded with more game equipment, which he put in the storage room, then went to the deck and watched the men arrive. As the four-hour leave neared expiration, men came running along the lawn to the gangplank, but Chavez was not among them. If the private didn't show, Sam could imagine the conversation he'd have with the officer who'd told him to keep an eye on Chavez.

He checked his watch. Chavez had under five minutes before they'd pull in the gangplank and set sail. The returning soldiers had dwindled to just a few, men stumbling from too much alcohol, red in the face, and smiling from ear to ear.

No Chavez.

Sam wondered if Chavez would go absent without leave, or even downright desert. He could just see the son of a bitch convincing himself he needed to remain in Hawaii and settle down with his hula dancer. Sam would be in all kinds of trouble.

Soldiers shouted from below, readying the gangplank to be pulled in. Then Sam heard a familiar voice, hollering at the men: "Hold up! Hold up!" A taxicab had pulled to a stop, and Chavez yelled, "*Un momento*, guys!" He jumped out and slammed the door. His hula dancer leaned out the window, a huge, pretty grin on her face. Chavez took a step toward the plank, then turned back and planted a big kiss on the young woman's lips. On deck, the men, now used to Chavez's big personality, hooted and cheered the love scene. Chavez broke off the kiss and dashed up the gangplank.

Eventually, Chavez made his way to the deck, where men greeted him with laughs and shouts and pats on the back, fully expecting to be entertained with another of Chavez's stories. But this time the young private didn't indulge them. They persisted for a bit, then tired and moved on.

Chavez joined Sam, his forearms on the ship's railing, staring out at the island paradise as the ship departed.

"Go ahead," Sam said. "Tell me how great it was."

"When this is all over, I'm going to come back and ask that girl to marry me."

Sam laughed, thinking it another of Chavez's jokes, but Chavez wasn't laughing. "You're not serious," Sam said.

"Deadly serious."

"You just met her, for what, two hours."

"When you know, you know, Staff Sergeant."

Sam was going to push the issue, then thought of that moment in the classroom when he'd seen Sarah tell off Mr. Pembroke and noticed her as much more than the smartest person in the class.

"Then we better be sure to make it back here," Sam said.

Not long after leaving Hawaii, the *President Coolidge* was joined by the heavy cruiser USS *Astoria* and the USS *Guadalupe*, a replenishment oiler. The ships crossed the international date line on Tuesday, September 16. On September 26 at 07:00, the floating palace left the South China Sea and entered the inlet to the vast Manila Bay.

Sam and the other soldiers rushed to the ship's railing to view the fortified island of Corregidor and its massive guns guarding the bay. Behind Corregidor, Sam spotted another alien landscape of steep mountains and a dark-green forest shrouded in mist, like the island jungle in the movie *King Kong*. The trees along the shore shimmered in a breeze and made the jungle look alive, both enchanting and frightening.

"The Bataan Peninsula." Chavez stood at the railing beside Sam, wiping perspiration trickling from his temples. "Who would have ever thought a couple of young guys from Salinas, California, and Eagle Grove, Minnesota, would stand on the deck of a luxury liner and view paradise?"

Certainly not Sam.

The ship continued thirty miles across the bay, then docked at Manila's Pier 7, in what looked like a large modern port. Behind the bustling waterfront, Sam spotted elegant houses among swaying palm trees, and the opulent Manila Hotel.

"That's where MacArthur is living," Chavez said.

"How do you know?"

"Chaplain told me. Said that's his headquarters. Think they have a few rooms left for us?"

"Wouldn't count on it," Sam said, though after the lavish accommodations Chavez had finagled on ship, he wasn't putting anything past him.

At 15:00 hours Sam, Chavez, and the others stepped off the ship in single file and boarded buses that would carry the soldiers through Manila's busy streets and past the stately mansions and posh hotels, where well-dressed patrons sipped drinks and admired the bay from verandas. But the neighborhoods near the wharf turned out to be just another facade, like the hula dancers: Beyond the waterfront, the city turned gritty. Wooden stalls lined the streets, and vendors hawked boiled duck eggs. Water buffalo swayed under the burden of heavy loads, and taxi drivers honked and swerved through a maze of carriages pulled by donkeys.

As Sam's bus slowed, the searing heat and humidity seeped through the windows, carrying a pungent, complex aroma of sweet flowers, exotic spices, burning incense, garbage, raw sewage, and exhaust.

The buses rumbled north, past the countryside's banana trees, rice paddies, and gardens. The poverty affected Sam, especially the Filipinos' bamboo shacks, what somebody on the bus called *nipas*, which were built on stilts with thatched roofs and slatted floors so the occupants could drop food scraps to the pigs and chickens below. By comparison, Sam had grown up in comfort, even during the Depression.

What struck him most, however, was the Filipinos' smiles and upbeat demeanor as the bus passed. Children and adults waved and smiled at the soldiers, and when the bus slowed, the people shouted "Hello!" and "Welcome!"

After an hour-long, forty-mile drive, the bus pulled into Fort Stotsenburg and its adjacent air base, Clark Field, what Sam's superiors called the center of American power in the Far East. Sam's tank battalion moved into moldy tents that had been assembled along the main road between the two facilities at the end of a runway used by B-17 bombers. Several times each day, the giant planes passed over Sam's tent camp at just one hundred feet, blasting the soldiers below with dust, the smell of burning fuel, and a deafening roar.

Immediately upon arriving, Sam mailed a stack of eighteen letters to Sarah, one for each day on board the *President Coolidge*. Over the following weeks, he settled into the Philippines, though the searing humidity and the mosquitos at night made him think someone had played a cruel joke on him and served up the worst that Eagle Grove summers had to offer. On October 18, his unit moved to newly constructed barracks built on stilts, with five-foot walls of weaved matting called sawali. Above the walls, the barracks were open, which allowed breezes to blow through, a sort of natural air-conditioning.

Days began early: 05:15 reveille and breakfast at 06:00. Sam spent mornings working on tanks and other equipment. Lunch was from 11:30 to 13:30, then another hour of work. After 14:30, it was too hot to do anything productive. Instead, the men performed light duties and relaxed until the workday officially ended at 16:30. During free time, they bowled and played horseshoes, tennis, softball, and badminton. Sam watched movies in the base's air-conditioned theater and had drinks on weekend evenings, usually with enlisted men but sometimes with his superiors. While Sam envisioned this was what it would be like to live in a country club, the kind of posh, tropical resort reserved for the Fred Astaires of the world, he also felt as though the men were just killing time, waiting.

He wrote Sarah nearly every day, though he had no idea if or when she would get his letters. *Next time I see you,* he penned, *we will make it official.*

Each letter he signed off *Your loving Sam.*

And each time he did, he paused and wondered when, and sometimes *if,* he'd ever make it back home to her.

9

A FEW GOOD WOMEN

Mankato State Teachers College
November 1941

Sarah clutched the unexpected envelope as she walked a path cleared of knee-deep snow across campus to Memorial Library. She had received the letter from Frank D. McElroy, university president, inviting her to a meeting in a library conference room. The letter referenced an exciting job opportunity for someone with Sarah's academic course of study. Sarah had no idea what that job opportunity could be, other than perhaps a university teaching position. She remained an anomaly, being the only woman in her master's program. She'd called the president's office but had been told all her questions would be answered at the meeting.

During a call home she had mentioned the letter and the exciting opportunity referenced. Both her parents had been excited. Sarah had said she intended to come home to Eagle Grove to teach, but her father had told her to go to the meeting with an open mind. "Nothing ventured, nothing gained," he'd said.

She'd borrowed a friend's navy-blue wedge dress and black pumps. If this was some type of job interview, she'd look the part. When she entered Memorial Library, Sarah showed a woman seated at the information desk her letter and was directed to a room on the second floor, behind the stacks. Sarah was even more surprised when she walked into a room of college-age women, some of whom she recognized. Each looked equally confused and intrigued as to the meeting's nature, their conversations hushed but animated.

Sarah saw a familiar face and moved to an empty chair. "Hi," she said. "I'm—"

"Sarah Haber," the woman said and extended a hand. "We were in a philosophy class together second year. Alicia Jones."

"Do you know what the meeting is about?" Sarah asked.

"No. No one seems to know anything more than what is in the letter. I can tell you this, though: they picked girls from a variety of colleges and majors—I've spoken to girls who majored in astronomy, philosophy, language, biology, and now, math."

After several more minutes, two men in dazzling white uniforms and a woman in civilian dress walked into the meeting. The presence of men in uniform on campus was not strange, given the times, but these were not college students. The men were older and had colorful ribbons above their left breast pockets.

"Good evening, ladies," the civilian woman said to get the room's attention. "If you could all take your seats, we can get started."

Eager to know what the meeting was about, Sarah and the others quickly sat.

"Captain Russell," the woman said.

A tall, trim, good-looking man resembling the actor Jimmy Stewart stepped forward. "Good evening, ladies, and thank you for coming. I'm going to cut to the chase here so as not to keep you in further suspense. Two months ago, US Navy rear admiral Leigh Noyes wrote a letter to Ada Comstock, president of Radcliffe College, seeking to recruit women, primarily because he was running out of college-educated men."

"There's a real opener," Sarah said under her breath to Jones.

"We've since expanded our search nationwide. We are seeking bright, native-born students who have the sense and ability to keep a secret, to work for the United States Navy, assuming you pass a qualifying course. The course will be daily for up to eight hours a day. You will be tested weekly, and your tests will be sent to Washington, DC, to be scored. Those of you who pass these tests and are selected will receive further training and earn $1,842 a year."

"Did he just say what I think he said?" Jones said. She was not the only woman to react to the amount of money, which was twice the salary Sarah would make teaching at Eagle Grove, and more than what most teachers would make at urban schools, which remained the most likely career choice for even the brightest women in the room.

Russell seemed to revel in the women's excitement. "Let me also tell you that character matters. We will be considering your compliance with your school's code of comportment." Which basically meant the Navy would consider whether the women had broken curfew or other rules set down by housemothers, like no smoking or drinking or inviting men to their room. "We will interview persons who know you here at school and back in your hometowns to ensure you are women of strong moral fiber. If you are interested—"

Sarah raised her hand. The captain seemed taken aback. "Yes, Miss . . ."

Sarah stood. "Haber. Sarah Haber. What field would we be working in for the US Navy?"

"Ah yes. Good question, Miss Haber. The field is called communications intelligence, but you will be forbidden from telling anybody the field or what you are doing—not your friends, not your parents, not your siblings, not your roommates, nor your boyfriends. You are not to disclose what you are doing in a letter or utter the words 'communications,' 'intelligence,' or 'security.' If you go out in public and are asked what you do, you will say you are a secretary. You will say you perform menial tasks, like filing and typing and emptying trash cans and sharpening pencils. You will swallow your egos and tell them you sit on the laps of your male officers and make them happy. Sadly, people will believe you."

Sarah didn't know whether to be insulted or grateful Captain Russell understood the plight of women in the workforce.

"What will we *actually* be doing?" she persisted, still on her feet.

"If pressed, you will say you are studying communications."

"And in reality?"

Russell seemed to be contemplating whether to answer further. He looked to the other officer in the room, who shrugged. "That remains confidential," Russell said to Sarah. Then to the rest of the room he said, "But let me be clear, ladies. Given the sensitivity of the tasks you will be performing, to tell anyone will be considered an act of treason, punishable by death. The fact that you are women will not be considered toward leniency."

Sarah voiced her next question louder, as several women were now mumbling to one another. "Isn't an act of treason usually reserved for times of war?"

Again, Russell hesitated. "Usually. Not always."

"Is the United States going to war?" Sarah pressed, thinking of Sam.

"I can't answer that, Miss Haber, but we must be prepared for any possibility." But he had answered. She took her seat.

"Did you say those selected for the program would work in Washington, DC?" Alicia Jones said from her seat beside Sarah, sounding almost giddy.

"I did."

Another woman raised her hand. "Is the course offered for college credits?"

Alicia spoke to Sarah. "College credits? Who cares? For eighteen hundred dollars a year and a chance to live in Washington, DC, I'd give the college back some credits. Where do I sign?"

As Russell discussed the possibility of college credits, Sarah sat back, in shock. Sam was in the Philippines, and now this naval officer stood before her talking about acts of treason and America needing to be prepared for anything. Captain Russell could hem and haw all he wanted, but Sarah knew better. The country was headed to war against the Axis powers—Japan and Germany.

And Sam would be in the thick of things in the Philippines.

"If you are interested," Captain Russell was saying, "please raise your hand, and Miss Pensky will provide you a packet containing your first problem set—a series of problems we'd like you to solve."

Miss Pensky stepped forward as Captain Russell stepped back. "Inside the envelope you will find numbered problems and strips of paper with letters. You are to complete the problem sets and return them to me in one week. No extensions for any reason. You may work in teams and help one another. I would encourage you to do so because speed is of the essence, as is accuracy. As Captain Russell stated, your answers will be sent to Washington to be graded. If you are interested, please come forward. You will be asked to sign an oath of secrecy before being issued an envelope."

Sarah stood but didn't immediately step forward, unlike nearly every other woman in the classroom. She didn't blame them. Most, like herself, came from rural areas and likely had lived on dying farms or in dying small towns. Most had had their futures mapped out long ago, and not even a college education would allow them to deviate from that course. They would return home to teach at jobs that paid almost nothing, in classrooms well beyond capacity. They would get married, have babies, cook, clean, and otherwise care for their families and their homes. The US Navy was giving them an alternative script, a chance to see the country, to live with friends, to go out on the town in a big city, unencumbered by the weight of responsibility that society thrust on their shoulders, a respite between the demands of being a daughter and the responsibilities of being a wife. They could simply be themselves, young women with all the same aspirations as young men.

"You look undecided."

Sarah turned. Captain Russell stood just a few feet to her left. She'd be graduating at the end of fall quarter and had already accepted an offer to teach at Eagle Grove High School, starting in the new year.

"Very," she said.

10

A Day of Infamy

Clark Field
Luzon, Philippines
December 8, 1941 (December 7, 1941, Hawaii Standard Time)

Sam's platoon of five tanks sat parked in a patch of bushes and tall cogon grass next to Clark Field's main runway. The crushed grass beneath the tanks emitted the smell of kerosene and rotten eggs, strong enough for some men to tie cloths over their noses and mouths. They had been stationed there day and night for seven days, when reconnaissance pilots had first reported Japanese transports milling around in a large circle in the South China Sea. The men were on pins and needles.

This morning, Major Paul Jones came out and climbed atop one of the tanks. The tall redhead spoke with a Tennessee twang.

"Boys," he shouted, to gain their attention.

"Listen up," Sam said to the men in his platoon.

"This morning Japanese planes bombed Pearl Harbor in a cowardly sneak attack," Jones said.

"What the hell?" Anderson shouted.

"America is at war," Jones said.

"I hope we blasted those bastards out of the sky," Anderson said. "Gave them a taste of what they're going to get." The other men cheered and pumped their fists.

"Those at Pearl Harbor fought bravely," Jones said. "Though not without some casualties and the loss of a few ships. Reports are still coming in, so I can't tell you a lot, only that you tankers have orders not to fire unless you encounter enemy paratroopers. The base's antiaircraft batteries and interceptor planes will handle any Japanese bombers."

"Damn right," someone shouted.

"I hope they land here so we can beat the hell out of them in person," Anderson yelled. "The sneaky bastards might have got the jump on us at Pearl Harbor. Let them come here when we have our heads high and our eyes wide open. We'll make them eat dirt."

More men in Sam's platoon shouted and raised their fists. Sam was not among them. Something in the major's tone made Sam cautious. He sensed the major had not given them the straight scoop. He approached Jones. "Major," he said. "What are the chances the Japs are coming here?"

"Everyone in the Pacific Theater has been put on alert, Staff Sergeant. That includes us."

"Is that why the Army Air Corps planes took off at eight this morning and are still up in the air?"

"They'll fly all morning," Jones said, looking up. "To avoid being caught on the ground, which is what happened at Pearl Harbor."

"How bad was it? Pearl Harbor?"

Jones shook his head. "Have your men ready, Staff Sergeant."

Sam didn't have to worry on that end. The men, now fired up, took great care going over the jeeps and the machine guns atop their tanks, and checking to make sure the barrels were cleared and ready to fire. Others paced in the grass, checking and rechecking their M1 rifles and Colt pistols. The men were talking tough, but Sam felt an anxiousness about what had happened and what could come. The Japanese soldiers had been at war in China for years. The men in Sam's platoon had never fired their tanks or their rifles except in practice.

Just after midday, the B-17 bombers and P-40 fighters returned and landed at the base, then taxied until aligned in a row on the tarmac.

"What the hell are they doing?" Chavez said.

"Must need to refuel," Sam said.

"All of them at once?"

"If they took off at the same time, I'd guess so."

"Well, pardon my lack of education, but does that strike you as loco?"

The pilots stepped down from the planes and moved toward the mess hall, presumably to grab chow.

"They came in to eat? Seriously?" Chavez said.

"Does seem like questionable judgment," Sam allowed.

"Questionable judgment? Seems like insanity, if you ask this beet farmer."

"Maybe Jones was exaggerating the situation. Or maybe they're not picking up anything on radar. As much as I hate to admit Anderson had a rational thought in his thick skull, the Japs had the jump on us at Pearl Harbor, but they have to know we'll be ready and waiting for them now."

"Waiting for them," Chavez said, frowning, "but not exactly ready. Not with our planes and pilots on the ground."

At 12:45 Chavez pointed to two V-shaped formations approaching the base. "Looks like more planes coming in, Sergeant?"

Sam scanned the planes already lined up in a row on the landing strip. He didn't know the number of planes Clark Field held, but it seemed to him that most remained on the tarmac. He adjusted his binoculars.

Something was wrong.

"Must be fifty or more planes," he said. "That's way more than we've ever had here, counting the ones on the ground." Then he spotted what looked like drops of water or confetti sparkling beneath the aircraft. "What the hell is that falling?" He adjusted the binoculars and realized what he was seeing. "Shit!" he yelled. "Those are Jap bombers dropping bombs." Sam slid off his tank and ran down the line, yelling at his men. "Bombs! Bombs! Take cover! Get down, goddammit. Get down!"

The explosions were deafening, and the concussive blasts shook the ground and created their own wind, knocking those still standing to the earth. Great balls of fire, red and yellow, twisted into the sky with plumes of black smoke. Sam lifted his head, then got to a knee, watching as American pilots raced from the chow hall for their planes. A few managed to scramble into the cockpits, but even as the first few planes taxied down the runway, Sam sensed they were too late. More bombs dropped, and the planes, freshly filled with aviation fuel, detonated like bombs themselves. Those trying to taxi swerved to avoid large craters in the runway, crashed, and burst into flames. Pilots jumped from the planes and sprinted for cover in the tall grass; some were launched into the air when their airplanes exploded.

Dazed, Sam felt like he'd been knocked silly on the football field. Words seemed stuck in his throat. Around him, his men had lost all discipline—running without direction or diving under the tanks. They pressed the palms of their hands to their ears to dampen the deafening sound. Some shouted, silent screams drowned out by one blast after the next.

Sam looked again to the mess hall. The remaining pilots were rushing from the building, some realizing they were too late and abandoning any attempt to reach their doomed airplanes. Those perfectly aligned planes exploded in flames and black smoke, one after the other, like dominoes falling. Fuel trucks caught on the runway also exploded, along with nearby buildings. Sam felt the heat from the balls of flames and could smell the pungent burning gasoline. The base's gasoline storage depot ignited, and a thunderous blast knocked Sam from his feet back to the ground. He again rose up, his nostrils filled with the acrid, burning odor of fuel.

When his head cleared, Sam heard the air raid siren wailing and saw chaos everywhere. Panicked men ran in all directions and seemingly without purpose. Their movements matched the muzzy half functioning of his brain.

He had to *think*. Had to think and act. Command.

He was responsible for these men, for keeping them alive.

Some men in Sam's unit climbed into the tanks, but Sam knew that was a mistake. The 37-millimeter cannons mounted on their turrets could not track the high-altitude bombers. Other men dove beneath the tanks, seeking cover, but Sam sensed that was also not good. The Japanese would target the defenseless tanks with their bombs after they attacked the runway and the planes.

Finally snapping from his confused state, Sam ran down the line, grabbing soldiers by the shoulder from under the tanks, while shouting and pointing in the direction of the nearest trench. Some men, wide-eyed, stared back with a blank expression, paralyzed by fear. Sam shoved them toward the trench to get them moving.

When he'd pulled the last man from beneath the last tank, he sprinted and dove headfirst into a trench as more bombs thundered all around them. He lay on his chest and covered his ears with his palms. The ground vibrated against his ribs, and his heart pounded within them.

When the explosions at last ceased, he sat up and looked to the sky. A second wave of Japanese bombers was descending, the roar of engines again deafening. They arrived with fresh bombs that demolished the remaining parked airplanes, but not the tanks, which surprised Sam.

Kristiansen, his company commander at Brainerd, lurched to his feet and ran from the trench toward the jungle. A mistake. "No—" Sam had begun to shout after him when a bomb exploded, and Kristiansen disappeared like it was a massive, unthinkable magician's trick.

A brush fire kicked up at the jungle's edge and quickly grew into a sudden living thing, snaking toward them, its smoke adding to the stench of rotten eggs, its flames crackling and producing denser smoke that obscured the field.

Another soldier tried to bolt for the jungle but Sam grabbed him, then shoved him down. "Stay down, goddammit. Stay down."

Something struck Sam in the back of the head, knocking off his helmet and shoving him off his feet. He had the sensation of flying before he hit the ground, the wind knocked out of him. He thought he'd been shot. When he opened his eyes, he couldn't see out of his left eye. He reached up and touched blood flowing down his forehead, then probed the top of his head and felt a wound.

Someone knocked Sam back flat to the ground and sat atop him. Panicked, he thought a Japanese soldier was attacking and kicked and punched.

"It's Pete! It's Pete!"

Sam looked up at Chavez through his one clear eye. Chavez ripped off a piece of his shirt and pressed it against Sam's head, then grabbed Sam's hand and put it on the cloth. "Keep pressure on the wound. Do you hear me? Keep the pressure on it. Head wounds bleed like crazy. It looks worse than it is."

"They're leaving," someone shouted.

Chavez pointed to the sky. "They aren't dropping any paratroopers."

Sam sat up, squinting at the bright sunlight and looking out of his one clear eye. The bombers indeed looked to be departing.

"Fighter escorts," someone else yelled.

The Zeros, so many, looked like a swarm of locusts. Sam stood and wiped the blood obscuring his vision in his left eye. Some semblance of his training took hold and he shouted, "They're coming in low to finish the job. Now, get to your tanks! Get to the guns! Now. Move! Move!"

Sam ran up and down the trenches imploring the scared men to climb into and atop the tanks. When he'd done so, he climbed atop his tank, and Chavez slid through the hatch. Sam locked on a Zero and fired the .30-caliber machine gun, screaming in anger and exhilaration. The Zero sped past him so fast it was almost a blur, but so low Sam spotted the pilot's eyes as he tried to pepper the plane.

The attack went on for what seemed an eternity, but when the Zeros finally departed, just two hours had passed. Chavez opened the hatch and climbed out onto the tank to sit with Sam. They looked at what had been Clark Field. The base had been transformed into a tangle of bomb craters, metal debris, bodies, and burned-out aircraft. The smell was nauseating and suffocating; rubber tires and fuel blazed, and black smoke billowed and twisted in clouds, so thick it obscured what remained of the runway and the barracks.

For the next several hours, Sam and his men helped load hundreds of dead and wounded men into trucks, onto bomb racks, and anything else with wheels. The area smelled of scorched flesh and bodies already beginning to decay in the steaming tropical heat. Persistent flies swarmed over the bodies of men Sam had served with in Minnesota, Washington, and Kentucky; men he'd sailed with on the USAT *President Coolidge*. Some had gotten married just before boarding the ship; others, like Chavez, had danced with the hula dancers in Hawaii and played games on the ship's deck. To Sam's horror, many wounded and dead had lost arms and legs, what remained just stumps, some cauterized by the fire, others tied off with crude tourniquets. Sam helped to carry one man whose intestines hung from a hole in his belly. He nearly dropped his end of the makeshift stretcher when he turned to vomit.

After Sam unloaded the mangled soldier at the base hospital, a doctor noticed the crusty smear of dried blood on his face. "Hey. Get back here, Sergeant, and sit down. Let me take a look at that wound."

"I'm fine," Sam said. "Treat the others who need help."

"You're not fine. Sit down, Sergeant," the doctor ordered.

Sam sat.

"You got shrapnel in your scalp. I don't have time to numb it."

"Just pull it," Sam said.

The doctor did so and Sam winced in pain, then again each time the doctor stitched the wound. As the doctor worked, Sam listened to the officers discussing what had happened. They argued over why the planes had returned at the same time and about why they didn't have better communication that the Japanese bombers were inbound. Sam learned all but one of 142 American airplanes had gone up in smoke and the air base had no air defenses left. You didn't need to be an officer to know that Clark Field could not repel another Japanese attack, that they were now sitting ducks, and Sam suspected the same was true of Pearl Harbor, that Major Jones hadn't been telling Sam or the rest of the men the whole truth about what had happened there. What this meant for those still able to fight remained to be seen, but it didn't look good, not from any perspective. He wondered if the Navy could send warships fast enough to make a difference, maybe bring more planes, but how many? And how long would that take? Until then, the men were on their own with what they had—tanks. And judging by the speed and destruction of the Japanese attack, it didn't seem near enough.

Sam quietly slipped from the hospital to find who remained of the men in his unit. He felt uneasy on his feet, though not just from the blow to his head. As he walked the field, his heart ached. He wasn't naive. He'd played sports, lots of them. He knew when his team had won and when it had lost, and his team had lost this battle. Worse, they hadn't even had the chance to fight. And the consequences were far graver than the loss of a game, or pride. Men, good men he'd come to care about, had died, and he couldn't help but wonder if he had done something wrong, if he had done something or failed to do something that had led to their deaths. He feared this attack was but a preview of what was to come.

America was at war.

From this point forward, people would be shooting at him and his men, trying to kill them. Any mistakes and Sam and his men would pay with their lives.

He passed where his barracks once stood but only saw a crater. He found what men remained near the tanks in the burnt grass. They would sleep there tonight. If the Japanese returned during the night, perhaps paratroopers, they would be ready.

"You think they'll come back?" Chavez asked as dusk fell and the first stars appeared in the sky.

"Tonight?" Sam said. "I don't know. But I know what happened here today and at Pearl Harbor is just the start. The Japs are knocking out what we can use to fight, our ships and our planes. They're softening us up. Once they do, they'll come for us. We can be sure of it."

For once, Chavez didn't have a snappy reply.

As Sam lay under his tank and stared up at its steel underbelly, he gently touched the white bandage on his head. It was real. This was no dream. He rolled onto his side and peered out from under his tank, northward, beyond a row of burned palm trees that now looked like broken toothpicks sticking up from the ground. The blood-red sky faded from dusk to dark, and a lone star appeared on the northern horizon.

"Star light, star bright, first star I see tonight," Sam whispered. He longed to feel Sarah's presence, and for her optimism, but it would not come, not this night.

"I wish I may, I wish I might, have the wish I wish tonight." Sam closed his eyes and squeezed the ring he carried in his buttoned shirt pocket, near his heart. Sarah, his family, and Eagle Grove had never felt farther away.

11

Poking the Bear

Luzon, Philippines
January 1, 1942

Sam's superior officers had informed him that on the day of the Clark Field and Pearl Harbor attacks the Japanese had struck other sites across the Pacific, and the next day, the United States Congress had declared war on Japan. Three days later, Japan's allies, Germany and Italy, had declared war on the United States. Sam was told that in hundreds of cities and towns across America, young men were lining up to enlist. He didn't know if that was true or just propaganda to lift the men's spirits. What he did know was the United States, with its years of isolationism, was far behind the well-oiled Nazi and Japanese war machines, which had been gearing up for years. What had transpired in those first twenty-four hours illustrated how well prepared the Japanese had been, and how far the United States needed to go to catch up.

America had entered the war, but they were a long way from winning it.

—

"Blow it," an officer barked into his radio.

Seconds later, a bridge behind Sam—the one his tank had just crossed—erupted in a ball of fire as seven tons of dynamite blasted chunks of concrete and metal high into the sky. The pieces arced through the air, lit by an orange glow, then splashed into the broad Pampanga River.

Sam knew the pattern all too well. In just weeks, the Japanese military had established four beachheads on Luzon, then took Manila and everything else in their path. Time after time, Sam's tank platoon and others sped forward to engage and delay superior Japanese forces, called suicide missions by many. The tank crews had orders to "hold at all costs" and buy precious hours and days to allow outgunned Allied forces to retreat along a series of defensive lines.

Each time the Allies set up a new line, usually along a river's southern bank, Sam and the other tank commanders would hold until given the order to turn and get out, fleeing farther south, often under heavy fire.

In a battle west of Carmen, the Japanese had fired armor-piercing shells, and one had cut through a tank under Sam's command, taking off arms and legs. John Anderson had lost an arm and had been rushed to the nearest hospital. Anderson had not been well liked in the unit, constantly needling the others, but he wasn't an anonymous face; that was maybe why his injury hit home so hard. He was one of them. Now he was gone. The real tragedy, Sam quickly learned, was there existed little to no time to mourn those killed or injured. As soon as the wounded were taken from the battle, Sam was told to give the order for his men to soldier on.

He had lost other men in his unit at the Agno River, and during a battle near Lingayen Gulf, a Japanese shell had decapitated one of Sam's bow gunners. Sam had not been in the tank, but those who had been were in a horrified state of shock, unable to speak and covered in blood and pieces of human flesh.

Again, the order had come down to bag the dead, get them out, and move on.

But it wasn't that easy. Each explosion shook Sam and the tankers to the core. Every casualty sapped his spirit and haunted his dreams when the exhausted men were given a few precious hours to try and sleep.

Tiny, safe Eagle Grove, Minnesota, was a world away, and not just geographically. Sam couldn't imagine ever actually living there again—turning off the lights at night, climbing up creaking stairs to his warm bed, and settling down into that silent, utterly secure world to sleep. How could this place and that place exist on the same planet?

Amid all the destruction, Sam could hear the lowing of cows and the howling of dogs deserted by their Filipino masters. He'd seen dogs feasting on human corpses and couldn't get the sight or the smells of scorched flesh, decaying bodies, and dead animals out of his head. The stench coated his lungs and seeped into his clothing. The dead were stacked so they weren't in the way of medics, and to try to prevent the bodies from being ravaged by the animals. But nothing stopped the insects. Buzzing flies blackened the corpses.

This was a horror Sam not only could never have imagined, but found himself unable to believe, even faced all day, every day, with the brutal evidence.

———

"Medic!" Sam yelled as his tank rolled to a stop after yet another engagement. He tumbled off the machine, exhausted, then reached for a wounded soldier draped across the tank's front, a young private from Wisconsin who had lost both legs at the knees when an armor-piercing shell destroyed his tank and killed the rest of his crew. Sam and Chavez had applied tourniquets to the man's legs, strapped him onto the tank, and driven him from the jungle.

"That's it, easy does it," Chavez said as he helped Sam lower the mangled soldier onto the grass. The private's face was blackened, as were his hands and what remained of his legs.

"Corpsman," Sam shouted as the war raged on. Tank guns thundered and shells whistled overhead, drowning out the screams of the injured and dying, and the shouts of others pleading for more ammunition. Machine gunners rattled off belts of bullets in metal canisters, one after the next, as fast as they could load the guns. The air soon filled with the smell of their guns overheating. Black soot from fires and from the oil spouting from disabled tanks covered the men struggling to repair them, darkening their perspiring faces, hands, and arms.

"Where are the goddamn corpsmen?" Sam yelled again above the din.

"They're tending to the other wounded," said an Army chaplain, Father Thomas Scecina, as he hurried forward, hunkered down, and knelt beside the dying soldier. "I'm here, son."

"What are you doing, Padre?" Sam said. "This is no place for prayers. We need a corpsman."

Chaplains of all denominations usually stayed well behind the front line—during battles, they staffed the battalion's makeshift hospitals to comfort patients and administer last rites—but Father Tom took a persistently hands-on approach. "We always need prayers, Sam, whatever else we might need. Lift his head for me so I can administer last rites."

Sam knelt, but a Japanese artillery shell exploded nearby and those not knocked down dove for cover, including Sam. When he lifted his head, Father Tom was on his knees, hunched over the soldier to shield him from falling debris. The priest then sat back on his haunches, finished his prayer, and traced a cross on the soldier's forehead with his thumb.

Sam looked past the padre as two corpsmen carried a stretcher through the grass and battle debris. "Over here." Sam waved them forward. When the men arrived, Sam looked down at the wounded man he and Chavez had worked so hard to keep alive. His chest no longer rose and fell. Father Tom reached with his fingers and gently closed the man's eyelids.

"Goddammit." Sam fell to the grass and pulled his knees to his chest as the corpsmen carried the body away.

"Get up," Father Tom said. "There are more dying. Do your job." Then the priest was gone, through the grass, to the next stretcher.

A little extra. That's how he'd heard one soldier in his unit characterize what Father Tom gave in these worst moments. The phrase had stuck. Sam had now witnessed why. Bombs raining down, shells exploding, elbow deep in gore, the padre could always be counted on to give a little extra.

Sam rose and turned to Chavez. "Spread the word. We've held as long as we can. Tell the men to pull back into the jungle and head farther south."

"We're running out of real estate," Chavez said. "We keep retreating, we'll be in the Pacific."

"Major Jones said reinforcements are coming," Sam said. "Until then, we need to keep fighting."

—

Reinforcements did not come. The Japanese had a blockade of warships around the Philippines, strangling Allied supply lines providing weapons, ammunition, food and water, and medical supplies. Two months later, in February, Sam's tank battalion joined the 192nd with orders to guard the airfields on Bataan that soldiers had quickly constructed, believing aid would come to the 12,000 American and 60,000 Filipino soldiers trapped on the peninsula after months of retreat. Chavez had been correct. They'd run out of land.

Fifty-gallon drums marked the runways and could be lit at night, the fire outlining the landing strip but also giving the Japanese warplanes an easy target to bomb. After each bombing run, Allied engineers repaired the airfields and the soldiers waited, night after night, for those reinforcements and supplies that never came.

Daily food rations dropped to 1,500 calories per person in February, 1,000 calories in early March, then were cut even lower. Starving American soldiers hunted for anything they could kill and eat, while Filipino soldiers found edible plants and roots. The only animals most men would not eat were the monkeys now displaced by the destruction of portions of their jungle; their faces made them look too human.

Maybe because Sam had subsisted on two small meals a day in Eagle Grove, his body had adapted better than most, though he, too, had lost weight. His uniform sagged on his shrinking frame. The Japanese frequently dropped surrender leaflets picturing a scantily clad blonde woman, prompting Chavez to say, "They'd be more successful getting us to surrender if they dropped pictures of a hamburger."

Gasoline rations had also been cut to fifteen gallons a day for each vehicle, except the tanks. Now, Major Jones advised Sam the allotment was about to be reduced to ten gallons a day.

"What the hell can we do on ten gallons a day, Major?"

"What we can," Jones said, his standard reply.

On April 3, 1942, the Japanese launched a major offensive supported by artillery and aircraft. A large force of Japanese troops came over Mount Samat and descended the volcano's south face, wiping out two divisions of Allied defenders and tearing a gaping hole in their defensive line. Word spread through the besieged battalion that General MacArthur had issued an order to his generals on Corregidor Island forbidding surrender.

"Easy for his generals to say, from their island fortress," Sam said to Chavez as they stopped their retreat to regroup.

Early on the morning of April 9, Sam returned to his platoon after a briefing by his commanders. "What did they say?" Chavez asked. "Are we getting off this peninsula? Are they sending supplies?"

"They said MacArthur wants us tankers to lead a surprise attack on Olongapo and capture Japanese supplies."

"Olongapo is more than ninety miles away," Chavez said. "How does MacArthur propose we get the tanks that far without fuel?"

"I don't know. I only know General King asked us tank commanders what we thought of the idea—if we could carry out the attack."

"I hope you told them MacArthur has lost his mind, along with the Philippines. It's time to get off these islands."

"We told him it would be impossible, even if we had enough fuel to get there."

"At least somebody's talking sense," Chavez said.

"Yeah, well. There's more," Sam said, pausing to search for the right words.

"More?"

"General King has decided further resistance is futile. Only about twenty-five percent of us are even healthy enough to keep fighting, and we have maybe two days of food remaining, even on one-quarter rations. We would be lucky to last another day. We have twenty-four thousand sick and wounded troops in the open-air hospital, plus forty thousand civilians to worry about."

"Got 'em right where we want 'em," Chavez joked bleakly.

"So we're being evacuated, right?" another soldier in Sam's unit said.

"There's not enough time," Sam said, "or enough planes or ships, even if they could get them in here quickly enough."

A black silence settled over the group.

"So . . . they're not coming?" Chavez said, the alternative dawning on him and the others. "Oh, hell no. No. No. No."

Sam drew in a deep breath. "General King made the decision at 03:35 to send a jeep with two unmarried officers—under a white flag—to negotiate terms of surrender with the Japanese commander, but the commander refused to meet them and insisted on King's presence."

"Needs the boss there to sign on the dotted line to humiliate us as much as they can," Chavez said. "Bastards. So when is King going?"

"It's already in the works. King will try to get assurance from the Japanese we will be treated as prisoners of war."

"As opposed to what?" someone asked.

"I don't know," Sam said. "I've been told to wait for an order to destroy all tanks, combat vehicles, arms, ammunition, radios, everything."

"I say no way," Chavez said. "I say we go down swinging. I'm not going to no POW camp."

"Yeah," the rest of Sam's men shouted. "Let's take down a few Japs with us."

"Damn right," Chavez said. "We make a run for the mountains, get lost, then link up with the Filipino *guerrilleros* fighting in the jungle."

"How much time do we have before King issues the order?" someone else asked.

"I don't know," Sam said. He looked at his watch. "But if you boys want to keep fighting until he does, then I'm with you."

The men cheered. "Let's go!" "The mountains!" "Let's do it!"

"Hang on. Hang on," Sam said over the shouting. "Let's take a vote. Make this democratic. Any man who no longer wants to fight, no hard feelings."

His platoon voted unanimously not to surrender and to head north toward the mountains. To get there, they would have to make a last, desperate attack on dug-in Japanese forces and do so without support from infantry, air, or artillery. The men never flinched.

Sam hoped he wasn't leading them all to their deaths.

They fell in and within twenty minutes were on the move. They had traveled three to four miles when, at 05:35, Sam received a command over his radio: "Blast. And we have one hour to comply."

"All tanks, stop," Sam said into his headset.

Now he had a dilemma. "Blast" meant their four-month battle against the Japanese was over. King had surrendered. All armored units were ordered to report to battalion headquarters and destroy all artillery and weapons. To disobey could be perceived as insubordination.

Sam spun around in the turret to make sure the single-file line of tanks behind him had received the same order. He waved a hand back and forth in a wide arc.

Chavez, who had been given his own command due to a shortage of personnel, shouted from atop his tank, directly behind Sam's, "Head for the hills?" and gestured to the nearby mountains covered in green forest.

Sam knew his men wanted to fight. He did too. He could lead them into the mountains to hide and cause trouble for the Japanese, but doing so now would disobey a direct order from battalion headquarters. Worse, it could put all the men who did surrender in mortal peril. Unless all the Allied forces trapped on the Bataan Peninsula surrendered, unconditionally, including Sam's platoon, Japanese forces would almost certainly overrun them in the morning and, in the absence of a surrender, kill them all. The massacre would start at the Allies' jungle hospital with its 24,000 gravely ill soldiers and the more than eighty Army nurses stationed there. In his meeting with his superior officers, Sam had been told that the "Blast" order was intended to avoid the worst slaughter in US military history. Maybe so, but it left them to endure the largest surrender in US military history.

As this debate raged inside Sam, a jeep arrived carrying a colonel.

"Where are you going, Sergeant? Didn't you get the order to Blast?"

"My men want to keep fighting," Sam said.

"We can still fight!" shouted a nearby soldier, who was immediately joined by all the men within earshot.

"No. You can't." The colonel stood in his jeep to speak to them. "You risk the lives of your fellow soldiers, the sick and the injured among them, unless you get these tanks back to headquarters and blow them. You'll be handing them to the Japanese to use on us. Now, you either turn these tanks around, or you will all be court-martialed."

Sam almost laughed. They were about to become prisoners of war. The prospect of being court-martialed paled in comparison. But he wouldn't sacrifice the sick and wounded.

"You heard the colonel," he said to his men. "Turn them around."

The men cussed and shouted, but they returned to battalion headquarters. In a nearby field, they destroyed their equipment and their tanks. Sam and his men plugged the tank turret barrels with oil, rags, and metal cleaning rods, loaded a shell into every chamber, and ran a lanyard from each firing pin to a point a safe distance away. As Sam clutched a lanyard, he recalled the church bell prank—the miracle of Eagle Grove. This time he wasn't ringing bells, or staging a miracle. This time, the shell exploded in the clogged barrel, destroying it. His tank went up in flames, along with his hope of returning to Eagle Grove and to Sarah.

Sam and his men were going to a prison camp, and how they would be treated by the Japanese, who were said to have committed atrocities and horrors on thousands of men, women, and children across China, was anything but certain.

12

THE HIKE

Luzon, Philippines
April 10, 1942

Sam and his exhausted men were asleep when Japanese soldiers overran their bivouac early in the morning. The soldiers yelled and screamed and kicked Sam and his men with their hobnail boots, then jabbed them with their bayonets. Outside, the mistreatment continued; the men were shoved and beaten until they formed two columns. The soldiers then stole everything they could, taking the POWs' watches, rings, money, and anything else they wanted. They took glasses off men's faces then smashed the lenses and crushed the frames. Sam had sewn Sarah's ring and his pocketknife into the lining of a vest he'd made from a green Army blanket. At least for now the soldiers did not take it.

The Japanese then separated the officers from the enlisted men.

"Typical," Chavez muttered. "Even now, they're riding at the front of the train and we're cargo."

"The Japanese are extremely rank conscious," said Major Jones, who'd opted to stay with the enlisted men. "It goes without saying that they'll treat the officers better than they treat us."

"Lucky us," Chavez said.

"Why are you still with us?" Sam asked.

"This is where I belong," Jones said, without adding anything more.

The enlisted POWs, and any officers who chose to, stood sweating in the unrelenting sun the remainder of the day. For some already exhausted men, it was too much. When they collapsed from the heat, the Japanese guards beat them further and dragged them off into the jungle, where the POWs heard gunshots.

That night the Japanese again kicked and clubbed the men into ranks of one hundred, then ordered the columns to march north.

"Going on a hike, boys," Chavez called out. "Walk in the park for the likes of us."

Maybe, Sam thought, but his gut told him this would be like no other hike they'd yet endured.

The soldiers shuffled north, four abreast, along a dry, heat-cracked road, armed Japanese guards all around them. Already starved, sick, and exhausted, the POWs were forced on an exodus from Bataan at the hottest, driest time of year.

And their mistreatment worsened.

As Sam, Chavez, and the others marched, they heard an engine roaring. Sam turned. A Japanese guard on the back of a motorcycle raced alongside their column with his saber out and a murderous look on his face.

Sam had just said, "What the hell is he doing?" when the guard extended his saber and beheaded a POW. The sight of the man's headless body taking two more steps before crumpling to the ground made several vomit.

As the men continued their march, guards came into their ranks and grabbed a soldier in a cut-off shirt. On his right arm was an American flag tattoo. They dragged the soldier from the ranks, kicking and punching him and hitting him with the butts of their rifles until he could no longer raise his arms to fend off the attack. They dragged him to a wooden fencepost and held his arm over the wood railing. Then, to Sam's horror, a soldier screamed and swung his saber, severing the arm. As the soldiers drove the rest of the men forward with their swords, Sam looked back. POWs had put a tourniquet on the dazed soldier's arm and were carrying him forward with them, but for how long?

Farther ahead, Sam spotted a group of prisoners beside the road digging shallow graves in the hard, dry soil. He presumed the graves were for those who had died on the march, and whose bodies now lay along the road. He was wrong. A guard shot a soldier holding a shovel in the head, and his lifeless body pitched forward into the freshly dug hole. The process was repeated multiple times. Wounded men tried to climb out of the graves, only to be shot, bayoneted, or struck by the shovels they had used to dig the graves but had given back to their guards. Other prisoners, fearing they would be next, died by suicide, bolting into nearby fields, where guards were only too happy to quickly shoot or bayonet them.

When men fell and couldn't get up, the guards ordered the column to step over them. Fallen men held out their canteens, desperate for water, but the POWs had no choice but to implore the men to get up, to march. "The buzzard squad is coming," Sam would say, a term the prisoners had quickly given to guards who walked behind their formation and stabbed prisoners too weak to walk.

Each time Sam stepped over a fallen soldier, it felt like another betrayal.

Many of the prisoners had dysentery or diarrhea and could no longer control their bowels. They defecated as they marched and were soon caked with their own filth, the Philippine dust, and sweat. The smell, combined with the odor of the gangrenous wounds and death, was overpowering.

The POWs had left Cabcaben late in the morning and didn't stop marching until 03:00. Exhausted, Sam hoped they'd rest the remainder of the night, but at 04:00 the guards shouted and again jabbed the men with bayonets. Sam and the others struggled to their feet and marched on.

They reached Lamao at just after 08:00 on April 11. There, the POWs were allowed to scavenge for food, though little was found. Sam and Chavez ate grubs, insects, anything they could find until their guards ordered them to move out at 09:00. They reached Limay at noon. Sam noticed a lot of movement at the front of the column.

"What's going on?" Chavez asked, also eyeing the commotion.

"Looks like they're changing the guard," Sam said. "Different-style uniforms."

"What does this mean?"

"I don't know," Sam said, but they all quickly realized it wasn't for the better.

The new guards marched the POWs at a faster pace, which caused the weakest to fall farther behind. And for some reason the guards also seemed more nervous, on edge, and their nerves led to additional beatings and stabbings.

A few brutal days later, Sam, Chavez, and others from his unit came around a bend in the road and spotted Father Tom kneeling over a fallen soldier.

"Father Tom, no," Sam called out, trying to keep his voice low. The chaplain could have gone ahead with the other officers but, like Major Paul Jones, he'd chosen to stay with the men. As Sam and Chavez drew near, it became obvious the bloody soldier—a victim of what looked like two vicious bayonet wounds—was past saving. The buzzard squad would end his suffering.

"Stand up, Father Tom," Sam said. "Fall in. There's nothing you can do."

The chaplain ignored him and applied pressure to the soldier's belly wound. He had lain his crucifix on the man's chest and was now sketching a cross on his forehead with his thumb. "Through this holy anointing, may the Lord in his love and mercy help you by the grace of the Holy Spirit," he said.

"Let's get him," Chavez said to Sam. They did a quick check for Japanese guards, then angled toward the roadside.

"Come on, Father Tom," Chavez said. "We gotta move, or they'll kill all of us." He and Sam each grabbed the chaplain by an armpit.

"Wait." Father Tom shook one arm free and offered a final prayer for the dying soldier. "May the Prince of Peace who freed you from sin save and lift you up."

"Time's up," Sam said.

He and Chavez hoisted Father Tom to his feet, dragged him into the throng, and blended in with the sea of humanity.

—

They arrived at Orani, then Hermosa, where the road changed from gravel to pavement. A hot tropical rain fell that did not refresh but at least allowed the POWs to lean back their heads and suck in precious drops of water, momentarily soothing blistered lips and swollen tongues.

At 16:00 hours Sam's column reached San Fernando. There, the guards herded them into what amounted to a bullpen, not unlike the roundup pens Sam had seen for cattle being branded. The ground was already covered in human waste from previously penned POWs, yet the men still collapsed onto it.

At 04:00 the Japanese awoke the POWs and marched them to a train station.

"Dibs on a window seat," Chavez called out.

"What window is that, jerk?" another said.

The boxcars for the narrow-gauge Philippine railroad came in two sizes: steel cars thirty-three feet long by eight feet wide and seven feet tall, or wooden cars sixteen feet long, just as wide, but only six feet tall. They each had a single door and walls slatted so tight they could ship wheat and rice.

The guards packed the men into the cars until they couldn't sit. When Sam and Chavez stepped aboard, the car was already full, but the guards kept pushing, kicking, and prodding with rifle butts, forcing more POWs aboard, then bolted the door shut. The men were pinned against one another so tight it was difficult to draw a breath, and some panicked, thinking they would suffocate. When the rail cars moved, Sam felt fresh air seeping in through the cracks around the door he and Chavez were pressed up against. Other prisoners noticed it also and began shoving toward it, to the extent they could.

"Hold on. Hold on," Sam shouted. The men who had been in Sam's tank platoon listened to their staff sergeant and held the others at bay. "We're going to rotate every three minutes so everyone can get fresh air."

"For how long?" somebody said.

"For however long we're trapped in here," Sam said.

Four hours later, the train arrived at Capas. The guards opened the doors and shouted orders in Japanese, again striking the POWs until the cars were emptied. The men stepped off and felt the rush of fresh air, cool on their perspiring skin, but the reprieve was brief. They were again formed into columns and set off at a quick pace.

"Looks like the luxury section of the voyage is over, gents," Chavez said. "We're back to hiking."

They walked the last nearly eight kilometers to Camp O'Donnell in stifling hot temperatures with oppressive humidity. Sam didn't know how many men had started the hike. He knew only that many never made it to Camp O'Donnell.

13

FINDING HER PURPOSE

Eagle Grove, Minnesota
May 15, 1942

Friday night, Sarah worked in the Paradise Theater's projection room. Mr. and Mrs. Larsen had been on the verge of closing the theater after so many had left Eagle Grove in search of work, had been drafted, or had chosen to enlist, including senior boys at the high school, who lied about their age for the chance to teach the "Japs" a lesson for bombing Pearl Harbor. Between the Depression and the exodus for the war, Eagle Grove had become a ghost town. The Larsens saw no point in showing a film to an empty theater, but Sarah had a plan to get people to come, telling the Larsens that those who remained needed something to take their mind off the war.

"But a half-full theater will hardly pay for the film's cost," Mr. Larsen said.

"That's true," Sarah said. "But what if you show the film only Friday night through Sunday, but multiple times each day? Half a theater will still be $13.50 with candy, popcorn, and fountain drinks. Give or take. And I'm happy to run the projectors."

"But we won't be able to pay you, Sarah."

"I'll run it for free," Sarah said. Since returning home, she'd felt she needed to do something to help.

"We can't ask that of you," Mr. Larsen said.

"We all have to give something," she said. "And the movies will be an escape for everyone, myself included. You'll see, people in town will come, and if we do a little advertising in the *Eagle Courier*, we'll get some people living nearby too. The Paradise is the only theater close by. Anyway, we won't know unless we try."

The Larsens agreed to give it a go. When the showings were a success, the theater near capacity each weekend, no one was more grateful than Sarah. She needed the distraction. She hadn't received a letter from Sam since the Japanese invaded the Philippine Islands following the attack on Pearl Harbor, but she didn't want to think about what that might mean. She'd poured herself into her new teaching job to dull her pain, decorated and redecorated her classroom, distracted herself solving crossword puzzles, and given piano lessons at night to stay busy. Most recently, she had helped to organize scrap metal drives.

None of it had helped.

She remained restless. She knew she could do more. She thought often of the night Captain Russell and another naval officer had come to Mankato to recruit female students to Washington, and she wondered if she'd been wrong to turn down the opportunity to help the war effort. Teaching had not fulfilled her the way she had hoped, not with many of her students shipping off to fight. It didn't seem right for her to be safe at home in Eagle Grove.

She loaded the first reel of *Sergeant York* onto the projector. The film had come out the year before and had been highly acclaimed. Sarah had seen it six times, and each time, she bawled. The WWI account of Alvin York hit too close to home.

Shortly after she'd started the movie on this night, someone knocked on the projection room door. She thought it might be Mr. Larsen. He was so grateful for Sarah's idea to keep the movie house open, he often brought her dinner, or a dessert Mrs. Larsen had made.

"Come in," Sarah said without shifting her eyes from the movie screen.

"Hi, Sarah."

She turned at the familiar but unexpected voice. "Mr. Carlson. What are you doing here?" But even as she said the words, an acidic burning inched up the back of her throat.

"Now, don't panic, Sarah," Mr. Carlson said. "We just received a letter from the War Department and—"

"Oh God." She jumped to her feet, knocking over the table on which she'd put her bag of popcorn and her Coke. "Not Sam. Please tell me Sam isn't dead."

Mr. Carlson raised his hands. "Not dead. No. No, not dead. But he's missing, Sarah. He was left behind in the Philippines when we surrendered. The Red Cross is trying to get more information, but they say we left behind many soldiers. It will take time locating all of them."

Sarah's legs collapsed and she landed on her butt in the chair. She didn't know what to say or do. "I can't just go on not knowing," she said finally. "Mr. Carlson, I can't *not* know." She pressed her face into her hands and wept.

Mr. Carlson wrapped an arm around her shoulders. "We have to be strong, Sarah. There's a very good chance Sam is still alive, that he was one of those forced to surrender. We need to assume he's alive."

"But where is he?"

"I don't know." He looked at her with hooded eyes, and Sarah realized he was in pain. She could only imagine the pain Mrs. Carlson was feeling, as well as Sam's siblings. He couldn't offer her any more than he already had, because he didn't have anything more but his faith and the slightest hope that comes from uncertainty.

"You're right," she said. "Sam's strong. He'll survive whatever it is, and he'll come home."

Sam's father fought back tears, his lips pinched in worry and uncertainty. He and Sarah consoled one another for a few more minutes, then said good night. As Sergeant York, a farmer, wrestled with killing German soldiers, Sarah thought again of the evening at Mankato when she'd been summoned to Memorial Library. She'd turned down Captain Russell. She'd rationalized doing so by telling herself it had not been her dream. Her dream had always been to teach at Eagle Grove. She looked to the movie screen, to Sergeant York, once a conscientious objector, who still wanted only to go home and farm, but who'd killed so many German soldiers they surrendered to him en masse.

Circumstances change, she decided. Life is not a straight line. There are bends in the road. We have to adapt, or we'll fail to make the turn and crash. This all struck her with the force of revelation.

Sarah needed to take the bend in the road.

After threading the last reel onto the projector, she hurried downstairs to the lobby. "I have to go," she said to the Larsens, who stood behind the counter looking grave. "I'm sorry."

"We know," Mr. Larsen said.

"Mr. Carlson told us about Sam," Mrs. Larsen said. "You go on home. Be with your family."

"No. I mean, I have to leave Eagle Grove. I have to do something more, something to help bring Sam home, and all those other boys. I can't just go on here day after day. Not anymore. Not with Sam missing. I'm sorry."

"Where will you go?" Mrs. Larsen asked.

"Where I can *do* something." She grabbed her coat and hat from the stand and moved to the theater's front door.

"Sarah, it's storming out there," Mr. Larsen said.

At that same moment, a lightning bolt lit up Main Street, and a nerve-racking thunderclap followed. Heavy rain pelted the street and sidewalk, then pebbles of hail fell, driven by a heavy wind. A spring thunderstorm.

Something unexpected. A bend in the road.

"Wait at least until the storm passes," Mrs. Larsen said.

Sarah spotted a crumpled empty popcorn bag on the carpeted floor and picked it up. She didn't know what awaited her in Washington, DC, but she did know she couldn't help Sam in Eagle Grove.

If she stayed, she'd simply be living day to day, wondering if Sam remained alive, if he'd ever come home again, and if he did, in what physical and emotional state? Men had come home from the Great War broken shells of their former selves, plagued by nightmares and terrors they could never name. Maybe she could help Sam, and the other young men who had shipped out of Eagle Grove High to enlist. Maybe working in Washington, DC, was the reason why she was so gifted in math, so driven to succeed.

She wouldn't know if she didn't at least try. Another lightning bolt lit Main Street. This time the thunderclap seemed to explode right above the theater, rattling the windows.

"I can't wait any longer," she said to the Larsens. "The storm is already here."

———

The following day, it took some persistence, a quality Sarah had never lacked, but she finally convinced her parents she needed to leave Eagle Grove. Then she reached Mankato State Teachers College president Frank D. McElroy by phone and explained her situation, that she had received a letter calling her to service, and while she hadn't immediately accepted the offer, she'd had a change of heart. She asked for Captain Russell's contact information.

Monday morning, she caught a bus to Mankato and walked from the bus stop to the historic four-story Saulpaugh Hotel. Inside the hotel lobby, she met a different Navy recruiter.

"I want to join the program Captain Russell spoke to us about at Mankato, the one in communications," she said. "I'm willing to take the course and the tests. All I ask is that you expedite the material so I can get to Washington, DC, and get started as soon as possible."

The recruiter raised his hands. "Slow down, Miss Haber. All of that won't be necessary."

"Please," she said. "I should have joined, but I had an obligation to teach back at Eagle Grove High School. Can't you make an exception for one more?"

The recruiter smiled. "Miss Haber, Captain Russell remembered you."

"He did?"

"You're the only woman from Mankato's master's program in mathematics. Am I right?"

Russell had done his homework. "That's right."

"Captain Russell was eager to have you, and disappointed when you turned him down. He believes you are uniquely qualified for the task, and he has waived the tests and already accepted you."

"He has?"

"Yes. We can presume that you are good at crossword puzzles?"

"Yes," Sarah said. "I am. Very good. I see patterns. Letters turn into words. They almost jump off the page at me."

The recruiter scribbled a few notes, then asked, "One other question. Are you married, or engaged to be married?"

Sarah's mind flashed to the balmy summer night almost four years before, when Sam, on bended knee, had proposed. She thought of Sam's phone call from a San Francisco pier, moments before his ship sailed for the Philippines, when she had said, "I'm finally ready." But before they could make their engagement official, the call had abruptly ended.

She'd made an offer, but Sam had not accepted her offer. And everyone knew a contract didn't exist unless it had been accepted.

"No," she told the recruiter. "I'm not married or engaged to be married."

Not technically.

It was a lie in every sense of the word, a comportment code breach. Lying was grounds for the Navy to dismiss her.

Let them try.

14

Home, Unsweet Home

Camp O'Donnell
Luzon, Philippines
April 17, 1942

Camp O'Donnell, a Philippine Army training camp under construction when the war started, had little shelter and no sanitary facilities, but the Japanese filled the camp with tens of thousands of POWs anyway. The Filipino POWs were separated from the Americans and imprisoned in the southern section of the camp. Once inside Camp O'Donnell's barbed wire fences, the American POWs were taken into a large field, counted, and again searched. Anyone in possession of Japanese money was presumed to have taken it off the dead body of a Japanese soldier, so they were separated from the other POWs and taken to the guardhouse at the camp's southeast edge. Any extra clothing, blankets, knives, and matches were confiscated. Sam managed to hold on to the vest he'd made by removing his shirt beneath and stuffing that into his pants, making the vest appear to be all that he had to wear.

After they stood for hours in the sun, the camp commandant arrived, a short, slightly built officer in a khaki uniform with a black belt, a Civil War kepi–style cap perched on his head, and a two-foot military saber in a scabbard dangling at his hip. The man stood on a box to stare down at the men. Sam thought of John Anderson, the insufferable redhead with the Napoleon complex, and sensed this would not be good. Just then Chavez made one of his off-the-cuff observations that hit home, like a burp or a fart in a quiet church.

"Geez, looks like something that fell out of a cereal box."

"Don't," Father Tom said. Too late. Despite their circumstance, Sam and others close enough to hear Chavez did a poor job of stifling their nervous laughter.

"Something is funny?" the officer said to the POWs in perfect English.

"Shit," someone said.

The officer stepped down from the box and quickly approached the men, going down the line and stopping in front of Sam. "You. What is your name?"

"Sergeant Sam Carlson," Sam said, standing at attention and looking past the Japanese officer.

"Tell me, Sergeant Carlson, what is so funny?"

"Nothing," Sam said.

"Try me," the officer said. "I am very familiar with American humor. I heard jokes frequently when I attended Princeton."

Sam glanced at the officer, unsure if he was serious about having an Ivy League education. If he was, Sam was certain the jokes he'd heard had been at his expense.

"It was nothing," Sam said.

The officer stepped forward, the top of his head barely reaching Sam's nose. In a flash he removed his sidearm and shot the POW standing next to Sam in the side of the head. The man crumpled and sank to the ground. The POWs recoiled in horror, some audibly shouting. The Japanese prison guards stepped in and struck those who had moved out of line, beating them back into formation.

"It was nothing?" asked the commandant. "So was that. Tell me it was nothing again."

Sam remained silent.

Major Paul Jones stepped forward. "We are prisoners of war, and I demand that we be treated under the rules of the Geneva Convention."

The little man blinked at him, then gave a long-suffering sigh and returned to his box. Mounting it again, he said, "I am Katsuo Yoshida, and from this moment forward *I* am your commander. You will do as *I* say. You were abandoned in the Philippines by your General Douglas MacArthur, a shameful man without honor who chose to flee rather than fight. He left you behind like dogs to fend for yourselves. You are enemies of the Empire of Japan, captives, not prisoners of war."

"Under the Geneva Convention—" Jones began.

"Which does not apply here," Yoshida said, nearly spitting his words. "That is an imperialistic document which the Empire of Japan did not ratify and therefore has no legal binding. You will be treated as rats, vermin, inferior and unworthy of respect or humane treatment."

"What does that mean?" someone asked quietly.

"It means we're not protected by the Geneva Convention," Major Jones said. "It means we can expect more treatment like we got on the march. It means the guards will kill indiscriminately."

Yoshida said, "Those POWs found to possess Japanese money have looted the bodies of Japanese soldiers, desecrated them, and have received an immediate death sentence." As if to support Yoshida's proclamation, a chorus of gunshots, like firecrackers popping, came from the guardhouse. Sam and the men around him flinched and turned to the sound, horrified by what it signified. Father Tom made the sign of the cross and closed his eyes.

Yoshida mocked the prisoners for another ten minutes, then dismissed them to the barracks. "You will find tight quarters." He smiled. "But not to worry. The laws of nature will thin your herd quickly." Yoshida stepped down from his box and the men turned toward the barracks. "You, Sam Carlson."

Sam stopped walking. Father Tom looked back at him, but Sam shook his head, a signal for Father Tom to move on with the others.

Yoshida approached. "You shall remain here with the body, until I decide what to do with the dead. You and I have unfinished business, Sergeant Sam Carlson, but we will have plenty of time to finish it."

Sam spent the remainder of the day standing in the blistering heat. Flies swarmed over the body and the pooling blood that seeped into the dry, dusty dirt. As the sun set, Sam was dismissed by a guard, but not before other guards beat him with rifle butts. With blood oozing from a cut over his right eye and pain in his ribs from the blows, he returned to the barracks, though Chavez grabbed him before he entered. He stood outside with Father Tom and Major Jones and a few other POWs.

"Shit, I'm sorry my crack got you in trouble," Chavez said. "And made you an enemy."

Sam spit a wad of blood on the ground. "Not your fault," he said.

"He was looking for a fight. I think we can expect more," Jones said.

"Why are you outside?" Sam asked. "No room?"

"The barracks were designed to hold forty men," Father Tom said. "Right now each has as many as eighty to one hundred twenty. They're lying on bamboo slats, without mattresses, bedding, or mosquito netting."

"We go in there and we'll catch every disease anyone is carrying," Major Jones said.

"What do you suggest?" Sam asked. "Monsoon season is coming."

Jones pointed to the ground beneath the barracks. "It looks more comfortable than the bamboo racks, and at least we'll have fresh air."

"What the hell did he mean we aren't prisoners of war?" Chavez asked Jones, but Sam answered.

"It means they'll kill us without thinking twice, as we all just witnessed firsthand, and heard coming from the guardhouse," Sam said. "Yoshida is like Anderson—a little chip-on-his-shoulder guy—but Yoshida is evil, not just a pain in the ass."

Chavez nodded. "A little Jap Napoleon."

"Don't let him hear you say that," Father Tom said.

"Right now, his sights are firmly fixed on you, Carlson," Major Jones said. "Watch your step and keep your head low. Don't give him any reason to single you out."

———

The POWs were allowed to run the camp, largely because the Japanese would only enter if there was an issue. They feared catching one of the rampant diseases within the camp, and they were superstitious about the dead, of which there were more each day.

The POWs initially received three meals a day, though it was hardly more than watery rice with a few vegetables. The POWs received no fruit. The Japanese used food as both reward and punishment, and they would cancel a meal seemingly for no reason.

"Psychological warfare," Major Jones explained.

"Never thought I'd be disappointed to pass up swill," Chavez said, which was what the men called the rice. The Japanese called it *lugaw*, which translated as "wet rice."

"It smells," Sam said the first time he'd raised a bowl to his nose. "How can rice smell?"

"Because they sweep it up off the floor and piss in it," Chavez said. "Bon appétit."

For breakfast, the POWs received a half cup of soupy rice and, occasionally, coffee. Lunch each day was half a mess kit of steamed rice and a half cup of sweet potato soup. They received the same meal at dinner. The POWs assigned to distribute the food used a sardine can to measure each man's ration, and fellow prisoners watched closely to ensure no one received extra.

All meals were served outside, regardless of the weather. Anyway, if it rained, the *lugaw* became *super lugaw*, according to Chavez. Once in a rare while, the cooks were given corn and made hominy. The prisoners were so hungry some men ate the corn cobs, which resulted in some dying when the cobs would not pass through the men's bowels. To supplement their diets, the men scoured the camp for grasshoppers, rats, snakes, dogs, and just about anything else edible.

Chavez soon learned through the grapevine that smuggling rings, or underground markets, sometimes emerged in POW camps, and he set out to determine if that was true at Camp O'Donnell. After a week of investigating, Chavez huddled with Sam, Major Jones, Father Tom, and a few other men who had been in Sam's platoon and could be trusted.

"The Filipino resistance is smuggling contraband into camp a few different ways," he reported. "It's hidden in the trucks delivering supplies. The Japs in the garage who do the unloading know about it, but they're on the take. The Filipinos also hide packages of food, medicine, money, cans of fish, wheat flour, beans, and coconut oil inside hollowed-out trees or buried underground but marked."

"How do they get it into camp?" Sam asked. "Guards check us every time we come back from our work assignments."

"POWs on the woodcutting crew smuggle the stuff hidden in the hollowed-out logs or buried under the piles of wood on the carabao carts," Chavez said, referring to the solid-wood-wheeled, low-slung carts hauled by carabao—water buffalo—to save on fuel, and which could get deeper into the jungle to collect firewood. "The drivers of the carts are also on the take."

"Okay," Major Jones said, "so how are we supposed to get it?"

"I'm on the case," Chavez said. "I've made friends with one of the Jap guards, and he can be bought."

"Great," Sam said. "I'll just call home and have my dad wire me some funds."

"He's also in charge of assigning work details, and I asked him to put me and you on the woodcutters work detail."

"And what do we pay him?"

"Leave that to me," Chavez said.

The POWs soon received work details, and Sam and Chavez were indeed assigned to woodcutting. Others were assigned to work in the rice paddies, or to build runways at Cabanatuan Airfield, which had been the home of a Philippine Army Air Corps unit. They soon realized the Japanese guards were not a hindrance. Most were more interested in sleeping in the shade during the sweltering heat or trying to stay dry under the canopy of leaves during the monsoon season. Sam and Chavez found packages hidden just where Chavez said they would be. They stuffed the contraband in the hollowed-out logs, which they put in with the piles of wood they cut, then smuggled it back into camp in the carabao carts through the camp kitchen.

As with everything Chavez did, he was soon successful, running an underground market inside the camp and keeping extra supplies of medicine and food to supplement the rations for Sam, Major Jones, Father Tom, and other POWs from the 194th Tank Battalion. "There's plenty of food to be had," Chavez said. "But the Japanese are holding it for themselves. I figure this is a way to take it out of their hands."

Jones didn't disagree, but he and Father Tom made sure the loot was shared with the other POWs in need.

"You know, Father," Chavez said, "Catholic guilt doesn't work when the alternative to feeling guilty is dying."

Nonetheless, Father Tom was soon smuggling contraband to POWs in the hospital with tropical diseases and in need of the extra rations, without saying where he got it.

The guards continued their psychological warfare, much of it at Yoshida's instruction. Truckloads of Red Cross medical supplies were frequently turned away at the camp gate. On the rare occasion Yoshida allowed supplies into camp, the Japanese took 95 percent for their own use.

The little Japanese Napoleon didn't make regular appearances inside the camp, and Sam had been able to stay out of his way when he did, but he would appear randomly and make bold proclamations about America losing the war, surrendering in cities across the South Pacific and Europe, and abandoning their POWs.

Yoshida also frequently ordered the guards to withhold water, making the prisoners stand in an insufferably long line in the blazing sun for up to eight hours waiting to sip water from the only spigot in the camp.

No water was wasted washing clothes. The POWs burned their clothing when it became soiled enough to rot on their bodies. Cooking water did not come from the spigot either, but had to be carried three miles from a river to the camp, a work detail Chavez quickly volunteered for. The water containers became another avenue to smuggle in his contraband, sunken by rocks.

One afternoon, as Sam waited in a long line with others to drink from the spigot, Yoshida strode into camp, turned on the spigot, and washed his hands, his face, and his neck with handfuls of water, letting precious drops spill into the parched soil. Then he ordered the guards to shut off the water. "I wish to bathe," he said. He turned to Sam. "You, Carlson." The man had not forgotten him. "You will fill my tub with water from the spigot. If you spill a drop, or drink it, no other captive will drink today."

Sam spent nearly an hour under the guards' watchful eyes carefully filling a small pail from the spigot and carrying the water to a metal tub behind a bamboo fence thirty yards away. When the tub was filled, Yoshida stripped off his uniform. Without it, he looked like a small boy. He climbed into the tub, luxuriating in the water, making no effort to keep it from splashing over the sides.

He leaned his head back against the tub rim and closed his eyes, cupping his hands and letting the water spill onto the dirt. "At Princeton, white-skinned boys like you, Carlson, with your pretty, blonde hair, took great pleasure in belittling me. I was 'the Jap' or 'the Nip.' To them I was not a person but something to be ridiculed and scorned. When my grades exceeded their own, their abuse became physical. I avoided them when I could and did my best to ignore them when I could not. They found amusement in my height, in the color of my skin, and in what I chose to eat. I was locked in lockers, beaten, and on one memorable evening, raped with a broom handle until I recited the Pledge of Allegiance."

Yoshida opened his eyes, lolled his head toward Sam, and stared.

"And now, it seems the shoe is on the other foot, as you Americans like to say, Sam Carlson. In Japan we say, 'Even Buddha's face only lasts until the third time.' Do you understand, Carlson?"

Carlson shook his head.

Yoshida scoffed. "It seems you are not very bright. This does not surprise me. I will tutor you: it means that even the most patient and tolerant person will lose his temper if he is provoked too many times." Yoshida stepped out of the tub, grabbed a metal can, and filled it partway with the water from the tub in which he had bathed. Then he allowed the rest of the water to drain onto the ground. After he dressed, he walked to where Sam remained standing and held out the can holding his bathwater. Sam, wary, didn't move.

"Take it, Carlson. And drink every drop."

Sam reached for it, but Yoshida pulled it back, unzipped his fly, and pissed in the can. He held it out to Sam. "Drink every drop."

Sam refused, shaking his head.

"No? Hmm."

Yoshida walked from behind the bamboo fence back to the spigot, where the long line of POWs had been forced to remain waiting in the beating sun, including Chavez, Father Tom, and Major Jones.

"I'm sorry to tell you," Yoshida said, "that Sam Carlson spilled a bucket of water on the ground."

The men in line groaned.

"But," Yoshida went on, "I want you to know that I am a fair man. Therefore, I will allow Sergeant Carlson to make amends for his mistake. All he must do is drink this water from the tub in which I bathed, and the rest of you shall drink from the spigot. If he refuses, or spills a drop, no one drinks today or tomorrow."

Yoshida held up the can.

Sam refused to take it.

The POWs in line urged him to drink it. "Drink it, Carlson." "Drink it, goddammit!" "What's wrong with you, Carlson?"

Yoshida smiled and tipped the can. "Last chance, Sam Carlson."

Sam looked at the men withering in line, their lips blistered, their eyes imploring him for the chance at a few drops of water. He took the can, looked Yoshida in the eye, and lifted the rim to his mouth. He tried to drink it without tasting it. Halfway through, he gagged, fought to hold the piss and dirty water down, but eventually coughed it up, puking repeatedly.

"A pity," Yoshida said. He turned to the men. "The spigot remains off." Then he turned on his boot heels and strode back toward the front gate.

The POWs near the spigot looked at Sam in disbelief. "What the hell, Carlson?" said one. "You screwed us all."

"Shit, Carlson," said another. "I would've given my left ball for a can of water. We won't drink for days, now."

The men trudged off, dejected and weak. Chavez, Father Tom, and Major Jones remained, looking at him, though not with anger or hatred, but curiosity.

"He pissed in the can," Sam said. "I'm sorry."

"You have nothing to be sorry for," Father Tom said, shaking his head. "My God, Sam. I can't believe you tried."

"I'll spread the word," Jones said, but Sam knew he could not spread it far enough, and even if he did, many POWs would not understand.

Sam looked to Chavez, who gave him a tired smile. "Hell, I would have imagined it was a big glass of lemonade, downed it, and asked for seconds." He wrapped an arm around Sam's shoulders and walked him back to the barracks.

———

The inadequate slit trenches dug for the POW's sewage soon overflowed. The smell was overwhelming. When monsoons came, Sam and the others used the rainwater to wash the dirt and filth from their bodies, but the rains also caused the sewage in the trenches to overflow onto the campgrounds. Flies swarmed everywhere, including the POW kitchens, and in their food. More and more men grew ill with any number of diseases. Dysentery caused rampant diarrhea, dehydration, fevers, abdominal cramping, and weight loss.

The camp hospital, such as it was, had no running water or disinfectant, the Red Cross supplies having been diverted.

The sickest POWs were taken to Zero Ward, so called because the Japanese didn't bother to count the men taken there, presuming they would soon be dead. Zero Ward was a study in collective misery. Naked, skeletal POWs lay sprawled on a wooden floor, covered in feces and coated in vomit. Their bodies twitched with bluebottle flies. They had no blankets, and only the water the men collected from rooftops or ditches. The stench from the building was horrific. Some POWs called it Saint Peter's Ward, a reference to the Bible's pearly gates, the last stop before heaven. The guards put a fence up around the building to protect themselves and would not go into the ward.

The death rate among the POWs soon reached dozens per day, what Yoshida called "culling the herd." Each morning, the POWs took turns searching the barracks, the hospital, and Zero Ward for soldiers who had died. The men carried the bodies on makeshift litters made from two bamboo poles and a blanket and placed the dead in the shade under the hospital building, waiting until the Japanese gave them permission to bury the bodies. Again, this became psychological warfare. Yoshida would refuse to give permission for weeks, and the POWs would have to live with the decaying and bloated bodies, and with the horrific smell. Sam did his best to ignore the bodies. He did not dwell on the dead or on the thought that someday he could be among them, but it became more difficult each day. He spoke with Father Tom, feeling guilt for having hardened himself to the dead, pretending they were not real so he wouldn't go crazy.

"God will not judge you for trying to stay sane, Sam," Father Tom said. "We all must do what we can to help those in need, and that includes ourselves."

As Sam, Chavez, Avery Wilber—a POW they called A&W or Root Beer—and a fourth POW carried bodies on their appointed day, Major Jones intercepted them. "Can't fit any more under the hospital until we clean the ground," he said.

"How are we supposed to do that?" Chavez asked. "And what are we supposed to do with the bodies in the meantime, stand them up in the yard and pose them like wax figures?"

"They're dying faster than we can keep up," Jones said. "This is the best I could manage from the little son of a bitch, Yoshida. The Japanese fear the dead bodies and risk of disease, so he's allowing us to move the bodies already under the barracks to one side, scrape the ground with hoes, spread lime over it, then shift the bodies back and do the other side."

"There must be eighty bodies under there," Sam said. "Why won't the Japs just let us bury them?"

"My guess is they're trying to hide evidence of war crimes and are still deciding where to put a mass grave."

When Yoshida finally granted permission for the POWs to bury the dead, Jones's suspicion was proven correct. The bodies had to be carried to a mass grave located two miles from Camp O'Donnell. The POWs' burial detail first stripped the dead of clothing. Any clothing not too tattered was washed in boiling river water and given to other prisoners. Those on grave detail tied strips of clothing over their mouths and noses to try to keep out the smell as they carried the naked, stinking corpses to the mass grave, sometimes moving as many as six bodies in a litter, and doing two trips a day, eight miles round trip in the grueling sun.

Sam hated the burial detail more than any of the others. It was inhumane in every respect, and he never got used to the dead POWs, with their mouths and eyes open, their bodies near skeletons. He could smell the graveyard a mile before they arrived. And because of the high water table, especially during monsoon season, they had to use poles to pin each body to the floor of the shallow grave. But no matter how deep they buried the bodies, or how hard they tried to pin them, by the following morning the dead would rise to greet them, either from water pressure, or having been dug up and partially eaten by wild dogs.

One morning, the POWs were awakened and ordered outside their barracks. Yoshida stood on his box wearing his ridiculous uniform and saber. He sought several hundred men to start work on a farm, which he said would be the largest work detail in the camp. Sam knew that was impossible. So few POWs were healthy enough to work, at least based on the prior day's roll call.

"You will garden your own vegetables," Yoshida said. "Okra, *talong*, corn, sweet potatoes. Think of how much better you will eat."

"Criminy. This guy should have been a used car salesman," Chavez said under his breath.

Apparently, no one else believed Yoshida either, because no one volunteered.

"Very well. Then we shall choose the workers, and any vegetables grown will be given to the guards."

"Surprise, surprise," Sam said.

Sam, Chavez, and others from the 194th were chosen for the detail.

"At least we'll be outside," Chavez said.

"In one-hundred-degree heat and humidity," A&W said.

As Sam and the others retrieved tools from a toolshed, a funnel of guards formed between them and the patch of ground to be worked. "What's that all about?" Sam asked.

"Maybe they want to give us a ticker-tape parade."

Sam didn't think so. He walked warily through the funnel with a hoe, one eye on the guards. They struck quickly, hitting the POWs with clubs, punches, and kicks, doing their best to knock the POWs down. When the beatings stopped after Chavez reached the garden and the guards exchanged money, Sam deduced that they had bet on which POW would be first to reach the garden.

Later that first afternoon, as Sam and the other POWs worked in the field, the hair on the back of Sam's neck stood on end, but before he could turn around, something hit him in the back of the head, knocking him face down into the mud. He felt the sole of a boot step on his head, burying his face. Unable to breathe, Sam nearly passed out before his tormentor removed his boot. When Sam rolled over, he looked into a bright sun that obscured the guard's face, but the voice was horrifyingly familiar.

"Tomorrow you will be first to volunteer, Sam Carlson," Yoshida said, "and you will tell the others to also volunteer. Or you will acquire a taste for mud, as you have for piss."

After that incident, the POWs on garden duty acted as sentries for one another.

"Big Speedo at three o'clock," Chavez would say. He'd nicknamed each guard. Big Speedo was fat, and when he wanted the POWs to work faster, he yelled, "Speedo! Speedo!" Another, smaller guard was Little Speedo. The guard Smiley *always* had a smile on his face but was a treacherous bastard; he'd beat the men if he believed they didn't work hard enough, then make them kneel on stones.

The POWs were informed the punishment for eating or stealing any vegetables was immediate death.

Sam didn't even question it. They'd already killed for far less.

15

RUDOWSKI

Camp O'Donnell
Luzon, Philippines
June 10, 1942

Day after day Sam worked harder, ate less, and grew weaker. His encounters with Yoshida continued whenever the little Napoleon came into camp. Yoshida seemed determined to embarrass Sam and alienate him from the rest of the POWs. Chavez, Father Tom, and Major Jones did their best to shield Sam from the despot, but they could only do so much to help without putting their own lives in danger. Sam didn't want that.

"This is my battle," he told them.

When beriberi hit, Sam's body was too ravaged to fight the disease, and he grew too weak to stand. Chavez's contraband medical supplies and food had also dwindled to trickles. The Japanese, having learned of the supply lines, made changes to how they inspected supplies and carts coming into camp. The Filipino suppliers had also grown scared of being discovered.

"Come on, Sam, you gotta get up." Chavez leaned over him as Sam lay in his bunk one morning. As Yoshida had predicted, the herd had been culled and overcrowding had been reduced. Sam and the others had moved inside a barracks. Chavez and Father Tom were doing their best to keep Sam hidden from the guards. "We got two minutes to get to roll call or no orange sherbet for dessert, buddy."

Sam knew that if they were late to roll call, everyone's meager food rations would be cut in half. "I can do it," he said, but when he tried to move his legs, swollen from fluid buildup, he couldn't budge them.

Sam had survived malaria, dysentery, dengue fever, and other diseases while in the Philippines, but beriberi crushed him. According to a camp doctor, beriberi, caused by a lack of nutrition, weakened the heart and circulation. Whatever was going on inside his emaciated body, Sam sensed death drawing near for the first time since he'd entered the camp. The body that had once excelled in any sport he played, that had done everything Sam had asked of it on their forced march across the Bataan Peninsula, and even more in this shithole, had reached its limit. He would be sent to Zero Ward to die in this humid, mosquito-ridden, godforsaken land. Then POWs would bury his wasted husk in the mass cemetery without giving him, or the life he might have lived, a second thought.

"Nah, nah, nah, you got it," Chavez assured him, working to prop Sam up in his bunk. "Maybe you'll get a good work assignment today."

Tasks inside the camp—cooking and cleaning—were less arduous. Most POWs, though, were sent out to build bridges, construct airfields, work the garden, and tend rice paddies. Men often did not return; they dropped dead from beatings or exhaustion, or their guards killed them for sport.

"Swing my legs over the rack," Sam said to Chavez. "Hoist me up."

Father Tom entered the barracks just then, knelt, and placed a comforting hand on Sam's shoulder. "You're not going anywhere." Like most of the POWs, Father Tom was emaciated; his limbs had withered to sticks, his elbows and knee joints now the widest parts. Yet the chaplain still moved ceaselessly among them. "You're staying here to rest. I'll take your place on whatever work detail you pull."

As a commissioned officer and religious figure, Father Tom did not have to go on work details, but the chaplain filled in for sick men daily. Their overseers didn't care, so long as the prisoners met each day's required quota of laborers.

"No," Sam said. "You can't take everyone's work detail, Padre." He looked to Chavez. "I'd rather you take me to Zero Ward."

"Too late," Father Tom said. "I've already volunteered. Lie down and rest."

Sam wanted to press the issue, but his body had other ideas. He fell back onto his bunk. "Thank you," he whispered.

After the work detail departed, Sam tried to fall back to sleep, but a noise woke him. When he opened his eyes, a large-framed POW was going through Sam's meager possessions, including the green Army vest in which he had sewn Sarah's class ring. "What the hell are you doing?"

The huge man looked down at Sam and grinned. "What do you care? You're not going to be here much longer. Just getting a head start on your stuff. You'd be surprised what even garbage like this can get. What size shoe are you?"

"Why aren't you on work detail?"

"I'm too sick." The man smiled. "Too weak."

He didn't look weak, or sick. He looked surprisingly well fed. "Who are you? What's your rank?"

"Me? I'm Private John Rudowski, 1st Infantry Division."

Rudowski. Rumors circulated about him in the camp. Other POWs said Rudowski angered easily, and disobeyed direct orders. He no longer saluted superior officers, and he stole food, clothing, and shoes from POWs who died.

"Put down my shoes and don't let me catch you avoiding work detail again."

Rudowski leaned down close. His breath was acidic, his teeth yellow. "Didn't anybody tell you?"

"Tell me what?"

"There are no ranks in hell. We're all in Satan's army now."

"I'll have you court-martialed."

Rudowski laughed. "Like I give a shit. Besides, the guards in here like me. I give them tips for their troubles."

"You're stealing from your fellow POWs. From the *dead*. Have you no conscience? No beliefs? You're an American soldier. There are rules."

"The only rule in here is kill or be killed, buddy, and I prefer one over the other." He turned back to Sam's things. "So, what else we got here?" He grabbed the vest and set about squishing it in his massive hands.

Sam reached beneath his bony back.

"Oh ho. What's this?" Rudowski felt Sarah's ring in the vest's lining. "A gold nugget?"

"Put it down," Sam said. "That is an order."

"Shove your order up your ass," Rudowski said, his attention on the vest.

Sam pulled the knife from beneath him, opened the blade, and drove it into Rudowski's leg with what little strength he had left. The blade, which he kept sharp using a stone, sunk to its hilt in the big man's thigh. Sam yanked it out, drawing a satisfying bloom of blood onto the man's pants.

Rudowski dropped the vest and clutched his leg, howling as he stumbled backward, knocking over bunks before crashing to the floor. The guards in the yard rushed into the barracks, chattering. Sam had slid the pocketknife back beneath him and had also pulled the vest under his body. Rudowski gripped his leg and moaned, both hands bloodied.

"No work detail," Sam said, pointing at him. "Faker. Faker."

The guards understood little English, but they understood a POW shirking his work detail. They set about beating Rudowski with their rifle butts and bamboo poles, but it still took four of them to get the wounded POW to his feet and usher him out the door.

"You're a dead man," Rudowski bellowed back at Sam. "You hear me? I'll kill you. First chance I get, I'm coming for you."

"Big deal," Sam called back. "Like you said, I'm already in hell."

16

INTO THE UNKNOWN

Eagle Grove, Minnesota
May 18, 1942

Sarah decided to stay at Eagle Grove High to finish the school year in early June—she owed it to her colleagues and to the principal who had given her the job, but mostly she owed it to the young women not to abandon them with just a few weeks left in the school year. The recruiter commended Sarah's loyalty and diligence, and gave her a week after the school year ended to report to an address in Washington, DC.

Her colleagues, students, and family took the news she would be leaving hard, especially since she didn't know when she would return. Her parents realized their daughter had made up her mind. When she did, no one could convince her otherwise. She no longer allowed herself to think of Sam as dead. He was a prisoner of war, but he was tough minded and strong of body. He'd take whatever his captors dished out. Besides, POWs were governed by the Geneva Convention, and the Red Cross had the right to inspect the camps to ensure prisoners received humane treatment.

After each teaching day, Sarah put a blanket across the windows of her classroom and read articles on the history of cryptanalysis and code breaking, then did the problem sets the recruiter had provided. Each packet contained a typed note reemphasizing the importance of absolute secrecy and the consequences of a breach. Sarah graded her answers using the key provided. Her initial scores were rough, barely 50 percent, but they steadily improved. She learned which letters reoccurred most frequently—*E, T, O, N, A, I, R,* and *S*; which often traveled together in pairs, like *S* and *T*; which traveled in triplets, like *EST, ING,* and *IVE,* and in fours, like *TION.* She studied terms like "route transposition," "cipher alphabets," and "polyalphabetic substitution cipher." She mastered the disguising of letters using methods dating back to the Renaissance, and she learned about rudimentary codes the Japanese had used in the past. She picked up basic Japanese phrases common in the messages.

On June 11, 1942, after the depleted Eagle Grove senior class graduated, Sarah's parents, brother, and sister again walked her to the train station, her mother in tears. Sarah was nervous, but also excited about this adventure and what lay ahead. She carried her raincoat, umbrella, and two hard-backed suitcases containing nearly every skirt and sweater set she owned and her pair of saddle shoes.

She boarded a crowded train—fewer ran to save fuel for the military—and found an open seat next to a young man she had known in high school. He told her he was 4-F because of epilepsy. She told him she was going to Washington, DC, to take a government job.

"A secretary?" he asked.

Sarah bit her tongue, hard. "Something like that."

"I always thought you'd go further."

She smiled, though inside she wanted to slug him. "Washington is about as far east as I can go."

"No, I didn't mean geographically—"

"I know," she said, cutting off further conversation by opening her book. Her mind was too amped up to concentrate on the words, and soon she turned her attention to the towns, trees, and farms streaking by the train window.

Late the next day, the land flattened as they drew closer to the capital and the train pulled into Washington's Union Station. Sarah stepped onto the platform amazed and bewildered. Around her the energy of a thousand commuters buzzed. Men and women of all ages and races hurried about dressed in suits and military uniforms. They had a look of determination she'd rarely seen in Eagle Grove since the Depression struck, and she immediately felt energized.

She walked into Union Station, a gigantic and imposing concourse with marble archways, white granite columns, and elevated statuary depicting ancient legionnaires—shields covering their private areas, for modesty's sake. High overhead a huge banner fluttered from the ceiling.

AMERICANS WILL ALWAYS FIGHT FOR LIBERTY

Other young women carrying suitcases—many looking just as confused as Sarah felt, not to mention wilted by the heat and humidity—were also among the commuters.

Outside the station, a blast of hot, humid air hit Sarah like a punch in the face. She wondered how the women survived the day in high heels and dresses. Her dress already stuck to her skin beneath her winter coat, which was too big to pack in her suitcase. Sarah worked her way through the crowd to a taxicab stand. She had never hailed a cab in her life, but watched others in line do it, then imitated them. A yellow cab pulled to the curb, and the cabbie, a middle-aged man with a scruffy beard and the butt of a cigar dangling from the side of his mouth, stepped out.

"Let me help you, miss. A pretty young lady such as yourself shouldn't have to carry her own bags."

"Thank you," she said.

"First time in Washington, DC?"

"Yes."

"You'll want to take off that coat before it kills you." Sarah removed her coat and folded it over her arm. The cabbie put her bags in the trunk, then opened the cab door for her.

"This being your first time in Washington, would you like to see some sights nearby? The monuments are truly spectacular."

"That would be lovely," she said, surprised and pleased by the man's kindness. She settled back in her seat with a sense of awe and nervous excitement as the cab drove past the Washington monument, the US Capitol, the National Mall, Lincoln Memorial, and the Arlington Memorial Bridge. Throughout the tour, the cabbie kept up a running dialogue. So much so, Sarah lost track of the time. She heard a click and looked to see a meter above the dash had ticked past seven. She leaned over the front seat, startled. "Does that mean seven dollars?"

"It does."

"I didn't think you were charging me."

"If the wheels are rolling, the meter is running, miss. It's a company rule."

"I can't afford this."

"No? Okay, where to?"

The Navy recruiter had provided Sarah an address to a building called Main Navy on Constitution Avenue. She gave the cabbie the address.

The driver smiled at her in the rearview mirror, but this time it had a leering quality to it. "My pleasure."

Sarah sank back into her seat, her face blazing. What an easy mark she'd been.

When the taxi finally stopped at Main Navy, Sarah's strong sense of direction deduced she was no more than a mile or two from the train station. Reluctantly, she paid the cabbie eight dollars, nearly half the twenty she had in cash.

She stepped up to a guard booth, poorer but wiser. Behind the booth, military officers passed beneath overhead wires strung between the buildings. When asked, she gave the guard her name and showed him her letter. The guard picked up a telephone and spoke for a few seconds, then hung up and directed her through the gate to the building lobby.

"What is this place?" she asked the guard.

"I'm not at liberty to say, ma'am."

Inside the building, a woman greeted Sarah, handed her a document, and ushered her into a room of other women about her same age. Some also looked to have just arrived, carrying suitcases. The woman spoke with a southern accent. "I've provided each of you a copy of a loyalty oath, which you are required to sign. By so doing, you swear to support and defend the United States Constitution against all enemies, foreign and domestic."

Sarah had no sooner read and signed the document than the woman handed out a second sheet of paper. "This is a secrecy oath. By signing this document, you swear you will not discuss your official duties outside this building, and you acknowledge that to do so could subject you to prosecution under the Espionage Act."

Though nervous, Sarah signed this document as well, then was given still more to fill out.

"These documents, including tax forms, need to be completed for your government employment. Since it is already after five o'clock on a Friday, you can bring them back Monday morning at eight. Welcome, ladies, to the service of your country."

The women started from the room. Confused, Sarah approached the woman who had handed out the papers. "Excuse me. I was told lodging would be provided."

"You don't have a place to stay?"

"No, I don't know a soul in Washington."

"Wait here." A minute later the woman returned with another woman who looked to be about Sarah's age.

"I understand you have no place to stay?" This woman spoke in a thick New York accent.

"No," Sarah said. "I was told—"

"Don't sweat it, honey. A lot of girls have the same misunderstanding. You can stay at the Meridian Hill. The military constructed it to house us g-girls."

"I'm sorry, 'g-girls'?"

"Government girls. That's what they call us. Some girls are scattered in boardinghouses in northwest Washington, but I figured a hotel beat living in someone's basement or attic, where I'd have to answer to the owners whenever I came and went. If I had wanted that, I would have stayed home." The woman laughed. "At least at the hotel I'm around people my own age not opposed to having a little fun. I'm Grace Moretti, by the way. From Cutchogue, New York."

"Sarah Haber. I'm from Eagle Grove, Minnesota."

"Eagle Grove? Never heard of it."

"Just a couple thousand residents, fewer now with all the men gone."

"And I thought Cutchogue was small. Same problem. No men. Hoping to meet some here in Washington looking to buy a young woman dinner." Grace struck a pose, hand on hip, and laughed again. "Come on. You can take the bus with me, Sarah Haber. Let me help you with those suitcases."

Some women on the bus were in animated discussions about weekend plans, dates to USO dances, picture shows, and the symphony. A few others looked much like Sarah felt—confused and a little overwhelmed. Fifteen minutes after boarding the bus, Sarah stepped off, and Grace escorted her to what looked like a hastily constructed hotel alongside freshly poured concrete sidewalks.

"I checked in last week," Grace said. "I was told the First Lady had these buildings built for us, but who knows."

"Really?" Sarah said. "Are there that many of us?"

"Didn't you see all the women about our age at Union Station?" Sarah had. "I guess Eleanor wanted to keep us all prim and proper." Grace struck another pose. "With so few men around, that shouldn't be too hard. What's a girl to do?"

Grace took Sarah into the building lobby, where a woman greeted them from behind a desk.

"This is my friend, Sarah Haber," Grace said. "Can you put her up in a room?"

Sarah was told a room cost $24.50 for the month, paid in advance.

"In advance? I don't have that kind of money on me. The cabdriver took me on an eight-dollar cab ride."

"They do that if they see a young woman with suitcases," Grace said. "Tried it on me, but a few weekends in Manhattan hardens you. I guess they got to make a living."

"It's Friday," Sarah said. "I'll send a telegram home and ask my mother to go to the bank in Eagle Grove first thing Monday and transfer some money from my savings to my checking. Can I stay until then?" Sarah asked the woman.

"Sorry, but if I do that for you, I have to do it for everyone."

"How about you let her stay in my room until her money arrives? She's a g-girl. She's good for it," Grace said.

"As long as you don't mind sharing a bed," the woman said.

"I don't mind. Do you?" Grace said to Sarah.

"Are you sure?" Sarah said. "That's awfully kind."

Grace waved it off. "Don't sweat it, honey. Shared a bed with my younger sister my whole life, and she snores. You don't snore, do you?"

"Not that I know of."

Grace laughed again, then walked Sarah through the lobby to a lounge. "Over there is the recreation room, and a shop that sells cosmetics and things. And that is the mail desk, where you can mail letters or pick them up. You can always find someone to play bridge or drink tea, and you can sit down here with a fella. No men upstairs. You got a fella?"

Sarah almost told Grace she wouldn't be sitting with any men, that she was engaged, then remembered the second question her Navy recruiter had asked her. "Boyfriend. He's enlisted. Overseas."

"You know where?"

"The Pacific Theater."

"Fighting the Japs," Grace said. "I think they're worse than the Germans. I don't see a ring. You're not engaged?"

"No. We're waiting until he comes home. He's missing in action."

"I'm so sorry, but good for you for waiting. There's a lot of high-speed marrying going on. Guys are proposing before they get shipped out, and women are rushing to the altar. Not me. I don't want to be married at twenty-two and widowed at twenty-three." Grace stopped walking. "Now, that was a dumb thing to say."

"It's okay."

"No. No, it's not. Here I meet someone I like, and I go and say something dumb. Don't think anything of it, honey. That's just my big mouth off and running. My dad says I talk faster than a roadster."

"I like you too, Grace," Sarah said. "And I appreciate your kindness."

"I'm not going to lie to you. Despite all the other women, it can get lonely. Know what I mean?"

Sarah did. She already missed her family and Eagle Grove, and she longed for good news about Sam.

Grace led Sarah to the third floor and explained that because so many girls were arriving, they were all doubling up in some rooms and maybe they could do the same. "Just a thought," she said. Doors lined long corridors. Grace pushed open her door and said, "Home, sweet home."

The one-window room consisted of a bed with two pillows, a desk and chair, a mirror, a closet, and a dresser. "Down the hall is the communal bathroom and showers. They have ironing boards and a kitchenette, also, though I've never used either. Never cooked. Mama always cooked at home."

Grace had put a sheet over the window to serve as a curtain. "Don't really need one on the third floor, but a gal on the first floor was in her pajamas and a man walked by, looked in, and tipped his hat. Can you believe it? Stow your stuff on my bed."

Sarah thought the room huge compared to the room she and her younger sister, Nora, shared at home.

"It ain't much," Grace said, dropping onto the bed, "but they make our life easy. We have a cafeteria at Main Navy, and we can send our clothes out to be laundered and dry-cleaned, and maids clean our rooms once a week."

Sarah startled. "I've never had a maid in my life, or my clothes laundered. I've always done it myself."

Grace bounced lightly on the mattress. "The military wants us singularly focused on our work."

"How is the work?"

"Challenging and mind-numbing. You'll find out more on Monday. So . . . why'd they hunt you down? What's your specialty?"

"Mathematics."

"You got a degree in mathematics?" Grace said, sitting up.

"A master's degree."

"Whoa. No wonder they want you. You're going to go far in this job, Sarah Haber. A little piece of advice?"

"Sure."

"We don't have a lot of leverage; you know what I mean?"

Sarah didn't. "No."

"We are the proverbial cog in the proverbial machine. What you have up here"—she pointed to her temple—"is like a gold mine. Use it to get what you want."

"I don't know what I want," Sarah said. "Except for my Sam and all the others to come home."

Grace smiled. "You're just one of those genuinely nice people, aren't you, Sarah Haber?"

"I don't know about that."

"I'm pretty sure I do. I think we're going to be good friends. Come on, I'll introduce you around."

Sarah soon learned the hotel had been hurriedly and cheaply constructed. Her first three nights she hardly slept, the noise in the hallway and the adjacent rooms sounding like it was in her room. Each time someone walked down the hall, the walls shook.

Grace explained the all-night traffic. "Other girls are 'hot bedding.' They share the room to save on rent and they share the bed, because they work different watches—that's military talk for an eight-hour shift. Three shifts each day around the clock. Just when you fall asleep, more girls come back, and other girls get up to leave. You'll get used to the noise. Like we've gotten used to everything else. The world is changing, isn't it, Sarah Haber?"

It was, Sarah thought, but not for the better. Definitely not for the better. She stopped herself.

"Things will turn around," she said. "For all of us."

17

THE LONG WALK HOME

Camp O'Donnell
Luzon, Philippines
June 26, 1942

Rudowski had been taken to the bamboo cage in the work yard. The cage was barely large enough to fit someone Sam's size; he couldn't imagine how they'd stuffed Rudowski into it. While the big man sweltered in the scorching afternoon sun for three days and froze in the chilly nights, the guards searched his bunk and found a treasure trove of wedding rings, gold crucifixes and Stars of David, and other items he'd stolen from POWs, both dead and alive. Rudowski had used the trinkets to bribe certain guards to get better work assignments, more food, and to remain in camp to rest.

Without his treasures, upon his release from the cage, Rudowski was given the same work assignments as everyone else, outside camp. Each time he and Sam made eye contact, Rudowski either ran a finger across his throat or otherwise reminded Sam they had unfinished business.

"First Yoshida, now Rudowski," Chavez said. "You attract nothing but the best, my friend."

Two weeks after his Rudowski confrontation, Sam remained weak, but Chavez had managed to get ahold of thiamine pills, and Sam was soon strong enough to at least pull a work detail. Not doubting the sincerity of Rudowski's threats for a minute, he had no interest in staying in camp alone. Nor did he want Father Tom to take another day of his work detail.

"In camp, you don't take a leak without one of us being present," Chavez had said, meaning the men in Sam's tank platoon who stuck together.

"Two or three of us," said Major Jones. "And that still might not be enough. Rudowski's so big he's likely to bang our heads together like coconuts, split them open, and eat our brains. You picked the wrong guy to make an enemy."

"And he still has a couple of guards on the take," Chavez said.

"How is that possible?" Sam asked, though he had noticed Rudowski was once again getting the plum work assignments.

Chavez rolled his eyes as if Sam was the most naive person on the planet. "Look at the size of him. He's obviously eating better than the rest of us too."

"You think he's got Yoshida in his pocket?"

"Not likely," Chavez said. "Since Yoshida is the one who ordered Rudowski to the box."

"He steals other prisoners' food," Wilber said. "If they gripe, he beats the hell out of them."

Rudowski again getting plum work assignments inside camp was fine with Sam, who always pulled work outside camp, either in the garden or the cemetery. It was ten hours he didn't have to worry about the beast gutting him like a fish. The full-time job of just trying to stay alive, his near-death experience, and the thought that death could be just around the corner—from guards or starvation or disease, if not at the hands of Rudowski or Yoshida—had pushed Sam to desperation. He needed to escape Camp O'Donnell.

The problem was, Yoshida had told those inside the camp that if one man escaped, those who remained would be punished. He didn't say how, and Sam couldn't imagine it could be worse than how the men were currently being treated. It would likely mean longer work details or possibly less food, but they were already working from sunup to sundown, and the food, if you wanted to call it that, was not much more than the watery rice.

On the other hand, if he could escape into the mountains and meet up with Filipino guerilla fighters who could get him to the coast and possibly to an American transport, he could let the military know of the mistreatment of the prisoners, and that the Japanese were not following the Geneva Convention.

Maybe they could put pressure on the Japanese to have the Red Cross admitted inside the camps and improve the POWs' treatment. If he could escape, Sam could also enlighten the world and not let the bastards—especially Yoshida—get away with the mass murders and other war crimes. He could save the lives of his fellow prisoners.

On a day when Sam and his other litter bearers—this time Chavez, Wilber, and Father Tom, who'd volunteered to take the place of another ailing POW—lugged corpses from Camp O'Donnell to the mass graveyard, Sam had his mind made up. He said to Chavez, who carried the other end of his litter, "I'm going home."

"Right. Me too," Chavez said. "Let's call General MacArthur and have him pick us up at the beach. Tell him to bring us some ice-cold beer while he's at it."

Sam had studied the guards on his prior grave details. They waited at the entrance rather than follow the men into the graveyard, deterred by the stench and their superstitions regarding the dead. They also appeared unconcerned about such frail POWs causing any trouble and didn't care how long the four men took to bury the dead, since it meant less walking for the guards and gave them a chance to catnap, smoke cigarettes, and otherwise relax. If the men stalled, Sam would have a four-hour jump on anyone chasing him, a better chance to get into the mountains and find the Filipino guerillas.

"I'm serious," Sam said to Chavez. "I almost went to Zero Ward. And now I got Rudowski running a finger across his throat every time I look in his direction, as well as Yoshida finding any opportunity to punish and humiliate me. I could end up just like these guys." He nodded at one of the emaciated cadavers they carried.

"What are you saying?"

"I'm saying, I'm getting the hell out of here," Sam said. "My tangle with beriberi was the final gun to my head. It forced the issue."

The group paused for a wild dog to cross their path, a human arm in its mouth. Three more dogs emerged from the bushes and gave chase.

"It's too risky," Chavez said.

Sam lowered his end of the litter. It forced Chavez to set down his end. Father Tom looked over at the two of them, but he and Wilber kept going forward. "You want to know what's risky?" Sam said. "What's risky is just sitting here waiting to die like sheep. Waiting until your number is called. Waiting to go to Zero Ward." He gestured at their dead passengers. "Look at these guys. That'll be one of us tomorrow. Or the next day. Or the next. Is that how you want to go out? Back on Bataan, we said we'd go down swinging."

"That was when we still had a fighting chance," Chavez said.

"We'll leave this camp one way or another, so let's go out fighting. We're down to our last chance. So I'm going to take it. I've got nothing to lose." Sam caught his breath. The rant had winded him, but also boosted his energy. "If I can reach the Filipino guerillas, they can get me to the coast, a transport. I can tell the military about the conditions in the camp."

"Then what?" Chavez said. "You think the Japs are going to just let the Red Cross waltz in here and waggle their finger and everything will change?"

"The Red Cross—"

"Can't get in here unless it's so that the Japs can steal all their supplies. And what makes you think the guerillas, if you could find them, have some way to get in touch with a transport? The Japs control the Philippines."

"I just know I have to try."

"Yoshida said we'd all be punished."

Sam laughed. "Like it could get worse? Come on, Pete. Since when did you just accept the Japs dictating your fate?"

"When I realized I had no options." Chavez lifted the litter, and Sam did also.

The men reached the graveyard's far edge, which butted up against a wooded hillside, and lowered the litters. Father Tom held his crucifix over the bodies and opened a small Bible but kept glancing out of the corner of his eye at Sam and Chavez, who continued talking.

"How do you plan to do this?" Chavez asked.

"I'll slip into the jungle right there," Sam explained. He gestured thirty feet behind Father Tom, where the terrain turned steep. "The guards won't know I'm gone for several hours. I climb into the mountains, find the Filipino guerillas, and have them get me to the coast and radio for pickup by a submarine."

"What are you talking about?" Father Tom said. He'd closed his Bible and moved to where Sam and Chavez spoke.

"Sam here is planning to escape," Chavez said.

Father Tom looked from Chavez to Sam and then back to Chavez, as if he'd misunderstood him. When Chavez just shrugged, Father Tom turned back to

Sam. "Sam, you are in no physical shape to endure the miles you would have to travel to reach help," he said, his voice sharp. "It would be suicide, even if the Japanese didn't catch you."

"What do I have to lose? Look at what we're doing, Padre. Someday it will be other starving POWs carrying *our* corpses out here to be eaten by wild dogs. All due respect, but no thank you. That will not be me."

"They'll kill you when they capture you."

"*If* they catch me. And I'd rather die trying than die in that prison camp."

"Yoshida said there would be punishment if anyone tried to escape, for all of us," Wilber said, sounding nervous.

"What more can he do?" Sam said. "We're already working from sunup to sundown and hardly eating. Look at us. We're all dying. If I get into the mountains and find the guerillas, I can let the military know. I can have them pressure the Japs to let the Red Cross into the camps to treat the sick and the dying. I can make a difference."

"I don't want to know what more Yoshida will do," Wilber said. "The little shit is liable to do anything."

"Which is why we need to let the military know what's going on. Given the time, Yoshida will kill us all."

"When do you plan to do this?" Chavez said.

"No time like the present. Another day in camp is another day to die. Anyone with me?"

"Not me," Wilber said.

Father Tom shook his head. "Sam, I'm asking you to rethink this."

"I have, over and over, Padre. I've thought until my head hurts. This is the best chance I have. That we all have." Sam looked to Chavez, his trusted friend.

"Not this time, amigo," he said. "I agree with the padre. It's suicide. If we can't talk you out of it, we'll stall for you, as much as we can."

"Okay then. I have to go to the john." Sam looked Father Tom then Chavez in the eye. "I'll see you boys back in the States. We'll raise a beer to victory and freedom."

"Sam," Father Tom called after him, but Sam slid into the jungle.

He climbed, at times nearly straight up. When he tired, he told himself the Japanese would also have to climb these hills to catch him. He moved as fast as his weakened body allowed, resting little. Jungle thorns tore his threadbare clothing and his skin, and the rough terrain bloodied his bare feet and hands, but every step higher onto the forest-covered mountain lifted Sam's spirits. His first goal was simply to get lost. His second was to find a Filipino village in the mountains and ask about guerillas in the area.

He had no choice now but to go forward. He could not go back.

Adrenaline fueled Sam for hours and miles. Night fell by the time he'd reached the top of the mountain and started down the other side. He followed a stream in the dark, guided by a full moon and the sound of flowing water. He'd been taught in Boy Scouts to follow water downstream, that it would lead to a village or to a larger body of water. In a village he'd find help; the Filipinos hated the Japanese. They would take Sam to the guerillas, and the guerillas would get Sam to safety.

When he stopped, Sam drank from the stream and the water became the Coca-Cola he once drank at the Paradise Theater. When he ate insects and grubs, he imagined popcorn kernels, and when he sat on the moss-covered ground to rest, he imagined his lumpy mattress back home. Though he was scared, he was more scared of getting caught. He pushed on.

At around 02:00, judging by the moon's position in the sky, Sam crested a high mountain ridge and spotted a village nestled in the valley below. The collection of houses with thatched roofs looked peaceful in the moonlight, but a wisp of doubt made Sam cautious. He hunkered down and studied the village. Eventually, he shook his worry. The Filipino villagers were also captives of the Japanese, just of a different kind. He recalled how they had smiled and waved at the American soldiers as they were bused through town on their way to their base, how they had shouted joyful welcomes, and handed the GIs food, flowers, and something to drink. He thought of how they'd risked their lives to smuggle needed supplies to the POWs. He started down the mountain.

As Sam walked into the village a dog sounded a frantic alarm that the village's perimeter had been breached. Uneasy faces emerged from their huts. They stared at Sam but did not smile or welcome him. They did not offer him anything to eat or to drink. His appearance, he thought. In his tattered garments, and iridescent moonlight, he looked like a ghost, like Jacob Marley in *A Christmas Carol.*

"American, American," Sam said quietly, arms raised to assure the villagers he was a good guy.

The villagers ventured farther from their huts. An elderly man approached Sam and studied him. Then he flashed a broken-toothed grin and extended both hands in a double thumbs-up gesture. "American GI."

Thank God. Sam nearly collapsed to the ground.

"Yes," he said, fighting back tears. "American GI." Sam asked about any guerillas in the area.

The village elder nodded and said, *"Mga gerilya. Mga gerilya,"* which sounded to Sam like "my guerilla."

Through a mix of gestures and broken English, Sam learned he would rest until dawn, when the guerillas would come and take him to the Americans. The elder hid Sam in a hut. Other villagers brought him water, bananas, and a soup of squash, okra, onion, and taro. Sam sipped the water, but his stomach, for weeks denied anything but handfuls of rice, rebelled. Still, Sam thanked each villager for their kindness.

He wished the guys had struck out with him. They would all be free, and soon he'd be getting word spread of the mistreatment and the killings. He allowed himself to think of Sarah, of walking into her classroom at Eagle Grove High School in his crisp uniform with a chest full of medals. There, in front of all her students, he would take Sarah in his arms, dip her like a Hollywood star, and kiss her deeply. Then he'd slip a ring on her finger.

He was going home.

18

LEVERAGE

Grace and Sarah had spent the weekend exploring DC and seeing the monuments up close. Everything was much faster paced than Sarah had experienced in Eagle Grove, and even on those occasions when she and Maryanne Dimple had gone to Minneapolis. At the end of each day, she had felt overwhelmed and exhausted. She had gone to a picture show Saturday night, and had been amazed at the theater's size, the picture's clarity, and the sound quality compared to the Paradise Theater. She and Grace had opted not to see *Casablanca* with Humphrey Bogart and Ingrid Bergman, feeling it hit too close to home, and had chosen instead to see *Road to Morocco*, a comedy with Bing Crosby, Bob Hope, and Dorothy Lamour.

They had both needed to laugh.

Monday morning, Sarah and Grace caught a bus back to Main Navy. Inside the building, a naval officer photographed Sarah holding a sign with her name and a four-digit number. He would affix her photo to a badge and told her she would need to wear it to enter and exit the compound. Forget the badge, he told her, and forget being admitted. Until she received her badge, he gave her a temporary pass. A Marine guard then ushered her and other women starting that day into a room. Captain Russell stood at the front in his crisp khaki uniform, colored ribbons over his breast pocket. He looked at Sarah and smiled.

"Ladies, hopefully you recall me. I'm Captain Russell, and I am here to welcome you to Main Navy. I'll get right to the point. Code breaking is one of our most fruitful forms of intelligence. Listening in on enemy conversations provides a verbatim, real-time way for us to know what the enemy is thinking, planning, worrying about, and carrying out. It provides information on their strategy, troop movements, shipping itineraries, battlefield casualties, pending attacks, and supply needs. It will play a key role in shortening this war and bringing our boys home, but we have a lot of work to do."

Which is why I'm here, she thought.

"We have different divisions to which you have been assigned. We have women who are testing America's codes to make sure they are secure. Others create dummy traffic—fake radio messages to fool the Germans and the Japanese. Some work to decipher the Japanese codes."

Sarah looked at the women in the room. It was a profound situation, psychologically. The women were brought to DC to free men to fight and, potentially, to die. Yet the work they performed was intended to bring the servicemen home alive, and sooner rather than later. Sarah would be protecting the very men whose lives she put in danger when she took their job.

Russell spoke for a few more minutes, then told the women to come forward and receive their assignments.

Sarah stepped forward and Captain Russell greeted her. "Miss Haber. I was pleased to learn you changed your mind. What caused your change of heart?"

"I guess I just wanted to do more for my country," she said. "I sound so altruistic. Will I be issued a soapbox, or should I have brought my own?"

"No," he said. "You sound like someone who has her priorities straight."

"I had boys in high school leaving to serve," she said, not wanting to mention Sam. "I thought maybe I could do something to help bring them home alive."

Russell smiled. "Well, you are uniquely qualified to help with that. A master's degree in mathematics is quite an accomplishment. Congratulations."

"Thank you."

"Given your unique qualifications, you will be working on my crew."

"Crew?" Sarah asked.

"My team."

"And what is your team working on?"

"Breaking Japanese codes," he said. "I'm not going to lie to you or try to glorify the work. It can be tedious and frustrating, but I believe you have what it takes to be very good at it."

"Then let me temper your enthusiasm, Captain. I'm not a genius. I'm more of what you'd call a grinder. I got my degrees in large part because I worked hard."

Russell again smiled. "First, the genius narrative is overblown. In many ways what you will be asked to do is the opposite of genius. Code breaking depends on flashes of inspiration, certainly, but more on carefully maintaining files so you can compare received messages with others from six months earlier. Your crew of six women will be like a giant brain. And I'm well aware of your propensity for working hard, by the way, as well as your view that a woman can do anything a man can do. You had a high school instructor who made the unfortunate mistake of discounting a woman's purpose, I believe."

"You checked up on me."

"We check up on every candidate, as I said we would, Miss Haber. Shall we get to work?"

"That's why I'm here, Captain."

Captain Russell took Sarah and half a dozen other women to a room he called Barracks D, where cryptanalysis was being done by a group referred to as OP-20-GY, which was in the process of being divided into GY-P for Pacific and GY-A for Atlantic. "Don't worry about all the acronyms. You'll get used to it," Russell told the women. "You will work in GY-P. Room assignments will be made and remade. The GY unit is already overflowing into three wings of this building, an arrangement that is neither convenient nor efficient."

Sarah was assigned to Room 1515, working under Vi Moore doing additive recovery. That is, she was told that the Japanese substituted numbers for letters, then used an additive to further complicate the code. "For instance, the number four might represent the letter A, but if the additive to the code is a six, the letter becomes an F, the sixth letter in the alphabet," her supervisor explained. "The Japanese are not simpleminded; their additives can often be a complex mathematical equation."

That's where Sarah came in.

Each day women crammed each room, and Sarah quickly recognized the difficulty of working in such tight confines. It appeared to her the shift size was determined by the number of available chairs. She and other recent recruits had to overturn metal trash cans to use as seats. They worked at tables using graph paper, cards, and pencils. The women all looked like they knew what to do, focused and intent. Some tables had stacks of index cards. Others had strips of paper hung on string like drying pasta. Fans circulated the air and rustled so much paper it was hard at times to hear yourself think. The cramped quarters provided little room to stow workbooks and offered no secure telephones, and with so many people coming in and out, secrecy became a constant headache.

After a few days, Sarah had learned her way around the complex, and she soon understood each room's distinction. In one room women worked at tabulating machines, punch-card machines, and strange sorts of typewriters. A thick array of cables hooked the machines together. Allied listening stations secretly intercepted messages from just about everywhere in the South Pacific, then encrypted them before sending them on to Main Navy. Once the messages were received, the crews would strip the American encryption, and the women would go to work trying to strip the enemy encryption. It was incredibly complex. Many of the women were also ex-schoolteachers, but their level of competency at breaking codes varied widely. With her math affinity, Sarah took to the numbers quickly, but her ability to keep a positive attitude was put to the test often. She kept telling herself that all the drudgery and painstaking attention to detail might break a code, maybe save a soldier's life, maybe Sam's.

She and Grace, who worked the same shift and in the same room, started out sorting messages, but after just a couple of weeks, Sarah was called into Captain Russell's office. She knocked before entering. "You asked that I report to you?"

Russell nodded and set papers aside on his desk. He stood. "I've been told that in the two short weeks you've been here, you've showed an affinity for untangling intercepts and recognizing certain digits at the beginning of a message."

"It wasn't difficult. I just looked for repeating patterns, then determined the designated station from which the message had been sent."

"That is outstanding work, Miss Haber. We've spent weeks trying to determine each message's origin. I'm transferring you to a crew analyzing four-digit numbers for potential patterns. It will be like trying to unravel a complex puzzle. Your salary will reflect the increased job difficulty. Are you game?"

"Yes, sir," she said, then remembered what Grace had said about using what little leverage the g-girls had. "I work well in a team. I work well with Grace Moretti, sir."

"Good. You'll both report to me tomorrow morning." Russell looked at the clock on the wall. "Another thing, Miss Haber. You are a civilian. You are not enlisted. You do not, therefore, have to call me 'sir.' Captain Russell or Bill is fine."

"I meant it as a sign of respect, sir."

"And I am appreciative." He checked the wall clock again. "It looks like I've kept you after your shift. I'd like to discuss your new position so you can hit the ground running in the morning. Have you plans for dinner?"

Sarah was so surprised by the offer, she stumbled for an answer or, better yet, an excuse not to go, but she couldn't tell Captain Russell she was engaged. Besides, maybe the invitation was harmless. Work related, as the captain had said. "No," she said.

"Good. I know a place where we can talk. Gather your things. I'll meet you in the lobby in, say, fifteen minutes?"

Sarah left the office and went to gather her belongings. Grace had waited for her, sitting on a worktable, her gloves on and purse in hand. She'd also collected Sarah's things.

"What did Captain Russell want?"

"I'm being promoted and getting an increase in pay."

"That's fantastic." Grace slid off the table. "Congratulations, though I'm going to miss you."

"Not for long. You're being promoted too."

"I am? How did that happen?"

"I guess they recognized your talent as well."

"Honey, as my father liked to say, 'Don't shit a shitter.' I'm nowhere near your level. Now what really happened?"

"I told Captain Russell we worked as a team, and continuing our relationship would bring greater success."

"You didn't."

"I did."

Grace hugged Sarah. "Honey, you catch on fast, and I'm not talking about code breaking. Let's go have a drink to celebrate."

"There's something else. Captain Russell wants to take me to dinner to discuss my new position."

Grace smiled knowingly. "Forget about catching on fast. Honey, you just zipped right to the head of the class."

"I'm sure it's just work related."

"Uh-huh," Grace said. "Did he ask me to accompany the two of you?"

He hadn't. Sarah thought of her cabdriver. He'd seemed the perfect gentleman, but he'd still taken advantage of Sarah's naivete. "Maybe I should tell him about Sam."

"Honey, you don't have to tell him anything of the sort. And I would recommend you don't. He's going to take you to a fancy restaurant serving food that girls like us rarely get to eat. Am I right?"

"I guess so."

"So . . . enjoy dinner, and when this war is over, you'll still go home to your Sam."

"Okay," Sarah said.

"Order the biggest, most expensive steak on the menu, a baked potato, and a Caesar salad. We'll have that drink to celebrate another time. Come on, let's go to the powder room and fix your face up nice."

Sarah followed Grace, but she remained uncomfortable, as if hiding her and Sam's relationship was somehow a bad idea.

19

BLOOD BROTHERS

Luzon, Philippines
June 27, 1942

A commotion startled Sam from sleep. He awoke confused, not recognizing his surroundings, nor remembering he had escaped Camp O'Donnell and was in a mountain village. He took a deep breath and regained his bearings. Then he heard what had awoken him. It sounded like broken English. The Filipino guerillas. He paused, listening. His stomach gripped and his panic spread. The accent was one he had come to know so well these past months.

Japanese.

He sprang to his feet and hurried to the window. The tribal leader talked with three armed Japanese guards. If they found Sam in the village, they'd kill the elder, and likely others. He moved to the small wooden door at the back of his hut and pulled it open. A Japanese bayonet jabbed at him, cutting his shoulder. The butt of a rifle struck him, and he fell backward, to the ground. After an efficient beating, they dragged him across the ground on his knees and dropped him between the elder and the officer.

"He didn't know I was here," Sam said from his knees, feeling his split lip starting to swell. "I hid in the night, before anyone was awake."

The Japanese officer crouched down. "You are a liar, Sam Carlson," he said in English nearly as proficient as Yoshida's. "He knew you were here all along."

"No. No, he didn't know."

The officer smiled. "Commendable, you should worry about a man who has betrayed you."

Sam looked up from the ground. "What?"

The officer laughed. "Pay the bounty," he said to a guard in English and while he looked at Sam. "Then bring the prisoner down the mountain. But don't kill him, yet. Yoshida has something special in store for him."

Two Japanese guards dropped a hundred-pound bag of rice at the elder's feet. The man would not look Sam in the eye. Emaciated villagers murmured excitedly. The elder had betrayed Sam to feed his people.

The guards lifted Sam to his feet, bruised, bloodied, and betrayed.

"Back to camp," the squad leader barked in Japanese.

The guards tied Sam's hands behind his back and secured a three-foot rope between his ankles, then prodded him down the hill, prodding him with bayonets and inflicting dozens of tiny cuts in his back, sides, and legs. The morning turned hot, and a searing heat radiated from the jungle floor. Within minutes, Sam was drenched in his own sweat and Philippine dust. His mouth became parched. When he stumbled and fell, the guards beat him until he got back on his feet.

"Don't kill him," the officer said, again speaking English. No doubt for Sam's benefit. "That would be too good for him."

Sam feared what awaited him, but decided he would not beg Yoshida to spare his life. He'd rather die.

After a long trek they arrived at Camp O'Donnell. The guards marched Sam through the main gate. POWs stood outside their barracks, including Chavez, Father Tom, Major Jones, Wilber, and the remaining members of Sam's tank battalion. They looked at Sam like they were already burying his corpse in the mass grave.

Now it was Sam's turn to be stuffed into the cramped four-by-four-foot bamboo cage Rudowski had been crammed into, where the other POWs could observe him, but not get close enough to speak to him. Sam's bones ached where he'd been beaten, and after hours in the cage, baking in the tropical sun, the muscles in his legs cramped, and he couldn't straighten his limbs to relieve the pain. Swarms of flies hovered over the cage and on Sam's body. Insects bit at his skin, but he grew too weak to kill them. He was grateful when he drifted out of consciousness. Dusk brought an unrefreshing warm, tropical rain. He tilted back his head and let the rain splash on his face, licking what raindrops he could over his cracked lips and into his swollen mouth. He told himself if this was to be his last memory of living, he would hold on to it no matter what Yoshida did to him.

Within minutes, Sam was drenched, and the sun receded. As night fell and the temperature dropped, his body shivered violently.

The process repeated for three long days, until the lock on the cage rattled and the bamboo gate opened. The guards pulled Sam, nearly unconscious, from the cage and threw him down onto muddied dirt. His limbs refused to straighten after being constricted for so long. The afternoon rain had come again. Sam was too exhausted to even shake the water from his face, though his vision had cleared. POWs again stood outside their barracks, staring at him.

"Ah, Sam Carlson." Yoshida appeared at Sam's side in his same ridiculous outfit. "So glad you could join us." He made a sweeping, unveiling gesture and Sam turned to see a row of blindfolded POWs, their mouths gagged, arms tied behind their backs. Rainwater streamed down their faces. Behind them, the rest of the POWs looked grave.

"Your blood brothers," Yoshida said.

"My what?" Sam muttered, barely above a whisper.

Yoshida spoke to his audience. "I advised all that there would be consequences should any prisoner attempt to escape." He turned to the gathering of POWs. "Surely you all remember. And I am a man of my word." Yoshida then spun and again approached Sam. "You remembered, Sam Carlson, but you chose to ignore my proclamation. You chose to put yourself ahead of your fellow prisoners, your blood brothers." He again gestured at the nine men.

Sam wanted to tell Yoshida he was wrong. He wanted to tell the men that he tried to reach the guerillas, to let the world know of the mistreatment in the prisoner camp. The words would not come.

Yoshida shouted for the other POWs to also hear. "It is now the law of Camp O'Donnell that for every man who tries to escape, successful or not, we will select nine prisoners to die because of that one man's selfishness. You are a selfish man, Sam Carlson. You have sacrificed the lives of these nine blood brothers."

"No," Sam said, not fully comprehending.

The rain picked up. Large drops splashed in the puddles in the yard. Sam struggled to shake the water from his eyes, to see. When he did, the row of POWs came in and out of focus.

Yoshida stepped to the first blindfolded prisoner. "Carlson, look here," he said over the rush of the rain. He grabbed the POW by his hair and lifted his head. "Do you know this man?"

Sam trembled. Even with the blindfold, he recognized Archie McGriff, one of his fellow tankers.

"Look closely, Carlson." He pulled off McGriff's blindfold and gag.

Sam's jaw locked. He couldn't speak.

"Carlson, you worthless piece of shit," McGriff said.

"He seems to know you." Yoshida laughed. "Still don't recognize him, Carlson? No final words? Then you won't miss him." Yoshida drew his Nambu service pistol, cocked it, and shot McGriff in the temple. McGriff crumpled to the ground, his blood mixing with the muddied water.

"You son of a bitch," Sam said, finding his voice, though struggling to speak. He tried to rise to his feet, but he was too weak and his injured legs wouldn't straighten. The guards struck him with rifle butts and bamboo poles across his back. Sam toppled over and rolled to his side, moaning. "Shoot me. Kill me, goddammit."

Yoshida said, "I want all your fellow prisoners to know that, unlike you, I am an honorable man. I said nine, and nine it shall be. You shall pick the order. Who's next? This one?" Yoshida stepped to a POW Sam did not know. "Do you know this one?"

Sam opened his mouth, but no words came.

"Yes? No? Maybe so?" Yoshida taunted. "Eenie, meenie, minie moe?" He pressed the gun barrel to the side of the POW's head and pulled the trigger. Another body. More blood colored the puddles.

"God damn you. Stop. I'm the one who escaped. Kill me."

"Now, Carlson, that is not the rule. I must stick to the rule, with specificity. This way I can be trusted, and you prisoners will have no excuses not to follow my rules." Yoshida turned to the POWs forced to watch. "And you shall follow them," he yelled over the rush of rain.

He stepped between the two dead soldiers and dropped to one knee beside Sam. "You think this is cruel?" he whispered. He smiled. "You should have seen what they made me do in Nanjing."

The Japanese officer lifted Sam by his hair to his feet. "You will watch, Sam Carlson. You earned this. If you do not watch, I will choose another nine." Yoshida stepped to the next POW, then moved behind him and pressed the barrel against his head. "I am highly educated from your country's finest universities. I am a man of honor and distinction."

He fired. The third POW crumpled to the ground.

"Stop!" Sam shouted.

Yoshida stepped to a fourth POW and put the pistol against the man's head. He fired, and he, too, collapsed. Yoshida returned to Sam, whispering in his ear. "When I initially refused to rape and kill Chinese students, my superior officers made an example of me," he said. "Now I will make an example of you, Sam Carlson." He stood, walked back to the line, and shot the fifth POW, then the sixth.

Yoshida danced a jig back to Sam and again knelt. "Some say I went a little crazy," he whispered. "Too unstable to fight on the front lines." He tapped the butt of his pistol on top of Sam's head. "What do you think, Carlson? Am I crazy?"

Yoshida turned and fired, like a gunslinger, making quick work of murdering the seventh POW. He danced his little jig. "A man can die but once," he said, quoting Shakespeare. He shot and killed the eighth POW.

Sam closed his eyes and screamed.

"One left, Carlson. You will please open your eyes—if you don't want me to draft another nine." Sam opened his eyes. Yoshida put his pistol barrel at the base of the next soldier's skull. Sam braced for the gunshot.

Click.

Yoshida cocked the hammer again.

Click.

"Uh-oh, Carlson. I'm out of bullets." Yoshida holstered his empty pistol. The two-foot blade sang as he drew it from its scabbard. Then he ordered the guards to force the ninth prisoner to kneel.

Sam sat on his heels, dizzied by the grotesque show. Around him the pools of blood had merged, creating a pond. He heaved, but nothing came from his empty stomach. The last POW squirmed and moaned, but he remained tightly bound. Yoshida lowered his sword and loosened the man's gag.

Sam had spoken with the soldier during the march from Bataan. He was another guy with a hometown and a story. He had a mother who loved him. A sweetheart who missed him. A little brother who wanted to be him.

"You selfish son of a bitch, Carlson. You'll burn in hell for this."

"He's really mad at you, Sam Carlson," Yoshida said with mock concern. He moved closer to Sam. "He's right, you know. You are selfish. And you will rot in hell."

"Right beside you," Sam said.

Yoshida smiled. Then he stepped behind the POW and lifted his sword high into the air. "Off with his head!" he shouted, again quoting Shakespeare, then brought the sword down and nearly decapitated the man. His skull hung from his neck by ribbons of muscle. "Almost," Yoshida said, shaking his head at his failure.

"Just you left," Yoshida said, his grin splitting his face. He sighed. "But you know what? I'm getting tired."

Yoshida took a pistol from a guard and walked back to where Sam knelt in the dirt. He removed all but a single bullet, then wrapped Sam's hand around the handle and lifted the barrel to Sam's temple. "Here in Japan, to take one's life can be an act of honor. Regain your honor." Yoshida put Sam's finger on the trigger. "Do it, Carlson."

Sam looked through the driving rain to the assembled POWs. In the front row stood Father Tom and Pete Chavez. Father Tom held out his crucifix to Sam, raised it, and slowly shook his head back and forth.

"End your pitiful existence," Yoshida said. "And start your eternity in hell."

Sam stared at Father Tom for what seemed hours, then fell forward, weeping.

Yoshida leaned down, speaking in Sam's ear. "As I suspected, Carlson. You have no honor. Killing a man like you would be too easy. I shall let you live to suffer the pain of your guilt, the torture of your shame, and the humiliation of your disgrace."

Sam turned his head and looked up at Yoshida.

Yoshida shuddered as if writhing in pleasure. "You will be a fine example each day for the other prisoners—if they don't kill you." Then he shouted to the guards, who moved and grabbed Sam.

The guards dragged Sam across the muddied yard and tossed him at the feet of the POWs. All but Father Tom, Pete Chavez, and Major Jones turned and left him.

20

A Proposal

Washington, DC
June 29, 1942

Captain Russell had a car and driver pick them up outside Main Navy. He held the back door for Sarah while she climbed into the seat, scooting to the far side. Captain Russell climbed in the back also and gave the driver, Jeff, directions to a place called Martin's Tavern on Wisconsin Avenue.

"Have you eaten there?" he asked Sarah.

Sarah shook her head and tried to look relaxed but had to consciously keep her knee from shaking.

"You'll enjoy it. Have you had a chance to see much of DC?"

"Some," Sarah said. "I had a taxi driver take a long detour when I first arrived."

Russell smiled. "Yes, they are known to do that. Not to worry tonight. Jeff and this car are provided by the Navy and will take you home free of charge."

Sarah wondered how the Navy could afford to pay for cars and drivers for its officers with a war going on, but she didn't ask.

Martin's Tavern was a two-story yellow stucco building with a hunter-green awning and shutters at the corner of Wisconsin Avenue. Captain Russell held out a hand to help Sarah from the car, then held open the door to the wooden vestibule with leaded windows. She stepped inside the interior door and the cozy, but opulent, surroundings nearly took her breath away. A wooden bar extended the room's length beneath half a dozen colorful Tiffany lamps. Customers sat at tables draped in white tablecloths with silverware, dinnerware, and wine glasses. It looked like a home decorated for the holidays.

"Captain Russell." The maître d' at the door bowed slightly. He wore a tuxedo.

"Sam, this is Sarah Haber," Captain Russell said, "a new employee in communications at Main Navy."

Sam. Sarah's eyes watered, but she pushed back her emotions. This Sam bowed gracefully to Sarah, as her Sam used to do in the projection room at the Paradise Theater, then led them to a table toward the rear and pulled out her chair. "May I take the young lady's coat?"

Sarah slid from her coat and handed it to Sam. Once they were seated, he asked, "The usual, Captain Russell?"

"Please."

"Can I get the lady a cocktail?"

Russell looked to Sarah. "Water is fine," Sarah said. "Thank you."

Russell placed his napkin in his lap. "How have your first weeks been?"

"A little hectic," she said. "Getting settled and all. New city. New surroundings. New friends. I've never worked in a place so large."

"You've certainly caught on quickly, as I knew you would."

"And how could you be so confident of that, Captain?"

Russell just smiled in answer. Then he said, "I majored in mathematics myself. I graduated from Georgetown and planned to go back to teach."

"Why didn't you?"

"My family had a small farm in Virginia. When the Depression hit, we lost the farm and just about everything else. Joining the Navy was the only path I had to get an education. Luckily, Mr. Hitler and Mr. Tojo allowed me to finish my studies before they commenced this war. Let's order and I'll tell you more about your new position."

Sarah opened her menu and nearly choked at the prices. How did anyone afford these prices during these times? Her shock must have shown on her face.

"Don't worry about the cost," Captain Russell said. "The Navy pays if it's a working meal."

Her shock became irritation. Soldiers were starving and dying all over the world. "How does the Navy afford a car and driver and pay for its officers' meals with a war going on?"

"Good question," Russell said, but the maître d' saved him by returning with his cocktail.

"Your old-fashioned, sir."

Russell took a sip. "It's perfect, as always. Thank you, Sam." He held the glass to Sarah. She raised her water glass to his glass, then set it down, again thinking of Sam and their ritual in the Paradise Theater's projection booth.

Russell said, "To answer your question, the Navy pays for a car and driver and an occasional meal, just as it pays for your laundry and a maid to clean your room once a week. Am I right?"

Sarah sat back. "Yes."

"There are going to be many long days and long nights, Miss Haber. You will be working odd hours. The Navy provides these 'accommodations' because it does not want me, or you, focusing on anything but our work."

"And how does Mrs. Russell feel about your hours?"

Captain Russell tilted his head, then moved his right hand to the ring on his left index finger, spinning it. "I'm widowed, Miss Haber. My wife died of cancer. It was slow, and painful, for all involved. Much like this war. I'd rather be married. I'd rather be on a ship in the battle, but God had other plans, and the Navy considers my skills too valuable and put me here. This is my fate."

"I'm sorry," she said. "About your wife. It was rude of me to ask."

"It was perfectly acceptable," he said. "In fact, I would have expected nothing less. You are inquisitive, attentive, and curious. You're not afraid to ask difficult questions. Add to those qualities your mathematics skills, and you fit nicely on the crew and, maybe, will end up leading it. You will be assigned to my team in Department K."

"Department K? What does the *K* stand for?"

"Not a thing. The terms are kept deliberately vague to preserve secrecy."

"And what exactly does Department K do?"

"Tomorrow you and Grace Moretti will begin attending lectures on code breaking and code making. Your salaries will be increased to $2,600 a year."

Sarah couldn't help but widen her eyes at the increase in pay.

"I'm sure it sounds like a lot of money to a young woman from Eagle Grove, Minnesota; it sounds like a lot to an officer from Virginia. But trust me, they can't pay you enough for the hours you will be working, the tedium you will endure, and the frustration you will often experience. But break the Japanese codes, and you affect the war's outcome."

"That's exactly what I want."

"Be careful what you wish for. You will be working on one of Main Navy's most urgent tasks—trying to break the JN-25 codes the Japanese use to direct their ships, including their marus, around the Pacific Islands."

"What are marus?"

"Merchant ships. Tankers, freighters, barges, cable layers, motor transports. They sail between ports all across the Japanese Empire, including Hiroshima, Yokohama, Wewak, Saipan, Tokyo, and Manila. Anything the enemy needs is sent by water, which means the marus are always sailing. Crack the code and we will sever the enemy's lifeline of food, fuel, reinforcements, weapons and machinery, and other critical supplies. It will allow General MacArthur and Admiral Nimitz to push back against the Japanese in the Pacific, where thousands of American soldiers are currently imprisoned and the war's balance remains undecided. Do you understand and accept what I am asking you to do?"

Sarah Haber did understand. She understood all too well.

She would be sinking ships.

PART 2

1

Breaking the Code

Main Navy Building
Washington, DC
February 3, 1943

Captain Russell had not understated the hard work or the long hours. Sarah's days could be tedious, frustrating, seemingly hopeless, and often grim, but she and her colleagues plowed forward, heads down.

Since arriving in Washington, DC, Sarah had called home every Sunday to speak to her mother and father. It was expensive, but the Navy paid for the call, an expense her family didn't need to bear, but that wasn't the reason Sarah always initiated the calls: she feared bad news each time the phone rang. Many of her fellow workers at the Annex had also instructed their families not to call them. When she did call home, she told her mother to begin their conversations with "There's no news of Sam," so Sarah didn't have to hold her breath. At work, Sarah and her team struggled to decipher the newest batch of messages encoded using the JN-25 machine. The Allies had never seen the machine and therefore did not know its inner workings. The analysts in her crew had earlier deciphered a four-digit code at the *beginning* of each message, which indicated where the message had originated. But the Japanese had again changed their code, and now Sarah and her colleagues were seeing the same four digits repeating in various locations in each Japanese message. Sometimes at the beginning of the messages, other times in the middle or at the end.

For weeks and months no one had been able to decipher what the moving code meant, and her commanding officers lamented that unless their crew figured it out, the US might lose the war.

Sarah noticed that many things the Japanese did intending to make their code harder to break actually made it easier, and she started to operate under the less-is-more principle. Just because she had an advanced degree in mathematics didn't mean the Japanese cryptographers did. Thinking "less is more," Sarah studied multiple messages spread out on her desk. Having stared at the messages for days, she suddenly had an epiphany as to why they could find the four-digit code in different areas of different messages. If correct, she'd feel foolish for not having thought of the solution earlier. She checked and rechecked multiple messages, then compared half a dozen side by side, and was both certain and embarrassed that she had the answer.

She grabbed the messages and hurried from her table and down the hall, avoiding naval officers and civilians. She ducked into Captain Russell's office and bypassed his secretary, who'd been told to admit Sarah day or night. She pushed into Russell's office as his secretary called after her, "He's in a meeting."

Sarah stepped into Russell's conference room and pulled up. Naval officers in their khaki-colored uniforms filled the seats at the long table. Russell sat near the head of the table, where a rear admiral—judging by the two stars on his shoulder boards—stood speaking. He stopped and looked at Sarah as if she had two heads. The others seated at the table also diverted their attention to the distraction.

"What is the meaning of this intrusion?" the rear admiral asked.

Sarah looked at Russell, whose eyes had widened. "I'm very sorry, sir. I have a standing order to immediately speak with Captain Russell if I find something pertinent regarding the Japanese JN-25 code."

The rear admiral looked to Russell, who had pushed back his chair from the table. "I'll step out, Admiral," Russell said.

The rear admiral raised a hand, then returned his attention to Sarah. "What's your name?" he asked.

"Sarah Haber."

"What department do you work in, Miss Haber?"

"I'm in the classification room," she said.

"If what you have to tell Captain Russell is of import—"

"I believe it is, sir."

"Then we would all benefit from hearing it."

Sarah looked at the men seated at the table, each staring at her. She didn't know if the rear admiral was being sincere or testing her. Some older naval officers weren't keen on having women in their midst.

"Go ahead, Sarah. Tell us all," Russell said.

Rather than be intimidated, she pictured the naval officers as her students at Eagle Grove High School, then moved to the head of the table. The rear admiral stepped back and gave Sarah the floor.

She looked to Russell. "For months we've been struggling to decipher the newest iteration of JN-25. The messages seemed garbled and did not make sense. But that's because we were starting in the wrong location."

"Where were you starting?" the rear admiral asked.

Sarah again looked to Russell. "At the beginning."

"And why would that be wrong?" the rear admiral asked.

Sarah looked to the admiral. "Because the enemy cryptographers aren't starting their messages at the beginning of their transmissions. Not anymore. They're sending garbled nonwords to throw us off, then beginning the message in the middle, or sometimes at the end. That's the purpose of the four-digit code we've struggled with. It signifies the beginning of the message." Seeing the blank looks before her, she said, "Here, maybe it's better if I demonstrate."

She placed the messages on the table. Russell and the others drew closer, looking over Sarah's shoulder, or leaning in to view the messages, palms pressed to the table. "When the Japanese cryptographers do this, they include a four-digit code telling the recipient where the message starts. Look at these four messages. Each contains the same four-digit code, but at a different location in each message, so we know it is not the code for any station of origin."

"What is it?" the rear admiral asked.

"The code, I believe, is not an actual word but simply means 'Begin message here.'"

Russell looked up at her. The others looked skeptical that the solution could be so simple.

"It gives us the point of entry into the actual message," she went on. "Next you will see the four-digit code 2468."

Sarah and her team had also struggled with that code for months.

"Thinking logically, after communicating where to begin reading the message, the next logical piece of information the person transmitting the message needs to let the recipient know is—"

"From where the message is being transmitted," Russell said.

"Each city and port," Sarah said, nodding. "I'm sure of it."

She spent the next several minutes deciphering each message for the naval officers. None were earth-shattering in their content, but she knew her discovery might be.

"If correct," Russell said, looking to the admiral, "this is the main Japanese water transport code."

Sarah looked from Russell to the rear admiral, then to the others in the room. Pandemonium broke out, and Russell pulled Sarah from the room and raced down the hall with her, one arm clutching her elbow. He ushered her into the room used to decipher suspected urgent or priority messages.

"Listen up, ladies," Russell said. "This is Sarah Haber. I believe she just broke a critical piece of the newest iteration of JN-25. Sarah, explain to them what you just told me."

Sarah did so, and the mood in the room changed instantly. The women were reading messages they'd struggled to decipher for weeks, sometimes months, establishing Japanese ship locations and transports. The Navy quickly tested the accuracy of certain deciphered messages and, when satisfied they'd been correctly deciphered, radioed Submarine Force, Pacific Fleet, in Hawaii, which radioed American submarine captains throughout the Pacific Theater the information they needed to intercept and sink ships.

Late that afternoon, Russell came into Department K and said to Sarah, "Grab your stuff. You've been promoted to the 'urgent' room. Your pay will reflect your promotion."

Sarah was grateful for the recognition and the increased pay, but what she really wanted was to leave the Meridian Hill Hotel, with its flimsy construction and paper-thin walls. She hated always having to stand in line—for the mailboxes, the showers, the cafeteria food, the phone, the bus. It was a waste of precious free time.

"What is it?" Russell asked.

"Don't think I'm not grateful for everything you've done for me."

"I don't," Russell said.

"It's just . . . I hate living at Meridian Hill." She detailed the list of problems. Russell listened intently, then said, "Grab your things. Come with me."

Sarah did and found herself once again in the back of Russell's car. During her eight months at Main Navy, she and the captain had continued what he called their "weekly work dinners," though they often did not discuss work. He told her they both needed a break from the pressure, and the short reprieve would only make them better equipped to tackle the next day.

Sarah was often torn. She had no doubt she still loved Sam, but she couldn't deny her attraction to the captain, and she knew he liked her for more than her exceptional code-breaking skills. He'd been the perfect gentleman throughout their time together, never even tried to kiss her, though sometimes Sarah wished he would, and when she closed the door on another date, she'd often lean against the wood and wonder if she was saving herself for someone who might never be coming home. She hated to think Sam could be dead, but she couldn't avoid it. Some of the few married girls in her section had received messages delivered by naval personnel telling them their husbands were dead. Each message received punched a hole in Sarah's and her colleague's hearts. Why should she expect Sam to come home when so many others were not? She could have turned down Russell's dinner invitations, but each time, she said yes, and she wondered if that meant more than she was letting herself believe.

She also felt guilty taking her forty-eight or seventy-two-hour leaves, when she and Grace would climb onto trains and buses to visit places like New York and Philadelphia. On shorter leaves, they would hop buses and trolleys to USO dances, or to get a drink at a bar. In nice weather, they took the bus to the beach to sunbathe and swim for the day. It was a life Sarah had never imagined herself leading, and she found herself enjoying her time. Should she feel guilty?

On a Sunday evening train ride back from New York, Sarah had broken down and confided in Grace her mixed emotions about having a good time, and how she felt about her weekly dinners with Captain Russell.

"So what's the problem?" Grace said, which was so like her. Practical, pragmatic, and quick to decide.

"Well, for one, Sam and I are supposed to get married when this war is over."

"Honey, do you know how many g-girls at Main Navy are engaged to get married to a fella after the war is over and are out dating now?"

"It doesn't seem right to me."

"You're looking at this the wrong way."

"How am I looking at it the wrong way?" Sarah asked, though she knew the answer. Grace was dating half a dozen men and making each believe he was the one for her. *He is,* she'd tell Sarah. *For the evening, anyway.*

"For one," Grace began, "no one knows when this damned war is going to end. It's been years already."

"Sam's alive, Grace. I know it."

"I'm not saying he's not. I'm just saying no one knows when he's coming home. It could be another year, two, maybe longer. Sam wouldn't want you sitting around moping your life away. You said after you turned down his marriage proposal, he never pressured you again. You finally had to tell him you were ready to get married."

Sarah had eventually confided in Grace about Sam after they'd become good friends. "That's true, I did. But what—"

"My point is, Sam knows you. He knows you're independent and adventurous. He'd want you to live your life to the fullest." A crooked smile escaped her. "Besides, what Sam doesn't know isn't going to hurt anyone."

"Grace—"

"I'm serious. Hear me out, honey. There's a war going on. And people are doing what they can to survive, to get through this without going crazy. You have that right too."

"So, then, what should I tell the captain?"

"You don't have to tell him anything. That's my point. Just enjoy the ride, and when the war ends, you'll both go your separate ways—him back to Virginia and you to Eagle Grove, where your Sam will be waiting for you."

When Sarah didn't respond, Grace said, "Oh, now, what's this? You're having a change of heart?"

Sarah rushed to explain. "Don't get me wrong. I love Eagle Grove, and it will always be home, but . . . it's just, after living and working here in Washington, and traveling to New York and all the other places we've gone, I'm not sure I want to go home to Eagle Grove and live on a dairy farm, raising kids, which is what Sam wants. I want to live my life . . . my dreams."

"And you think Captain Russell might be able to make those dreams come true."

"Well, I don't know. Maybe."

———

Captain Russell's car pulled up to an apartment building not far from Main Navy.

"What is this place?" Sarah asked from the back seat.

"Developers are building apartments everywhere for all the workers flocking into town. This one has a two-bedroom apartment available. If you split the rent, it's not much more than what you're paying now at Meridian Hill, though you won't have the same perks, like a cafeteria or a maid."

"I can do my own laundry," Sarah said. "And it's high time I did my own cooking and cleaning too. I know Grace is tired of Meridian Hill also, and Margaret Addington. And since Margaret works a different watch, we can hot bed. At least I'll be getting a decent night's sleep."

"And you can walk to Main Navy," Russell said.

Sarah smiled. "Thank you, Captain. I hope you don't think I'm trying to take advantage."

"What if you are?" He returned her smile. "Who would blame you?"

"Is that what you think?"

"No. But I thought maybe if you felt a little guilty, I could convince you to accompany me to the USO formal dance Friday night."

Sarah thought about Sam, her conversation with Grace, and her joy and awe experiencing places like Philadelphia and New York. The other girls had spoken of the USO's formal dances, how glamorous they felt in formal dresses, the officers in dress uniform, a big band orchestra playing. Dances had never been something that made Sarah swoon, not in high school and not now, but she couldn't deny she had feelings for the man sitting across the car from her waiting for an answer and a chance to make her feel glamorous. And she couldn't deny she wanted an experience with him that wasn't *work related*, whether real or just a convenient excuse to be seen out together.

"Is that a no?" Russell asked.

"It's a—" She almost said, "Not yet," but caught herself. "I'd be honored to attend, Captain."

Russell smiled. "Wonderful. However, we still have a problem."

"We do?"

"You're still calling me Captain. How about at Main Navy I'm Captain Russell. Outside of those confines, I'm Bill Russell. Could you live with that?"

"I believe I could, Bill," Sarah said.

———

Friday night, Sarah paced her room at the apartment.

"Honey, you're going to wear a hole in the floor, you keep up like that," Grace said.

Sarah had borrowed a dress from Grace, royal blue with a swan neckline and a waist tie, that Grace said would have every officer at the dance picking their jaws up off the floor.

When she stepped from her bedroom to the living room, Grace gave her a mischievous smile.

"Too much?" Sarah said.

"Too much? There is no such thing as 'too much.' The color brings out your eyes, and the fabric hugs you in all the right places."

"Maybe I should wear a sweater over it?"

"Nonsense. As my mother likes to say, 'If you got it, flaunt it.' And you got plenty. Come on, let's do your face."

When Captain Russell arrived, Grace insisted on answering the door so Sarah could "make an entrance."

"She's just touching up a few things," Grace said to the captain. "Let me get her."

Grace left him in the front room, swept into the bedroom, and clapped her hands over her mouth. "Oh my God. He's wearing his white uniform and looks like a movie star."

Sarah, nervous, said, "I don't think I can do it, Grace."

"The heck you can't, honey. As good as he looks, I might knock you out and go myself. Now get out there."

Sarah took a deep breath and stepped into the living room. Captain Russell had his naval cap in one hand, his other hand behind his back. He *did* look like a movie star, and his eyes lit up upon seeing her.

"You look lovely," he said.

"Thank you," she said. "And you look handsome."

He removed his hand from behind his back and held out flowers, white lilies. "These are for you. I didn't know the color of your dress."

"They're lovely, thank you. Shall we go?"

Grace came out from the bedroom, like a mother sending her daughter off to a high school dance. She held a white sweater and her winter coat out to Sarah. "Have fun," she said.

Sarah took the sweater and coat on the way to the door. She looked back at Grace, who gave her one last wide-eyed smile and mouthed the words "Oh my God!"

Captain Russell was, as Sarah expected, a perfect gentleman. Except for offering his arm to help her into and out of the car and placing his palm at the small of her back to introduce her, he kept his hands to himself.

The orchestra started and Captain Russell held out his hand. Sarah took it, and he escorted her onto the dance floor, where they danced to Judy Garland singing "Everybody Sing," "You'd Be So Nice to Come Home To" by Dinah Shore, and Bing Crosby's duet with the Andrews Sisters, "Don't Fence Me In." Sarah gradually left behind her guilt and allowed herself to enjoy the evening. She couldn't remember the last time she'd smiled so much. Everyone at the dance seemed to be blowing off a little steam. The work, especially code breaking, required such intense focus, it was wonderful to forget all about it for a night. Everything was magical until the orchestra played Bing Crosby's "Swinging on a Star." It made Sarah think of Sam and the wishes they'd made on the North Star.

"Another dance?" Russell said, holding out his hand.

Sarah tried to smile through her tears. "Maybe we could sit this one out?"

Russell smiled, but from the look on his face, he saw the sadness in her eyes. "Sure. Let me grab us some punch."

When Russell left, Sarah struggled to regain her composure. She removed her compact from her case and checked her makeup. At least it hadn't smeared. She kept thinking of what Grace had said, that there was nothing wrong with dating and, when the war ended, going home to Eagle Grove and to Sam. Up until the last song she had allowed herself to believe it. Now she wasn't so certain.

Russell returned and handed her a glass of punch, then said, "I have an idea. How about we take a stroll outside. Get some fresh air."

Sarah was glad for the distraction. They donned their coats, and Russell led her outside. They walked a path winding through boxwood hedges. The air was cold but the sky clear, revealing a full moon.

"Better?" Russell said.

She smiled at him. "Yes. Thank you."

"Not too cold?"

"It feels good," she said. "Reminds me a bit of Eagle Grove."

"But the cold isn't the only thing that reminds you of Eagle Grove, is it?"

She took a deep breath. Bill Russell was an observant man. "No," she said. "Not the only thing."

"You looked like you were enjoying yourself . . . up until that last song."

"I was—I *am*, Bill. I'm having a wonderful time." She did not want him to think her ungrateful. "It's been such a lovely evening in so many ways, that . . ."

"That you're feeling a bit guilty?"

Sarah nodded. "Yes."

He nodded and they strolled a bit longer. Then he said, "When Claire died, I didn't know how I was going to go on without her. How I would even date again."

When he didn't continue, Sarah asked, "How did you?"

He stopped and turned to her. "Slowly. One day at a time. I'm in no rush, Sarah. I'm just enjoying the company of a beautiful, intelligent, charismatic young woman."

She took a deep breath. "Thank you, Bill."

The orchestra started up again. "I think they're getting ready to play their last song," he said. "Are you up for one last dance?"

"I would enjoy that, very much." She linked her arm through his, and he escorted her back inside to the dance floor.

2

The WAVES

Naval Reserve Midshipmen's School
Smith College, Massachusetts
March 12, 1943

Sarah did not stay long at Main Navy or in her new apartment. When President Roosevelt signed a bill into law creating a Women's Naval Reserve, Sarah, at Captain Russell's urging, accepted a commission to the WAVES—Women Accepted for Volunteer Emergency Service. The women were not *drafted*, and their commissions were temporary—to appease the older naval officers dead set against women in the military. Sarah's commission would expire six months after the war's end.

Still, Sarah would now be "in" and not merely "with" the Navy. She would become a commissioned officer in the US Naval Reserve and receive another bump in pay, which she and her family could always use. So, just as she was settling into her work at Main Navy, Sarah and others who joined the WAVES, including Grace, departed Washington, DC, for the Naval Reserve Midshipmen's School at Smith College in Massachusetts.

The break from Bill—she was at last able to dispense with "Captain Russell," even in her thoughts—was for the better. Their situation had become complicated. Sarah enjoyed his company and their conversations; he was well educated and could talk on various subjects, and she couldn't deny he was both a gentle-man and quite good looking. He'd kept his word and had been patient. He never pressured her for more than she was ready to give, but Sarah knew he was wondering where they were going.

She didn't know.

On one occasion he had dropped her off at her apartment after a night out, and when he'd bent to kiss her, Sarah had willingly accepted. It felt comforting to be kissed, his hands on her back in a warm, strong embrace. She returned his kiss eagerly, and when they parted lips to take a breath, she saw only his beauti-ful, soft blue eyes and was tempted to ask him in. But then she realized she was not seeing Bill's eyes but Sam's when they necked in the projection room of the Paradise Theater.

She put her hands on Bill's chest. "I'd better go in," she said, sounding breathless.

"Are you sure?" he asked.

She wasn't. She wasn't sure of anything anymore. "Grace is home," she said. "Expecting me." She'd said good night and slid in her apartment door but did not go to bed. She went to Grace's room and woke her, and they talked into the early morning.

On another night, Grace had been home and awake when Sarah finally stepped in. "Those kisses at the door are getting longer and more passionate," she said.

"You didn't hear us," Sarah said.

"I don't have to hear to know," Grace said. "How do you feel?"

"Conflicted."

"Meaning?"

"My body wants to feel Bill, but my mind keeps seeing Sam."

"Give it time, honey. And don't judge yourself. What you're feeling is what all of us are feeling. What the whole country is feeling. We all just want to slip away from this war and feel human again, even if it's only for a moment."

The seal with Bill had been broken. On subsequent dates their kisses became more passionate, their hands roaming. Sarah could always end their entangle-ment by warning that her roommates were home, and it wouldn't be appropriate for them to see their superior officer out of uniform, though Grace had said on more than one occasion she'd like that opportunity very much.

The truth was, on occasion, Sarah would also.

Leaving for officer school gave both her and Bill a chance to maybe rethink their courting.

At officer school, Sarah and Grace absorbed rudimentary naval words like "deck" for "floor" and "mess" for "meal," as well as what it meant to be a naval officer—instruction containing nothing useful to code breaking. Main Navy had been reluctant to let their code breakers go. They were making great progress on the most recent version of JN-25. So after just four weeks of drilling and marching in officer training, Main Navy recalled the women to Washington.

On the train ride back, Sarah and her fellow WAVES felt giddy in their fitted navy-blue wool jackets with shoulder braids, their flattering skirts, white shirts, and cloche hats. While it was only a uniform, it acknowledged they were not secretaries sitting on officer's laps. What they did was important, a part of the war effort.

On the train, young children stared and pointed at them, and one young girl was bold enough to approach Sarah.

"I was just wondering," the girl said, "what order do you belong to?"

"Order?"

"Yes. What order of nuns?"

All the girls laughed. Okay, maybe the uniforms weren't the ticket.

When they arrived back at Main Navy, the Marines at the gate clearly resented the female naval officers and took pernicious pleasure in making them salute over and over until they "got it right."

Sarah saluted once and started past a Marine on guard. "Hold on," he said. He looked no older than the boys Sarah had taught back at Eagle Grove. "That wasn't a proper salute. Do it again."

When she'd arrived in DC, Sarah likely would've done as the Marine asked, but she was no longer that person. She stepped to within inches of the Marine.

"What is your name, Marine?"

"Excuse me?"

"Excuse me? You are speaking to a superior officer, Marine, and you will address me as Ensign Haber. Is that clear?" Ensign was the lowest rank of a commissioned officer, but it outranked a private.

The Marine looked stunned. He turned to his cohorts, who appeared equally perplexed.

"I asked your name, Marine." Even Sarah was startled by the steel in her voice.

The Marine snapped to attention. "Ma'am. Private Arthur Bensone, ma'am."

Sarah went down the line of other Marines, each of whom snapped to attention, saluted, and stated their name.

"We don't have time for your foolishness," Sarah said. "We work for Captain Russell, and we have soldiers to save, including your fellow Marines. Is that clear?"

"Ma'am. Yes, ma'am," the Marines responded.

"Let's go, ladies."

Grace was jubilant. After they'd left the Marines behind, she said, "Good Lord, honey. I don't know what bee buzzed in your bonnet, but I wish it would sting me."

The Navy had developed a top secret code-breaking operation at 3801 Nebraska Avenue, once home to Mount Vernon College with its brick buildings, spires, and expansive lawns with trees emerging from the long winter. It made Sarah feel as though she were back on campus at Mankato. Navy leaders called the facility the Naval Communications Annex, but most referred to it as the Annex, or WAVES Barracks D. Captain Russell would be one of the operation's lead officers, and he brought along Sarah, Grace, and other cryptanalysts from his team.

Sarah gave up her apartment for a bunk and locker in a temporary Quonset hut in a huge encampment set up across the street from the code-breaking compound. That solved the problem she'd had about inviting Bill into her apartment. On dates, Sarah also found herself thinking of excuses for why she couldn't go to his home, but she never had to use them. When she told Grace this, Grace laughed and said, "Oh, Sarah Haber, if I could take you back to when you first arrived and have you listen to yourself now." She said Bill and the other officers lived in officer quarters on the naval base. His bringing Sarah home, someone who worked for him, would not go unnoticed and would not be met with approval. "They'd likely ship you out to another division under different command. And selfish though it might be, I would miss you."

The compound, surrounded by a fence and secured by Marine guards, was intended to eliminate distractions to maximize their production. At least Sarah saved more money, thinking it a nest egg for her and Sam.

Captain Russell gathered the women in Barracks D and emphasized the importance of their work. "The early Japanese victories have begun to work against them," he said. "They have become more and more spread out over Asia and the Pacific archipelagos: China, Hong Kong, the Philippines, Thailand, Burma, Malays, the Dutch East Indies. Their radiomen have had to increase the power of their transmissions to communicate, making those transmissions easier to intercept. The problem we now face is we are intercepting thirty thousand messages a month, which means we need to decipher a thousand messages a day."

Sarah blanched, knowing the workload that entailed.

"The situation in the Pacific is at the tipping point. Since our victory at Midway, a pushback plan is being formulated to retake the Philippines and invade Japan. Your skill at code breaking has never been more important or imperative."

A Philippines invasion would mean freeing the soldiers from the prisoner of war camps, including, she hoped, Sam.

Sarah worked at her table on the messages needing to be decoded quickly—and which might require action. These messages were short, straightforward, and no nonsense. They consisted of sailing schedules, harbormaster reports, reports on the water levels at ports, and the transportation of cargo. Her team soon discovered the sailing schedules, which included each ship's transport number, shipping route, and the dates, times, and ports of departure and scheduled arrivals.

Whenever Sarah or one of her team determined the meaning of a particular four-digit code, the code and designated word were placed in a book each cryptanalyst used, making decoding subsequent messages quicker and more efficient. The department's growing number of code breakers and their increased efficiency led to increased productivity and success. When Sarah's crew identified the movement of marus supplying the Japanese army, the findings were quickly transmitted to Submarine Command and routed to submarine captains. It led to the sinking of one ship after the next. Japanese soldiers were deprived of food and medicine. The Japanese army didn't receive aircraft and other machinery, or spare parts, which delayed or prevented missions. Troops could not receive munitions or reinforcements.

At one of their weekly dinners, Bill told Sarah, "Less than fifty percent of Japanese transport convoys are reaching their destinations, and less than twenty-five percent make it back. We are weakening Japan's outlying bases, making them susceptible to heavy bombers and amphibious assaults."

The Allied war effort was on the upswing, and each day closer to the war's end was one day closer to Sam coming home alive.

If he was still alive.

3

The Safest Secret

Naval Communications Annex
Washington, DC
April 20, 1943

On a Tuesday morning, Sarah returned to the Annex to work the first watch, which often meant working twelve hours instead of eight, since she'd get embroiled in a message and then have difficulty leaving her post until she'd decoded it. As she decoded the latest messages before her, mostly routine Japanese transmissions, a naval officer entered Barracks D and approached her worktable.

"You have a phone call, Ensign Haber."

Sarah looked up and immediately felt sick to her stomach. "A phone call? Who is it?"

"Your mother. Said it was important and she needed to reach you. You can take the call in Room 1632, the conference room. It's not being used at present."

Sarah looked to Grace, then the other women at her table. The WAVES had forged close friendships working in such an intense setting, bound by their shared secrets. They all had left their homes, were relatively close in age, smart, resourceful, adventurous, and filled with a sense of duty. They lived together, ate meals together, and worked long hours together. They went out together and protected one another. But they also shared each other's disappointments and heartbreaks when bad news arrived. The most heartrending moments came on the surprisingly frequent occasions when WAVES decoded radio messages relevant to their loved ones—learning that German forces planned to retreat, thus moving away from a brother's unit rather than toward it, or that an uncle would face a massive frontal assault at dawn, or a cousin would be bombed overnight. The women were often tormented by what they knew, and always utterly powerless to do anything about it.

This time, news had come for Sarah. She couldn't seem to push her chair away from the table. Struggled to even breathe.

Grace reached across the table and squeezed Sarah's hand. The women no longer said things like "I'm sure it's nothing" or "Everything is going to be all right." Far too often, the news was bad. Sam remained Sarah's first thought, but she also worried about her parents and her siblings, that something could have happened to one of them—a heart attack, stroke, or other injury. The money she was earning had helped improve their day-to-day living situation, but some things money couldn't fix.

Sarah, who'd once prided herself on seeing a glass half-full, wouldn't allow herself to think the call was good news. The weight of the calls her friends had endured had become a harsh reality she could not ignore. The letdown would be too steep and the landing too painful.

Sarah, at last, left her workstation and picked up the phone in the conference room. "Hello?"

"Sarah."

"Mom." *Oh God,* Sarah thought. "What is it?"

"It's about Sam. He's alive."

Sarah jumped to her feet and jammed the black phone tight against her ear. "Sam's alive? How do you know? Was it a telegram? What did it say?"

"The Carlsons got a letter from the Army yesterday—"

"Is he okay?" Sarah interrupted.

"He's a prisoner of war."

This wasn't new information. Not really. Sarah had long suspected it. But alive. "Where?"

"The Philippines."

"What else?" Sarah asked. "Tell me what else."

"Sweetie, the letter was just two sentences," her mother said. "I knew you'd want the exact wording, so I wrote it down for you."

A paper crinkled before her mother read the letter. As she'd said, just two brutally short sentences.

"That's all?"

"That's all. I'm sure a more detailed letter will come."

Not likely, Sarah thought. "How old is the letter?"

"The Carlsons just received it."

"No. How old is the news that Sam's alive?"

"I don't know."

Sarah took a deep breath and wiped at tears streaming down her cheeks. The message wasn't much. The report could have been from last week or last year, but it was enough, for now. Sam was alive. For now. Her world shifted, back to Eagle Grove. She'd forgotten much about her small town, enamored by the nation's capital and the other big cities she had visited. She loved being needed, of excelling at her work. She loved the excitement of going out with girlfriends and eating in fine restaurants with Bill Russell at a table draped with a white tablecloth as spotless as his uniform. She loved the attention he gave her and the compliments, an outlet from the tremendous stress she was under both at work and not knowing anything about Sam.

But now she knew.

Sam was alive. And she would believe that to be so if and until . . .

Sam was reality. Her reality. Eagle Grove was reality.

Her dream was of a life with Sam. This life she was now leading was not reality. It would end, just as Grace said it would. One way or another. The WAVES would all go home again, but to what and to whom? No one knew for certain, but they all hoped life would get back to—maybe not to the way it had once been, but to what they made of it.

"It's enough for now," Sarah said to her mother.

After hanging up, Sarah walked slowly back to her table, drying her tears with her hands. Her friends and work colleagues stared at her. She sat and let out a breath, then more tears. "Sam's alive. He's a prisoner of war in the Philippines."

The women burst into tears of shared relief. They came around the table and surrounded Sarah, hugging her, and wiping their tears. When they separated, Grace said, "That's great news, honey. That's something to hold on to."

Sarah nodded. Grace had summed it up perfectly, as she usually did. *Something to hold on to.*

"I've made another decision," Sarah said. "I'm going to seek a transfer to the JICPOA facility in Hawaii." JICPOA was an acronym for the Joint Intelligence Center, Pacific Ocean Area. Sarah had been thinking about the transfer for a while. She would be closer to Sam, and she would be working in the Navy's newest top secret decoding facility.

"It's next to impossible to get in," Grace said. "First, you have to apply to the Navy's Japanese Language School in Colorado, and I've heard they only take one out of every hundred who apply. And no woman has ever transferred to JICPOA."

"I'll get into Boulder," Sarah said. "And I'll be the first woman at JICPOA." She knew someone who could help her.

She left the table, went down the hall, and entered Bill's office. His secretary waved Sarah in. Bill sat behind his desk, finishing a telephone conversation. He gestured to a chair, but Sarah remained standing, which caused Bill's brow to wrinkle. When he hung up, Sarah said, "I need a letter of recommendation."

"Okay. For what?"

"To get into the Navy's translation school in Boulder, Colorado."

Bill looked like he wanted to ask her why she would want to leave, but he didn't. That she had a fella in the military and intended to go home to him after the war was either an answer he didn't want to hear, or already knew. "Okay. I can make that recommendation," he said. "You realize it is a long shot."

"And I'll need a second letter. I plan to apply to JICPOA in Hawaii."

His brow again furrowed. "No woman has ever received an assignment to JICPOA."

"Then I'll be the first." When Bill smiled, Sarah, perturbed, said, "You don't think I'll get in?"

"No. I think you will," he said. He took a deep breath and let it out. "I have news also, Sarah. I was waiting for a better time to tell you, but I guess there's no point now. I'm transferring out."

"Oh," she said, feeling a bit, perhaps, unimportant to him. She also couldn't help but wonder if his transfer had anything to do with her inability to commit to him. "Where are you going?"

"To a battleship in the Pacific. It's an assignment I've sought for a while. I wanted to tell you in a better setting. You've come to mean so much to me. The hardest part will be leaving you."

"What about your job here?" she said. "You said you were uniquely qualified to train code breakers."

He smiled and came around the desk, taking her hands. "We've trained enough code breakers that my job here is not as urgent as it once was. The Navy needs intelligence officers to help process the mountains of documents and other intel coming into US hands as we take over more islands on our way to Japan. It's a real chance for me to save lives."

Sarah had mixed emotions. "You'll be in harm's way, Bill. It's—" She almost said it was hard enough worrying about Sam. Worrying about him as well would be too much.

"Others have done their duty, Sarah. This is my turn."

Bill didn't say it, but maybe they both knew that leaving DC at the same time would make goodbye easier. "I don't know what to say," she said.

He smiled. "Let's not say anything. I've thought about this moment also. Let's just let the chips fall where they may. You've done great work here, Sarah. What you've done has had real meaning. You saved American lives." He paused and looked to be searching for the right words. "And you made my life better as well. You're the first woman since Claire's death who I've loved, Sarah. I hope I'm not putting you in an awkward position telling you this."

"No, Bill. I care about you, and you've made my life here easier too. I'm grateful. I don't know what I would have done if I didn't have someone I could talk to outside of work."

He nodded. She knew he had wanted to hear her say she loved him also, but Sarah couldn't say that. She couldn't say exactly what Bill meant to her, what they had been to one another. Each had certainly been someone the other could confide in; someone to embrace on the dance floor; someone to let the other know that, even in a world that had gone dark and mad, there still existed some sanity and a faint light of hope.

"I will miss you, Captain," she said. Then, feeling a compulsion, she threw back her shoulders, raised her right hand, and gave him a stiff salute.

"I will miss you, Ensign Haber," he said and returned the gesture.

4

OFF AND RUNNING

Naval Communications Annex
Washington, DC
May 17, 1943

Sarah's letter arrived three weeks after she applied to Boulder, and to the surprise of everyone but Sarah, the language school instructed her to board a train immediately. She hurriedly packed her bags, which wasn't difficult, given the few possessions she maintained. The uniform had eliminated the necessity of shopping for clothes or shoes; what she owned fit in the two hard suitcases she'd initially brought to Washington, DC.

Grace sat on her bed, dressed in uniform and preparing to leave for her watch at the Annex. She wiped tears from her cheeks. "I wish I was going with you," she said, "but not even you could get me accepted to that place. I still don't know any Japanese words."

"I wish you were coming too." Sarah closed her suitcase and clicked the two latches, then looked around the Quonset hut. "I guess that's it."

Grace struggled to hold back more tears. "I guess it is."

The two friends hugged. "This isn't goodbye, you know," Sarah said. "I'll see you again."

"You bet your ass you'll see me again, honey. You and that fella of yours are coming to New York when this war is over. You won't see celebrating like in New York anywhere else in the world. You can kiss in Times Square."

"And you'll come to Eagle Grove," Sarah said. "You won't experience watching a movie at the Paradise Theater anyplace else in the world. Now go to work. It'll be too hard for me to leave with you here."

Fifteen minutes after Grace left for the Annex, Sarah walked downstairs and hailed a cab. Exhibiting God's occasional fondness for ridiculous symmetry, who should arrive behind the wheel but the very cabbie who'd picked her up when she arrived at Union Station on June 12, 1942. Sarah had kept her eye peeled for him ever since that encounter, and here he was, delivered to her eleven months later.

Only eleven months? It seemed a lifetime ago. In some ways, it was.

He didn't recognize her, she could tell. Probably it was the uniform.

"Where to?" he asked.

"Union Station," Sarah said.

"You're one of those female military personnel."

"WAVES," she said. "Women Accepted for Volunteer Emergency Service."

"You volunteered?"

"I did."

"So, what, you're a secretary?"

Sarah smiled. "I'm an officer," she said.

"No kidding. I'll be damned. You shipping out?"

"I am."

"Would you like to see the monuments on your ride to the station?" he asked. "I mean, who knows when you might be back, right?"

It was all she could do to suppress a laugh. The man was nothing if not consistent. She reminded herself what Grace had told her, that he was just trying to make a living for his family in a difficult time. "Sure," she said. "Turn off the meter."

"What's that?" He looked in the rearview mirror.

"I said turn off the meter." She handed him a ten-dollar bill over the seat back.

"Thanks," he said. His eyes squinted, uncertain. "Do I know you?"

Sarah thought of how much she had changed, how much she had learned since she arrived as the naive young girl from Eagle Grove. She hardly recognized herself. "No," she said. "I don't think you do."

5

DREAMING IN JAPANESE

JICPOA
Honolulu, Hawaii
August 3, 1943

When Sarah stepped off a Navy transport plane, she was surprised to find a car and driver waiting to take her to the Navy's Joint Intelligence Center, Pacific Ocean Area, or JICPOA. She knew little about the center, only that the military had established it under a cloud of secrecy at the US naval base in Pearl Harbor and that it was originally called the Intelligence Center, Pacific Ocean Area, or ICPOA.

She remained exhausted from the pace of her classes at the language school in Boulder. The nearly three months had been grueling, despite her having picked up some Japanese while deciphering codes. She had eaten, drunk, and conversed in Japanese, but her instructors had told her she would not be fluent until she dreamed in Japanese.

At the end of her rotation there, her commanding officer and chief instructor, Captain Reedy, had called Sarah into his office. Now in his late sixties, Captain Reedy and his wife had lived in Japan before the war's outbreak. Too old for an overseas assignment, but eager to serve, he headed up the language program.

"You wanted to see me, sir?"

"I understand you applied to JICPOA," he said. Unlike the Army, the Navy had refused to allow female code breakers to serve in Hawaii, let alone overseas, but as US military forces advanced across the Pacific, and the Navy rotated its intelligence officers from Hawaii to forward posts, Sarah knew things would have to change.

"Yes, sir."

Reedy smiled. "Can I ask why you want to go there?"

She knew that saying she wanted to go to be closer to a fiancé serving in the military would never fly. The military would view that as rash and emotional, or just angling for a rendezvous in an exotic location. "Serving in Hawaii would put me closer to the action in the Pacific, sir," she said, "and offer opportunities for advancement. More than anything, I wish to do my duty to bring our soldiers home. I am at the top of my class here, sir. JICPOA only takes the best. That's me."

Reedy nearly laughed. "You certainly don't lack for confidence."

"A lack of confidence is not what the military needs at this juncture."

"Certainly not." He paused as if considering the veracity of her responses. "You have a guardian angel looking over your shoulder, Ensign Haber."

"An angel, sir?"

"An order came down from on high. For every cryptanalyst JICPOA ships from Hawaii to an overseas base, the Navy will allow one woman officer from the mainland to replace him. You speak Japanese. You were one of the best code breakers at the Annex. I think the first position should belong to you."

Sarah had subsequently passed three rounds of interviews before boarding the Navy transport plane for Pearl Harbor.

Once inside the JICPOA compound, Sarah stepped from the car to an awaiting Marine. He snapped to attention and gave her a crisp salute, which she returned. "If you will follow me, Ensign Haber."

"I have to get my suitcases." She turned to the car.

"That won't be necessary. Your belongings will be taken to your locker and stowed. Later today, I will lead you to your assigned barracks. If you would follow me, please." The Marine turned on a dime and led Sarah inside the building to a room with bunks and two chairs facing one another.

"Can I get you a glass of water?" the Marine asked.

"No. Thank you."

"The colonel will be with you shortly." He again snapped to attention and saluted.

Sarah had come a long way since the Marines at Main Navy had disrespected her and her fellow WAVES. She returned the salute, whereupon the Marine spun again and exited, shutting the door. Sarah knew enough about military procedure to know her only job now was to wait, though this time it wasn't long.

Only minutes later, a naval officer entered the room and shut the door behind him. Sarah threw back her shoulders and saluted.

"At ease, Ensign Haber." The officer gave her a haphazard salute and gestured to the two chairs. "Take a seat."

They faced one another, so close their knees almost touched.

"I'm Commander Jasper Holmes. Do you know of me?" Sarah guessed him to be midforties.

"No, sir."

"I'll give you the *Reader's Digest* version. I spent thirteen years as a commissioned officer and commanded the submarine *S-30*, based at Pearl Harbor, but chronic back pain got so bad I could no longer hide it during my annual physical exams. The Navy put me out to pasture in 1936. I'm neither a linguist nor a cryptographer, but after the war broke out, the Navy lured me back to create and lead a top secret code-breaking operation to track and decipher Japanese radio communications and pass the information to Allied commanders. My section is known as the Fleet Radio Unit, Pacific, or FRUPAC. Have you heard of it?"

"No, sir."

"Good. No one outside this building should have. We joined ICPOA to form JICPOA."

Holmes zeroed in and asked Sarah a question with which she was intimately familiar.

"Do you like to do crossword puzzles?"

Sarah hid a smile. "I do, sir."

"I'm told you're very good—excellent, as a matter of fact—at decoding Japanese messages. And you're fluent. Expect orders by the end of today. You will be working in FRUPAC under my command. We have an urgent need for which we believe you are uniquely suited."

"Uniquely suited?"

"You helped decipher the JN-25 code, did you not?"

"I was part of a team, sir."

"Your commanding officer said you were much more than a part."

Bill. Whatever he had written in his letter of recommendation, it had captured the attention of the highest brass in the US Navy's most secretive center.

"FRUPAC needs code breakers who are fluent in Japanese. Any questions?"

"No, sir." Sarah liked Holmes immediately. He had a fatherly way about him, but she suspected he could also be tough as nails and didn't tolerate nonsense.

"Good. The Marine outside this door will take you to your barracks. Have you eaten or slept at all?"

"Not much of either, sir."

"Get some chow and some rack time. You're working the second watch."

The Marine reappeared and escorted Sarah to her barracks, but she didn't sleep, both excited and a little intimidated. She hoped Bill hadn't oversold her abilities.

Her orders arrived near the day's end, directing her to FRUPAC, located in the other half of the JICPOA building. The personnel going in and out of JICPOA wore yellow-banded plastic photo identification badges around their necks. A Marine provided Sarah a red badge identifying her as assigned to FRUPAC. He told her to display the badge at all times. "When you leave the front gate, make sure to tuck the badge securely out of sight. It should never leave your person while in uniform, nor should you take it anywhere while out of uniform. When entering the building, day or night, a Marine guard will inspect your card. There are no exceptions. Not even for Commander Holmes. Off base, if you are asked about your job, you are not to respond."

"Not even to tell them I'm a secretary?" she asked with a thin smile.

"Not even to tell them you're a secretary. You simply do not respond. Understood?"

"Understood."

"Let me emphasize that not even flag officers or ship captains are told anything about what goes on in FRUPAC, although they regularly receive our intelligence. The origination is sanitized. Security takes the highest priority, even higher than operational success."

"What does that mean?"

"It means, if we judge that the information we decode will reveal to the enemy that our intelligence has broken the Japanese code, then the information will not be disseminated. No exceptions."

During her first week in FRUPAC, Sarah was shuttled from one internal section to the next to better understand its inner workings. In each section the senior officer explained the elements of their work and answered her many questions. Eventually, she was taken to Commander Jasper Holmes's office in combat intelligence, but Holmes wasn't there.

He was in the workspace, with his team.

PART 3

1

New World

Sam lay flat on his back, looking up at a square of light. Heads blocked the light and stared down at him. He had a moment of panic, thought he had died and was in his coffin, people mourning over him. He recognized faces—Pete Chavez and Father Tom—then looked past their concerned expressions to the metal ribs over their heads and realized he was in the hold of the ship they'd been boarding. He'd been on a step when the POWs above him had surged forward, and he'd lost his footing and fallen backward. He must have struck his head.

"Give him room," Chavez was shouting. "Give him room."

Sam, with Chavez and Father Tom's help, sat up. He had no sooner done so when their guards began shouting and descended the narrow makeshift staircase.

"Speedo! Speedo!"

A guard held a broom handle, swinging it like a sword. POWs dodged and ducked and shoved one another to get out of the way. The guard swung the handle at Sam, but Chavez bent over Sam, shielding him, and absorbing the blow across his back.

"Dios," Chavez said, the blow nearly knocking him over.

"Speedo! Speedo!" The guard reared back and struck another POW. Sam spotted three additional guards, also armed with broomsticks, rifles, and bayonets, coming down the stairs.

"Get up, Sam," Major Jones said. "On your feet."

The major and Chavez slid their arms under Sam's armpits, lifted him to his feet, and pulled him back from the entrance just before the guards arrived. Sam, dizzy and unsteady, reached up, fingering an aching welt on the back of his head. He shook the cobwebs and heard the din of more than a thousand male voices echoing inside the hull of the metal ship, some shouting, others pleading for air and for water. The stench of the men, cramped together, was nearly overpowering.

"We got to move." Chavez pushed them farther back into the lightless depths of the hold.

"Stop pushing," a man up ahead shouted.

"No more room," another yelled.

"Christ, Jesus help us," Father Tom muttered.

"Sardines get more space in the can than this," Chavez said.

Each time the crowd stopped, the guards used rifle butts and bayonets to prod the POWs farther forward. "Speedo! Speedo!"

"Heads up," a POW called out, and soldiers in front of Sam raised their arms to pass an unconscious body overhead. Moments later, another motionless body passed overhead, then a third.

"No!" the guards yelled. "No up. Only down."

As Sam, Chavez, Major Jones, and Father Tom were pushed deeper into the hold, Chavez pointed to the metallic struts, barely visible in the dim light, girders that framed the ship's hull. "Ribs," Chavez said. "We're in the belly of a whale."

"Swallowed whole, like Jonah," Father Tom said.

The comment pulled Sam from his fog. He looked back over his shoulder at the light and air from the hatch, then looked forward into the darkened hold. He knew being forced further back was certain death, but lingering too close to the front would merit a crack in the head from the guards. That left only two ways to move. Left or right.

"This way." Sam stepped to his left. "Move to the side."

He leaned his shoulder hard toward the tall struts and kept a wide, sturdy stance to maintain balance. POWs protested and tried to throw elbows at Sam and his group, but they couldn't move their arms in the cramped space, and they gave Father Tom a pass. "Come on, Father," Sam said. "Lead the way. To the side. The side."

Soon the priest was clearing a path. Sam hooked a bamboo pole running from floor to ceiling. Then he grabbed ahold of Father Tom's shoulder, pulling him back.

"Hold on to the pole like your life depends on it," Sam said, believing it surely did.

The priest, seeing what Sam intended, did so, then linked elbows with Chavez, who grabbed Major Jones.

His friends gripped the bamboo support pole and clung tight as one surge of POWs after the next exerted more force, then swept past them like rogue waves curling deeper into the darkness.

"What the hell are those?" Chavez pointed to tiered bamboo shelves running along the side of the ship. They looked like bunks, three levels high, with three feet of vertical clearance between each platform. They likely had been used for storage. Now, dozens of POWs had clambered onto them thinking they could rest, but those who did were soon shouting muffled, increasingly desperate cries that they were pinned against the ship's steel hull by the bodies layering in next to and atop them. When the stifled cries stopped, did that mean the men had suffocated? There was nothing Sam or anyone else could even think of doing to help them. None of them could help themselves, let alone anyone else.

"It's a slave ship," Father Tom said. "This is inhumane."

"News flash, Padre," Chavez said. "The Japs are not human."

More bodies swarmed into the racks, prodded by the guards' rifle butts. POWs who managed to hold a position on the lower tiers without being crushed got soaked by sweat dripping from the men on the rack above them. Those on the top bunk appeared to have escaped the bedlam, but the air had to be hotter near the top of the hold. Soon they, too, cried out for water. All up and down the racks, prone men kicked and shoved for space.

"It's okay," Chavez said to Sam. "I don't need no window after all. Give me the aisle."

Another wave of bodies tried to drive Sam and his group deeper into the hold. Sam's weakened arms ached, but he clutched the pole until the surge pushed and rippled past them.

Sam lifted one foot and stepped up onto the edge of the lowest bamboo rack, using the pole for balance. The elevated perch gave him a broad view. Hundreds of human heads surged deeper into the ship's belly. Sam guessed the hold might be seventy or eighty feet long. He figured about three hundred men could fit with reasonable comfort, but the guards appeared to have crammed close to two thousand POWs into the space.

He'd been wrong about the prison camps. The POWs hadn't been in hell. *This* was hell.

"Between Scylla and Charybdis," Father Tom said.

"Gesundheit, Padre," Chavez grunted, fighting against another surge.

"Greek mythology," Father Tom said. "Sailors either get crushed on the rocks or sucked into the whirlpool. Take your pick."

"Ah," said Chavez. "I got you now. Like sleeping between my brothers Carlos and Marco." Chavez grinned. "Carlos wets the bed, but Marco farts."

Chavez somehow drew a smile from Sam, despite the unfolding chaos and the horror he was witnessing. For months after Sam's failed escape and Yoshida's execution of the nine POWs, Sam could not even smile, riddled with guilt. Father Tom had spoken with Sam daily to help him deal with his guilt, telling Sam he couldn't blame himself for Yoshida's cruelty. "You could never have predicted the horrors he would inflict on those men. This was his doing, not yours. Do not give him a pass."

Even after Camp O'Donnell closed and they were moved to the slightly better Camp Cabanatuan, escaping Yoshida for some time, none of the other POWs said they forgave Sam, but some at least said they understood, that the blood brothers rule had not existed when Sam had tried to escape. Others didn't care. They said the prisoners had been warned of dire consequences, and Sam had run anyway. Sam had to be careful to never be alone. He had Rudowski gunning for him and who knew who else.

Despite Father Tom's counseling, Sam remained racked with guilt. When a POW was too sick to work, he volunteered to take his place on the most difficult work detail. When another needed food or medicine, Sam gave up his, including the contraband Chavez had obtained.

Slowly, those in the camp took notice, and many granted Sam a pardon. But he couldn't pardon himself.

Day after day he returned from work detail exhausted and collapsed on his bunk. Father Tom forced him to eat and drink what little rations they were given.

"How long do you think you can keep doing this before you collapse and can't recover?" Father Tom asked Sam after he returned from a particularly grueling work detail.

"As long as it takes. Until we get out of here."

"I told you, Sam, God has forgiven you. So have most of the men. You have to forgive yourself."

"This is how," Sam said. "By making amends."

"And what about going home alive to the family that loves you. To Sarah?"

Sam fingered the ring, still sewn into the lining of his vest. "I'll get home," he said.

"Not at this pace, Sam. Chavez says the contraband is drying up. If you get beriberi again, or malaria, he can't get the medicine you'll need to keep you alive."

Sam had not cared. The world had become shades of black and gray. Food had no taste or smell, not that the swill they received had much of either to start with.

This went on for months, until one night when Sam, unable to sleep, ventured outside the barracks to sit on the ground, his back against the building wall. He stared up at a starlit sky and fingered Sarah's ring. He found the Big Dipper and followed the tail to its bowl, which pointed to Polaris, the North Star. He wondered if she, too, was looking up, seeing the same star. And he recalled Father Tom's words about getting home to his family, to Sarah. Then he realized something else. He was being selfish. He realized what his death would do to her, and to his parents and his siblings. He might be making amends by working himself to death inside the camp, but his death would kill his family.

"Star light. Star bright," he said.

First star I see tonight.

Sam looked about, certain he'd heard Sarah's voice. It wasn't possible, he knew, but it sounded as clear as his own.

"I wish I may, I wish I might, have the wish I wish tonight," he said. And he forgave himself. "I'm coming home to you all. God willing."

In the following days, color returned to his world. So did his sense of taste and smell, and gradually he forgave himself for what he'd done.

But now he had another problem. Rudowski was on this ship, and still intent on killing him. Sam's only defense was that no one, not even the beast, could move anywhere in these cramped quarters, and certainly not quickly.

But Sam would sleep with one eye open, just in case.

2

SETTING SAIL

The **Arisan Maru**
Pier 7, Manila Harbor, Philippines
October 11, 1944

By the time the *Arisan Maru* was ready to sail, its human cargo of eighteen hundred POWs had descended into chaos. The men yelled and cursed, pushed, and shoved. They clawed and scratched for air, space, and water. Then machine gun fire echoed through the hold and the men froze. Guards had descended halfway down the staircase and shot their machine guns through the open hatch into the sky. Gaining the men's attention, they pointed the gun barrels at them, causing them to recoil.

Yoshida calmly stepped down three stairs but would come no farther. He held a handkerchief over his nose and mouth.

"Sit down. Please sit down now," he said to the POWs, gesturing with his hand. "The next shots will not be warning shots." The guards swept their machine guns over waves of ducking POWs.

"There's no room to sit," Chavez called, stating the obvious. "It's worse than a Chavez family reunion in here."

Other POWs voiced their agreement.

"Sit down," Yoshida said again. "Or we will have no choice but to make room." His three guards again swept their machine gun barrels, this time faster.

"We're sitting ducks," Father Tom called out to the men. "One blast will kill twenty of us. Sit where you stand."

Major Jones, who had made his way back to the opening in the hold, stepped onto the staircase, arms raised to show Yoshida he posed no threat. Then he turned and addressed the POWs. "Everyone, listen up," he hollered in his southern drawl. He motioned the men to the floor. "Y'all heard the chaplain. Sink where you stand, and sit. Or we're dead."

POWs nearest the hatchway sat first. The others followed. Sam had less than two square feet of floor space—not much, even for emaciated bodies starved for two and a half years. He drew his knees tight to his chest, clasped his arms around his shins, and leaned back to back against Father Tom. Other POWs didn't have even that much room and could only sprawl across one another, their arms and legs spaghetti-like weaves of interlocking limbs.

The ship's horn emitted a sudden high-pitched blast that ripped through the hold, and the men covered their ears. Shortly thereafter, the freighter's giant diesel engines roared to life, a loud bell clanged, and a mix of shouts in Japanese preceded the sound of boots running on the deck above. Yoshida said something in Japanese, and the guards sprang to attention as he left the hold and ascended to the deck.

"Saved by the bell," Chavez said.

Minutes later the freighter jolted and eased from the pier. "We're casting off," Sam said.

"But to where?" Father Tom asked.

"Formosa?" Sam said.

"Nope, nope, nope," Chavez insisted. "It's Honolulu. I got a hot date with that hula dancer as soon as this war is over, and I plan to keep it."

"That was three years ago," Avery Wilber said. "She isn't going to remember your sorry butt."

Chavez stretched his arms over his head and tried to wiggle his hips. "You underestimate the Chavez charisma. Women cannot resist. And they never forget."

"That's an elephant," Wilber said.

"They'll put us up at the Royal Hawaiian on Oahu, don't you think?" Chavez said to Father Tom.

"Miracles happen," Father Tom said, smiling.

The ship's movement brought much-needed fresh air sweeping into the hold. Sam savored his decision to remain near the hatch as the breeze blew across his face and the freighter chugged out of Manila Harbor toward open water. But things in the hold soon went from bad to worse. The seas turned rough beyond the harbor, and the *Arisan Maru* rose and fell with the large swells. Seasickness gripped the POWs, and the sound and the smell of men puking created a chain reaction throughout the hold. Vomit rose to the back of Sam's throat several times, but he gagged it down.

"Our bodies can't take this," Sam said. "Not after Bilibid." Six weeks prior to boarding the ship, Sam and the other POWs had been taken from Camp Cabanatuan to Manila's notorious Bilibid Prison, where some, though not all, survived starvation rations.

Two hours after they left the harbor, the fading light seemed to quiet the hold.

"Must be near sunset," Sam murmured to Chavez and Father Tom.

"Might cool things down," Chavez said.

A rumor started in the hold, speculation that the prisoners were part of an exchange for Japanese prisoners and the men were on a ship to freedom.

"I'm not buying it," Major Jones said to the group, but kept his voice down. "Just a baseless rumor likely started by Yoshida to get our hopes up so he can crush them again. More likely we're being taken deeper into the Japanese Empire to work in the mines—even farther from freedom, not closer to it."

Just before dark, guards lowered five-gallon metal benjo buckets into the hold by ropes. Though usually used as toilets, these contained rice, and word spread fast. Hundreds of starving POWs surged toward the hatch in a rush for food.

Major Jones quickly ascended the staircase again, and despite his own weakened condition from worsening malaria, he managed to maintain some order. "Everyone *sit!*" he thundered. "Sit, or we're going to spill the buckets in all this shit and puke, and nobody will get anything."

When the POWs sat, Jones and a few other officers disconnected the buckets of cooked rice from the ropes, then distributed them in different directions.

"Take them back," Jones ordered his officers. "One handful per man. We officers eat last."

Major Jones's eating last was in keeping with Sam's experiences with him in the camps and the stories told about him. Jones had led on Bataan, holding out for as many weeks as possible. He'd been shot in battle, transported to a make-shift jungle hospital to have the bullet removed, then demanded to be returned to the front line. At the camps, he'd insisted that he pull his own work detail each day, though as an officer he could have declined. It had surely damaged his health, as had his malaria and other killer tropical diseases.

If Major Paul Jones were a cat, he'd used up eight of nine lives.

They all had.

"Okay, here it comes," Sam said several minutes later when an officer and bucket drew close. The soldier scooped out a handful of rice, about the size and shape of an orange, then plopped it into Sam's cupped hands. He did the same for Father Tom and Chavez.

Sam savored the rice and tried to make it last as long as possible. Father Tom, however, stooped over a man who had collapsed to the floor and started hand-feeding his rice to the fallen soldier. "Padre, you have to stop giving your food away," Sam said. It was a line he had spoken dozens of times before.

"He needs it more than I do," Father Tom said, his standard reply.

"Here, take half of this." Sam unfurled his fingers and shoved a golf ball–sized lump of rice into his friend's hand. "I'm serious, Padre. You have to eat, or we're both going to starve to death."

Father Tom grudgingly accepted the rice and, after eating, helped the fallen soldier to sit up.

The sun set, and a deeper darkness gripped the hold. As the temperature cooled, men cursed the Japanese. Others pleaded and moaned, and more than a few whimpered for their wives or mothers. Some talked to one another in hushed voices.

Sam kept his eyes open, scanning the darkness, worried that Rudowski hadn't given up on his promise to kill him. The *thought* of Rudowski was, at present, more terrifying than the man.

The giant propellers churned the sea and the ship settled into a gentle rocking motion, but it did nothing to quiet Sam's mind. He wondered where this hell ship was taking them, and whether any of them would survive.

3

First Full Day at Sea

The **Arisan Maru**
South China Sea
October 12, 1944

The *Arisan Maru*'s moans mixed with the screams and groans of POWs, a ghastly chorus that sounded like demons in the darkened hold. These had been strong, disciplined men, men of character and faith, but years of starvation and torture, and now this new reality, had shattered their hopes and taxed their sanity. Sam covered his ears, but he could not block out the voices. Through the night he heard arguments break out, leading to what sounded like fights—twenty or thirty men shouting, cursing, and pummeling one another. The battles never lasted long. The men were too worn out to sustain them.

Sam fell in and out of sleep. The putrid stench and his cramped muscles added to his misery. When, at last, a faint dawn light crept through the open hatchway, Sam said, "Made it through the night."

"Thank God," Chavez said.

Sam peered up at the nearest bamboo rack. "Wonder how many guys suffocated in there."

"Or got killed." Chavez glanced toward the back, where the most intense arguing and fighting had been.

The *Arisan Maru* chugged onward, and the ship's hold heated as the sun rose. The temperature radiating off the metal hull had to eventually approach 120 degrees, baking the POWs in a floating oven. In the early afternoon, a merciful downpour cooled the ship, and wind pushed fresh air into the hold and gallons of rainwater rolled off the deck into the hatch. Men below the hatchway opened their mouths to catch the drops and filled empty canteens passed forward from the hold's darkened reaches, anything to ease their thirst.

Desperate for any distraction, Sam and others around him swapped memories of loved ones and favorite foods. They described what they would do when they returned home. As usual, Chavez's stories were the most vivid and colorful and therefore the most anticipated, especially since they could always be counted on to feature a scantily clad woman and an improbably gymnastic sexual interlude.

As the afternoon waned, the *Arisan Maru*'s engine noise dropped, and the ship slowed.

"Are we stopping?" Sam asked. "It feels like we're stopping."

"Must be a bay," Father Tom said. The seas had calmed. The freighter rocked less.

"Could be anchoring for the night," Jones said.

"Honolulu already?" Chavez stood and swayed his hips. "Bring on the beaches and the broads, boys."

"It's time," Father Tom said to Sam. "The men are calm now."

"Don't do it, Padre," Sam warned. He'd been against Father Tom's idea when the priest first shared it with him, but the padre was not to be deterred. He stood and moved toward the stairs.

"Where the hell is he going?" Chavez asked.

"He wants to lead a prayer service," Sam said.

"In here? Seriously? My prayers for broads and booze got a better chance of coming true."

"I tried to warn him."

Father Tom squirmed and twisted his way to the wooden staircase. Not an easy task. Desperate POWs near the hatchway guarded every inch of their real estate, with its better air and light, and the occasional rainwater, but they made room when they realized it was Father Tom. The priest climbed halfway up the staircase. Father Tom was just five foot eight, but after years of continually taking sick POWs' work details, he looked to have shrunk, his shoulders rounded and his spine bent like a feeble old man's. His once round, symmetrical face had become gaunt and angular, his cheekbones and the bones in his nose visible. The Army cap he had worn cocked to one side and his wire-rimmed glasses were both long gone.

Just as Father Tom was about to speak, a soldier threw an empty canteen and hit the priest in the head. "Sit down," the man growled. "God don't exist. Not in here. We're in the belly of a goddamn demon."

The POWs nudged one another and murmured uneasily under this barrage of blasphemy.

Major Jones leaned closer to Sam and Chavez. "Be ready. We may have to save him before they lynch him."

Sam moved as if to get up, but Chavez grabbed his arm. "You don't exactly have a lot of credibility in here, amigo. You stand up, you're just giving them a larger target—not to mention flagging your location for Rudowski, wherever that sadist might be."

Father Tom touched his head where the canteen had struck, but he stood his ground just as Sam knew he would. Father Tom had told him a bit of his life story during the many hours they'd shared in the POW camps. The priest had been born in rural Linton, Indiana, in 1910, and had grown up during a boomtown culture war. Coal discovered near his quiet little town had attracted a flood of miners. Vice crimes soon followed. At its peak, he said the once-sleepy town had more than three dozen bars and an equal number of churches. With five sons to raise, the stakes were high for Father Tom's Czech immigrant parents, who steered each of their five boys away from the vice and into a Catholic education at Saint Peter's Elementary School, where Tom, the quiet middle child, melted into the background.

When his oldest brother, George, chose the priesthood, Tom followed. They both attended Saint Meinrad Seminary and embraced its contemplative lifestyle and focus on service. Father Tom told Sam spiritual life was his passion, and its values—humility, kindness, compassion, and concern for others—his life calling.

Ordained in June 1935 at age twenty-four, Father Tom joined the Army Chaplain Reserve Corps and was sent to the Philippines in 1941. He served as regiment chaplain. Major Jones told Sam and the others that although Father

Tom carried a Bible instead of a gun, he had earned many medals for service, bravery, gallantry, and heroism. Sam didn't doubt it, having personally witnessed Father Tom pull men from a burning building and rush into raging battles to comfort fallen soldiers when he should have been in the rear. He had even married a young soldier to an Army nurse on the front lines as enemy shells exploded all around them.

Now, in the stinking, cramped hold of this Japanese hell ship, Father Tom wasn't about to let getting beaned by an empty canteen stop him from what he rose to do.

He made the sign of the cross and raised his arms. He held the five-inch crucifix made of wood and silver, an ordination gift from his parents that not even the guards had dared to take. A reddish-orange glow angled into the hatchway from above, bathing him in a column of light.

"Wow," Chavez asked. "Did he just dial up that theatrical lighting?"

"I don't put anything past the man," Sam said.

Father Tom rotated the crucifix in the light. The restless POWs grew quiet and still. Some crossed themselves. "Let us pray with confidence to the Father in the words our Savior gave us," he said. A sea of POWs bowed their heads in unison, though they were a mix of Catholics, Jews, Protestants, agnostics, and even a few atheists.

When they had finished the Lord's Prayer, Father Tom said, "O Lord, we are eighteen hundred Jonahs in the dank black belly of this whale. We humbly beseech Thee, O Lord, to cast us out of this whale and to deliver us safely to our families. In your mercy, keep us free from sin and protect us from all evil as we await in joyful hope the coming of our Savior, Jesus Christ."

"Amen," the great bulk of the soldiers called out.

"The peace of the Lord Jesus Christ be with you always," the chaplain said.

"And also with you," the POWs said.

"Let us offer each other the kiss of peace."

Many of the men who, hours before, had been fighting, shook hands. Father Tom offered a few more prayers, a brief sermon, then said, "Go now to love and serve the Lord and each other, my brothers." The chaplain lifted his arms and the crucifix, gave a final blessing, and stepped off the staircase. Men reached out a hand to touch Father Tom as he worked his way back to his spot, and the last bit of streaming golden light faded.

"The man's a goddamn miracle worker," Chavez said to Sam.

Sam didn't disagree.

But the peace that Father Tom's worship service instilled in the men only lasted until nightfall, when darkness again took the hold and prisoners' angry screams shattered the fragile calm. Fights flared, and the brutal black hours crawled by.

Sam kept one eye open, searching for his own demon.

"Satan comes in the dark," Chavez said softly, quietly, fearfully.

"Satan has no place here," Father Tom said, his eyes closed.

Maybe not, Sam thought, but after what he had witnessed the last three years, he was certain the Prince of Darkness had his talons in the men on this hell ship, used darkness as his weapon, and was laughing demonically at them all.

When dawn broke, Sam again hadn't slept much, the specter of Rudowski hanging over him. Each time he dozed, a gnawing premonition that the worst was yet to come awakened him.

"Made it through another night," Chavez said.

Buckets dropped through the hatchway by ropes. "Slop time," Chavez said. "More fine dining aboard the *Stinko Maru.*"

As before, Major Jones and the other officers detached the five-gallon buckets of rice for distribution. Sam scanned the jammed bamboo racks. "A lot of guys not getting up for chow."

"Too sick," Father Tom said.

Chavez squinted into a nearby rack. "Or dead."

An officer arrived and scooped rice into Sam's cupped hands.

"I'm watching you, Padre," Sam said. "I'm not taking a bite until I see you eat yours."

Father Tom balked, but when Sam refused to eat, the priest made the sign of the cross, thanked God for his food, and slowly ate.

The ship's twin diesel engines roared back to life and Sam heard the clanging of the anchor rising, crushing his hope they'd be taken off the ship and not have to endure another day at sea.

"Anchors aweigh, my boys, anchors aweigh," Chavez said. "We're off to another exotic location."

4

The Beast

The **Arisan Maru**
South China Sea
October 13, 1944

On the second full day at sea, the dehydration became unbearable. Two men drank from a canteen, and Sam asked if they could spare a swig. Father Tom stopped Sam just before the neck reached his lips. "They're drinking urine," he said.

Later, Sam helped Father Tom pin down a POW who had gone berserk, screaming and thrashing about like a man possessed. They held him until the man passed out.

"We're losing our way," Father Tom said. "Sanity. Civilization. It's all fading away."

"Civilization said, 'Adios, muchachos' days ago, Padre," Chavez said.

By the third day, Sam knew the next food drop would be every man for himself. He wriggled to the hatchway area, where he found Major Jones and two other soldiers piled atop another crazed POW.

"There are more and more of them," Major Jones said. "Getting even worse in the back, though." He glanced toward the stern. "Rumor has it a gang, led by Rudowski, is biting throats and sucking blood. Murdering men."

Rudowski, Sam thought, ever thankful he had steered Father Tom and Chavez away from the ship's stern, where the beast apparently now dwelled.

The fourth day at sea, three POWs managed to restore power to two large electric blowers inside the ship's hold. For a few glorious hours the large fans blew impossibly delicious fresh air over the throng of sweating bodies, but the Japanese guards discovered the blowers the following day and cut the power supply. Fouled, sticky, toxic air refilled the hold like warm syrup.

As dusk descended, the hold again quieted, most of the men either asleep or too tired to speak. The space reeked of the pungent blend of excrement and sweat, mixed with the unmistakable odor of the dead and the dying—an odor Sam had become all too familiar with inside the burial ground two miles from Camp O'Donnell. The ship moaned and creaked, for now gently rising and falling. Sam sat with his back to Chavez, Father Tom at their side. All three men had their legs pulled up, their forearms resting on their knees.

Sam heard a scurrying from somewhere in the hold behind him and thought of rats, then realized there wasn't room on the ship for rats. He lifted his head when he heard the sound a second time, this time accompanied by protesting men disturbed from sleep. "Where are you going?" "Hey, there's no room here!" "What the hell?"

Sam looked up in time to see Rudowski hurling himself over and through the men. He lunged the final few feet and bowled into Sam, Chavez, and Father Tom. "I *told* you, Carlson. I'd kill you."

Sam struggled to free Rudowski's hands from his neck, the disturbed men now awake and protesting loudly. Sam couldn't breathe. He felt elbows and knees and other bony body parts hitting him. Fists and forearms pummeled Rudowski, but seemingly without effect.

Chavez repeatedly shouted, "Get off him. Get him off!"

Sam saw stars, his vision going black. Then, just as quickly, he felt Rudowski's grip relax; the big man's body went limp and finally collapsed.

"Get him off. Pull him off," Chavez shouted.

Chavez, Father Tom, and others pulled Rudowski from Sam. Above him, Major Jones held one of the metal benjo buckets the Japanese had put in the hold for the men to defecate and urinate in. The major had apparently used it to hit Rudowski in the back of the head, how many times Sam didn't know, but enough to finally knock him out, given the dents in the can.

"Are you all right?" Father Tom asked.

Sam sat back up, rubbing his neck where Rudowski had choked him. His throat felt raw and sore. The other men slowly scurried back to their designated places they had so carefully guarded, especially those near the stairs.

"Yeah. Yeah, I'm okay."

"The question is, what do we do with him?" Jones said. "Not like we can lock him up somewhere or tie his hands together."

"Let's start by getting him out of here before he comes to," Chavez said. "Now that we know he's still gunning for Sam, we'll be on guard. I say we shove him into the back where he came from."

"That, too, won't be easy," Father Tom said. "He's too big and the men are too tired to pass him overhead."

"We'll have to drag him," Jones said. "Only way."

Jones, Chavez, and several other officers stood, and with Jones clearing a path by shouting at the men on the ground to move aside, they managed to drag Rudowski deep into the dark stern.

"He's back there," Chavez said when he returned. "But when he wakes up, he's going to be angrier than a bull with three swords in him."

"We'll sleep in shifts," Jones said. "Until we see just how serious Rudowski is about a repeat performance."

5

BURIAL AT SEA

The **Arisan Maru**
South China Sea
October 17, 1944

On the sixth day, Major Jones asked Sam, Chavez, and Father Tom to join him near the main hatchway. "Grab some water," Jones said when the men arrived. One of Jones's officers gave them each a spoonful of water from a closely guarded bucket. The latest food drop had included buckets of dirty water, enough for one spoonful per man. Distribution would begin soon.

"How are you holding up, sir?" Sam asked. With no quinine tablets to treat his malaria, Major Jones exhibited the telltale shivers and a fever.

"Reports from the back are getting worse," Jones said, ignoring Sam's question. He turned his gaze to Father Tom. "The reason I called you here is we need to get the dead bodies out of the hold. It's unsanitary, and the decay is adding to the smell. But beyond all of that, the men deserve a proper burial at sea, with last rites. That's your department, Padre."

"I'll be happy to, but will the Japanese allow it?"

"I've put in a request and I'm waiting to find out. Figured it wouldn't hurt if you asked, maybe say it's a religious thing . . . or some such thing."

"How many dead do you figure?" Father Tom asked.

"At last count, forty-three," Jones said. "It could be more, maybe a lot more. I sent three officers to check the rear, but they haven't come back yet."

"Okay, then," Father Tom said, glancing up the staircase. "Should I ask now?"

Jones drew a deep breath and started up the staircase, Father Tom behind him. Sam and Chavez remained at the foot of the stairs.

Jones stopped his ascent when the Japanese guards topside pointed their rifles into the hold. "Down! Down!"

Father Tom and Jones saluted and bowed, then gestured and explained. A minute later, a guard disappeared. Tense moments passed before Katsuo Yoshida appeared above the hatchway, his body casting a shadow down the staircase. "Well, well, what do we have here?" he said, dabbing at the back of his neck with a small towel.

Father Tom and Major Jones gave the Japanese officer his required salute.

"So, you want to remove bodies from the hold?" Yoshida said. "I am sorry. That is not possible."

"They're entitled to a decent burial," Jones said. "The Geneva Convention on the treatment of prisoners of war—"

The little Napoleon became animated. "I told you! We are not in Geneva. And I have told you the *rules* created by Western imperialist countries do not apply to us."

Yoshida had calmly refused every request Jones had made since the men boarded the ship. More food. More water. Chances for sick men to get on deck and get fresh air.

"Please," Father Tom said. He climbed a step higher. "For the love of God. These men are Christian and must have a Christian burial."

Major Jones was counting on Yoshida being like the other Japanese officers, respectful of rank, and especially of a religious leader. While Yoshida pondered Father Tom's request, his aide approached, a young lieutenant whom Pete Chavez had nicknamed Snookie, after a housecat back in Salinas who didn't do much but was always around. Snookie bowed to Yoshida, then addressed him in urgent Japanese.

Yoshida studied Snookie but said nothing. Tense moments passed. Finally, he turned back to the hatch and delivered a terse history lesson to the POWs, one they'd heard many times. "I have dedicated my life to international peace and understanding. But Western countries keep doing the opposite with your imperialistic wars of aggression in Asia."

"He's like one of those dolls with a string you pull and he says the same thing over and over again," Chavez said quietly to Sam.

Yoshida pointed to the air as if pointing at an invisible map on a lecture stage. "France stole Indochina. Portugal took Timor. The Netherlands enslaved the East Indies. England conquered Burma, Malaya, and Borneo. Spain occupied the Philippines until the American military seized it in 1902. Do you see the pattern here?" He didn't wait for an answer. "Enough is enough. The white men have left Japan no choice but to fight back before you colonize us too. Ours is a war of liberation, of independence. Asia is for Asians. Island by island, Japan is freeing its neighbors from the rule of Western colonial powers." Yoshida flicked an imaginary speck of dust from the right shoulder of his crisp uniform. The POWs waited. Without looking at them, he said, "You may bury the bodies at sea. Tonight, after dark." Then he turned and calmly walked off.

Jones and Father Tom descended the staircase. "Thanks, Padre," Jones said. "You made this happen." He spoke to Sam and Chavez. "Rest up, boys. We have a long night ahead of us."

Sam dreaded the thought that he would again be on burial duty.

———

"Listen up," Major Jones shouted from the stairway as dusk settled over the hold.

Chavez pinched his lower lip and blew out a shrill whistle. The hold quieted.

"The Japs are letting us bury our dead at sea tonight. I'm not sure how many more chances we're going to get at this, so pass our fallen brothers forward."

The men fell to it.

As Sam did his part to move one body overhead, he startled. "This guy's still warm," he said.

Father Tom peered down at the figure from the bottom step, probed the POW, then shook his head. "He's dead. The heat in here keeps the bodies warm."

A chill crawled up Sam's back as he thought of the soldier probably suffocating in the unrelenting heat—another nightmarish way to die. The list kept growing.

With little room, they had no choice but to stack the bodies atop one another at the bottom of the staircase. "Take whatever clothes they have," Major Jones said. "We may need them for bandages."

In time, they had built a mound of more than fifty naked cadavers. Now to get them out of the hold. Guards dangled three ropes through the hatchway, then gestured for POWs to attach the ropes around the ankles of each dead body, one at a time. Major Jones fashioned a slipknot around the first and tugged the rope. The line went taut, the naked body rose a few feet, dangling and swaying in the air. Jones and the others connected ropes to two more corpses, and they, too, rose, feet first. The sight of three upside-down corpses suspended in midair, their jaws open in silent screams, caused Sam to look away. He noticed other POWs doing the same. Sam saw the bodies of the deceased he'd buried in the mass graves, their arms reaching up from the ground as if digging out from the dirt.

This was another nightmare.

"That ain't right, man," Chavez said, speaking for all the men nearby, for once his voice flat. "These were American soldiers. They deserve better. They shouldn't go out like this."

Father Tom stepped forward and gently held the head of a corpse as the guards drew him aloft. He traced a cross on the man's forehead and whispered a prayer. Then he saluted. The others close by followed the padre's lead and saluted.

Minutes later, the three empty ropes fell back into the hold and the next grisly round began, the process repeating itself for the next hour. When the last body rose through the hatchway, the final bit of daylight flickered out and the sky went dark.

Around 20:00 hours, when the full moon had risen, Yoshida sent word for the burial detail to come on deck.

"Let's go," Major Jones said.

Sam, Chavez, Father Tom, and a tall, soft-spoken major named Robert Lothrop, whom they'd all first met when transferred to Camp Cabanatuan, followed Jones up the wooden staircase. Sam stepped onto the deck for the first time in days, and his skin tingled as fresh, cool air caressed him. The smell of the sea wafted into his nostrils and onto the tip of his tongue. He sucked in the fresh air like drinking a cold glass of water.

The Japanese guards broke his revelry. "Speedo! Speedo!" They steered Sam and the other members of the detail to the portside railing, where the naked corpses had been stacked like firewood. The bright moon tinted the dead men's contorted limbs, faces, and torsos a ghostly gray.

With the ship anchored and the engines silent, the men stood in solemn stillness. Sam looked about where the ship had anchored. It was a bay, near as he could tell. In the distance, he could make the outline of a darkened forest on a nearby island, but he could not determine where the maru had set anchor.

"No blankets to wrap the men," Sam said flatly. "No slabs to set the bodies on. No weights to sink them below the surface. No twenty-one-gun salute. No taps playing."

"We just going to toss them overboard like they were nothing?" Chavez asked.

"Not exactly the most civilized burial." Sam sighed.

"But it's the best we're going to get," Jones said. "Father Tom will make this dignified."

The priest collected his thoughts, hands folded beneath his chin. Then he stepped forward, raised his crucifix, and said, "In the name of the Father and of the Son, and of the Holy Spirit."

Sam and the other Americans snapped to attention, some making the sign of the cross.

"We gather here to commend our brothers to God our Father and to commit their bodies to the sea." Father Tom squeezed a small white cloth in his fist and sprinkled water over the piled bodies. "Those whose lives of faith began when the waters of baptism washed away their original sin we now commit back to the water and to the Lord our God, in whom all sins shall be forgiven. Almighty God, you created the Earth and shaped the vault of heaven. You fixed the stars in place."

Sam checked the sky for the North Star, his "Sarah star," but could not find it. Clouds were rolling in.

"We have been trapped in the snares of death, but you have set us free."

"Faster!" Yoshida yelled. He stood fifteen feet above the men on the ship's superstructure with his arms folded across his chest. "Talk faster."

Father Tom ignored him. He lifted his crucifix above the corpse pile for the final prayer. "Eternal rest grant unto them, O Lord, and let perpetual light shine upon them. May they rest in peace. This we ask through Christ our Lord."

For the next half hour, the men committed the bodies to the sea. Sam and Major Lothrop lifted one body after the next and slid them over the metal railing. Chavez worked with Jones. The bodies dropped fifteen feet, splashed in the calm water, then joined an eerie platoon of corpses floating in a wedge of moonlight, the current pulling them farther and farther from the ship until darkness swallowed the last glimpse of the bodies.

"It's dark, but I can see so clearly," Lothrop said, the first words he'd uttered since they'd been on deck. The major sucked in a breath of air. "And the air is so clean." Lothrop didn't appear to be directing his words to Sam or anyone else. "It's been a long time since any of us has been clean."

"I know what you mean, Major." Sam bent to retrieve another soldier, but Lothrop failed to join him. "Need a hand here, Major." Sam looked to the guards to see if any had noticed Lothrop had stopped working.

"Where do you think you're going, anyway?" Lothrop said over the railing.

Sam stood, his first sense something was wrong. "Who are you talking to?" He glanced again at the guards, who had still not noticed Lothrop. "Major?" Sam snapped his fingers, drawing Lothrop's attention. "We have to keep going here or the Japs will shoot us and throw us overboard."

"Right." Lothrop resumed the gruesome task. But a short time later he again stopped. "Which island do you think is closer? That one? Or the one over there?"

"Hey, are you okay, Major?" Sam touched Lothrop's narrow, bony shoulder. "You okay?"

"Yeah, I'm okay." Lothrop looked around the deck. "Do we have more? How many?"

"A dozen or so."

In his two and a half years in the camps, Sam had learned every person had a breaking point. The major had seemingly reached his. Sam's goal now was to finish their task and get the man back down into the hold.

But Lothrop did not bend for the next corpse. He moved to the railing and squinted at the closest moonlit island. Then he pointed. "I see my son."

"Faster! Faster!" Yoshida urged, above and behind them. The guards, alerted, prodded the men.

Sam bent for the next body. "No, you don't see your son, Major. It's just an illusion."

Lothrop became animated. "I do. He's right there, on the shore. My entire family is with him. They're all waving to me." Lothrop lifted his arm to return the wave.

Sam quickly tugged down Lothrop's arm. "Dammit, sir, pull yourself together. Your family isn't here. We're prisoners of war. We're burying the dead. Do your duty."

Sam gripped Lothrop's shoulder. The major's muscles tensed, straining to pull away from him. "Tom," Sam said as loudly as he dared. "Padre!"

When the chaplain looked his way, Sam pointed at Lothrop with his free hand, then tapped his own temple three times.

"I'm going home." Lothrop wrenched himself free of Sam's grip and lunged for the railing.

6

Escape

The Arisan Maru
South China Sea
October 17, 1944

Lothrop gripped the ship's railing and, before Sam could react, vaulted over the side. He dropped like a stone, arms straight above his head, into the bay.

"Nigero!" a Japanese guard yelled as he rushed to the railing. Other guards repeated the escape alert. *"Nigero!"*

The freighter's deck, quiet a moment before, erupted in confused commotion.

Sam spotted Lothrop swimming, already about a hundred feet from the ship, headed toward the nearest island, to the illusion of his wife and children waiting on shore. The men could do nothing now but silently urge him on.

Guards lifted their rifles and fired. Each time one missed, the others jeered and ribbed him. The major swam harder, giving Sam and the others hope.

Almost out of range, Sam thought. *Keep going!*

"Stop it. Fools." Katsuo Yoshida's voice made his guards freeze. He climbed down the ladder to the deck. Scared guards lowered their rifles and made room at the railing. Yoshida pressed past Sam, drew his pistol, extended his arm, and took aim. Instinct took over, and Sam was about to grab Yoshida's arm when Father Tom gripped Sam's hand, looked him in the eye, and shook his head.

Tense seconds passed. Yoshida lowered his gun, sighed, and holstered it. He turned to a guard and held out his hands.

The guard handed Yoshida his rifle. Yoshida braced his hip against the railing, licked his thumb, and took aim. He fired four shots. Major Lothrop stopped swimming. A moment later he floated face down in the water. Yoshida turned from the railing and faced Sam and the others.

"Shot while trying to escape," he said. "You know the rules. Nine blood brothers must be executed."

"He didn't jump," Sam said. "We were holding a body over the railing, and he slipped."

"Maybe you want to join him, Carlson?" Yoshida smiled. "Even better. I have a deal for you. To show how generous and civilized I am. You can jump overboard like your friend and swim for that island," he said. "If you make it, then I will not kill nine men. You'll be a hero."

Sam looked to the island. Ordinarily he could swim the distance, but in his weakened condition he wasn't so sure. Still, the chance to save the lives of nine men pulled at him. He would be square again.

"I'll even give you a head start," Yoshida said.

Lothrop had swum on the surface. Sam would swim underwater and pop up only for air. Yoshida wouldn't be able to draw a bead on him, even in the bright moonlight.

"Of course, if you don't make it, that would be yet another failed escape attempt. Nine additional prisoners would be executed."

The stakes had just doubled.

"Don't do it, Sam," Chavez said.

Yoshida laughed. "What do you have to lose, Carlson? You are already a complete disgrace."

He signaled for guards to drag Sam to the ship's railing. "And now, class," Yoshida said to all, "Sam Carlson gets a second chance."

Sam studied the moonlit island, still thinking he could make it if he zigzagged under the water, avoided the wedge of moonlight on the surface.

"Here, let me help you decide." Yoshida jabbed the rifle barrel into Sam's back, pushing him up against the railing.

Sam gripped the railing, and once again measured the distance to the island. But what then? What if he made it to shore without getting shot? Yoshida would never let him simply slip away. He'd come after him, call it another failed attempt. And then kill eighteen more men?

"You seem stuck," Yoshida said. In one swift motion he flipped his rifle and cracked Sam on the back of the head with its butt. Sam dropped to a knee. "Did I loosen things up a bit, Carlson? Go, you coward," Yoshida said. "Time's up."

Sam struggled to his feet, and again gripped the railing like a gymnast about to mount the pommel horse.

—

Father Tom tilted a canteen to Sam's lips. The lukewarm water slid down the back of his throat. He sat up and shook his head, which felt as heavy as a bowling ball, then moaned from the pain caused by the sudden movement. "What happened? My ear hurts; my whole head is splitting."

"Another crack and Yoshida would have split it like a coconut," Chavez said. "Good thing he knocked you out the second time he hit you."

"You'd be dead if he hadn't, and maybe the rest of us as well," Major Jones said. "He was baiting you. He would have used you as target practice, just like Major Lothrop."

"How long have I been out?"

"All night," Father Tom said.

"Did Yoshida kill nine blood brothers because of Lothrop?"

"Not yet," Chavez said. "But the major is right. We can't give him an opportunity. The sick son of a bitch lives for this shit."

As if on cue, the hatch cover slid open, and Yoshida stepped down three steps. "I need nine prisoners." He smiled. Those in the hold receded from the staircase in a human tide of self-preservation.

"No volunteers? Then I will choose. Carlson first."

A hushed silence gripped the hold.

Yoshida lowered himself to the top step. "If you do not come up willingly, I will have the guards bring eighteen men."

Sam, not about to let any more die because of him, climbed the staircase. On deck the guards seized Sam and dragged him across it. They tied his bony wrists behind his back and turned him to face the ocean. Behind him, Sam heard the guards drag more struggling POWs on deck, beating them to their knees. "Please kneel," Yoshida said as if Sam had a choice. Two guards put hands on Sam's shoulders and shoved him to his knees. Yoshida drew his two-foot saber from its scabbard, and the guards stepped back. The Japanese officer gripped the handle and stood where Sam could see him. He stepped to Sam's side and brought the blade over Sam's head. Sam shut his eyes. He felt the blade touch the back of his neck and flinched. Yoshida laughed. He derived pleasure from the POWs' fear. Sam would not give the bastard the pleasure. He kept his gaze on the watery horizon and his thoughts on Sarah and his family. He hoped someone on board would live and tell them what became of him.

Yoshida twirled the blade overhead, the sound like fan blades gaining speed. Then he pulled a deep breath into his lungs and cried out. Sam shut his eyes and felt the blade slice lightly across the skin on the back of his neck, like a razor. A trickle of blood rolled onto the deck.

"This isn't right," Yoshida said.

He stepped forward and slid his sword back into its scabbard. He was playing with Sam, like a cat with a mouse. Sam would not take the bait.

"Untie him," Yoshida said. The guards, looking perplexed, loosened Sam's bindings.

Sam rubbed one wrist, then the other to get the blood flowing again, but kept his eyes on Yoshida.

"I'm not going to kill you, Carlson." Yoshida dropped to one knee and nestled close to Sam's ear. "You will do it. Your Western books and movies call it 'hara-kiri.'" Yoshida's voice turned solemn, almost reverent. "But we call it . . . 'seppuku.'"

Yoshida slowly pulled a ceremonial dagger from its sheath and lifted it so Sam could see the blade, the light of the moon glinting. He continued to whisper. "Like a samurai warrior, you can restore your honor, Carlson. You have brought shame upon your country, your family, and yourself. I am giving you the chance to die a heroic death. Show them you have the courage." He gripped Sam's chin and turned his head to the men on their knees.

Sam looked back and stared Yoshida in the eye. "Suicide's a coward's way out."

"Oh, Sam Carlson," Yoshida said, his voice soft. "You have much to learn. Let me teach you." Yoshida knelt behind him, then wrapped his arms around Sam's emaciated waist. He pressed Sam's hands around the dagger handle with his perfectly manicured fingers and guided the blade's tip to Sam's belly. "Start here, on the left," Yoshida hissed into his ear, his breath acidic and foul. "Insert the blade to the hilt. That's important."

Yoshida's hands squeezed tighter. The dagger's tip, razor sharp, poked through Sam's thin vest and nicked his skin. "Then cut sideways across the belly, left to right." Yoshida traced a line across Sam's stomach, slicing the vest and leaving another thin trail of blood. "Now, this is where many falter," Yoshida said when the blade reached the right side of Sam's belly. "They collapse from the pain. But if you can, Carlson, turn the blade and cut upward to finish the job. You will inspire everyone."

Sam knew what would inspire the men. He just wasn't sure he could do it. Could he move his body to the side as he shoved the knife, plunging it into Yoshida's stomach before he or his guards could react? Better to die in a hail of bullets than by suicide, Sam thought. Better to take Yoshida to hell with him.

"Do it, Carlson," Yoshida whispered. "Free yourself from your pain. Restore your honor."

Sam drew a deep breath and gripped the dagger handle. He tensed every muscle in his body. His next move—the last he would ever make—needed to be fast and sure.

7

BREAKING POINT

The **Arisan Maru**
South China Sea
October 18, 1944

Snookie rushed to Yoshida's side, shouting in Japanese and momentarily distracting Sam.

Yoshida kept his arms wrapped around Sam, his hands on the blade handle. *Now!* Sam thought. *Shift to the side and kill him now, while you have the chance.*

Snookie gestured to the *Arisan Maru* bridge thirty feet above. The ship's captain gripped the railing, his other hand pointed at Yoshida, then swept toward the ship's bow. He shouted something, looking and sounding animated.

Sam shifted to the side, about to strike.

Yoshida yanked the hilt from Sam's weakened hands and stood. He shouted a response in Japanese and bowed to the captain, then pointed his dagger at the bound POWs on deck as he spoke to his guards.

Snookie and the other guards poked and prodded the POWs to stand, then herded them forward, toward another square hatch at the ship's bow.

"This is your lucky day, Sam Carlson." Yoshida slid the dagger back into its sheath.

Sam watched a stream of nearly naked POWs rise, forced, from the hold, prodded by Japanese bayonets across the deck to what Sam deduced to be the ship's forward hold. They descended through another hatch, though a few POWs collapsed on deck and were rolled to the side.

Twenty minutes later, when the POW parade had finished, Yoshida returned to where Sam remained kneeling. He barked commands, and two guards jerked Sam to his feet and escorted him back to the main hatch. "We've rearranged the rats," Yoshida said to Sam. "Gave you a little more room to run around." Yoshida gestured to Snookie, who drove his fist into Sam's belly, knocking the wind from him as he pitched backward into the hold's darkness.

"Nice of you to drop in," Chavez said. He and Major Jones had cushioned Sam's fall, and Father Tom caught Sam's head before it cracked against the floor.

"What's going on?" Jones asked.

Sam sat up. "I don't know. But it looks to me like the captain ordered some of the men to the forward hold."

Jones shook his head. "We thought maybe we'd reached a port and were finally getting off. Then the guards shouted, *'Mō iya. Mō iya.'* No more. No more."

"It will at least give everyone here more elbow room," Chavez said. "But I'm gonna be upset if I hear they have a bowling alley up front."

One by one, the remaining men drifted back into the darkness, disappointed they had not reached a port, but the additional room at least allowed them to lie down.

A short while later, a POW bolted up the staircase, despite Major Jones and others trying to grab him. Too late. When the POW poked his head through the opening, a guard bayoneted him in the neck, and the POW's body pitched backward, tumbling down the steps to the floor.

Chavez approached Sam and Father Tom. "We need to do something to occupy their minds or we're all going to go crazy."

Father Tom turned to Sam. "Tell the men a movie, like in the camps."

In the POW camps, Father Tom had called on Sam frequently to "tell movies," and said it was the only thing the men looked forward to each night. Sam didn't know about that, but he did know that during the hours he'd passed retelling *Carefree, Shall We Dance,* or *The Gay Divorcee,* the barracks had fallen blissfully silent as he transported the men into those glittering stories and escapes.

Sam could still remember nearly all the lines, and he painted luxurious land-scapes and settings with a passion that sometimes startled even himself. What lines he couldn't remember, he made up.

But that had been back in the barracks, and as bad as their experiences had been, it was far better than this hellhole. "Now?"

"Now more than ever," Father Tom said.

"Yeah," Chavez said. "Serve up one of them you're always talking about, one of those Fred and Gingers." Chavez turned to the men in the hold. "Movie night, boys!" he bellowed, sounding like he had when he'd announced the mov-ies shown on the *President Coolidge*. "Gather 'round. Tonight we're showing . . ." He turned to Sam. "What are we showing?"

Every sunken eye redirected to Sam. "*Carefree*," he said.

"Tonight's feature film is *Carefree*, starring Fred Astaire, Ginger Rogers . . ." Chavez looked to Sam, and Sam fed him the other names. Chavez got as far as "Ralph Bellamy as Stephen Arden, Luella Gear as Aunt Cora" before he shrugged and said, "and a bunch of others. Come on, get your popcorn and soda, and get a good seat."

To Sam's astonishment, some of the men came forward and sat, and Chavez went from man to man in the front row, handing each an imaginary bag of pop-corn and a Coke and telling them to pass them back. Sam saw smiles on POW faces for the first time since they'd been imprisoned in the hold.

"Are you ready?" Chavez shouted.

"Yeah," the men responded.

"That wasn't good enough. Are you ready?"

"Yeah!" they shouted louder.

"All right, then." Chavez made a beeping sound like the radio antennae at the start of the RKO Radio Pictures, then mimed a curtain opening across the screen and did his best to also imitate an orchestra. "Gentlemen, welcome to tonight's premiere of *Carefree*."

The seated soldiers hooted and hollered.

Sam did his best to explain what was happening, while acting out the part of Fred Astaire. He enlisted Chavez to play Ginger Rogers, which brought more laughter, and Father Tom played multiple other roles. Sam couldn't dance a lick, but that didn't matter in the cramped space—despite the extra room cleared by the transfer of some men to the forward hold. Chavez, ever the ham, spun about the men, whirling Ginger's imaginary dresses and skirts. It was absurd, but in the camp and now this hold, everything was absurd. The men calmed. They laughed and made catcalls. Sam kept them entertained for more than an hour. Then, exhausted, he bowed to huge applause and sat.

When he'd finished the movie, Sam looked to Father Tom, who nodded and said softly, "Good show, Sam."

—

The next day, at sunset, with checkered rays of light streaming into the hold through the hatch, Father Tom climbed a few steps and faced the men in the faint light. He raised his crucifix to begin the nightly prayer. "Our Father, who art in heaven . . ."

The number of POWs joining Father Tom each night had dwindled. Sam didn't know if it was due to POWs dying or simply losing hope. The transfer of several hundred to the front hold had also eaten into the numbers.

"God's dead," a POW shouted from the darkness.

Father Tom snapped upright and glared at the crowd. Sam had rarely seen him angry, but he was angry now. "Who said that? Who said God is dead?" Father Tom bounded from the staircase into the seated crowd. A sea of soldiers parted, leaving a man wearing only a loincloth, maybe twenty years old.

"Did you say, 'God's dead?'" Father Tom knelt beside the soldier. "God is not dead." He stood and shouted to them all. "You'll find him in your heart, men. Without fail."

"Aw, bullshit," another man shouted.

"If God is here, why hasn't he saved us?" a third POW asked.

"Yeah," another shouted. "Haven't seen hide nor hair of him in more than three years now."

The shouts became a chorus and the men grew more animated. Some surged toward Father Tom.

Father Tom did not back down. His jaw firmly set, the priest elbowed his way through the crowd and remounted the staircase. He raised both arms in the air, and tried again, but this time without success, to quiet the bedlam. Sam, Chavez, and Major Jones, growing ever weaker from malaria, stood at the bottom of the steps to keep an errant fist from finding the priest.

For two and a half years, Father Tom had always been able to reach the men. But not now. Something had tipped. The men no longer listened.

Maybe the POW was right. Maybe God was dead, and this was hell.

Father Tom descended and sat with his head down, more dejected than Sam had ever seen him.

"Don't sweat it, Padre," Chavez said, patting the priest on the back.

"It's the circumstances," Sam said. "Not the message."

"Yeah," Chavez agreed. "Lazarus rising from the dead wouldn't swing these guys."

"Maybe they're right," Father Tom said in a new, hollow voice.

"What do you mean?" Sam said.

"Where *is* God?" Father Tom asked. "That soldier's right. I haven't seen any sign of him in almost three years. Day after day I pray, and day after day those prayers go unanswered. Men die. So many. Where is Christ? I can't hear him anymore. I can't feel him."

"Hey, Padre," Sam said, shooting a glance at Chavez. "Come on. If you lose hope, we all lose hope."

"That's right," Chavez said.

"Well, stop looking to me for your hope," Father Tom said, voice now angry, "because I'm out of hope. And I'm done trying. Find your own hope." Then he stood.

"Padre—" both Sam and Chavez began.

"Enough," Father Tom said, more anger in his voice. "I'm no one's padre and no one's priest. I'm just a man like all of you. Stop looking to me for your salvation. I don't know the way anymore. Find it on your own." He stepped to the side of the staircase and sat alone.

Sam moved to follow, but Chavez grabbed him. "Let him be. He has a right to feel the way he does. Maybe more so than all the rest of us."

—

As darkness fell, Sam became aware that guards had gathered atop the stairs. Major Jones saw them too and went up to speak to them. Sam had the sickening thought that Yoshida intended to finish what he'd started and execute Sam and the others.

Major Jones came back down the stairs and walked directly toward Sam, Chavez, and Father Tom, who'd drifted back to take a seat near his usual station. "I need you all on deck, pronto. Burial duty."

Sam looked to Father Tom, uncertain what he would do, but the priest stood and dragged himself up the stairs behind Major Jones. Sam and Chavez followed. The guards herded the burial crew to another pile of naked corpses. Sam looked all about, but Yoshida was nowhere to be seen. Clouds obscured the moon, making the deck nearly pitch black.

"Look," Chavez said as he and Sam lifted another body over the railing. He nodded to the lights of what looked like a large port city. Sam bent to pick up the next body and snuck a glance behind him at the lights. It did look like a port, but it was difficult to see any definition.

"What is it?" Sam whispered to Chavez as they bent for a body.

"I don't know. But in my head, it's Honolulu. God might be AWOL, but my hula gal is there waiting for me, clear as day, every time I look for her. Second this war is over, I'm gonna be right there with her."

After nine days aboard the hell ship, Sam didn't care at which port they disembarked. He didn't know how he could last another hour in that hold.

"Might be Osaka," Major Jones said under his breath as he and Father Tom carried another body suspended between them. "Maybe Tokyo."

After Sam and Chavez delivered the next body to the water, Chavez momentarily slung an arm around Sam's shoulder and took a longer look at the port. "It's a big city, for sure," he said. "Say one more prayer, Padre, that this floating hell is finally over."

As the burial crew went about their grim labors, the *Arisan Maru* eased ever farther into the bay. Overhead, the clouds shifted, allowing more moonlight to illuminate the port and the city.

"I'm gonna kiss the ground the moment we land," Chavez said. "Get right down on my knees and give it a big smooch."

"Put me in a camp again," Major Jones said. "I don't care where—Japan, Formosa, anywhere but this death ship."

"Whoa, look at all the ships in the harbor," Chavez said. Then he straightened from his burial task. "They're on fire." All four of them stood and stared.

Flames rose above what was left of the shattered ship nearest them. Sam spotted another burning vessel beyond that one, and then another. One after the next.

"Somebody bombed the hell out of this place," Major Jones murmured.

"Why does it look so familiar?" Chavez said.

"Oh no," Sam said, the realization hitting him. "God, no."

PART 4

1

Back in the Hunt

FRUPAC
Honolulu, Hawaii
October 19, 1944

Sarah had hit the ground running at FRUPAC. She had learned much of what she was asked to do during her work at the Naval Annex. She understood codes, as well as traffic analysis, ciphers, additives, false additives, and transposition. Holmes had assigned her to the translation and code recovery section. The room was all business. No idle chatter. Sparsely equipped, it had ten tightly organized desks. Unlike in Washington, DC, here Sarah was the *only* woman in the room. She and three other junior officers worked under a watch officer and two experienced translator-cryptographers. If she found anything of interest, she brought it to two senior officers seated at large desks on opposite ends of the long room.

Though she was the only woman, Sarah knew her work was generally on par with or ahead of the other code breakers, and she had quickly gained their respect. Their watches consisted of dry spells when they accomplished little, then flared into days of intense activity. Excitement took over and the cryptanalysts put off sleep and meals until Holmes ordered both.

Her section had broken the latest Japanese code, supplying better intelligence to submarine commanders, resulting in more sunken Japanese ships, and hopefully getting one step closer to ending the war and bringing everyone home, including—and especially—Sam.

2

CRUEL TWISTS

The **Arisan Maru**
Pier 7, Manila Harbor, Philippines
October 20, 1944

"It's Pier Seven," Sam said.

"But it can't be," Chavez said. "Can it?"

They had seen the pier twice before: when their luxury ocean liner, the *President Coolidge*, arrived in the Philippines, then again on October 11, when they boarded the *Arisan Maru*.

"That big building back there," Father Tom said, approaching the conclusion Sam had already reached. "That's Bilibid?"

The *Arisan Maru* drew closer.

"Manila," Sam said, still disbelieving.

"The whole goddamn trip was one big circle," Chavez said. "All the shit on this can. All the dying. Why?"

As the freighter drew nearer, it became clear why they hadn't initially recognized the port. Damaged and half-sunk ships dotted the harbor, the bows and sterns protruding from the water. Others looked as if they'd rolled onto their sides. Fires smoldered on other vessels and spewed black smoke.

"Our boys got a little payback for Pearl Harbor and Clark Field," Chavez said. "That's something. Must be thirty ships they hit."

"Shore got hit too." Sam pointed to the waterfront, now littered with bomb craters, overturned vehicles, and burning buildings.

"This looks like a bombing to soften up Manila for a landing. We must be retaking the Philippines," Major Jones said, sounding as though he was trying to temper the enthusiasm in his voice.

"This boat trip was a living hell, but it might've saved our lives," Father Tom said as he made the sign of the cross. "All the POWs' lives. God is certainly not dead."

"*Dios mío,*" Chavez said, mimicking the priest's movements. "What if we had survived the Bataan march and the camps only to get slaughtered by our own flyboys?"

"But we didn't," Father Tom said. He looked to the sky. "We didn't." He shook his head. "Everything happens for a reason. God didn't abandon us. He saved us."

Chavez climbed atop the railing and balanced there, staring at Manila Harbor.

"Jesus, Pete," Sam said. "What the hell are you doing?" He sneaked a glance over his shoulder to see if any guards had noticed, but they, too, were staring at the battered port. "Get down. This is no time for clowning around. The Japs are going to be pissed our boys bombed them. They won't need an excuse to shoot us."

As if on cue, the guards turned toward the men, but they didn't raise their rifles, shout, or otherwise react. They, too, appeared shell shocked, as if they were only now starting to process what had happened and what it meant.

Japan was losing the war, and a massive retribution stared the guards in the face.

————

The *Arisan Maru* tied back up to Pier 7, and Sam and the others were again locked in the hold. They strained to hear any clues about what was happening on deck.

After three hours of silence he heard a familiar noise and got to his feet. "Listen," Sam said. "Those are cranes."

"Same sound we heard nine days ago," Father Tom said, "when we first set sail."

"They're loading supplies again?" Sam said.

More hours passed. Shortly after midnight, the ship's diesel engines roared to life and the anchor chain scraped against metal as it rose.

"Oh, shit," Sam said, standing up quickly. "We're setting sail."

"Do you know what this means? Why we're in the hold?" Chavez said. "They never intended to drop us anywhere. The Japs must be using us as human shields to protect their warships."

"If that was true, then why didn't they put a red cross on the boat?" Father Tom said.

"We aren't much good as human shields if our boys don't know we're here," Major Jones agreed.

It hit Sam then. "Because they're losing ground to the Allies. And when our boys invade the Philippines, the Japs don't want them to find us alive," he said. "It's the same reason you said they had us bury the dead a couple miles away from the camp: they don't want those bodies found, and they don't want witnesses to all the crimes they've committed. They're sending us out on these ships to die."

"Sam, keep your voice down," Father Tom said, but it was too late. POWs nearby overheard Sam and Chavez speculating, or did so on their own. They shouted and pleaded, a cacophony of misery.

Sam wished the Allied planes would return and bomb them again, damage the ship or even sink it, anything to stop them from going back to sea. He listened for the sound of airplane engines, thought he heard bombs, then realized it was thunderclaps from an approaching tropical storm. "I don't think I can survive another trip, Padre."

"That's the whole point," Chavez said. "Maybe none of us is supposed to survive. And the kicker is that we four"—he gestured to himself, Sam, Father Tom, and Major Jones—"have been doing their dirty work for them. Dumping our own bodies overboard and disposing of the best evidence of all they've done."

Major Jones said, "Hang on, Chavez. Don't start blaming yourself or any-one else. No one is to blame, except the Japs. They aren't marking the ship, but not because they want us to die and to dump our bodies at sea. Who knows, maybe those cranes we heard were loading military supplies on board, too. And the Japs might want us for slave labor in the mines in Japan and Formosa. I'm not sure what's happening at present, why they haven't off-loaded us yet. It may have to do with the Jap shipping schedule, or that storm we ran into when we first shoved off."

"Those of us on burial duty gave those men dignified burials," Father Tom said, sounding again like his old self.

"Maybe so," Chavez said, defiant. "Maybe we will get off-loaded somewhere. But when? And in what condition? How many of us died last trip? A hundred? A hundred and fifty? And we're all weaker now. They'll give us less food and less water. We're going to drop like flies, and our bodies will litter the Pacific Ocean." He turned his eyes on the men around him. "I say we revolt. Take our chances next time we're on deck for burial duty. Surprise the guards, grab their rifles, and tell the boys in the hold to rush the deck when they hear us shooting."

"The Japs have a .50-caliber machine gun pointed at the hold. It would be a slaughter," Major Jones said.

"Then let's take out the machine gun first," Sam said, on board with Chavez. If he was going to die, let it be by a bullet and not starvation. "Turn them on the guards. I'm with Pete. Better to fight when we still can than wait to be slaughtered like sheep."

"And what then?" Jones asked, raising his voice. "Even if we managed to take the ship, the radio operator would just call a Jap destroyer to come sink us."

Sam knew a freighter was no match for a destroyer, not even close.

As the debate raged on, the ship departed Manila Bay into a typhoon. For three days, the convoy sailed north in stormy seas with the men again locked in the hold and denied the chance to bury the dead. Powerful winds battered the ship. The *Arisan Maru* groaned when it pitched upward on swells, then shook as it plunged down hard into the trough. Sam, Chavez, and Father Tom clutched the bamboo pillars to keep from rattling around the hold like gravel in a tin can. Waves of puke and crap sloshed over their feet.

On the third day, they caught a break. The weather cleared and the seas calmed. The guards appeared topside and instructed Major Jones to again bury the dead.

"Don't do anything foolish," Jones said to Sam and Chavez before going up the staircase.

"This is it," Chavez said to Sam under his breath as they started up. "We may not get another chance. If I get the opportunity, I'm going for a weapon. I don't care what order the major gives. I'm not going to stand down."

"I'm with you," Sam said, looking back. "Let's take out the machine gunners first."

"Like Wyatt Earp and Doc Holliday at the O.K. Corral."

"Right," Sam said. Then he stopped. "Wait—didn't Doc Holliday get shot?"

"He did. So did Wyatt Earp's brothers. But Wyatt didn't."

"So who am I?" Sam asked.

"Doesn't matter," Chavez said. "It's their legend that will live forever."

3

FRUPAC

FRUPAC
Honolulu, Hawaii
October 22, 1944

At her desk, Sarah went through hundreds of messages each day, decoding and deciphering each transmission, then converting the five-digit numerical strings into Japanese characters and words written in the Japanese scripts called kana. She'd then translate the Japanese words to English.

Fifty tons of rubber loaded on a freighter to Sumatra, she read.

Routine. She placed the message in a wooden box at the corner of her desk and worked on the next message.

The Fujiki Maru *will arrive in Singapore eight hours late due to mechanical issues.*

Routine. She put the message in the same box.

Sarah's FRUPAC unit focused on the maru code—specifically the ships' cargoes, as well as their locations, destinations, and other details as they crisscrossed the Pacific. Each freighter reported its daily noontime position to Tokyo, which made the ships easy for Sarah and her team to track.

Sarah picked up the next intercept and decoded it. *The* Taiko Maru *is diverting to Leyte with eight hundred troops to help defend the island.*

General MacArthur had landed at Leyte Island in the Philippines two days earlier, and Allied forces were advancing. Any news related to the Philippines therefore qualified as urgent. Sarah placed the decoded message in her "Urgent" box above the one labeled "Routine." A woman would come through the room, gather the messages, and distribute them to the appropriate office up the chain of command. Sarah had yet to receive a "Frantic" message, one that would require her to bolt from her chair and personally deliver the information to Commander Holmes. If Holmes also deemed the message to be "Frantic," he would rush it to Admiral Chester Nimitz's office in the building next door. Nimitz would decide whether the message warranted being sent to Washington.

A frantic message was the reason for MacArthur's abrupt return and invasion of the Philippines. The Allies had intended to retake one island at a time, but a colleague had deciphered a "Frantic" message that buckled knees. The Japanese Minister of Defense had sent a telegram from Tokyo across Japan's occupied territories, instructing those running the POW camps to execute all POWs if Allied troops were approaching their camps, to prevent the POWs from being liberated to fight again. He instructed them to use bombs, decapitation, and any other means, then hide the evidence. Within hours, FDR had the telegram in his hand at the White House. Sarah knew the chances of Sam's survival grew ever slimmer as the war raged on, and this lessened those odds further, if he was still alive. Worse, unlike in Washington, DC, she didn't have Grace to keep her calm or the other girls to help console her. She had to keep her mouth shut and do her best to hide her worry as she and her colleagues at FRUPAC awaited the president's response. The president's decision would either change the entire war strategy or, should Allied forces continue to advance one island at a time and get near the POW camps, it would give the Japanese time to carry out the death sentences of tens of thousands of American POWs.

After what seemed an eternity, word trickled into their command center that FDR had ordered a direct invasion, General MacArthur had waded ashore, and the Allies were quickly fighting their way across the Philippines. It was now a race to reach the prison camps before the thousands of POWs could be executed.

Sarah pushed back from her desk, exhausted from worry and a lack of sleep. She raised both arms overhead and stretched, careful not to knock over the tall stack of white index cards perched on her blotter. At the other nine desks, her colleagues had also forgone sleep and were frantically processing stacks of intercepts, clacking typewriter keys, and studying a large wall map. The room was a giant brain, singularly focused. Those inside the room ignored even the large wall of windows that provided sweeping million-dollar views of Pearl Harbor and the Pacific Ocean.

Sarah got back to deciphering the next message.

Twenty tons of coal going to Tokyo.

Routine.

Thirty-five soldiers on the Awa Maru

have fallen sick from food poisoning.

Routine.

She pulled the next index card and decoded each letter and each word. As she did, she felt something she had not felt deciphering the other messages. Something about this message did not feel routine. Far from it. Finished, she stared at her work, then forced herself to decode and translate the message a second time.

For accuracy.

Then a third time, because she simply couldn't fathom what the message said, despite knowing the Japanese Minister of Defense had ordered the murder of thousands of POWs if the Allies neared the camps.

No mistake.

No doubt.

Frantic.

When she tried to stand, her legs betrayed her. She rubbed one sweaty palm on the front of her skirt, then the other. The other officers at their desks paid her no attention, focused on their own work. She held the message under her desk, trying to catch her breath and decide what to do.

She wanted to destroy the message.

She didn't want to be the person taking it to Commander Holmes.

But she had to. She'd taken an oath and that oath was the reason she was at FRUPAC.

She'd received a letter from Captain Russell written from an undisclosed location somewhere in the Pacific. In it, he told her that Commander Holmes had chosen her from among four hundred candidates because Russell told Holmes he could trust Sarah to always do the right thing. To do her duty.

She had an obligation not just to her country, but also to the WAVES she left behind at the Annex who might someday want to follow her to work in Hawaii.

She knew her duty.

But God, she didn't want to do it.

She took a deep breath, stood, and walked down the hall to Commander Holmes's closed office door. His doorway threshold marked a point of no return.

She might hold Sam's life in her hands if the message was accurate.

She had no reason to doubt it wasn't.

She studied the paper one last time. Then she rapped hard on the office door.

"Enter," Holmes said.

Sarah stepped in. Commander Holmes wore the Navy's standard tan khaki pants and collared shirt. His shoes, belt, and narrow necktie were regulation black. Holmes was just forty-four years old, but the war's strain had aged him. It had aged them all.

"What is it?" Holmes asked. He was packing his signature pipe with tobacco. He pointed it at the large Far East map on the wall and smiled. "And can it possibly top MacArthur wading ashore in the Philippines?"

Sarah and millions of other Americans had listened to General MacArthur's live radio address from the beachhead. Called A-Day, the massive amphibious landing involved more Allied ships and troops than the D-Day operation four months earlier. "People of the Philippines," General MacArthur had bellowed from the island of Leyte, two hundred miles south of Manila. "I have returned. By the grace of Almighty God, our forces stand again on Philippine soil."

It had brought them all hope.

Now, most of Japan's navy sailed toward Leyte for a decisive encounter. The largest naval battle in history would begin within hours.

"A seventeen-ship Japanese convoy just left Manila, sir. It's headed to Formosa, then Japan," Sarah said.

"How many freighters?" Holmes asked, putting the pipe in his mouth, striking a match, and drawing the flame into the bowl.

"The MATA-30 convoy has twelve freighters."

"What's on board?" he asked, extinguishing the match.

"A mixed bag," Sarah said. She started down the list, struggling to keep her voice calm as she read from her roughed-up paper. "The *Kimikawa Maru* is sixty-eight hundred tons and carries bauxite ore, fuel oil, and aviation gasoline. The *Kokuryu Maru* is seventy-four hundred tons and full of Japanese troops. The forty-seven-hundred-ton *Shikisan Maru* is loaded with manganese ore."

"Great targets," Holmes said, becoming animated. Sarah knew it was enough tonnage to make it a priority. "Escorts?"

"Five escorts," Sarah said. "Subchasers *Kurasaki* and *Kusentai No. 20* plus three destroyers—*Take, Kuretake,* and *Harukaze.*"

"*Harukaze,*" the former submarine skipper said, puffing on his pipe, the sweet aroma of tobacco filling the room. "She's a tough old SOB."

Holmes stepped to the wall map where small black magnets represented Allied subs. Every morning the vice admiral from Submarine Command updated submarine positions and collected Holmes's "book" of suggested targets. "Looks like we have three wolf packs in the general area," Holmes said, studying the map. "Nine subs, total." He dragged a finger across the map. "They could each intercept the convoy along this path, attack it, and get out before the destroyers have a chance to attack." Holmes turned to Sarah and said, "Good work, Ensign. I'll let Submarine Command know right away to order the submarines into rendezvous positions."

Sarah knew what would happen next. The submarines would sink the freighters and cut off supplies.

"There's something else you should know," Sarah said.

"What is it?"

"It's about the POWs in the Philippines. MacArthur might already be too late."

Holmes's brows knitted together. "What do you mean, 'too late'?"

Sarah started to reply but choked back her words. Another sentence began, but it, too, halted. She started a third time and again stopped, fighting to get her emotions under control and doing a poor job of it.

"Ensign?" Holmes said.

The words rushed from her lips: "A freighter in the MATA-30 convoy carries Allied POWs in addition to military cargo."

Holmes lowered his pipe. "Is it marked?" he asked.

"No indication of any marking," Sarah said. "No requests for safe passage. Eighteen hundred men from multiple Philippine POW camps have been moved onto the maru. If we give this message and Allied submarines attack that convoy, that ship, those POWs will die."

Holmes's head jerked back as if he'd taken an invisible punch. "How certain are you?"

"Positive." Sarah handed the paper to Holmes. "It's the *Arisan Maru*, sir. Last freighter in the convoy."

Holmes scanned the typed message she had translated. "The *Arisan Maru* is also reported to be carrying fifteen tons of aluminum and nickel, and thirty-six boxes of airplane parts. The captain can't request safe passage."

Sarah released the air from her lungs. The POWs' fates—and possibly Sam's—were now out of her hands. She had made her choice and done her duty in telling Holmes.

Holmes would make his.

"Intercepts like this are winning the war," Holmes continued. He put his pipe in an ashtray designed to hold the bowl, turned, and stared at the board and the magnets. "We're choking off enemy supply lines one torpedo at a time. We're starving Japan's war effort." He stepped closer to the map. "If we don't sink these ships because of that one freighter . . . If we let this convoy escape, Japan could extend the war." He swept an arm across the Pacific Islands. "All those ships, troops, and supplies could do more harm. They'll help protect Formosa and other islands near Japan." Holmes spun around to face her.

"Then tell Submarine Command to sink the other ships, but not the *Arisan Maru*." But even as Sarah said it, she realized the problem with her suggestion. One Holmes had already considered.

"If we sink every ship but the *Arisan Maru*—the lone freighter carrying American prisoners—then the Japanese will know we broke their code," he said. "They'll change it, and it could take us months to break it again, possibly years. How many more men will die?"

Sarah knew his logic made perfect sense. She also recalled that when she'd started at FRUPAC, a Marine had told her that secrecy took priority over operational success.

But a submarine attack was a death sentence for the POWs on board the *Arisan Maru*, and with the war possibly entering its final stages, those POWs were just weeks, or months, from freedom.

"Sir. These aren't just any POWs."

"I know," Holmes said. "We abandoned these boys two and a half years ago. Left them without food or ammo. We owe them." Holmes didn't give her time to respond. "And just so we're clear," the commander said. "I know this is personal for you. I know your hometown sweetheart, the one you've been searching for, is a POW in the Philippines and you fear he could be one of the eighteen hundred on that freighter."

Sarah blanched. "How did you know, sir?"

"Captain Russell advised me, but I chose you for the position anyway, because he also told me of your strong sense of duty and commitment, and of your integrity."

Sarah swallowed hard. "His name is Sam—Sam Carlson."

Holmes nodded grimly. "What are the odds that he's on that ship? I imagine you've already worked it out."

Sarah had indeed already divided the eighteen hundred POWs on the freighter by the estimated number of Allied prisoners still alive in the Philippines, based on the initial number of captives and their projected death rate over time. The result was rough, but all she had.

"Twenty-five percent," Sarah said. "A one-in-four chance he's on that freighter, give or take."

"And your gut?" Holmes asked. "What does it say?"

Their work relied not just on numbers but also on hunches. The same brain wiring that made Sarah and other cryptanalysts so good at creative pursuits also gave them strong instincts. It was like a sixth sense.

"One hundred percent certain, sir," Sarah said.

Holmes reached for his pipe, took several puffs, and turned to study the wall map again. A heavy silence and pipe smoke smothered the room. He spoke through clenched teeth as he again considered the message. "I'll show this to Admiral Nimitz right away. He might even run it by Washington." The commander jerked a brown leather briefcase off his desk and stuffed the communiqué inside. "But I already know what Nimitz will say and do." Holmes locked the briefcase latch. He made direct eye contact. "And I think you do too. I'm sorry. God help us all."

"God help us all," Sarah repeated.

4

WAR PATROL

The USS **Shark**
Luzon Strait, South China Sea
October 23, 1944

Submarine commander Edward Blakely received the coded message from his ensign. "The first word is 'Ultra,' sir," his ensign said. "I stopped decoding it right there."

Submarine Command had sent the coded radio message to a radioman at Pearl Harbor, who'd broadcast the message several times over the next twenty-four hours. When the sub surfaced at night to charge its batteries, they monitored their specific Pearl Harbor frequency from inside the submarine's tiny radio room. The radioman received and decoded the messages, but stopped immediately if the first word was "Ultra," short for "Ultra Secret." Only the submarine commander had the authorization to decode an Ultra Secret message and only in a locked radio room. He was to memorize its contents, then light the paper on fire and burn it.

Blakely, thirty-two years old, commanded the USS *Shark*. He entered the Navy upon the sudden death of his father at forty-seven, after reading Alec Hudson's adventure stories about submariners in the *Saturday Evening Post*. On December 9, 1941, just two days after the Japanese attack on Pearl Harbor,

Blakely transferred to the USS *Tuna* and served in various roles while the submarine operated in the Pacific—then he returned to the East Coast and assumed his command of the fleet's newest submarine, the USS *Shark*.

Blakely dismissed his ensign and made his way to the closet-sized radio room. Once there, he closed the door and locked it. At a small table surrounded by electronics, he deciphered the message, hoping it detailed a convoy of Japanese ships. The *Shark*'s first war patrol had been a smashing success, sinking four ships totaling 32,000 tons and incapacitating a fifth. Blakely had received a glowing commendation, and his executive officer, John D. Harper, had moved a big step toward fulfilling his ambition to command his own submarine. However, the *Shark*'s second war patrol, from July 10 to August 29, had been a bust. They'd largely been on "lifeguard duty," picking up downed American pilots, and had returned to Pearl Harbor without sinking a single ship.

Four weeks into the *Shark*'s third patrol, their drought was continuing. They had yet to sink a ship. Blakely and his crew desperately wanted to get back into the fight.

Blakely decoded the opening lines and pumped his fist. The message ordered him and his wolf pack of nine submarines, called Blakely's Behemoths, to intercept a large flotilla of Japanese vessels, and provided each sub with a specified longitude and latitude the ships in the flotilla were expected to reach by a specified date.

"It's about damn time," he said.

The next several lines revealed the Japanese convoy's ships' names and their tonnages. Blakely's pulse raced. He tallied over ninety thousand tons, enough ships and tonnage for each submarine to feast well. But when Blakely decoded the message's final lines, everything changed. The message detailed each freighter's suspected cargo, including the cargo of the last ship in the convoy, a six-thousand-ton freighter, the *Arisan Maru*. Military supplies, but also something else.

"Oh my God," Blakely said.

He checked and rechecked his work decoding the message to ensure he hadn't made a mistake. He hadn't.

He sat back, stunned.

Per protocol, he memorized the message and lit a match, but as the flame neared the paper, his hand stopped. He blew out the match and committed the kind of protocol breach that ended careers—he folded the Ultra message and slipped it into his shirt pocket.

———

Thirty-six hours later, when the USS *Shark* reached the provided coordinates, Blakely popped through a round hatch and climbed onto the open-air bridge. He gripped the gray metal railing to brace himself against a stiff breeze and rolling sea and stood beside his XO, John Harper. "You wanted to talk to me, John?"

Harper let loose the railing and folded both hands behind his back. "Permission to speak candidly, sir?"

"Permission granted."

"Sir, the men want to know why we're not attacking these bastards. We've arrived at the coordinates provided. Everyone is hitting it but us."

Over the radio, Blakely had been kept advised that the Japanese convoy was spread out over many miles, as were the submarines in his wolf pack. The submarines had been given intercepting coordinates, and several had arrived and begun sinking the first freighters in the convoy.

The *Shark*, having arrived after the attack began, had to be more careful. The destroyers would now be on high alert to submarines in the area and ready to quickly respond with depth charges.

Harper unfolded a piece of paper providing radio updates from nearby submarines. "*Drum* sank a cargo vessel twenty-four hours ago. *Seadragon* and *Snook* both got ships early this morning." He tapped the paper. "*Sawfish* got a freighter too." Harper stuffed the paper back into his pocket and gripped the metal railing against another ocean swell. "All due respect, sir, why aren't we attacking?"

Blakely couldn't tell Harper what was inside the hold of the last freighter besides military supplies. Nor could he tell his executive officer the last words his mother said to him before the USS *Shark* and its eighty-seven-person crew departed Groton, Connecticut, on February 14, 1944. "Promise me you won't harden your heart," she'd said. "I worry about the cost of this war, the toll it's taking on our young men, including you. I fear all the hardness and killing could destroy an important part of you." She tapped his chest. "You have a big heart. A good heart. Don't lose it."

"We have to be patient, Harp. And careful," Blakely said. "We need to let this convoy and its ships come to us. Remember there are three destroyer escorts out there, and they're now on high alert and searching for us using radar."

In his left shirt pocket, Blakely felt the folded Ultra message. The commander hoped they wouldn't court-martial him. After all, he had followed the Ultra's instructions. He ordered his wolf pack—Blakely's Behemoths—to the designated coordinates, and the attack *was* on.

"But sir, it's a goddamn turkey shoot out there," Harper said. "We're missing our opportunity."

Blakely wanted to sink ships—they all did—but Harper obsessed about it. The more ships the *Shark's* crew sank, the faster Harper would get his own submarine command.

"We'll sink ships, Harp. You'll get your tonnage."

"Conn, radar," a voice crackled over the bridge intercom.

Blakely clicked the intercom switch and leaned close. "Radar, conn, go ahead."

"Sir, we have contact, seven thousand yards, bearing zero-zero. She's dead ahead, sir."

"Anyone see her?" Blakely shouted to the two lookouts with binoculars perched high above him and Harper.

"Nothing yet, sir," one replied.

"Nothing, sir," said the other.

"Increase speed to one-half," Blakely said into the intercom. He called to his lookouts. "Boys, let me know the moment you spot this rig." Then he said a silent prayer it was not a freighter, the *Arisan Maru*.

"Aye, aye, sir."

A minute later, the intercom squawked again. "Conn, radar, six thousand yards, sir. She's getting closer. Looks like a lone freighter."

Blakely's heart sank.

"Sir, what are your orders?" Harper said.

The Ultra message burned in Blakely's shirt pocket. This freighter had to be the *Arisan Maru*, given its position so far behind the other ships in the convoy. The decision tore at him.

"Any indication of destroyer escorts in the area?"

"No, sir."

Blakely looked to his executive officer. "Harp, prepare to dive."

"Aye, aye, sir," the XO said, elation in his voice. Harper dropped through the round hatchway and scrambled down the ladder into the submarine's conning tower.

"There she is, sir." A lookout perched high above Blakely pointed to the horizon.

"Confirmed. Dead ahead," the other lookout said. "Freighter. Big one."

"Any sign of the destroyer escorts?"

"Negative," both lookouts said.

The destroyers were likely hunting for the subs in his pack that had already fired torpedoes.

"All hands below," Blakely said.

Blakely descended halfway through the open hatchway, then paused to take a final look in the Japanese freighter's general direction. He tried to imagine the POWs locked in the hold, then wished he hadn't. He climbed down the metal ladder with that image in his head but forced himself to take command—confident, focused, on the hunt, and ready to kill—even if he did not feel that way.

"Secure the hatch," he ordered.

"Secure the hatch. Aye, aye, sir." A seaman climbed the ladder and cranked the round lid shut.

The hatch secure, Harper clicked on the 1MC, the ship-wide intercom system. "1MC," he said. "This is the XO. General quarters. Dive the boat. Dive. Dive. Dive."

Harper punched the dive alarm and a Klaxon sounded throughout the ship, the distinct *ah-OOH-ga, ah-OOH-ga.*

"Put us at periscope depth, full ahead," Blakely said.

"Periscope depth, aye, sir," the helmsman replied. "Full ahead."

In fifty-eight seconds, the *Shark* disappeared below the surface. The excitement on board was like an electric charge.

"Up periscope," Blakely said when the submarine leveled off. He grabbed the two black handles on the silver column as it rose from the floor. "Helm. Steady as she goes," Blakely said. He flipped a switch on the periscope, then leaned into its viewfinder. The submarine and its crew fell silent. "There she is," Blakely said, his voice almost a whisper. "Freighter. Six, seven thousand tons.

Down periscope." Blakely turned to the helmsman as the device retracted. "Slow to one-quarter."

"Slowing to one-quarter, aye, sir."

"Up periscope," Blakely said minutes later. The metal column again rose from the floor.

Blakely leaned into the viewfinder and spotted the Japanese ship. "Definitely a freighter." He moved away from the periscope for Harper to step to the glass.

The XO grabbed both its handles and peered through the viewfinder. "Confirmed, Skipper."

"Can you see any markings, Harp?" Blakely asked.

"Negative, sir. She's still too far."

"Let's get a little closer. Think they see us yet?" A submarine's periscope caused a visible wake on the water's surface.

"Negative, sir. She hasn't changed course." Harper stepped back from the periscope.

"Down periscope," Blakely said. "Let's make sure she isn't marked. Helmsman, change course, left to zero-nine-zero."

"Left, zero-nine-zero, aye, sir," came the reply.

"Up periscope," Blakely called a few minutes later. He spotted the freighter again, then added, "Twenty-five hundred yards. Harp, check me."

Harper slid in for a look. "Confirmed, twenty-five hundred yards."

"Any markings?" Blakely needed an excuse not to fire and hoped the target had red or blue crosses signaling nonmilitary cargo.

"Negative, sir," Harper replied. "Target is clean."

Excitement suffused Harper's voice. Blakely knew the entire crew ached to sink another ship. Harper stepped away from the periscope. Blakely stepped in for a final look. Tense seconds ticked by as the pressure built. Finally, Blakely said, "Full stop."

"All engines stop, aye, sir," the helmsman said. He eased the throttle back.

The submarine's two diesel engines cut, and the vessel coasted on momentum. Crewmen glanced around the room. Harper's voice broke the confused silence.

"Sir, shall we load forward torpedo tubes?"

"No," Blakely said. Feeling his face burning, he pressed it tighter against the periscope viewfinder, avoiding his crew. "We'll wait right here. See if she zigs back this way."

Blakely pulled back. When he did, he noticed Harper scanning the faces of the other men. As second-in-command, only he could challenge the skipper. He stepped to the periscope and spoke straight into Blakely's right ear, louder this time.

"Sir, should I alert the torpedo room?"

Blakely eased away from the eyepiece, struggling to give the order.

"Enoe," Harper said, using Blakely's nickname at Annapolis. "What is it?"

Blakely shook his head.

Harper studied him. "Sir, the torpedo room?" he asked, loudly enough for everyone to hear.

"Radio *Seadragon*," Blakely finally said, meaning another submarine in the pack. "Inform them we're going after this freighter." He spoke the words but could not swallow, his mouth and throat dry, an acidic burn inching up from his gut. He cleared his throat and spun around. Perspiration trickled from his temples. This was an order he did not want to follow—but it had to be done. The only question was whether he could do so without taking lives. "Load forward torpedoes, one, two, and three, ready four."

"Load forward torpedoes, one, two, and three, ready four, aye, aye, Skipper," Harper repeated, his voice thrumming with excitement. He punched the intercom. "Torpedo room, conn. Load forward torpedoes, one, two, and three. Ready four."

"Rev her up, Willie," Blakely said to his chief motor machinist. "Ahead one-quarter."

"One-quarter, aye, sir."

A calm, muffled response crackled over the intercom from the sub's front section. "Conn, torpedo room. Loading forward tubes, one, two, and three, ready four, aye, sir."

Every man on the sub moved with purpose, as trained. Blakely knew they had joined the Navy and chosen duty as submariners just for moments like this. They lived packed in cramped quarters, went weeks without showers, and breathed in dank air, but the next few minutes could make it all worthwhile.

"Stand by for my mark," Blakely ordered.

"Aye, sir, standing by," his chief torpedoman's mate said. He would wait for Blakely to confirm the TDC, or torpedo data computer, which calculated a valid firing solution based on a set of parameters including the torpedo's course and speed and the target bearing, range, speed, depth, and impact angle. If Blakely's torpedoman responded "Solution satisfactory," it meant the solution met certain criteria, such as having a lower error margin, a high probability of hitting the target, and a reasonable time to impact. It all depended, however, on Blakely's mark.

"Helm, maintain position," Blakely said. He pressed hard against the periscope viewfinder and took careful aim at the stern, the propeller. The shot would require all the skill the commander could muster, no room for error. "Steady . . . steady . . ." Blakely timed the freighter's speed and distance. "Mark."

The torpedoman shouted back, "Solution satisfactory, sir."

"Fire one," Blakely ordered.

"Fire one!"

The USS *Shark* shook as a blast of compressed air ejected a three-thousand-pound torpedo. Its steam-driven propellers whined as it cleared the submarine. The soundman listened through his black headphones as the torpedo sped away. "Running hot, straight, and normal, sir," he said.

Blakely peered through the periscope and raised an open hand.

Harper studied his stopwatch. "C'mon, c'mon."

The seconds ticked by. The Mark 14 torpedo quickly reached a top speed of forty-six knots.

"Missed her off the stern," Blakely said after ninety seconds. The men groaned. The *Arisan Maru* now knew it was under attack and had likely radioed the destroyers in the area. He didn't have much time.

Blakely turned to his chief torpedoman's mate and said, "Wait for my mark."

"Aye, aye, sir."

"Harp, ready two."

"Ready two," Harp said into the communications intercom.

"All right, here we go." Blakely pressed his face into the periscope again. When the little black crosshairs lined up exactly where he needed them, Blakely shouted, "Mark."

"Solution satisfactory," the torpedoman said.

"Fire," the skipper ordered.

"Fire two!"

"Fire two. Torpedo's running hot, straight, and normal," the soundman confirmed.

Another ninety seconds passed. "She missed off the bow," Blakely said. "Wait for me."

The destroyers now had additional precious minutes to respond before the submarine dove. Blakely pulled away and arched his back. He knew the eyes of his crew were upon him. "Okay, on my mark." He leaned into the periscope again. "Mark."

"Solution satisfactory."

"Fire three!"

"Fire three!"

Blakely hugged the periscope. He spun it left, then right. "What happened? Where is it?" His face mashed harder into the viewfinder.

Harper glanced at the radioman, who put both hands on his black headset, then shook his head.

"Conn, torpedo room," a voice crackled over the intercom. "Third fish is stuck in the tube."

"Full stop," Blakely yelled. He needed to shut down the engines before their vibration detonated the stuck torpedo.

The crew fell silent. The warhead lodged in the ship's bow carried six hundred pounds of volatile Torpex. It could explode any second. The blast would shear off the submarine's front third.

"Down periscope," Blakely said. He flipped the intercom switch and hoped his voice sounded calm. "Torpedo room, conn. What's going on down there, gentlemen?"

"Conn, torpedo room, aye, sir. Got a fish stuck in tube three. Elko's in there trying to wrench it free, but she's jammed good."

"Please urge Mr. Elko to make haste," Blakely said.

He clicked the intercom off and closed his eyes. Minutes were ticking by, time for the destroyer to find them on the surface.

Blakely had deliberately timed the first two torpedoes to comply with the TDC solution and hit the freighter, but to cause damage, not to sink it. Both had just missed. Now he wondered if the stuck torpedo's detonation would be his judgment.

5

BLASTED

The **Arisan Maru**
Luzon Strait, South China Sea
October 24, 1944, 4:50 p.m.

An impossibly loud siren pierced the hold. POWs covered their ears. In between blasts, Sam heard boots pounding on the metal deck.

"What's going on?" Father Tom shouted to Sam.

"I don't know, but it sounds like the Jap crew's running. Dozens of them."

"Attack," a raspy-voiced officer said from behind them. "The ship's under attack."

The ship's siren blasted a second time, then a third. The boot sounds returned, then stopped.

"Why have they stopped?" Father Tom asked.

"Don't know," Sam said.

Minutes later, the soldiers again stampeded across the deck, and the freighter turned so sharply Sam and the others lost their balance. He took a small step to regain his perch.

"Evasive maneuvers," the hoarse POW shouted. "Must be a sub launching torpedoes. They wouldn't bother turning if it was an airplane attack."

The hold came alive with chatter and cheers.

"Hit us, Navy!"

"Here we are! Don't miss."

"Please, God, help them sink us."

Sam, too, got caught up in the excitement, cheering like the others until hoarse. Then he realized the potential ramification of the attack and looked at Father Tom. "Hey, wait a goddamn minute," he said. "If this ship goes down, we go down with it."

The POWs around him fell quiet, an eerie silence. Then a POW yelled, "I don't give a shit. Just get us off this shithole."

"Damn right. C'mon, boys," another man shouted. "Sink us!"

Sam turned to Father Tom. "Pete's up top with Major Jones," he said. "They were stacking the bodies on deck for tonight's service."

The guards had only allowed two men on deck, a change in their routine.

Sam plunged into the crowd. Father Tom followed. They navigated toward the staircase leading to the hatch as the anxious POWs waited and listened. A sharp boom ricocheted through the hold, followed by two more explosions.

"Deck gun," Sam shouted. "They're firing the cannon."

"Torpedo," the hoarse POW officer called out. "They're trying to explode an incoming fish."

The deck gun fired yet again. The men leaned as the ship swerved and its diesel engines revved.

"Hang on," Sam said.

"The deck gun can't hit anything," the POW said. "The boat's rocking too much."

"What's that?" Sam said. The men paused, quiet, listening.

A new sound. Getting louder but difficult to discern over the thrum of the ship's engines.

"Sounds like a boat engine coming our way," Father Tom said.

"That's no boat engine," the officer said. "Torpedo! Hang on!"

The freighter lurched with the violent explosion, then shuddered and heaved out from under the POWs' feet, tossing them like rag dolls. Men screamed. The wounded vessel creaked. Father Tom recovered first and helped Sam to his feet. Sam felt stunned, the same sensation he'd felt during tank battles on Bataan.

"You okay?" Father Tom yelled, snapping Sam out of his moment of paralysis.

"Yeah, I'm good."

Sam scanned the devastation inside the hold. A tangled mess of twisted steel, bamboo, and bodies obscured by dust and smoke. The injured moaned and screamed. Some POWs got to their feet, but others lay still.

A second loud explosion again jolted the ship, and the concussive blast again floored the men. Father Tom and Sam scrambled to their feet and made their way toward the hatch. Sam started up the still-intact wooden staircase to find Chavez, but just three steps up, a commotion blocked his path. Major Jones tumbled down the stairs.

"Look out!" Sam shouted, dropping back down, but not before Major Jones hit him and knocked them both to the ground. The explosions had colored Jones's face and arms with a black mixture of soot and oil.

"I gotcha, sir." Sam assisted Jones to his feet. When he realized Pete Chavez had not dropped down the hatchway he said, "Where's Chavez?"

Major Jones grimaced in pain.

"Where's Chavez?" Sam repeated.

"Big explosion," Jones said through gritted teeth. "Fire everywhere."

"What about Chavez?" Sam leaned closer and clutched Major Jones's shoulders. His voice quaked. "Where is he?"

"I'm sorry, Sam," Major Jones said, shaking his head. "I don't know."

6

Careful What You Wish For

The USS **Shark**
Luzon Strait, South China Sea
October 24, 1944

As he had attempted with the first two torpedoes, Blakely had carefully aimed the third fish to disable but not sink the Japanese freighter, hitting it at the bow, forward of midship. But by the time the torpedo room had freed the fish, the *Arisan Maru* had maneuvered straight into its path.

"Direct hit," Blakely said in a thick voice, looking through the viewfinder and feeling a flood of emotions as flames swirled in a ball and shot skyward from the wounded vessel. "Hit her just aft of center."

The crew cheered.

Blakely pushed himself away from the periscope to make room for Harper, who would provide the verification required by Submarine Command. The thought of having just murdered hundreds of helpless POWs sickened Blakely, and he fought to keep his chow down and his emotions in check as his crew celebrated.

"Fish three detonated," Harper yelled, his face pressed into the periscope. "Fish three detonation confirmed."

The radioman announced the hit to the entire crew, and more cheers erupted throughout the sub. Their drought was over. The *Shark* and her starving crew had once again feasted.

Blakely flicked the intercom switch and cleared his throat of what felt like sludge. "Torpedo room, conn," he said. "Well done getting that fish out. Thought we were goners there for a second."

"Conn, torpedo room," came the reply. "Thank you, sir. Won't happen again."

Blakely returned to the periscope to study the burning freighter. A column of black smoke swirled hundreds of feet into the sky and obscured much of the ship. What remained of the four-hundred-foot Japanese vessel already listed. "God forgive me," Blakely whispered.

"Begging your pardon, sir," Harper said. "Shouldn't we dive? Those destroyers have been on alert for twenty-four hours searching for subs."

For a US Navy submarine in the South China Sea, it wasn't fight or flight: it was fight *and* flight. Firing a torpedo at a convoy, especially after the attack was already underway, was like swatting a hornet's nest. You took your shot and quickly fled before the Japanese destroyers gave chase. Subs on or near the surface were no match for a destroyer's firepower.

Blakely scanned the burning freighter, his eyes still glued to the periscope. He could not say it out loud, but he needed to know if any POWs had lived through the explosion.

"Sir," Harper persisted. "The convoy's escorts could spot us any second now that we've fired."

Blakely studied the wreckage. "Just need to confirm—"

"Oh, she'll sink," Harper interrupted. "Might take a while, but she'll go down. It's a kill for us, sir. All due respect, we need to get the hell out of here."

"Okay," Blakely conceded. "Fifteen-degree bubble. Dive the boat."

"Dive the boat," Harper ordered. He punched the intercom. "This is the XO, general quarters, alarm, dive. Dive. Dive." The entire sub sprang to action. The Klaxon horn again blared its alert. Harper slid in for a final look, spun the periscope full circle, then jerked back a quarter turn. "Contact!" he shouted. "Enemy destroyer. Bearing two-five-zero-zero yards and closing fast. She came in behind the smoke."

Blakely yanked Harper's elbow away from the periscope, looked through the viewfinder, and spotted the destroyer. "How long, Harp?" he asked.

"We'll be down in thirty seconds."

Might not be quick enough. "Go deep," Blakely called to his helmsman. "Left on two-seven-zero."

"Aye, sir. Left, two-seven-zero."

"Down periscope."

The submarine pitched downward, and the men grabbed the *Shark*'s ribs to stay on their feet. Seawater flooded the opened ballast tanks, helping the sub to dive. Sailors cranked the bow and stern plane wheels to angle the sub's descent.

"Make your depth four-zero-zero feet," Blakely ordered.

"Aye, sir, four-zero-zero feet," the helmsman replied.

Click-boom! The first depth charge exploded, and the submarine lurched. Men crashed to the floor. Lights flickered.

Blakely lifted himself off the floor onto one knee. "Full throttle, Leo."

"Aye, sir, full throttle."

Click-boom! A second explosion knocked more men to the floor. Again, they scrambled back to their feet. Blakely's crew had survived three different depth charge attacks during their first war patrol—a total of 179 explosions, many of them at close range. His crew would not panic.

"Harp, did you get a look at that destroyer?"

"Looked like the *Harukaze*, sir."

"Agreed," Blakely said. "She's got sonar now, according to other sub crews back in Pearl." Sonar bounced signals off objects in the water, making it possible to locate submerged submarines.

Click-boom! Another depth charge exploded. Men again fell to the floor like prizefighters taking punches. Again, they got back up. The *Harukaze*'s propellers rhythmically thumped as it passed overhead.

The men studied the ceiling, listening.

Blakely silently cursed himself. He should not have fired on the *Arisan Maru* at all. Then he had made a second mistake, lingering near the surface for too long to check for POWs. He'd put his sub and his men in grave peril.

"We can shake her, right, Skipper?" Harper asked.

"We're about to find out," Blakely said.

7

TRAPPED

The **Arisan Maru**
Luzon Strait, South China Sea
October 24, 1944

The absence of Pete Chavez pierced Sam's heart. War had taken so many friends, so many brothers-in-arms, but this cut was the deepest.

"Don't write him off just yet," Father Tom said. "He's probably hiding, waiting for his chance to escape."

"You're right," Sam said. "If anyone can make it, it's Pete. Probably gonna swim to Honolulu."

"But, Sam, right now, we have to save ourselves and everyone else."

"Water's rising fast," Major Jones called above the din. Seawater lapped at their ankles. "If we don't get out, we'll drown."

"Could be dangerous up top," Sam said to Jones. He studied the hatchway and strained to hear over the sound of rushing water, which had reached the first step. The level of tension rose. Chavez would not have hesitated to have a look up top. Sam wouldn't either. He didn't really have a choice, anyway. They couldn't stay in the hold.

"I'm gonna have a look. Japs or no Japs. Someone's gotta check."

Sam climbed the staircase. Halfway, he remembered the POW who'd tried to climb on deck only to get stabbed to death by a bayonet. Sam ascended high enough to poke his head through the open hatchway.

"What do you see?" Major Jones said. "Are they gone?"

Sam swiveled to check the view, then froze. Just twenty feet away, three Japanese guards crouched over a .50-caliber deck-mounted machine gun, the barrel pointed at the hatch. They locked bullets into the gun chamber with a metallic click.

Sam ducked, shouting, and scurried down the steps. "Machine gun. Take cover!"

Shots rang out, pinging against the metal. When the machine gun silenced, Sam got up from the floor and said, "They're waiting to mow us down as soon as we climb out."

"We can either drown in the hold or get machine-gunned to death," Major Jones said. "Not exactly the options I was hoping for."

"Wait a bit," Father Tom said. "They can't stay long. They'll have to abandon ship to save themselves."

"Begging your pardon, Padre," Sam said, looking at the rising water, "but we don't have a lot of time to wait them out."

A loudspeaker bellowed from above. Sirens wailed. More boots thumped on the deck. Minutes passed. Water had risen to the third step, above the POWs' knees.

The deck grew quiet. The footsteps and shouts faded.

"I'm gonna take another peek," Sam said.

Sam mounted the staircase. Halfway up, Yoshida appeared at the top. Sam froze.

"Going somewhere?" Yoshida snapped his fingers, pointed, and gave an order in Japanese. Snookie appeared beside him, holding the wooden hatch cover. "End of the line for all of you. I have enjoyed your company." Yoshida spat through the opening. "Now die like the rats you are."

Yoshida took one step back and Snookie lowered the six-by-six-foot cover across the opening.

Sam scrambled up the stairs and pounded on the cover, but it would hardly budge. Jones and Father Tom joined Sam, using their backs to try and raise the lid. Several other men also took turns, alone and in groups, but also gave up from exhaustion.

"It's no use," Major Jones said.

The engines stopped. The hold listed to the side with a slope upward toward the stern. It wasn't bad yet, but Sam felt the ship would eventually sink stern down.

The hold's usual din changed to the sound of rushing water.

The deck had also grown quiet. "Japs must've left," Sam said. "Saved themselves but left us to die."

Father Tom took a deep breath, gripped his crucifix, and recited the Lord's Prayer, a prayer Sam's mother had said every night during the Depression. The thought of home made him grip the hem of his vest. He felt Sarah's hidden ring. The thought of never seeing her again, or his family, broke his heart. During his years in camp and through all the abuse, the ring had always brought him hope. Not this time.

His fingers touched the pocketknife. "Holy shit," he said. He looked to Father Tom. "Holy shit," he said again, louder.

"What is it?" Father Tom said.

Sam tore at the hem.

"Sam?" Father Tom said.

Sam slid Sarah's freed ring on his bony middle finger and pulled out the knife. "Maybe a damned miracle, Padre," he shouted. "I can cut the ropes . . . if I can reach them." He scrambled back up the stairs. Those below him gathered, chins tilted up, watching, cheering him on. Sam tried to get the knife blade between the hatch cover and the deck, but he didn't have enough room to reach the rope tying the cover closed. He climbed down and sat, mentally and physically exhausted.

Father Tom turned to Major Jones and asked, "How long do you think we have?"

"An hour or two, max," Jones said. He looked to the ship's stern. "But if that bulkhead collapses, we're gone in minutes."

POWs shouted throughout the hold. Hysteria and panic set in.

"Stop!" A shout rang out. "Stop, dammit." The POWs gradually silenced. "For God's sake, stop it." Major Jones's entire body shook. Men froze in place. Jones took a deep breath. "Boys, I don't have any words of encouragement. We're in a hell of a jam. But we've been in jams before. Remember who the enemy is. Remember who we are fighting for." He straightened and spread his shoulders. "We're American soldiers. Remember that, above all else. We are American soldiers. And we're going to play it that way to the very end. We don't quit and we don't panic. Not while any one of us can still draw a breath."

It was more rah-rah than reality, but hundreds of POWs cheered. Major Jones let the emotion run, then raised a hand for silence. "Men, I've asked Father Tom to say a few words." Jones turned to the chaplain and Sam heard him whisper, "I hope they're good ones, Padre."

For the moment, the POWs ignored the rising seawater now lapping at their knees. They focused on the staircase and Father Tom's dimly lit figure.

"Please, Lord," Father Tom said, his voice strong and confident, "if it be Thy plan to call us now, give us the courage to go as men." He lifted his crucifix high into the air and raised his voice. "The Book of Isaiah says, 'When you pass through the waters, I will be with you, and through the rivers, they will not overflow you. When you walk through the fire, you will not be burned, and flame will not scorch you.'" Father Tom paused. "Do not give in to your fear. This is not yet the end."

"Nice going, Padre," Sam said from where he sat on the top stair. He pointed at the closed hatchway. "Now, can you order us up a miracle and get that goddamn hatch removed?"

A voice boomed from the darkness. "Let's get the hell out of this shithole." *Rudowski.*

The man, still enormous, emerged from the shadows. And charged up the staircase like a bull released from its chute. Rudowski squared his feet on a stair, bent at the waist, and pressed his broad back against the roped hatch cover. Then he moved his feet up a step and straightened his legs. His back heaved and he roared a primal scream. The hatch creaked and lifted. Not more than an inch, but it lifted. Rudowski adjusted his angle and growled, straining, and expelling great blasts of air. The wooden hatch cover moved another inch, enough that sunlight danced around the edge.

"Hold it up," Sam said, climbing the stairs as he flipped open the pocket-knife's blade.

Rudowski took a deep breath, again put his back to the hatch, and strained, lifting it. Sam slipped the knife blade outside the opening created at the edge and sawed back and forth. "Keep pushing," he told Rudowski, his arm quickly numb from exhaustion.

"Do it," a soldier shouted from below.

"Do it, Carlson! Get us the hell out of here."

Sam refused to give in to the pain, or his exhaustion. He screamed and continued sawing. Seconds later, the wooden hatch cover made a cracking sound, the rope snapped, and the hatch popped up on one side. Rudowski climbed one step higher, arched his back again, and raised the open hatch until it tilted at an angle. Light embraced him and flooded in.

"Hold it," Sam shouted. "One more rope."

Sam stepped up, switched the blade to his other hand, and cut at the second rope. It was easier with more room. He sawed until Rudowski sprang up with a loud grunt and pushed the hatch so hard it popped into the air. The giant paused, then turned and looked down at Sam. "We're even, Carlson." Without another word, Rudowski stepped from the hold onto the deck and marched off.

Sam climbed to the top step. The *Arisan Maru*'s deck was empty of guards. The ship listed at an angle, with the stern higher than the bow but not so steep that the men could not walk on it. Not yet anyway. He moved to the railing. Their Japanese captors were rowing lifeboats to a destroyer two hundred yards away. Sam hurried back to the hold and yelled, "It's all clear. Japs are gone. Let's go. Move!"

The POWs were free for the first time in two and a half years. Still in one hell of a predicament, but free. Sam reached down a hand to help others climb the staircase to the deck. It was made easier because the stern was pitched upward. "Let's go. One at a time."

The men did not rush the staircase. Many were too weak to do so. Major Jones reached topside, and he and Sam helped the others. Father Tom refused to go up, staying at the bottom to push soldiers too weak to climb, ignoring the rising water.

The POWs emerged from the hold as they had descended into it, after what now seemed a lifetime ago: one at a time. Some collapsed to their knees and lifted their arms to the sky, as if reborn. Others, animated skeletons, looked like walking dead, swatting at the bright light, haunted and crazed by it. A few stumbled to the railing and toppled overboard. Others threw them pieces of wood and other debris that would float.

The ship moaned and creaked, then listed farther, the stern rising another few feet.

By the time the last man had emerged from the hold, the water had nearly reached Father Tom's thighs. Sam helped the chaplain climb through the hatchway onto the slanted deck. Emerging, Father Tom tilted back his head and whispered, "Thank you, Lord."

"Don't thank him just yet, Padre. Look for life jackets. The Japs in the boats weren't wearing any. I'm going to look for Pete."

Sam stumbled across the deck shouting Chavez's name, not seeing him, not hearing a response. He also didn't see bodies on the deck. Those that had been stacked for the burial service had likely gone overboard when the ship was hit. He could only hope Chavez had somehow gotten off.

Father Tom called out to him from beside two large lockers. When Sam looked back, the priest lifted a life jacket. Sam hurried to him and found the lockers filled. He'd never worn a life jacket but knew from scuttlebutt that the stuffing inside—a tropical tree fiber called kapok—would keep a person afloat for about three hours. After that, the waterlogged jacket sank like a rock. Sam picked up a jacket from the pile, started to put it on, then stopped. He raised the life jacket high above his head for the others to see.

"Come and get 'em, boys!"

He tossed the jackets to the men on deck. Father Tom, Major Jones, and Sam helped dozens don the jackets and lace up the sides. As the men got their life jackets, some jumped over the railing, saying they feared the suction when the ship sank.

The exodus underway, Sam grabbed a life jacket for Father Tom. "Put this on."

Sam threaded the chaplain's arm through a hole, then spun him around to insert the other, but the chaplain grabbed Sam's arm, stopping him. At the ship's bow more POWs were staggering from the forward hold, covered in coal dust, soot from burning fuel and oil, and blood.

Sam and Father Tom rushed to the opening in the deck and knelt to help those crawling out. Their Japanese captors had taken the ladder they'd used to load the men, so the survivors had stacked corpses and used the human pyramid to climb out. Behind them, waves lashed at a hole in the bow. When the waves receded, they took lifeless floating bodies.

Father Tom made the sign of the cross. "Lord have mercy." He slipped from his life jacket and gave it to another POW. "There aren't enough."

Sam didn't know much about ships, but he was now confident from the listing, which raised the stern, enough now that the men had to lean forward, that the wounded freighter would soon sink, and he did not want to be sucked down with it. He looked to the Japanese destroyer, where dozens of desperate American soldiers had swum. Japanese sailors lined the railing, using long poles to force the struggling swimmers away from the boat. Others pinned the POWs under the water, drowning them.

Sam spotted another Japanese destroyer farther away, slicing through the water and launching fifty-five-gallon canisters off its stern into the sea. "Depth charges," he said to Father Tom. "They're chasing the submarine that fired the torpedoes."

"Poor guys are catching hell," Father Tom said as another depth charge hit the water.

The deck was chaos. POWs holding anything that might float jumped over the railing.

Others shuffled on the slanted deck toward the ship's galley, emerging with food, and Sam realized that no matter what happened next, he and Father Tom would need food and water to survive in the South China Sea.

"I'm going to see if there's any chow or fresh water left." Sam followed other POWs into the ship, the doorways perched at an angle.

In the ship's galley, a surreal orgy of eating had begun. Starved POWs ate from twenty-pound bags of uncooked rice spilled on the floor. Others poured vegetable oil, ketchup, or sugar down their throats. Sam stepped past them and ripped open drawers and cupboard doors, hunting for food, finding them empty. Then he opened a cabinet and found stacks of shoebox-sized Red Cross packages. He tore a box open and found powdered milk, coffee, margarine, vitamins, a can of jam, peanut butter, and toiletries.

Sam stuffed a whole chocolate bar in his mouth, grabbed as many packages as he could hold, and quickly went back out, handing the packages to any man still on deck and keeping a few for himself and Father Tom. Where was the priest? Sam spun in a circle, searching, and spotted Father Tom near the hatch.

Then, to Sam's horror, the priest descended back down into the ship's hold.

8

Run Silent. Run Deep.

The USS **Shark**
Luzon Strait, South China Sea
October 24, 1944

The USS *Shark* descended, but not quickly enough. Depth charges exploded all around the hull. The men were repeatedly knocked down and scrambled to their feet.

"Passing two-five-zero feet, sir," the helmsman said in between blasts. "Approaching the thermocline." A thermocline, a layer of colder water, had a different density that distorted sonar signals from above. Submarines used them to hide from enemy ships.

"Continue to four-two-five feet," Blakely repeated. The skipper pulled a white handkerchief from his hip pocket and dabbed sweat from his upper lip and forehead.

Click-boom!

The *Shark* rang like a bell and shuddered. Sailors again fell, and again struggled back to their feet. This explosion felt closer than the first dozen. Reports indicated that pipes sprang leaks, and high-pressure water sprayed crewmen fore and aft. Light bulbs, spritzed by cold seawater, popped. A few men vomited from fear, turbulence, or both.

Click-boom!

The next concussion blew out the *Shark*'s lights. Emergency lights cast the crew in an eerie red glow. Pipes split, releasing geysers of steam, and cork insulation fell on the crew. The sub yawed and tilted to one side, pinning crewmen to the walls.

"Damage report," Harper said to the radioman. "Damage report. All stations."

"Right one-quarter turn," Blakely said, his voice urgent but not panicked. "Wiggle us down."

"Approaching four-two-five feet, sir," the helmsman said. "We're below the thermocline."

"Level off at four-two-five feet," Blakely said. He turned to Harper. "Rig her for silent running, Harp. Now."

The ship leveled. The crew shut down the ventilation blowers, air-conditioning, and refrigerator motors. Men took off their shoes to reduce noise. Nonessential crewmen climbed into bunks to conserve air. An anxious sailor stood between every compartment, ready to seal its watertight door to limit flooding. The submarine inched forward at two miles per hour on battery power. The depth charges became more intermittent, then stopped.

Harper broke the silence. "Did we shake her?" he whispered.

"Maybe." Blakely stared at the ceiling.

A faint pinging sound broke the silence. All eyes scanned the ceiling and walls as the *Harukaze*'s sonar grew louder.

Ping. Ping. Ping.

The destroyer's propellers churned straight overhead.

"They found us," Blakely said just before another depth charge exploded.

Click-boom!

The *Shark*'s stern lifted, tossing crewmen. The hull popped and clanged.

"Damage?" Blakely whispered, getting up from the floor.

The radioman gripped his black headset. "Electrical damage, forward torpedo room," he whispered. Then he gestured at his control panel and ran a finger across his throat. "Radio's out. Radar screen is frozen." He paused, listening to more updates. When he spoke, his voice was quiet but urgent. "Leaks but no flooding. Half a dozen minor injuries."

Click-boom!

Another depth charge exploded. This one closer still. The men all knew an explosion closer than twenty-five feet—within the "kill zone"—would destroy the sub.

"They found us, all right." Harper rose to his knees, then stood. "Now what?"

"Pray," Blakely said.

9

Give That Little Extra

The **Arisan Maru**
Luzon Strait, South China Sea
October 24, 1944

Sam knew Father Tom was looking for soldiers too weak to climb out of the hold on their own, that he refused to leave even one man behind. But to reenter the ship's hold was surely suicide, as fast as it was filling with water. Sam dropped the Red Cross packages, swore, and rushed down the angled and listing deck to the hold. He descended halfway down the staircase, shouting Father Tom's name over the spray of water, and searching for him in the murky air.

"Over here," Father Tom replied.

Sam jumped down the remaining steps into the water, which now reached his waist, and shoved it aside with each step forward.

"What are you doing? We have to go, Padre," Sam said when he reached the priest.

"Quickly, this way." Father Tom led Sam to a makeshift platform just above the water level. An injured POW lay on it, still conscious. Two other POWs stood by holding a blanket.

"Shit," Sam said. "How many still down here?"

"Maybe a dozen," one of the two men said.

"Too many, Padre," Sam said, shaking his head.

"Not if we hurry. If we hurry, we can get them all out before the ship goes down." He held out the blanket. "Grab a corner. We'll take them out one at a time."

The four men lifted the dying soldier onto the blanket, grabbed the ends, and carried him.

"Good news, buddy," Sam said, doing his best to imitate Pete Chavez. "You've been upgraded to a new cabin. Finest view on the *Stinko Maru*."

A faint smile crossed the injured soldier's face.

The stretcher crew struggled around and over broken rafters, beams, bamboo bunks, twisted metal, and other hidden debris. When they reached the stairs, they struggled with the POW, but at least the angled stairs, not nearly as steep as before, helped them. On the slanting deck, they lowered the man, and Sam and the other litter carriers put their hands on their knees, utterly depleted. No way they could haul the rest out on their own.

What the hell was he going to do?

If he wanted to get the priest off the ship, he needed to think fast, and *act*.

"I'm going to find more help," he said to the others. "We can't do this by ourselves."

Sam now had to watch his footing as he climbed up the stern to Major Jones, seated in an area with other wounded men. He told him Father Tom needed help. Jones spread the word to men who had not yet jumped overboard, most of them officers. About a dozen grabbed whatever they could find to use as litters, and they descended back into the hold.

Each time Sam's team descended that staircase, fear gripped him, as he knew it gripped the others, some of whom made no secret of their feelings, muttering that the task was foolish, not least because the men in the hold were too weak to survive. *That may be*, Sam thought, but he also knew Father Tom wouldn't stop until they were all out. And in that moment, Sam realized maybe that was the only thing that separated a hero and a coward. The coward faced mortal danger and fled. The hero kept doing his job. This was his turn to do his job. Foolish or not, he wasn't going to run.

One by one, they hauled the dying men up onto the deck and to the stern, the highest part of the sinking ship. When Sam at last lowered the final POW from the hold, he was so spent it was all he could do to not just lie down beside him. He looked down at the soldier he had momentarily saved. His arms, covered in blood, rested over his torso, where entrails oozed from his stomach.

"Come closer," the man whispered.

Sam dropped to a knee beside him. A peaceful expression washed over the man's face. "Thank you," he said. "I didn't want to die alone down there." Then he shut his eyes.

Sam rocked back onto his ass, hugged his knees, and wept. When he had recovered enough to survey the deck around him, he saw Father Tom rolling clothing collected from the dead into makeshift pillows and offering the soldiers lying on the deck reassuring words. Father Tom lowered a man's head and approached Sam. "Help me hear these men's last confessions. Hold them up. Comfort them."

"I'll do it, Padre, but you have to promise me that when we finish, you'll get off this ship with me."

"Hold their heads up for me," Father Tom said.

Though his arms and legs ached, Sam did as Father Tom asked. The chaplain stepped to a supine man, and Sam gently lifted the soldier to a seated position. Father Tom leaned close to the man and whispered, "Go ahead, son."

The injured soldier made the sign of the cross. "Bless me, Father, for I have sinned. My last confession was eight months ago. These are my sins."

The dying soldier confessed to shooting a fellow American during the confusing heat of battle, to stealing food from another prisoner, and other sins.

"May God grant you pardon and peace," Tom said, using his wooden crucifix. "I absolve you of your sins. In the name of the Father, and of the Son, and of the Holy Spirit."

Sam laid the soldier's head down, and he and Father Tom moved to the next soldier in line. The *Arisan Maru* groaned, shifted, and listed further. The stern raised a little higher still. Their time was nearly up.

Father Tom and Sam traveled from dying man to dying man. Sam tried not to think about the end—how the ship could suck him into the dark ocean depths. He looked to the line of soldiers remaining and put a hand on Father Tom's arm. "Not enough time to hear every confession, Padre. We can't get to them all."

Father Tom looked over the dozens of remaining men. "I'll absolve the entire group—a general absolution. Before I do, would you like to confess your sins, Sam?" Father Tom didn't wait for an answer. He placed his hand on Sam's forehead and traced the sign of the cross. "Your sins are forgiven, Sam."

Sam moved to where Major Jones lay on the deck. Injuries from the torpedo blast, the major's malaria, and other ailments had weakened him to the point that he could no longer stand. Sam gently raised Jones to a seated position. Jones grimaced. "How many're left on board?"

"Maybe a hundred," Sam said.

Jones nodded to Father Tom, who approached down the line. "You two need to get off. That's an order." He began tugging at his life jacket. "Help me out of this thing."

"No, Major," Sam protested.

"It isn't going to do a dead man any good."

Free of his life jacket, Jones gave it to Sam but nodded to the priest as Father Tom reached them. "Make sure he puts it on, and the two of you get off this ship. That's an order." Jones again grimaced in pain. When it passed, he asked, "Father, what's your rank?"

"First lieutenant."

"Not anymore." Jones put his hand on Father Tom's shoulder and took a deep breath. "US military regulations authorize me to make battlefield promotions. I hereby promote you, for exceptional service above and beyond the call of duty to these men and to your country, *Captain* Thomas Scecina."

Something detonated somewhere inside the ship, causing it to shudder and groan. Sam dropped the major, but Jones used what strength he had left to prop himself up on his elbows and continue speaking. "I gave you a direct order, Captain. You should not have even been on this ship. The Japanese excused you."

Sam looked to Father Tom. "Is this true?"

"Of course it's true," Jones said. "The Japanese excused chaplains. Tom volunteered to stay with the men. Go on. Both of you. Now."

As if on cue, the ship again shifted and the bow dropped violently, toppling Sam and Father Tom. Sam rose to his knees, then his feet. "You heard the major, Padre. We gotta jump ship now."

Father Tom looked out over the dying, then glanced to the heavens before he reengaged Sam. Sam grabbed the priest's arm and threaded it through an opening in the life jacket, then turned him and pulled it around his back to his other arm.

"You've done more than I had a right to ask of you," Father Tom said. "You need to go, Sam. You need to get home to Sarah and your family."

Sam threaded the priest's other arm and began tightening the strings around his emaciated body. "That makes two of us, Padre."

"This is my purpose, Sam. These men. This moment."

Sam shook his head. "I can't leave you here, Padre. Direct order."

"I know. Walk with me for a second." Father Tom gripped Sam's elbow and guided him to the ship's railing, which, because of the boat's angle, was at Sam's hip.

"You have to live, Sam. Someone needs to tell the people back home what happened here and in the camps. Someone needs to show them where the bodies are buried. You need to be a witness for all these men. That's your new mission, Sam. Your new purpose for being."

"We'll both do that, Father."

"Not me," Father Tom said.

Sam realized what the priest was saying. Orders or no orders, he didn't intend to jump. "I can't go without you," he said.

"I know." Father Tom pulled Sam close, hugged him, then whispered, "May God bless you. And forgive me."

He shoved Sam hard in the chest. Sam's backside hit the railing and he pitched backward, tumbling over it, off balance, and descended into the South China Sea.

10

Baptism

The cold water took Sam's breath away, disorienting him. Thanks to the life jacket, he shot upward and breached the surface. It took a moment to get his bearings. All around him debris and men floated. Some POWs swam awkwardly away from the sinking freighter in their life jackets. Sam looked back to the ship and spotted Father Tom at the railing, a shadow backlit by the fading sun. The priest raised his arms, one holding his crucifix, high above his head in what was no doubt one final blessing.

Then he stepped back, until Sam could no longer see him.

"No!" Sam yelled.

A man swimming nearby called out to him. "Hey! We gotta get clear!"

Sam swam a few strokes toward the ship, which now rode just five feet above the water, but waves, current, and wind pushed him away.

"No," he again shouted, unsure and disbelieving. Men and debris floated past, the men issuing warnings about the ship's pull when it sank.

With nothing left to do, Sam whispered a silent goodbye to the friends who had helped keep him alive in the camps and on the ship. First Pete Chavez, now Father Tom and Major Paul Jones. All gone.

Then he turned and swam.

A strong current pulled Sam from the wounded freighter, a hundred yards, then more. His muscles quickly tired and he took a break, letting the current do his job for him. A dozen POWs clinging to a large piece of wood from the ship floated by him, paddling with their hands, bits of wood, and other debris. He spotted another group of perhaps two dozen men gripping a cluster of boxes, poles, crates, oilcans, boards, and other items lashed together using strips of clothing and wire ripped from the crates. Sam stroked toward them and called out, "Coming in." He reached for a handhold.

"Got to be the ugliest raft ever," a POW said, pulling Sam in. "But at least she floats."

Minutes later, another POW on the raft pointed over Sam's shoulder. "The ship's going down."

Sam turned and looked back into the fading light. The *Arisan Maru*'s stern rose like the head of a whale breaching the surface, seemed to bob for a moment, then sank beneath the waves. Great bubbles boiled at the surface as the ocean claimed six thousand tons of metal. The whole ending struck Sam as not violent, but peaceful.

A man on board the raft pointed to the water and shouted. "Good piece off the starboard side."

Sam spotted the square piece of wood roughly twenty yards away and yelled, "I'll get it." He rolled into the water and swam. His heavy arms chopped the water in slow strokes, and the bulky vest made it feel like he wasn't getting anywhere. Doubt crept in and he turned back to the raft, but the current, wind, and waves had pushed it too far away. Sam would never catch it. Without options, he summoned what strength he had left and swam to the wooden square. He grabbed it, caught his breath, then dragged his upper body from the water.

The strong currents pulled Sam and the others farther from where the *Arisan Maru* had sunk, and the debris field increased in size. Sam could see men splash and hear them scream, but in time their voices, too, grew faint. He floated past corpses, turning them over when he could, hoping to find a canteen of water. Anything to eat.

Then, the corpses were gone too.

Darkness descended, and for the first time in nearly three years, Sam was alone.

PART 5

1

LETTING GO

As night fell, a strong wind had picked up, chilling Sam to the bone. Distant shouts in the darkness had floated across the water, though it could have been his imagination playing tricks on him. He'd heard voices shouting "Sharks!" and had pulled his feet and arms from the water, tucking his knees tight to his chest. For hours, desperate and drowning men had pleaded for help, until those voices had faded to silence. An eerie quiet took their place, and Sam had wondered if he was the last man alive.

After what seemed an eternity, but was just a matter of hours, a faint reddish-orange light broke on the eastern horizon. Sam had lived through the night. The glow quickly grew into the most radiant, beautiful sunrise he had ever seen. He shielded his eyes to witness it, a swell rose, and he spotted something in the water, though so out of place, so unlikely, he couldn't bring himself to accept it as real. Was he delirious? Seeing things? He squinted hard and moved his hand to shield his eyes. When the next swell rose he saw it again.

A white lifeboat.

He opened and closed his eyes, still disbelieving. The lifeboat disappeared in another trough, then rose again on another crest.

Not a dream. Real.

He flopped onto his stomach and paddled for several minutes, but his hatch cover spun in circles, getting him nowhere. The sun on the horizon silhouetted the lifeboat, and he recognized it as one the Japanese had used to escape the sinking *Arisan Maru*. He tried to judge the distance, cognizant of what had happened when he'd left the raft and swum for the hatch cover. The cover would drift too far away in the current and wind for him to return if he abandoned it. He would drown.

He laughed at the absurdity of his reasoning.

He was alone, adrift in the Pacific Ocean, without food, water, or shelter from the sun during the day or the frigid night air, and he was worrying he might drown?

He took a final look at the lifeboat and chose his only real option if he wanted to survive. He tipped off the piece of wood into the South China Sea. The cold water again shocked his senses, more intensely this time. His chest tightened and he struggled to breathe. But the jolt also rejuvenated him, and he pushed himself into motion. He took a single stroke, then another. He didn't swim for the boat, but for where he hoped to intercept it. He lowered his head and kicked and stroked with his arms using everything he had, knowing exhaustion or hypothermia would quickly claim him.

A grueling fifteen minutes passed. Fatigue did indeed creep in, but Sam refused to give in to it. He sang movie tunes in his head to beat back negative thoughts. When he looked up, the lifeboat bobbed in the swells. Closer. He drove himself toward it.

He kept closing the door to exhaustion and doubt and fought to keep his head above water. He told himself he was making progress, to keep going. He had to survive. Like Father Tom had said, he had to get home. He had to let everyone know what had happened to all these men.

Fifty feet from the lifeboat, he sucked in a deep breath and mustered what little energy he had left for a final push.

The lifeboat grew closer still.

Ten more strokes.

Another ten.

A dozen.

He reached the boat after a final ten, utterly spent, and realized another, unconsidered problem. The gunwale, the lifeboat's edge, rocked four feet above the water's surface. Sam couldn't reach it. His legs felt as heavy as lead. He knew he had no chance with the water-soaked life jacket weighing him down. He tried not to dwell upon the irony of having swum all this way only to drown inches from the lifeboat. He removed the jacket, then took a deep breath, and slipped below the surface. He launched himself upward, kicking as hard as he could and reaching up with his arms. His fingers gripped the edge for a moment, then slipped. He fell back, descending beneath the surface. He gathered himself and kicked a second time, reaching. Again he grabbed the edge only to feel it slip from his grasp.

"Dammit."

As he descended beneath the surface a third time, he knew it would be for one final push. He kicked and rose from the water. This time something, or someone, clasped his wrists—the salt water blurred his vision and his rescuer's face. Hands shifted to his armpits and pulled even harder. *Chavez,* he thought. It would be just like the son of a gun to commandeer a Japanese lifeboat. Probably had a smorgasbord of food and water on board with him too.

Sam's torso flopped over the hard, narrow gunwale and he tumbled into the boat's basin. He balled into a fetal position, violently coughing, gagging, and spitting up seawater. When he stopped heaving, he clutched the lifeboat's edge and pulled himself to a seated position. The sun silhouetted his rescuer in shadow. Sam leaned his head to the side so the man's body blocked the bright sunlight.

His Good Samaritan was not Pete Chavez.

"Nice of you to drop in," Rudowski said.

2

More Bad News

FRUPAC
Honolulu, Hawaii
October 25, 1944

Three days had passed since Sarah had told Commander Holmes about the maru carrying eighteen hundred POWs. His response—the Allies would have no choice but to sink the ship, which also contained military supplies, lest they reveal they had broken the Japanese JN-25 code—had made Sarah question everything she had done since leaving Eagle Grove. She had wanted to increase Sam's chances of surviving. Now she wondered if her good intentions had doomed him and those she had sought to help.

This morning, Sarah again carried grave news to Commander Jasper Holmes's office. "Sir," she said, knocking as she entered Holmes's open office door without awaiting his reply. Two other analysts squeezed past her on their way out. Analysts within FRUPAC had been updating Holmes nonstop since MacArthur's troops landed on Leyte and pushed inland against nearly half a million Japanese troops. At sea, the Imperial Japanese Navy had arrived for a final, all-or-nothing battle between hundreds of ships, and earlier in the day, reports trickled in of Japanese forces crashing squadrons of airplanes into US ships, emphasizing how desperate Japan had become. According to JICPOA intercepts, the Japanese called these "kamikaze" raids, which meant "divine wind." The explosions had resulted in the sinking of two dozen US ships.

Holmes turned from the wall map and looked at Sarah through bloodshot eyes. "What do you have, Ensign Haber?"

"Radio intercept from the MATA-30 convoy—" Sarah had to stop to catch her breath. "I'm sorry, sir."

"Take your time."

Sarah hadn't slept much since delivering the message about the *Arisan Maru*. She was running on fumes. "In the Luzon Strait. The Japanese destroyer *Harukaze* reports sinking a sub." She extended the white index card toward Holmes, who took and read it. News of a US submarine trumped all other messages in terms of priority. Holmes read the index card out loud. "*Harukaze* dropped seventeen depth charges. Bubbles, heavy oil, clothing, cork rose to surface. *Gekichin.*"

Sarah had not bothered to translate the last word. Everyone in FRUPAC knew *gekichin* stood for "sunken enemy ship."

Holmes plucked a piece of paper off his desk, then moved to his large wall map and cleared his throat. "We've had nine subs hitting the MATA-30 convoy off and on for more than forty-eight hours." He studied the black magnets. "Let's see who's checked in." Holmes read from the paper. After a moment, he said, "All but the *Shark*. Haven't been able to raise it on the radio either. I know the skipper, Edward Blakely. Izzy and I had him over for supper during their last layover."

"Sir," Sarah said, "if I may ask, what was the last communication from the *Shark*?"

"Certainly." Holmes went back to his desk, shuffled through the messages, and picked up another card. "Looks like *Seadragon* got a radio message already," Holmes said. "*Shark* reported radar contact, a single freighter trailing well behind the convoy. Said they were commencing to attack."

Sarah stepped to the wall map and touched a finger to it. "That would put them about here." She placed her right index finger on the map to mark the submarine's location. She turned. "Commander, where exactly did the *Harukaze* report sinking the sub?"

Holmes scanned the intercept for the coordinates. "North twenty degrees, forty-one minutes," he said.

Sarah slid her left index finger to the correct latitude.

"East one nineteen, twenty-seven," Holmes said.

Sarah traced her left finger eastward across the map. Her two index fingers met—one for the Japanese destroyer, the other for the missing submarine—and the last wisp of hope evaporated from the room. Neither Sarah nor Holmes needed to speak. They both knew the sub sunk had been the *Shark*.

Holmes had explained official procedure to Sarah in the event of a submarine sinking after the USS *Seawolf* went down. He would walk to Submarine Command in the building next door and deliver the bad news in person. By evening, Submarine Command would send a typed form letter to the head of Pacific Command.

> *It is with the deepest regret the Commander, Submarine Force, Pacific Fleet, reports the USS* Shark *is overdue from her third war patrol and must be presumed to be lost.*

Next, the Navy would send telegrams to the families of the *Shark's* eighty-seven men, informing them their husbands, sons, and fathers were missing.

> *The Navy Department deeply regrets to inform you your [husband/ son], [name and rank], is missing following action while in the service of his country. The Department appreciates your great anxiety but details are not now available and delay in receipt thereof must necessarily be expected. To prevent possible aid to our enemies and to safeguard the lives of other personnel, please do not divulge the name of his ship or station or discuss publicly the fact that he is missing.*

Sarah knew one more detail about the process that she had also learned from Holmes. The crew and the sub were not "missing." Just as she had after looking at the wall map, Submarine Command would have a strong idea where the sub and its men would forever lay at the sea's bottom. And Sarah couldn't help but think she had also sent those husbands, sons, and brothers to their deaths, along with the eighteen hundred POWs on the maru the *Shark* had sunk.

As a commissioned officer, Sarah could never tell anyone what she had done. She would have to live with her horrific secret, alone.

Her penance.

3

SURVIVORS

The USS **Shark**
Luzon Strait, South China Sea
October 25, 1944, 6:30 a.m.

"Status report," Blakely whispered, reclaiming his position next to the periscope.

"Still running silent. Eight hours since we logged a depth charge," Harper replied, also in a whisper. "All repairs complete except for radar and radio. It's a short somewhere. Engineering will have to check about two miles of wire to find it. But it looks like our trick worked."

Desperate to escape the *Harukaze*, Blakely had ordered his crew to blast debris from the torpedo tubes. A mass of cork, pillows, clothing, and oil had floated to the surface as if the submarine had sunk. Then the *Shark* had quietly circled, returning to where they had attacked the *Arisan Maru*. Blakely had other intentions.

"Let's hope. Surface and take a look. The sun will be up."

"Aye, sir."

Harper quietly issued the orders, and crewmen busied themselves. After playing dead for ten hours, the USS *Shark* climbed to the surface. Blakely flipped an overhead intercom switch and said, "Helm, take us to periscope depth. Tell the men we may be taking on passengers."

"Aye, sir. Periscope depth," the helmsman said from the control room. "Prepare to take on passengers."

"Passengers?" Harper asked. "All due respect, why take the risk to save a few Jap sailors? We're damn lucky to be alive. We need to get back and make repairs."

Blakely ignored Harper's comment. He'd expected this pushback.

"We don't have room for a bunch of Jap prisoners," Harper said to Blakely, inches behind him. "Not enough food or water either."

Harper was correct. The *Shark* had left Pearl Harbor on September 23 with orders to return home in forty days. Their war patrol was more than two-thirds complete, and their finely calibrated supply of food two-thirds depleted.

Blakely traced a finger on his map, down current from where they had torpedoed the freighter.

"Five-zero feet," the helmsman called. "Periscope depth, sir."

"Up periscope," Blakely said. He took a deep breath and stepped toward the cylindrical column as it rose from the floor. He scanned the sea while the *Shark* glided just below the surface. "No planes or ships in sight. Clear. Take her up. Prepare to charge batteries."

"Aye, aye, sir, coming up," the helmsman said. He brought the submarine to the surface, and it cruised northward in the first light of dawn. Clear skies and calm seas.

"Give me five lookouts," Blakely barked. "If there are men in the water, we'll spot them from up top."

Five sailors climbed onto the open-air bridge, scanning with binoculars. Deep in Japanese territory, they knew to watch not only for floating men but also for enemy planes, subs, and destroyers.

"Man the deck gun," Blakely ordered after he and Harper had joined the lookouts on the bridge.

"Aye, Skipper," Harper said. He leaned toward the open hatchway on the floor and shouted into the conning tower, "Man the deck gun."

A voice from below repeated the order. "Manning the deck gun. Aye, sir."

The sub's forward hatch opened, and three men climbed out. They unstrapped the five-inch MK-17 deck gun with its ten-foot barrel, then loaded ammo.

"Contact, sir," a lookout called. "Floating debris."

Blakely lifted his binoculars and looked where the man pointed. Seconds later, he flipped the bridge intercom switch and said, "Ensign, turn the boat right standard rudder, twenty-five degrees. Idle in."

"Aye, aye, sir. Right standard rudder, twenty-five degrees. Idling in."

"Could be a trap," Harper warned. "Japs have started using debris to lure our subs to the surface."

"Maybe," Blakely said. "But my gut tells me this is no trick."

As the sub cruised near the debris field, lookouts called out a mix of planks, timbers, and other debris tied together as makeshift rafts. Men riding atop the rafts waved and shouted.

"Jap sailors," Harper said. He lowered his binoculars. "Maybe a half dozen."

"Armed?" Blakely asked.

"Hardly. They're nearly naked."

"Get a boarding party up top, pronto. Let's fish 'em from the water," Blakely said. "You lead it."

"Aye, sir. With pleasure." Harper dropped through the hatchway to organize the boarding party.

The sub turned and circled back, closer to the debris. Harper and eight crewmen ascended through the forward deck hatch. His team specialized in boarding sampans and other small vessels. They carried a 12-gauge double-barrel shotgun, a .45-caliber Thompson submachine gun, and various pistols. If it were a trap, they'd fight back and kill all but one Japanese sailor, keeping the one alive for questioning—common practice, though not an official policy.

"Ready for some target practice?" Harper said to the sailor operating the machine gun. He responded by locking an ammo clip in place as the sub drew near. Harper counted seven men on the makeshift raft, their faces blackened. Three men sat or knelt on boards and other debris. Four others clung to the debris from the water. They yelled and slapped at the surface, but the sub crew couldn't understand them given the water and engine noise and the distance. They raised their weapons, ready to fire.

"Hey. Whoa, whoa," a clear voice called from the debris. "First you bastards sink us. Now you're gonna shoot us? We're American POWs, for Pete's sake." The speaker, a gaunt figure wearing only a loincloth, tried to stand on the makeshift raft but, unsteady, dropped to his knees.

One by one the boarding party lowered their weapons, confusion on their faces.

"Who are you?" Harper shouted.

"Just some guys trying to get to Honolulu." The soldier grinned. "You headed that way?"

Harper's men looked stunned. One said, "That guy is speaking English. Holy shit, Harp. Did we sink a US ship?"

Harper, still cautious, tossed a rope to the makeshift raft and yelled, "Only one man. The one who speaks English."

"Of course I speak English. I'm from California," the soldier yelled back. He grabbed the rope and held it tight while the crewmen reeled him closer.

Other survivors jumped from the raft and started swimming, but Harper yelled at them to stay on the raft, and his crew aimed the shotgun and machine gun, ready to fire.

The crewmen hauled the man onto the submarine's fin and helped him to stand.

"Permission to come aboard, sir?" The soldier saluted, then grabbed Harper and hugged him, soaking the lieutenant commander's khaki shirt. "Thank you." He wept.

Harper grabbed the POW by the shoulders, held him at arm's length, then turned to the bridge and shouted to Blakely, "They're Americans, sir."

"I told you. We're American POWs." The man collapsed to his knees and hugged Harper's legs. His body heaved deep sobs.

Blakely descended the bridge ladder to the forward deck hatch. He helped the POW back to his feet. "What's your name?"

"Pete Chavez, sir." The POW tried to salute, but his arm stopped halfway to his forehead. "Last I heard, I was a private."

"Where did you come from?" Harper asked.

"They loaded us on the freighter the *Arisan Maru*." Chavez paused to catch his breath and steady his voice.

"Loaded you where?" Blakely asked.

"Out of Manila. Pier Seven," he said. "Eighteen hundred of us. Packed in the hold like sardines for days without food or water. Got torpedoed yesterday."

Blakely took a deep breath, fighting back a surge of emotion. He cleared his throat. "How many more? Where are the rest?"

"I don't know how many of us are still out there." Chavez shook his head. "A lot of men didn't make it. A lot died in the hold."

"Where were you imprisoned?" Blakely asked.

"The Philippines. Marched from Bataan, sir. A lot of us, at least. We tried to hold Bataan but got beat up, bad. Ran out of everything. After the surrender, they marched us all up to Camp O'Donnell, where we stayed until it closed two months later. We've been in camps ever since. Cabanatuan. Bilibid."

"The Battling Bastards of Bataan." Blakely's voice broke.

"What's that?" Chavez said.

"You're a Battling Bastard of Bataan."

"Well, if you say so, sir. Then I'm proud to say I'm one of those bastards."

"You guys have a bit of a reputation," Blakely said.

"We did our best, sir."

Blakely pointed toward the hatchway. "Head below. They'll get you some warm clothes and food."

"Yes, sir." Chavez pinned his narrow shoulders back, tucked his chin, and lifted a perfect salute.

Blakely returned the salute but held it a second longer.

Chavez shook off a sailor's help. "You heard your skipper. I'm a Battling Bastard of Bataan," he said and marched unaided to the open hatchway and descended into the *Shark*.

Topside, a lookout called from his elevated perch. "Contact, sir. Vast debris field. More men, sir. Port side, port side." The lookout paused, then shouted, "Holy cow, sir, there must be a hundred—No, sir. *Two* hundred men in the water." He lowered his binoculars and crossed himself.

"Harp, get all available hands on deck, pronto," Blakely ordered. He turned to the conning tower and called below, "Lower us down a bit, Leo. Get those bow planes flat on the water." The ten-foot metal appendages served the submarine like wings on an airplane. They tilted to make the sub climb or dive. Blakely wanted them lowered to make it easier to get the survivors on board.

Word spread through the sub of American survivors, and more men rushed on deck to assist in the rescue. Blakely climbed back to the bridge, where he barked orders and directed traffic. Over the next hour, the *Shark*'s crew worked quickly. Navy training manuals didn't cover situations like this, so they made it up as they went. Harper formed sailors into teams. The first team took the most dangerous job, swimming rope lines out to the rafts. If a Japanese plane appeared and forced the sub to dive, they would leave this team stranded, alone and defenseless. A second team crawled onto the sub's bulging saddle tanks to pull survivors aboard. A third team worked like a bucket brigade, passing, or carrying, survivors to the aft battery compartment hatch, where they lowered them. Inside, crewmen took the men to the pharmacist on board, or to an open rack. For the USS *Shark* crew, this marked their first encounter with the grim reality of war. Seeing the emaciated POWs brought some to tears.

Blakely recognized he couldn't get all the survivors. He didn't have the time or the space on board. His sub could only fit a few dozen extra passengers. He needed more submarines and pronto. "Do we have radio yet?" he said into the intercom. "We need *Seadragon* and *Blackfish*, pronto. *Snook* and *Drum* too. Get me subs."

"No radio yet, Skipper," the helmsman's voice crackled. "That last depth charge really did a number on it."

"Harp? Keep watch." Blakely dropped below deck to the crew's sleeping quarters. "Two per bunk," he ordered. He had done the math and realized they'd run out of rack space soon. "God knows they're skinny enough to fit."

He found the chief pharmacist's mate. Subs did not carry doctors on board.

The pharmacist was instructing the crew. "Sit those in the worst shape over here. I'll give them morphine shots to knock back their pain. Take the healthiest ones to the rear and give them a water-soaked rag and two slices of bread. Nothing else."

"What's the situation?" Blakely asked his pharmacist.

"They're in bad shape, sir. Starved, dehydrated, diseases, exposure. You name it."

"Do the best you can."

For the next hour and a half, the sub inched through enemy waters, recovering more half-dead POWs.

"How many on board, Harp?" Blakely asked when he came back up top to the bridge.

"Forty-four survivors recovered so far," his XO said. "At least two hundred spotted, probably more. It's a huge debris field."

Blakely raised his binoculars and scanned the vast ocean. He could hear floating survivors calling out. His goal was to rescue as many as possible and safely deliver them back to Hawaii.

"They say the Jap freighter was jam-packed with our boys," Harper said. "Why the hell didn't they mark the ship? We checked it before firing, right, sir?"

"We both checked it before firing. The target was clean."

"Some of our boys are so upset they can't even look at the POWs."

"We did as ordered," Blakely said. Then he changed the subject. "We have to get the radio working. We can't fit them all. We need more subs."

"Contact," a lookout shouted from above. "We got company, sir. Jap destroyer." The sailor pointed toward the horizon.

Blakely and Harper wheeled and rushed to the sub's starboard side, opposite the debris field. Blakely raised his binoculars to the horizon. "Jap destroyer, Kamikaze class."

"I'll tell everyone to speed up the rescue," Harper said. "We've still got time."

"Do it and be quick about it, Harp," Blakely said, his voice calm.

"Aye, sir." Harper dropped down a ladder to the deck and yelled orders to get a move on.

"Leo?" Blakely leaned over the open hatchway near his feet. "Rev 'er up. We're gonna need a quick getaway. All hands, prepare to dive the boat."

"Aye, sir," a voice rose from the conning tower below. "All hands prepare to dive."

Blakely clicked the bridge intercom and said, "Chief, go to 1MC." Then he yelled into the conning tower hatchway again. "Tell them to strap the passengers in and prepare to dive the boat. Battle stations."

"Aye, sir," came the reply. "Battle stations. Battle stations."

The alarm went out via the ship's intercom: "1MC, all hands, alarm, prepare to dive the boat. All hands, general quarters. Prepare for battle. Secure our passengers." The Klaxon blared. *Ah-OOH-ga, ah-OOH-ga.*

Harper shouted to his crew. "Faster. Jap destroyer bearing down on us." *Shark* crewmen on the bow plane hustled to assist more survivors. Everyone knew a submarine caught on the surface stood no chance against a destroyer.

Minutes later, Blakely lifted his binoculars to check the inbound destroyer. "Looks like the *Harukaze* has come back again," he shouted.

The first shell exploded seventy-five yards off the sub's bow.

"We're out of time," Blakely said. "We have to dive."

"Sir, we've got a few more within reach," Harper yelled back to Blakely on the bridge. "Stand by."

"No time," Blakely said. Another *Harukaze* shell exploded.

"One minute, sir," Harper screamed. "I need one minute."

A third shell exploded. Seawater doused Blakely. He turned to the debris field full of floating POWs reaching out and pleading for the sub not to leave. Blakely's awful dilemma tore at him, but his crew faced grave peril.

They could all die.

He had no choice.

"Dive," he shouted through the hatch. "Now."

4

RESURRECTION

South China Sea
October 25, 1944, 7:20 a.m.

Sam scrambled back against the lifeboat wall, and seriously contemplated jumping overboard and taking his chances in the South China Sea. It would be certain death, but so too might be staying on board.

"Irony or fate, Carlson?"

"I'm hoping irony," he said, studying Rudowski. Then he said, "Thanks for the help."

"I'm not sure I would have, had I known it was you." Rudowski bit a piece of firm, dry biscuit in half, then extended the rest toward Sam. "Here."

Sam hesitated.

"Take it," Rudowski said. "For getting me out of that hold. I won't offer it again."

Sam reached for the biscuit, cautious at first, then snatched it. He shoved the food into his mouth and chewed hard, like a starving dog. "Got any water?" he asked.

Rudowski gestured at a canteen on the wooden floor. "Just that."

Sam scrambled to the canteen, unscrewed the cap and, about to take a gulp, stopped and sniffed the opening. He didn't smell urine. He drank a swig, then spewed salt water onto the floor. "It's contaminated."

"Now we both know," Rudowski said. "Damn."

Sam sat back. After a few minutes he looked around the boat. "What else we got?"

"No more food. But we got a boom." Rudowski gestured to an eight-foot wooden pole on the floor of the boat.

Sam considered the boat and the pole. Both had Japanese letters on them. He leaned over the gunwale to view the exterior. "This lifeboat is from the *Arisan Maru*," he said. "I saw them when I went on deck for burial detail. Japs used them to row over to the destroyer. They probably cut them loose and tried to sink them. This one must have floated away."

"You know how to rig it?"

Sam wondered if the only reason he was still alive was because Rudowski needed someone who knew how to rig the boom and to sail the boat, though they couldn't do the latter without something to use as a sail. "I think so," he said. The problem was, they didn't have all the necessary parts, though he didn't tell Rudowski that.

Rudowski recited his inventory. "Tiller's okay. No mast. No sail. No oars. Hoping to find something floating out here to make a sail."

More minutes passed. Neither man spoke. Fatigue made Sam dizzy. After more than twenty-four hours without sleep, his body shut down. He slumped against the gunwale.

"Why'd you do it?" Sam asked.

"Do what?"

"Help me out of the water."

"I told you. I might not have, if I had known it was you." Rudowski paused. Then he said, "I told you on the ship. We're square. You saved my life cutting that rope and getting us the hell out of the hold."

Maybe. But Sam was having a hard time believing Rudowski was sincere. Maybe he saved Sam to have something to eat if, and when, that time came. Each time Sam's eyes closed, he forced them open and found Rudowski staring at him, as if waiting for him to fall asleep. Though he fought against his exhaustion, eventually it overtook his will to stay awake.

"Hey, what's that?"

Sam startled. He sat up. The light of day had faded. He'd been asleep for hours. "What's what?"

"That." Rudowski pointed.

Sam didn't initially see anything. "Where?"

"Right there. Looks like another pole."

The long wooden object rose and fell on the swells. Sam estimated it to be two hundred feet away. "Might come in handy," he said.

"We gotta get it," Rudowski said.

"No oars," Sam said, looking around the lifeboat interior. "Gonna have to swim for it." Still weak from his hours in the water, Sam waited for Rudowski to volunteer to fetch their distant prize. He didn't. Sam looked to the sky. "Gonna get dark soon. We'll lose our chance."

A tense minute passed.

"You going?" Sam asked.

Rudowski shook his head. "Can't swim. Never learned how."

"You're a goddamn liar," Sam said. Rudowski hadn't just fallen off the ship and into the lifeboat. If he had, more men would be in it. "You had to swim long and hard to reach this lifeboat."

Rudowski shook his head. "Nope. Bumped right into me as I floated by with a life preserver."

Sam considered all the reasons why he shouldn't try to retrieve the pole. Even if he could reach it. The current might prevent him from getting back to the boat. Sharks might be drawn to his splashing. Rudowski could get the wooden beam from Sam but not let him back into the boat, the way the Japanese used poles to keep the POWs away from the destroyer. And the pole might be useless.

"Not much time left," Rudowski said.

The sun indeed approached the watery horizon. Fear engulfed Sam at the thought of wasting what could be a precious gift. He rose, found his balance, and dove into the ocean. The frigid water squeezed his chest and his body shuddered, but he got his bearings and stroked toward the pole. He moved more quickly without the life preserver. Rudowski stood in the boat pointing the way.

Ten tough minutes later, Sam reached the pole. He hooked his arm around it and floated alongside it for a second, exhausted and out of breath. He was only halfway done, and swimming back would be more difficult because he would have to pull the pole. When Sam checked for the lifeboat, he saw it bobbing in the distance, Rudowski perched on the edge, watching.

He no longer worried about sharks, the strong current, or even Japanese ships. He feared being alone again. He checked the setting sun, an orange sliver on the horizon. Time was running out. No real options. He checked the lifeboat one last time. Reaching it would take every ounce of strength he had left.

5

QUICK DESCENT

The USS Shark
Luzon Strait, South China Sea
October 25, 1944, 7:40 a.m.

"Take her down!" Blakely boomed.

Harper shouted from the deck to the bridge. "Thirty seconds, sir."

"Now, Harp. That's an order."

Sailors pulled one last man from the closest debris pile onto the submarine and stuffed him down the forward hatch, then followed, half climbing, half falling down the ladder.

Harper paused at the hatch and pointed off the *Shark*'s port side, where twenty men kicked and paddled their way closer to the sub. "We can get them."

"No time, Harp," Blakely said. "Get below." Blakely started for the ladder.

"I'm not leaving American POWs with that warship bearing down on them," Harper said and launched himself onto the deck.

Blakely lunged and wrapped him in a bear hug, then wrestled him back toward the open hatch. "That destroyer is bearing down on *us*," he said, straining. "We can lead it away from the survivors." A crewman emerged from the hatch. "Grab his legs," Blakely said.

The sailor gripped Harper's feet and pulled him down the opening. Blakely followed. He slipped halfway into the submarine, then took a final look. The *Harukaze*'s frothing white bow was plowing directly at the *Shark*, its guns blazing.

Another shell exploded nearby.

Blakely dropped down the ladder into the conning tower. "Secure the hatch." A crewman sealed the door and spun its wheel lock tight while Blakely rushed to the periscope. "Take us down to five-zero-zero feet. Fast!"

"Aye, aye, sir," the helmsman said. "Five-zero-zero feet. Dive. Dive." The sub descended at a sharp angle, as quickly as its twin engines could take her. The crew braced as the sub dove.

The first depth charge exploded starboard but caused no damage.

"Chief, we need that radio!" Blakely yelled.

"Negative, sir. Still no radio or radar. We're deaf, dumb, and blind."

"Harp, get that passenger up here, the one I talked to on deck."

"Aye, sir." Harper wiped his eyes and turned to a seaman stationed at the hatch. "He's outside the control room. Chavez. Bring him here."

"Aye, sir."

Blakely queried Harper, "How many men did we get?"

"Fifty-six. Two died. Four are unconscious. They were starved and dehydrated. Sir, I wasn't . . ." Harper trailed off. "I didn't . . ."

"I know, Harp," Blakely said. "I know."

The seaman returned with Chavez.

"You wanted to see me, sir?"

"We've got a couple of minutes before the *Harukaze* destroyer finds us on sonar," Blakely said. "I need to ask you a few more questions."

"Fire away, sir."

"When did you depart Manila?"

"We left there twice," replied Chavez. "Last time might've been three days ago." He shook his head, then added, "Hard to keep track of time stuffed down in the hold."

Blakely knew the *Arisan Maru* had left Pier 7, Manila, on October 20. "Hear this, Private," Blakely said. "You're a free man. You're on board a United States Navy submarine, the USS *Shark*."

"Thank you, sir," Chavez said. He smiled at the others in the cramped control room. "I had that basic idea, but I appreciate hearing it spelled out. Now, sir, about how long will it take us to reach Honolulu? I got a date with a certain hula dancer."

The men around them smiled, but they all knew they were a long way from Honolulu and safety. It's why Blakely had brought Chavez to the control center: if they didn't make it, he wanted Chavez to know he died a free man.

Click-boom!

A depth charge exploded. It was closer, but no damage was reported.

"We've got some business to take care of before we drop you in Honolulu." Blakely turned and checked the depth gauge spinning as the sub dove. He prayed the *Shark* could stand the emergency descent after the beating it had already taken. His sub was about to dive deeper than ever before.

6

LIFE AND DEATH AT SEA

South China Sea
October 25, 1944

A brutal half hour after he started swimming, Sam neared the lifeboat. He guided the twelve-foot pole toward Rudowski, who grabbed it and hoisted it over the lifeboat's gunwale. Rudowski and their prize disappeared from Sam's view.

"Hey," Sam called, exhausted. Without the floating pole, he was slipping beneath the surface. "I need a hand."

No answer.

"Rudowski." Sam swallowed a mouthful of the South China Sea and coughed. "Dammit, help me."

Sam kicked hard and reached for the gunwale but, weaker now from the swim, he missed it by several inches. He sank below the water's surface, kicked hard, but failed again. Then Rudowski's hands seized his outstretched wrists and pulled him up and over the edge. Sam flopped into the boat, struggling to catch his breath.

Rudowski said, "I had to secure the pole."

"I thought maybe you'd had a change of heart."

Rudowski's eyes narrowed. "I told you, Carlson. We're square." He thought for a moment. "You made the swim. I rescued you. So we're still square."

"Let me take a closer look at the pole." Sam got to his knees and looked more closely. "Damned if it ain't the mast built for this style lifeboat," he said. "Or one just like her."

"Doesn't do us much good without a sail, though, right?" Rudowski said.

"No, it doesn't." Sam looked at the clouds on the horizon, red, yellow, and orange. *Okay, Padre, that's two miracles. Hoping you can ask that good Lord of yours for one more.* "But it gets us one step closer," he said.

The sun set. Darkness fell. Stars emerged, more than Sam had ever seen. He searched the sky until he found the Big Dipper and traced it to the North Star. He wondered if, wherever she was, Sarah, too, was looking at their star. He closed his eyes and made a wish—this one, though, was to get home and do what Father Tom had told him to do. Be a witness for them all. "I wish I may. I wish I might. Have the wish I wish tonight."

Sam could no longer see Rudowski, but he could hear the man's breathing and sensed his presence.

"Let's make a pact," Sam said.

"What did you have in mind?"

"No funny business; all right?" When Rudowski failed to reply, Sam said, "No matter how bad things get, no one knocks the other guy off and eats him. Deal?"

Rudowski laughed. "You're a suspicious son of a bitch, aren't you, Carlson?"

The response was not an answer, and Rudowski didn't supply one, but Sam figured if Rudowski meant to kill him, he'd had plenty of opportunities to do so, and hadn't.

As night deepened, the temperature dropped, the air frigid. Sam's teeth chattered, and he curled into a ball to conserve body heat.

When the eastern sky finally lightened, Sam willed the sun to quickly rise, though he knew they would eventually fry beneath it and he'd soon long for shade. As the day progressed, hunger and thirst gnawed at him. He sensed desperation mounting in Rudowski too. The two men talked little and moved less. They stared at the sea and sky. The boat rocked Sam into a fitful sleep, but he awoke when it lurched. He heard a loud splash and looked about. Rudowski was not in the boat. He looked over the edge. The big man was swimming away, already thirty feet off the starboard side. Had he gone mad?

Maybe, but Sam had been right about one thing—Rudowski could swim.

Rudowski paused and looked about. A hundred feet away, Sam spotted a floating corpse. The body rose and fell with each swell.

Sam stood and pointed at the body. "Left. Swim to your left."

When Rudowski reached the body, he poked and probed. A few minutes later, he turned toward the lifeboat and swam back, slower this time, towing something. Sam reached down to help as Rudowski neared the boat.

"Take this," Rudowski barked from the water. "And this." Sam grabbed both objects and tossed them to the floor, then bent over the lifeboat edge to clasp Rudowski's forearms. He leaned back, using what body weight he had left to pull the big man into the boat and keep it from tipping over.

Rudowski rested on the lifeboat floor breathing heavily, but he had his two prizes. He unscrewed a canteen cap and tested the water. "Fresh." He sipped more water until he coughed, then handed the canteen to Sam, who wanted to drink greedily but restrained himself. Rudowski opened the other item, a small leather bag. "Lookie here," he said. "Hardtack. And a couple cans of sardines." He tossed half the hardtack to Sam.

It would buy them another day, maybe two.

When the pair finished their feast, they settled back. They agreed to take turns sleeping while the other scanned the sea for more floating debris or bodies.

Rudowski pointed. "What's with the ring? You take it off a corpse?"

Sam had slipped Sarah's class ring on his finger before they opened the hatch. "My sweetheart gave it to me when I left the States for the Philippines."

Rudowski's brow furrowed. "How'd you keep it hidden from the Japs?"

Sam didn't want to mention he'd sewn it into the lining of the vest, along with the knife he'd used to stab Rudowski in the leg.

"Buried it under the barracks."

"Where is she now?"

Sam thought for a moment. "Eagle Grove, I imagine."

"Never heard of it."

"Minnesota. She teaches high school. Math. When I get home, I'm going to marry her."

Rudowski didn't respond. He looked out into the vast ocean. "You're a hell of an optimist, Carlson, given our circumstances."

"I guess she rubbed off on me," he said. "She always sees the glass half-full."

"Yeah? What if there is no glass?"

"We have two canteens," Sam said. "If it rains, we can catch the fresh water in the sardine cans and fill them."

"If it rains," Rudowski said, looking up at the cloudless sky.

"Where's home for you?" Sam asked.

"Wherever I lay my head," the giant said. "Right now, this boat is home."

That sounded sad to Sam, but he let it go.

Hours dragged by. The sun fell.

"We need to sleep front to back," Rudowski said. "Conserve what body heat we have."

Sam was both surprised and nervous. He couldn't help but be distrustful. He didn't like the idea of turning his back to Rudowski, but he also didn't like the thought of freezing to death.

"I don't like it any more than you do, Carlson," Rudowski said. "But I'm not queer and, given your story about your sweetheart, neither are you."

"So how do you want to do this?" Sam asked.

"I'll lie down behind you. When that side gets too painful, we'll roll over."

"Okay," Sam said. He slid across the boat. Rudowski smelled as bad as the sardines, but Sam likely didn't smell any better. Rudowski pushed up behind him, draped an arm around him, and pulled Sam close. It took a few minutes, but Sam felt heat emanating from the man's body.

"Carlson?"

"Huh?"

"Just in case your half-full sweetheart proves correct, and we both live: if you tell anyone about this, I'll kill you."

Sam couldn't help but laugh.

—

When dawn arrived, Sam awoke to Rudowski's back. At some point in the night, they had turned over. He rolled away, awakening the big man. They basked in the early morning warmth while their minds and bodies slowly thawed.

As the day wore on, their tongues swelled, their skin cracked, and their desperation grew. Neither said it out loud, but Sam knew they shared the same thought: if they found another corpse, they'd have to eat it.

Instead of a dead body, Sam picked up a small fish that flopped into the lifeboat at midday. He gave Rudowski half, and they managed to kill an entire hour eating it. The tiny fish somehow lifted Sam's spirits.

"Why the hell are you smiling?" Rudowski said.

"Because we're free."

"I'd hardly call this free, Carlson."

Sam searched for the right words. "Better than Camp O'Donnell and a hell of a lot better than the hold of that ship."

Rudowski gave three pathetic handclaps. "You're crazy, Carlson. The sun has fried your brain. We can't take much more of this freedom. We need a miracle."

The comment surprised Sam. "You believe in miracles, Rudowski?"

"I'm Polish Catholic. I don't have a choice."

"Altar boy?"

"What do you think?" Sam had a difficult time imagining Rudowski as a child, let alone wearing a cassock. "What about you?" Rudowski asked.

"Protestant," Sam said. "The only church in town."

"My father hated the Protestants. But he hated everybody."

Including Rudowski, Sam deduced from Rudowski's tone.

"You enlist?" Sam asked.

"The day I turned seventeen. Lied about my age."

"Given the size of you, I doubt anyone questioned it."

"Never looked back. Had to get the hell out of there."

"What will you do—after the war, I mean?"

Rudowski laughed. "You really do have endless optimism, Carlson."

"Humor me."

"I don't know," Rudowski said. "Haven't given it much thought."

Sam wondered if Rudowski had been lucky in that regard, not having anything or anyone at home to long for during these years of torture and abuse. Maybe it made the time pass a little easier. Then Sam thought of Sarah, of his parents and siblings, and of Eagle Grove. Thoughts of returning home to all of them had sometimes been the only thing that kept him alive. Rudowski had no such light to counter those dark and lonely days.

The boat drifted farther, both men falling in and out of sleep.

In the afternoon, something bumped against the boat and jolted them both awake.

"Sweet Jesus," Sam said, sitting up.

"Shark?" Rudowski asked.

Sam moved to the lifeboat edge looking for a dorsal fin, not seeing one. A large wooden box bobbed next to their vessel, bumping into the boat again.

"What is it?" Rudowski asked.

"Don't know," Sam said. "Give me a hand getting it in the boat."

Rudowski helped him hoist the heavy box from the shifting sea, but it was awkward—bulky and heavy. They dropped it into the sea several times.

"Pin it to the side," Rudowski said. Sam secured the box against the boat's side and Rudowski reached down into the sea, grabbed the bottom, and lifted it from the water. He and Sam and the box tumbled backward into the boat.

Both men rested for a moment, drained from exertion. Then Sam studied the box. It was about two feet square and a foot deep. Several screws held the lid tight. Japanese lettering ran in horizontal rows. "Get the sardine cans," Rudowski said.

The two men used the cans to work the screws. One by one, the screws loosened and popped free. Rudowski pried off the lid. He looked stunned, not believing what he was seeing. "I'll be damned," he said and tugged a long bolt of white fabric from the box. "A sail."

Sam nearly cried. Instead, he laughed. "Not a sail. A God-given miracle."

"Bullshit," Rudowski said, though he was also laughing. "The Japs didn't need the box to row over to the destroyer, so they tossed it overboard or just left it on board."

"Maybe."

"No maybe. That's what happened. The miracle will be us sailing some-place safe."

Sam didn't care. He knew the odds of the box bumping into their lifeboat, a scrap of wood in the vast South China Sea, were astronomical. Not to mention the box contained exactly what they needed.

It was a damn miracle.

Sam pulled ropes and pulleys from the box and held them high, again nearly crying. "We can rig a sail, Rudowski. It'll get us out of Jap waters."

"Which way's China?" Rudowski slapped Sam on the back.

For the next hour the men rigged the two poles and then ran a rope through the mast's tip, then Rudowski stood the mast upright into its position in the center of their boat. Their words were few. They rested often but never for long. A chance to control their destinies kept them going. Finally, they connected the eight-foot boom to the mast base, then added the other rope. Rudowski went to the boom's end and attached the sail.

"All set?" Rudowski asked. He gripped the horizontal boom so it couldn't swing out over the water.

Sam hoisted the sail with Rudowski holding the fabric to the mast. When the sail reached the top, Sam said, "Let it go."

Rudowski let loose the fabric. It fluttered, then filled with wind. The boat shot forward and leaned to one side. Sam pulled hard, tightening the sail. It glimmered in the bright sun and cast them in shade, a respite from the blistering heat as the boat churned through the water.

Both men laughed, the breeze blowing back their hair.

Without warning, Rudowski let the boom go. The eight-foot pole swung out over the water, making the boat jerk wildly then come to a halt. Sam hardly had time to react when Rudowski lunged at him. On instinct, Sam curled into a ball to protect his face, but Rudowski did not grip Sam's neck. Instead, he ripped the rope from Sam's fingers and quickly threw it down. Sam recoiled, fell backward to the lifeboat floor, and scooted to the side, his heart pounding. Rudowski yanked the white canvas down from the mast, a blur of frenzy and fury.

"What the hell are you doing?" Sam said.

Rudowski ignored Sam's question, gathering more sail and stuffing it on the lifeboat floor, panting like an animal and looking out over the ocean.

"Look," Rudowski said, out of breath. He quickly pointed to the horizon. The emotion on his face was one Sam would never have imagined seeing.

Rudowski was afraid.

Sam turned. An enemy destroyer, and it appeared to be headed right at them. Rudowski and Sam cowered, peeking over the gunwale.

"Did they spot us?" Sam said.

"Don't know, but they're coming straight at us, either way."

"What do we do?" Sam said. "Jump overboard?"

"You jump overboard, the Japs know you're alive and I'm alive. You saw what they did to those POWs who swam to that destroyer. They pushed them back in the water and drowned them. Now, shut up," Rudowski said. "Play dead. Or pray. I don't care, as long as it makes you lie completely still."

Rudowski did not wait for an answer. He pushed Sam onto the sail and sprawled his big body across him, pinning him to the floor.

They heard the massive ship's engines' thrum, drawing closer.

Rudowski lifted his head but only slightly. "It's circling, about two hundred yards away."

If the ship rammed them, it would be the end. The ominous gray ship reduced engine speed—a sound Sam had become familiar with inside the *Arisan Maru*.

"Don't move a muscle," Rudowski whispered. "It's circling a second time."

"How close?"

"Still two hundred yards."

Sam held still, but his mind raced. The wake hit the lifeboat and tossed it up and down. His heart pounded. Japanese voices spoke, and he was certain one belonged to Yoshida, still hunting him, still trying to kill him.

Machine gun fire erupted. Bullets splashed the water, a few ripped into the lifeboat wall. Shards of wood hit the side of Sam's face. Every muscle wanted to jerk in panic, but Rudowski's muscles tightened, and his weight pressed Sam down, not allowing him to move. The machine gun fell silent. An eerie calm fell over the ocean. More chatter came from the ship, Japanese gibberish. Another machine gun blast tore at the boat. Wood chips and water sprayed both sides of Sam's face, but again he did not move.

Not a muscle.

Not a twitch.

He slowed his breathing.

Seconds turned into minutes. Then the ship's diesel engines revved and the sound built to a thunderous roar. The destroyer departed, the wake again causing the lifeboat to pitch and twist. The two men remained perfectly still. When Sam could no longer hear the engines, he slowly raised his head. He expected Rudowski to push it back down, but the big man did not move. Sam was just barely able to see over the gunwale, still pinned beneath Rudowski's body. He did not see the destroyer.

"They're gone," he said, sighing. "All clear."

Sam tried to rise, but Rudowski's weight kept him pinned down. "Rudowski, they're gone."

Rudowski did not move.

"Rudowski?" Sam wiggled free, his movement rolling Rudowski onto his back. Rudowski's eyes were open, staring up at the sky. Empty. Lifeless.

"Oh no," Sam said. "No. No. No."

7

REVELATIONS

The USS Shark
Luzon Strait, South China Sea
October 25, 1944, 7:50 a.m.

Click-boom!

Another explosion shook the submarine. Lights flickered. Men struggled to remain upright.

"They found us," Blakely said.

Click-boom! Click-boom!

Two more explosions in rapid succession dealt a devastating blow. The red emergency lights dimmed. Tiny holes sprayed water. Black, acrid smoke billowed from an electrical fire in another compartment, and the odor of burnt rubber indicated the sub's batteries had been torched. Men coughed and wheezed.

"Damage report," Blakely ordered.

"We've lost propulsion. Bow plane's stuck," the helmsman shouted, his voice near panic. "We're still heading down. Can't stop our descent."

"Seal compartments. Blow the tanks," Blakely said. He clenched a fist, out of options. "Let's surface and fight the son of a bitch."

Confronting a destroyer would not end well, but at least they would go down fighting. Like David versus Goliath, maybe they could land a lucky shot.

"Can't do it, sir. Electricity is out," the helmsman replied. "The men are trying to throw the switch manually, but the forward compartment's flooding. The valve controls are shot, and we can't empty the ballast tanks."

With no way to stop their steep dive, the men had minutes to live, at most, before the ocean depth crushed the hull—every submariner's worst nightmare. A crewman wrenched the last hull leak closed, and the water stopped spraying. A tense quiet embraced the men. Chavez climbed off the floor and grabbed a periscope handle for balance.

Blakely could hardly believe this was the end. A part of his brain was still trying to think of things he could do to save his submarine and his men. But he was coming up blank. They were out of options. This was the end. This was how he, his crew, and the POWs he'd tried to save would die.

If so, then he would go out with dignity. For his men.

"I'm sorry, boys, it looks like this is the end," Blakely said. He knew that elsewhere on board the sub, desperate crew would keep trying to fix the broken sub until the very end, but he also knew their attempts were futile. "Listen, we only have a few moments left, so I'll be quick." Blakely turned to their passenger. "Private Chavez, there's something you need to know. What I'm about to say could get me court-martialed, but I guess I no longer need to worry about that now; do I?"

"Passing five-five-zero feet," the helmsman said.

Blakely and his men all knew a Balao-class submarine imploded from pressure at a depth somewhere beyond six hundred feet, even with its thicker, fortified walls. Only a few feet and seconds remained.

"I knew the freighter we sank last night contained American POWs," Blakely said. "I ordered the attack anyway."

His confession stunned his crewmen.

"We broke the Jap radio code," the commander said. "Our folks at Pearl Harbor get every Jap message and we know where every one of their ships is located, what it's carrying, where it's going. Round the clock."

No one spoke.

Blakely managed a low chuckle. "Hell, us skippers are so spoiled now, we complain if a convoy shows up ten minutes late."

"Approaching crush depth," the helmsman said. His usually calm voice quaked.

Thick, acrid smoke filled the room.

"So our code breakers told you the *Arisan Maru* was carrying American POWs?" Chavez asked.

"They did," Blakely said.

"But you had no choice but to sink us," Chavez whispered.

"The MATA-30 convoy started with twelve freighters," Blakely said. "If we sank eleven but left the only one carrying Allied POWs, the Japs would have smelled a rat. And if they changed the code . . ."

". . . the war would've been prolonged," Chavez said.

"By months, maybe years. More men would've died. Thousands more."

Blakely reached into his breast pocket and slowly extracted the printed Ultra message. The commander crumpled the paper in his fist and held it at arm's length. Then he unclenched his hand and dropped the wad to the floor. Blakely wanted to explain how he aimed the torpedoes to stop the *Arisan Maru* but not to sink it, but he was out of time.

"Seven-two-five feet," the helmsman said. "Hull breach imminent." He removed his black headset and gently hooked it on a radio dial. Then he leaned back, turned his head, and stared off into space.

"Men," Blakely said, straightening his posture as he scanned the room. He saluted his crew. "It has been an honor serving with you."

All eight in the conning tower, including Chavez, returned the salute, some with silent tears streaming down their cheeks.

Blakely lowered his salute and said to Chavez, "I'm sorry, soldier, but you're not going to meet that hula dancer."

"Don't be so sure," Chavez said. "Maybe we'll meet someday in heaven, sir."

Blakely looked at his men. "We saved a lot of American lives."

Blakely heard the crunching of metal, popping like a string of firecrackers going off, water spraying.

"Seven-five-zero," the helmsman said, the last words Blakely or his men in the control room would ever hear.

8

New Mission

South China Sea
October 27, 1944

Hours had passed since the Japanese destroyer had departed. Most of the machine gun fire had been high, and the bullet holes above the waterline. With tears running down his cheeks, Sam spent time plugging holes with whatever he could, wadded pieces of clothing. He'd have to periodically bail.

The sun had dipped below the horizon, and Sam had run out of tears. He didn't know if he had been crying because he'd realized Rudowski had saved his life, or because he feared being alone again. The big man had given him someone to talk with. So often, over the course of his two and a half years of captivity, Sam had been made to feel less than human because the POWs were treated worse than animals. Father Tom had always told Sam to remember he was human, that it was the world that was inhumane.

Having Rudowski alive in the boat had made Sam feel like he had a chance to survive.

They weren't friends.

Never friends.

But human.

He had not yet raised the sail again. Nor had he done the unthinkable. He had not shoved Rudowski overboard and cast him adrift, though he knew he couldn't keep him on board. Couldn't even be tempted.

He'd hated the burial detail in the prison camps, then on the *Arisan Maru*. But this last burial would be the hardest of all.

Sam moved to Rudowski, the light of day quickly fading. He estimated that even in his emaciated condition, the man weighed more than two hundred pounds. Dead weight. Even at full strength, the task of lifting him up and rolling him over the gunwale would be arduous, and Sam was far from full strength. He would move Rudowski's leg or arm, and the limb would flop back to its starting point. Eventually he succeeded in rolling Rudowski's body to the edge, face down. He lifted the right leg and hung it over the side. He moved the right arm and dangled it over the side. He had to be careful he didn't fall in or tip the boat. Rudowski was no longer there to save him.

With Rudowski's body balanced there along the gunwale, he said, "Father Tom's not here to do a proper burial, so you're stuck with me." He took a deep breath. "Dammit, you were . . . mean as hell. And I didn't know you. Not well. But I think I got some sense of why you were the way you were, from the little you said about your life. Let's be honest. You never liked me, and I never liked or trusted you. I was scared of you, especially in the hold." Sam shuddered at the terrible rumors within the ship's hold of murder, cannibalism, and vampirism, and at the cold, clear logic of Rudowski's survival-of-the-fittest, law-of-the-jungle choices.

But he wouldn't judge the man.

Who was he to judge? "That's something I guess you'll take up with the man upstairs, as will I someday."

He touched Rudowski's shoulder and tried to summon Father Tom. "You got us out of that hold when no one else could, and you covered my body and took the bullets that would have killed me. It might have been an accident, but that isn't how I'll remember it. And I no longer believe things happen for a reason. I can't logically explain why God would allow what has happened these past years."

He took a breath. "But I made a promise to Father Tom to make it home and tell everyone what happened in the camps and in that hell ship. I'm making that same promise to you. I'll let your family know what happened to you. How you saved my life." He paused again, thinking of Major Jones on the deck of the *Arisan Maru* when he promoted Father Tom.

"US military regulations authorize me to make battlefield promotions." Sam, a noncommissioned officer, didn't have that authority, but he really didn't care. "I therefore promote you, for exceptional service above and beyond the call of duty to me and to your country, *Corporal* . . ." Sam couldn't think of Rudowski's first name, or if he'd ever heard it. "Corporal Rudowski. And in the name of Father Thomas Scecina and the God he so fully believed in, I absolve you of all your sins and commit you to the ocean. May you rest in peace."

Sam struggled but managed to get Rudowski's body onto the gunwale edge. The boat tilted, and for a moment he thought it might tip over, but all at once Rudowski rolled and splashed into the ocean.

The big man's body floated there beside the boat for a surprisingly long time, like he was reluctant to part ways.

Sam knelt, said a prayer, and watched the swells rise and fall until the blood-red sky faded to dusk, then to night, and Rudowski disappeared.

Sam was alone again.

———

Sam kept himself busy rigging the sail, and when the canvas rose it signaled another chance at life. He looked to the vast array of stars and let the canvas luff rather than pull it tight. He realized he had another problem. He had no idea which way to sail. Wind and waves had spun his boat in circles for hours, and now darkness had fallen.

He recalled the day the *Arisan Maru* sank, when a Japanese crewman had told an American POW the freighter was one day from reaching the island of Formosa, and that the POWs might be off-loaded there. If Sam chose a northerly course and landed in Formosa, which Japan controlled, he would surely be either killed or captured and sent to the mines to work. Sailing south would be the same result, and east would take him farther from land. It would take longer tacking against the steady breeze, but he knew he needed to sail west.

Sam and Rudowski had figured sailing due west would get them to mainland China, or close to it. It was a long, hard-to-miss coast, and the Chinese hated the Japanese. It was his best chance.

First things first, though. Sam needed to find west. He thought of Sarah and the North Star. Could he find it?

He searched the sky and, after a moment of disorientation, he located the Big Dipper. He found the two stars forming the constellation's bowl, which pointed the way to the North Star. And there it was.

As bright and beautiful as ever.

He had north, which meant he could find west.

He tugged the halyard. The white canvas sail rose, then he scrambled to the stern and gripped the tiller. He turned the boat until the North Star shimmered on his right. The white sail billowed, and the lifeboat pitched forward, slow at first, then gaining speed under a steady breeze.

Sam held the course for three nights and two days. At dawn and dusk, he got bearings from the sun's position. At night, he kept the North Star on his right side. He took catnaps now and then, and fatigue and hunger played tricks with his mind, but he held his course. The sun baked his skin until his neck and shoulders peeled, but the sail provided some shade. Two squalls nearly sunk the boat, but also dropped gallons of fresh rainwater into it. Sam filled the canteens and the sardine cans, drinking as much as he could.

Each time Sam's body weakened, he thought of Father Tom and Major Jones, of Rudowski, and Pete Chavez, and his promise.

The War Department needed to know the Japanese were not marking prisoner ships. It needed to know the torpedo fired on the freighter had killed hundreds of American POWs. The War Department needed to know that thousands of POWs who had died in the prison camps lay rotting in mass graves, so they could bring those bodies home and give them a proper and dignified burial. The families of the men lost at sea needed to know their loved ones' bodies had been committed to the ocean after religious services by Father Tom.

An invisible clock ticked inside Sam. The longer he took to return home, the lower his chances of survival and the higher the number of American POWs who could die. To fill the time, Sam again replayed the movies he and Sarah once watched in the Paradise Theater's projection room—and recited the lines of both Fred Astaire and Ginger Rogers, at least what he could remember, this time for an audience of just one. What he couldn't remember, he imagined. Each time, Sarah sat beside him, head resting on his shoulder, or sipping Coca-Cola from her straw and eating popcorn.

He swore he could smell her beautiful fragrance.

At night, his boat glided through the water under a billion stars.

On the second night, an explosion of red, green, and blue lights danced in the water around the lifeboat's hull. As Sam glided through this colorful world, he didn't think it could be any more beautiful. Then a whale spouted and rolled to the surface. A second did the same. Then a third. The great mammals gently rose to peek at the odd contraption sailing alongside them.

Another time, a fin breached the surface, but Sam's panic subsided when a second, then a third rose from the water and a dozen white-sided dolphins appeared, some spinning high above the water.

With a lot of time to think, Sam realized he no longer feared death—only the consequence of it. He feared being unable to keep his word to Father Tom. He feared leaving Sarah at such a young age. It pained him to think of the agony his death would cause his mother and father and his siblings, the hole it would punch in his family's hearts.

On the morning of the third day, as Sam sliced through the sea with a full sail, a dark speck appeared on the western horizon.

Another Jap destroyer?

Sam considered dropping the sail, then decided he really didn't have that option. He had no food and only half a canteen of water remaining. He squeezed the tiller, willed the dark speck to be something good, perhaps a US submarine, and sailed on. Moments later, another speck appeared, then a third and a fourth. Soon he counted eleven objects on the horizon.

An entire Japanese convoy? They still controlled these waters. Would they dump him in yet another POW camp or shoot him where they found him?

Ten minutes later, Sam determined the specks were boats. Forty to sixty feet long, the boats looked like floating homes, made of sturdy, brown wood. They had house-like structures in the middle, and high sterns with platforms. A large brown sail, shaped like a half moon, puffed from each vessel.

Sam said a silent prayer. "Let this be the China coast and let those be Chinese fishing junks." He picked a fishing boat at random and sailed straight for it, calling out when he reached the boat's side, his voice hoarse and weak. "Hello?"

A dozen men, women, and children came from the cabin to stare at the strange man in a loincloth.

"American," he said, exhausted. "American GI."

Several men grabbed ropes, chattering, as the junk turned alongside Sam's rig. A middle-aged, leather-faced man threw Sam a line, and he secured it to the mast. Then the men reeled his lifeboat in against the junk.

"Thank you," Sam said when two young men helped him climb aboard. Sam was so weak he could hardly lift his legs, even with help. He fell on his back on the deck, weeping. The men, women, and children stood over him, muttering and studying him as if he were an alien. He knew he didn't look human, not in his current condition. He needed to pull himself together, present himself as more than a sobbing pile of bones. He lifted himself and leaned his back against the railing. He counted eight men. Two held machetes, another a hatchet. The women and children had slipped out of sight. Sam had no idea which way this was going to go, whether they would cut him to pieces or sell him to the enemy for a bag of rice.

An imposing six-foot-tall man emerged from below deck and strode to Sam, studying him. Seconds passed in tense silence. Then the man turned to the others and barked what sounded like orders.

The men advanced on Sam with their machetes and hatchets.

9

AMERICAN GI

South China Sea
October 30, 1944

The men stepped past Sam and climbed from the junk onto Sam's lifeboat. They chopped the wooden vessel into bits and tossed firewood-sized pieces onto the deck, where family members hauled them below.

They were hiding evidence.

Later, as the captain smoked a home-rolled cigarette, he scribbled a note using English letters. *British or American?*

"American," Sam said and pointed to the word.

"Ameddican," the captain said. His mouth inched into a crooked grin, minus one front tooth. He extended both arms straight in front of him and slowly pointed his thumbs up. "American GI good," he said.

"Yes," Sam said. "American GI." But he had been down this path before and had been traded for a bag of rice.

The captain gave Sam a home-rolled cigarette, scribbled another note, then pointed to his chest. "Chinese." He gestured to his large, extended family. "Chinese," he said. Then he shook his head. "Japan no good."

"Japan no good," Sam agreed.

After the workers sank what was left of Sam's boat, the captain ordered the men to pull up their fishing nets. The junk set sail, and the crew moved Sam below deck. Women brought Sam clothing and fish, a paste-like rice, and stale bread, which he moistened with warm tea, but he could only eat bits of food before nausea set in and he nearly threw up.

They brought out a towel and a bucket of heated water, and some of the men, including Sam, bathed. Afterward, Sam put on clean Chinese clothing. He refused to remove Sarah's ring to bathe until a woman brought him a cord of braided fishing line. Sam tied the ring onto the line, then draped it around his neck and tucked it inside his clothing. He stepped onto the deck, only to have the sarong tied around his emaciated waist unwrap and fall to the floor. The children on deck laughed as Sam lifted the cloth and held both ends, uncertain how to tie them. A child stepped forward and looped the loose fabric into an elaborate knot at Sam's hip.

The fishing boat sailed through the night. Sam slept in the crew quarters beneath warm blankets for the first time in years. He awoke early the following day and stepped onto the boat deck with a blanket draped over his shoulders against the morning chill. The fishing junk had anchored within sight of land. A broad bay stretched along a coastline of white sand and behind it, a dense tree line.

Sam gestured toward the landmass. "What's that?"

"*Zung Gwok,*" the captain said. China.

Sam nearly cried.

The crew raised anchor and prepared to sail just as another Chinese junk pulled alongside, its crew passing them a bunch of bananas but talking animatedly while glancing back over their shoulders.

Worried, Sam thought.

When their conversation became heated, he thought he might again be turned over to the Japanese. The junk captain walked to Sam. Sam shrugged and raised his palms to say, "What now?"

"*Jat Bun gwai,*" came the captain's reply. Then he added in English, "Japanese."

The captain pointed south to a small island on the horizon. A Japanese military outpost, Sam guessed. Then he produced a small piece of paper and a pencil. He scribbled a note, then handed it to Sam, who studied the writing and made out the words: "We go to China to day."

Sam wasn't sure if the captain meant today or two days, but he was relieved nonetheless.

A twelve-foot wooden sampan appeared, towed by the other fishing boat. Sam's hosts eased him over the railing into the flat-bottomed boat. The captain climbed in, grabbed a long sculling oar, and quickly set to work, though not toward the island. The captain rowed hard in the opposite direction. The fishing junks shrunk behind them. Every few strokes, the captain turned to check the Japanese military outpost for signs of approaching vessels. *So far so good,* Sam thought.

When they neared the coast, Sam split his focus between the outpost and the shore. He tried to calculate whether, if the Japanese sent a ship, the sampan could make shore. Ten minutes later, the sampan neared a bare stretch of beach. Instead of landing, the captain slipped through a narrow gap into a shallow estuary, the sandy bottom only three feet below. Japanese ships could not follow them.

"Japanese there." The junk captain took his hand off a pole he used to push them upstream to gesture north. "Japanese there." His long arm swept to the south. Then he gestured straight upstream and said, "We hide."

The silent countryside of rice paddies, low hills, and lush forests passed by for the next two hours before the captain broke his silence. He pointed to a dozen wooden sampans beached on the far bank as well as rudimentary buildings. "Kitchioh," he said.

The captain beached the sampan alongside others and helped Sam out and up the bank to dry land. Sam reached down and scooped up a handful of dirt, letting it pass through his fingers. It was the first land he'd touched since October 11, when the *Arisan Maru* left Pier 7.

The captain shouted to a young man tending fishing nets. The youngster sprang from his sampan and sprinted toward the buildings. "Come," the captain said. He took a step and waved for Sam to follow.

Sam had no choice but to trust the man.

He followed him along a dirt road past rustic homes, some made of cement with tin roofs. Others had mud walls and thatched roofs. Women and children stood watching them from windows, doorways, and gardens. They looked apprehensive. A foursome of seated men paused their board game to stare at Sam. Children froze or ran away.

The Kitchioh village looked to have suffered attacks during the war. Some homes had been burned to the ground, only their brick foundations remaining. They passed a brick building, bigger than the others, but with an entire wall blown out. Inside, a young woman with long black hair and wearing a white dress taught a class of maybe twenty kids of all ages. She moved her wooden pointer across symbols on the chalkboard but stopped when she noticed Sam.

Sam thought of Sarah back in Eagle Grove, no doubt teaching her own classes.

A boy, maybe five or six, trotted over and inserted himself between Sam and the captain. He gripped the fisherman's thick thumb and said, *"Ah ba."* Then he smiled and grabbed Sam's hand too.

"Mou si ge," the boat captain shouted at the bystanders, seemingly to reassure them. Soon, other children approached Sam. A pair of older men came next, then a trio of women, until finally a crowd of some thirty villagers surrounded him. The little boy first to approach Sam gently stroked the hair on Sam's leathery arm. Sam noticed two fingers were fused, and the wrist locked in a bent position.

They reached the village center. Three well-dressed men waited. The oldest looking had a long, thin gray beard. Sam thought of this man as the village mayor or elder and bowed deep and long to show respect.

The junk captain said something in Chinese, pointing at Sam, then in the direction of the ocean. The gray-bearded man studied Sam but said nothing while the captain continued speaking and gesturing to Sam.

Finally, the gray-bearded man smiled and extended a hand. After a moment of hesitation, unsure, Sam gave it a gentle shake.

Others present then also reached for Sam, and he shared handshakes and smiles with them also, bowing to them all.

The gray-bearded man, who Sam thought of as the "mayor," spoke and made a gesture for Sam to follow him. Then he barked *"Joeng hoi"* to clear a path through those who'd gathered.

Sam had no clue what the man had said, but he seemed friendly. He took Sam to the veranda of a building made of cement blocks with a tin roof and sat Sam in a comfortable chair. Sam sipped water and gingerly ate rice dishes and fresh fruit, though it remained too rich for him to eat much of or to keep down.

He excused himself several times to throw up, but always returned and slowly ate more, hoping his starving body would retain some nutrition. Curious villagers came and went, studying Sam as if he were a zoo exhibit.

Late in the afternoon, Sam got a warm bucket to bathe with and a clean set of Chinese clothes, pants and a shirt. Evening came, and he enjoyed another meal seated at a large, round table in the mayor's wooden house. Elders made emphatic speeches. Their words flew past Sam, but their expressions of friendship reassured him. The drinking and feasting did not end until late in the evening. The junk captain and mayor walked Sam to a building and showed him to a bed. Before drifting to sleep, Sam squeezed Sarah's ring, still on the cord draped around his neck.

He whispered, "I'm coming home."

And he wanted to believe this time it was so.

—

Someone touched Sam's shoulder, awakening him, but also held a hand over his mouth.

"You go now," the fishing boat captain whispered, his tone urgent.

Sam got out of bed quickly. "Japanese?"

"Shhh." The boat captain put a finger over his lips, looked out the window, then back at Sam. "Japanese soldiers coming," he explained. "Many."

10

QIU JIN

Kitchioh, Guangdong Province, China
November 2, 1944

Sam stumbled from bed, fumbled with his borrowed clothes, and staggered outside. The captain hurried him to the village center, where the gray-bearded mayor and another person waited in the moonlight. They, too, looked concerned. The fishing boat captain removed his round hat and placed it on Sam's head. "Go now."

Sam looked about. "Which way?" he said.

The person standing beside the mayor stepped forward. "I will take you."

A woman. The schoolteacher from the classroom looked up from under a green-and-red skullcap, into which she'd tucked her long black hair.

"You're the teacher."

"Qiu Jin," the woman said. "Daughter of Qiu Xinhou." She pointed to the captain.

The teacher had put on loose-fitting pants and a baggy shirt. She wore an embroidered gray-green vest, laced like shoes and tied along its sides. She'd swapped her pointer stick for a sword hanging in a scabbard.

"M hou ji si," the old man said. He gestured toward the silent houses while speaking to Sam. "He says he is sorry," Qiu Jin said. "Many spies here. A Japanese military outpost learned you are here. They are sending troops."

"Then we better go. I don't want any trouble for your village." Sam turned to the three men. *"Xie xie,"* he said, his only Chinese phrase. He gripped the old man's hand but spoke to Qiu Jin. "Tell them I can never thank them enough for all they have done for me."

The daughter translated and the mayor rattled off a final comment, which Sam didn't understand, but the three men looked saddened.

"He said this village always helps strangers in need," Qiu Jin explained.

"Xie xie," Sam said again. He turned to the fishing boat captain. "You saved me, and I will always remember you." Qiu Jin interpreted for the two men.

The fisherman spoke in Cantonese and again Qiu Jin translated. "He says war makes good men do bad things. So, we must do good when we can."

The fishing boat captain wrapped a tender arm around Qiu Jin's shoulders and spoke Cantonese. He was worried for her.

"Zau laa, aa baa," Qiu Jin said and hugged him. Then she turned to Sam and said, "We go now."

They had started toward the forest when the spunky boy who had held Sam's hand when he entered the village ran toward them carrying an old blanket. Qiu Jin knelt and hugged the child, stroking his hair and whispering to him. Sam felt guilty taking a daughter and a mother from her family, and for putting her in danger. Qiu Jin spoke to the child and gestured to Sam. The child stepped to Sam and wrapped his tiny arms around Sam's legs. The gentle kindness nearly overwhelmed Sam after everything he had been through. He patted the boy's head.

"No more time," Qiu Jin again urged.

Her father picked up the boy, and Sam followed Qiu Jin out of the village.

The next hour passed in nervous silence. Sam tailed Qiu Jin along narrow dirt trails. She kept a fast pace, and Sam asked no questions. He was too winded to speak. He struggled to keep up with her and hoped his depleted body would not fail and put them both in danger. They trudged through moonlit rice paddies interspersed with forests. The rural scenery at first reminded Sam of the Philippines, then of his Minnesota home. He tried to focus on the farm he and Sarah would one day own. *Lots of sweet corn. No rice.*

"Wait . . . please," Sam groaned. He finally doubled over, exhausted.

Qiu Jin turned back and knelt next to him. "Drink water." She propped Sam up and pressed the bottle to his lips.

"Xie xie," Sam said after several swallows. He stalled for time to catch his breath. "How'd you learn English?"

"Father encouraged me," she said, her eyes continually scanning the trees, assessing their surroundings. "We lived in the north, in Nanjing. I learned English at school."

"Nanjing?" Sam said. Every American soldier knew the capital city and what had transpired there when Japanese troops invaded in late 1937. Soldiers raped and killed thousands of Chinese civilians, barbarism on an unmatched scale. Sam also recalled Katsuo Yoshida saying he had been in Nanjing and had been ordered to rape the women and kill civilians.

"Were you in Nanjing when the Japanese attacked?"

"I was a high school student," Qiu Jin said. She gave Sam another drink. "Father was school principal."

"You're lucky you survived." Sam rubbed his bare feet.

"Lucky? Yes, maybe lucky," Qiu Jin said, her voice low. She rose. "Must keep moving. Bad soldiers chase us."

Sam followed orders and pushed on. His knees and feet ached. "Will the Japanese hurt your father for helping me escape?" he asked.

"They cannot hurt him anymore," Qiu Jin said over her shoulder, then hurried down the trail.

Two more hours passed. A faint light teased the eastern sky as Sam labored up a steep slope. They climbed into grassy hills overlooking coastal rice paddies, and Sam caught glimpses of a broad, south-facing bay in the distance. When the sun broke over the horizon, they stopped to rest on a large flat rock. Qiu Jin climbed atop it and scanned the landscape behind them for pursuers while Sam sipped water and bit into a piece of flatbread she had produced from her shoulder bag. Sam stood and spotted specks in the distant bay that he assumed were fishing junks. He hoped Qiu Xinhou was on one of them. He prayed the Japanese did not punish him.

"Where are we going?" Sam asked. He ate another piece of bread and drank more water. "Can you get me to Americans?"

"You go to Kunming," Qiu Jin said. "American base. Very big."

Qiu Jin pointed to the sky where, with perfect timing, morning light reflected off twelve specks flying high above them—long-range bombers heading east toward the rising sun, leaving vapor trails stretched across the brilliant blue sky.

"From Kunming," she said.

Sam glanced west. "How far?"

Qiu Jin thought a moment, then grabbed a long stick and scratched a number in the dirt. "One," she said. She drew another number and paused. "Seven."

"Seventeen kilometers," Sam said. He could make that trip.

Qiu Jin etched another number next to the previous two. A zero. Sam's heart sank. Then she made another zero. Sam's hope faded. He couldn't travel 170 kilometers, let alone 1,700.

He shook the thought.

He'd never believed he would live through the Bataan march either, or the abuse in the prison camps. He'd thought he would die on the hell ship and surely in the lifeboat. Somehow, he had survived. One miracle after another had kept him alive. He told himself that this walk through the hot, humid mountains was a piece of cake compared to what he'd been through. At least he had water, and no Japanese poked bayonets at him.

Sam intended to keep his word to Father Tom for all the friends he had lost.

Qiu Jin took a swig of water, then erased her numbers from the dirt and tossed the stick into nearby bushes. She picked up Sam's round hat from the ground and handed it to him. "You walk." She turned and marched down the trail.

11

BLISTERED STEPS

Guangdong Province, China
November 2, 1944

The miles dragged by. Sam's bare feet became raw and blistered. Each step shot pain through his body. He ached. By midday, the baking sun added to his misery.

He'd decided this would be his last walk.

If the Japanese came, and survival became unlikely, he'd kill as many as he could before they killed him. It wasn't bravery. It was fear. He would never again be a prisoner of war. He would not allow himself to be tortured, humiliated, or in any way abused again. That, at least, was over.

Stream crossings brought short relief. Sam lingered to allow the cool, flowing water to soothe his damaged feet. He splashed it on his face and aching body. The water cooled his skin but did nothing to wash away the doubts that crept into his thoughts about his physical endurance.

He pushed those thoughts aside and pressed on. One step after the next.

They reached a large river, and Qiu Jin summoned a ferry boatman with a whistle. While the flat, wooden boat crossed from the other side, Sam dangled his feet in the water.

"You can make it?" Qiu Jin asked.

"I'll make it," he said.

Qiu Jin, ever vigilant, pointed an index finger at her hat, then at Sam's hat, and gestured for him to pull it down low. Sam did so. His borrowed Chinese pants and shirt helped disguise his emaciated frame, but his Caucasian face stood out and, as the village mayor had said, spies lurked everywhere.

The little ferry docked, and they stepped aboard. Sam kept his head down and his gait like an old man shuffling forward. It wasn't difficult. He felt like he was ninety years old. The ferryman pulled on a thick rope stretched across the river until their raft reached the far bank. Qiu Jin paid the man, and Sam followed her a few hundred yards to a nearby village, where she bought rice cakes and tea from a street vendor. She told Sam to eat and drink slowly.

He had no sooner finished than she said, "We go now."

Additional hours and miles passed. Every three miles or so, they stopped at a stone gatehouse with an elaborate archway stretched over the road. They went into the villages to purchase more rice cakes, hard-boiled eggs, tea, and other items from vendors' stalls.

After one such stop, Qiu Jin said, "Vendors in the city say that Japanese patrols came through last week, but none since."

"Is that good?"

"Might be good. Might be bad. Maybe they no come no more. Maybe they are soon to return."

"Then we better keep moving," Sam said and got to his feet.

At sundown, they stumbled into a crowded city of rickshaws and carts weaving between stray dogs, live chickens in woven bamboo baskets, and other animals. Small stores sold pots, pans, and other household goods. Some cooked aromatic dishes that perfumed the air with exotic scents. The people carried heavy loads, their shoulders and carts weighed down with what looked to Sam like their life possessions. Even the children, with sad, dirty faces and ragged clothes, hauled large packs.

"Is this normal?" Sam asked.

"No normal in war," Qiu Jin said. "Refugees." She gestured toward the surrounding hills. "Those coming say Japanese attacking this region now. Major offensive."

Sam grew fearful thinking of the likely atrocities, and of having to pass through an area with Japanese troops.

Qiu Jin took a few more steps and said, "This city is Lukfung. We sleep here."

She led him through narrow streets and alleyways. Halfway down a path, she knocked on a nondescript wooden door. An old man opened the door a few inches and peeked out. Qiu Jin spoke in hushed Cantonese, and the man quickly ushered them inside. He checked both directions before closing the door behind them. Qiu Jin and the man again exchanged words in a rapid conversation. Then the host paused to study Sam as if waiting for an answer.

"He wants to know if you're a downed pilot," Qiu Jin explained.

"No," Sam said and shook his head. The man seemed surprised, perhaps even a bit disappointed, but remained gracious, taking them to a table filled with food, where they were served by a woman, barely five feet tall, likely the man's wife. Sam did his best to eat the food, until his stomach rebelled. The woman gave him a tea that Qiu Jin said would soothe his stomach. After, the woman poured him a warm bath, and Sam soaked his bloody feet in water laced with herbs. The woman cleaned Sam's blisters, applied a soothing ointment to his feet before wrapping them, and helped him climb into a firm, comfortable bed.

Sam slept hard. In his dreams, a platoon of Japanese soldiers burst into his bedroom, guns drawn. He calmly informed the Japanese platoon captain it had been a grueling day, and he was too tired to get up. They'd have to either shoot him or come back for him in the morning.

When Sam awoke, he realized he'd slept until long after dawn. He rose and stumbled into a light-filled interior courtyard, his muscles knotted and sore.

The woman of the house guided him to the table, again set with enough food for a large feast. She slid back a chair and urged Sam to sit, then removed the covers of various dishes and named them in Cantonese—what looked like pork, eggs, rice, and cakes, and more of the tea, which had indeed helped to settle his stomach.

"*Xie xie,*" Sam said. He gave the hostess a grateful bow, then ate what he could keep down.

"How do you feel today?" Qiu Jin asked when she arrived halfway through his breakfast.

"Okay," he said. In truth it felt like every muscle in his body was rebelling, but he wasn't about to tell her that.

She pointed to his swollen bare feet. "Can you walk?"

"I can walk," he said. "If I can't, I'll crawl."

She laughed, reached into a bag, and pulled out a pair of traditional Chinese shoes, placing them on the floor next to Sam's feet. "No crawl necessary."

"Oh God, thank you," Sam said. He slipped the shoes on gently and marveled at the fit.

Qiu Jin pulled pants and a shirt from the bag and gave them to Sam. Then she flashed a coy grin and said, "One more surprise. Come outside."

Sam followed her to the front door. Outside, two men stood next to an oversized wood-and-wicker chair strapped atop two horizontal poles. Sam had seen photographs of ornate British colonial sedan chairs with enclosed boxes and a side door. This one was rustic and open-air.

"You ride today," Qiu Jin said.

Sam ran a loving hand along one of the two twelve-foot bamboo poles supporting the semireclined chair. "Thank you," he said to Qiu Jin. "You're an angel."

"And you're a hunted man," Qiu Jin said. "When shopping, I hear in market the Japanese search hard for you. They say you must not escape. They say you know things. Information that must not reach America."

The Japanese had repeatedly broken international law. If Sam and others could get back alive, their tormentors would be prosecuted for war crimes. "Then let's get moving," he said to Qiu Jin.

The porters carried Sam up steep terrain and across valleys. A mix of low shrubs and emerald grass coated the hillsides like a green carpet, dotted by the occasional scraggly tree. Qiu Jin moved fast along dirt trails, no longer slowed by Sam's weakened condition or ruined feet. She told Sam to continue to keep the hat low on his head and to bend forward, like an old man, so those they passed would not pay him any attention. They soon encountered many other sedan chairs on the road, and Sam realized it was part of the culture and helped him blend in.

Ten miles and three hours later, Qiu Jin came to a sudden halt. So did the porters. She looked up, listening. Sam did also and recognized the sound. An airplane engine. A plane with a large red circle painted under each wing flew over the hill, low and slow. When it had passed, Qiu Jin said, "Looking for you."

The plane reached the end of the valley, then circled back.

Sam felt his anxiety rise. "We're caught in the open," he said. He glanced at the low vegetation. No forest for cover. "Should we run?"

"No. Be normal. Keep head down. We look like everyone else."

Qiu Jin turned and hissed in Cantonese to the porters. They waited for three sedan chairs and six other porters to join them, then proceeded as a larger group. Sam lifted his wide-brimmed hat to steal a peek as the plane made yet another pass. The pilot flew lower this time. Sam felt defenseless, knowing the plane could strafe them at any moment.

"I don't like this," Sam said.

"Stay calm," Qiu Jin barked. "Control your mind."

Her comment made him think of Rudowski sprawled on top of him to keep him from jumping overboard to flee the destroyer's machine gun. He had willed himself not to move, not to panic. He could do that most difficult thing again. Absolutely nothing.

The plane circled once more, then banked toward the nearby ridgeline. Seconds later, it disappeared.

"Do you think they'll be back?" Sam asked.

"Maybe." Qiu Jin studied the distant ridgeline for the plane's return.

"How will we know?"

"Easy," she said. "If they spotted you, then we will walk around a corner, and the soldiers will be waiting."

12

A PRISONER WITHIN

Haifeng, Guangdong Province, China
November 3, 1944

Qiu Jin waved at a stone-and-wood arch and told Sam it marked the entrance to the city of Haifeng. The arch was broken on one side, and only a few mounted Chinese characters remained in place. "We stay here." She paid the porters, and they picked up the sedan chair to leave.

"*Xie xie,*" Sam said to the departing men, clasping their hands and bowing. "*Xie xie.*"

Sam and Qiu Jin moved quickly along the city streets. His feet and legs felt refreshed. He kept his hat tilted low but sneaked sideways glances at the poorly clad people bustling along the dirt roads and deduced many to also be refugees of war. Copper-colored brassware hung on storefront pegs. Washed linens swayed on clotheslines, and tea shops did brisk business. Bamboo chimes danced and played tunes in the breeze.

Qiu Jin led them through a maze of narrow side streets before she knocked on a small, blue door. A stooped elderly woman answered. She and Qiu Jin exchanged words. The old woman straightened and turned to Sam, whispering in Cantonese, though Sam caught an English-sounding word, "Doolittle."

The woman stepped back, and Qiu Jin checked the street in both directions before leading Sam through the doorway.

Inside, Qiu Jin interpreted what the woman had said. "She say, many people searching for you. But you are safe here."

"*Xie xie,*" Sam said to the old woman. He turned to Qiu Jin. "Can you tell me what this word 'Doolittle' means? I heard it yesterday too."

"A famous American pilot," Qiu Jin said. "When the Americans surrendered in the Philippines, and you became a prisoner, the Americans were losing the war badly. They need something good. One week later, they attacked Tokyo. Sixteen planes from an aircraft carrier. Doolittle was the leader."

"They bombed Tokyo?"

"Yes. It surprised Japan. Gave us all hope. The planes did not have enough fuel to return to the aircraft carrier, so the pilots flew to China and parachuted over the coast. Chinese people helped Doolittle and the other pilots escape the Japanese. Hid them. Got them to safety." Qiu Jin's expression turned somber. "The Japanese came like a swarm of locusts and destroyed everything, looking for the pilots. They burned entire villages. They tortured, raped, and killed many of my people."

Qiu Jin and her family faced even greater risk than Sam had realized, as did the occupants of each house at which they stopped.

Sam again soaked in a hot bath and changed into clean clothes. The woman bandaged his feet, then brought plates of food. Sam was able to eat a little more each meal. Afterward, Qiu Jin arranged a traditional massage, and Sam relished the idea of gentle hands kneading his sore muscles. Instead, he spent the next hour in agony. A small, wiry man came into Sam's room and motioned for him to undress and lie on the bed. Then he hopped on Sam and used the edges of his hands and his elbows to strike nearly every inch of Sam's emaciated body. He paused only to shift positions or to get Sam to roll over. Last, he cracked Sam's toes and fingers, then his neck. He departed without having spoken a single word. Though it had been painful, afterward Sam's body felt better than it had in years.

That evening, in a quiet corner of the house, Qiu Jin made them tea. "You have suffered," she said, handing him a steaming glass of orange-scented tea. "This I know. Tell me about your better days."

Sam recounted the world he'd left behind in America, specifically in Eagle Grove. He talked about his Minnesota childhood, the Depression, his family losing their farm, and him often going hungry.

"You know hunger," she said.

"I thought I did, but not like what I experienced in the prison camps."

"You have someone?" Qiu Jin asked. She pointed at the ring on the string hanging around his neck.

Sam described Sarah and told Qiu Jin he had not heard from her in three years. "She's a teacher," he said. "Like you. She's strong and smart also. You remind me of her."

"My father says teaching is a great act of hope," Qiu Jin said. "An old Chinese proverb says, 'If you plan for one year, sow rice. If you plan for a decade, plant trees. But if you plan for a lifetime, educate people.'"

"He's a wise man, your father. And brave."

"Yes," she said. "He is so."

"Tell me about your life," Sam said.

Qiu Jin shared how she grew up an only child, how her parents instilled in her a fierce independence and a love of learning. They named her after a famous educator and activist who fought for women's rights, and they bought Qiu Jin books in English and took her to see a few Western movies.

In time, the conversation shifted to their war experiences. Qiu Jin turned solemn as Sam described conditions inside the POW camps and on board the *Arisan Maru*, then its sinking. "I'm ready to leave it all behind," Sam said. "Ready to get back home."

"You're not ready," Qiu Jin said.

Sam set down his teacup. "Why not?"

"Your bad memories will follow you to America. They'll haunt your sleep."

He wondered if he screamed when he slept, or if she had noticed his hands trembling.

"You will be free on the outside, but still a prisoner inside." She touched her chest.

Sam suspected she was right. "What can I do?" He didn't expect any words of wisdom, but he underestimated Qiu Jin.

"Each time you have a bad memory, gently replace it with a good one," Qiu Jin said. "You have suffered much war, but you had happy moments before."

"Many."

"Replace bad with good."

Sam thought about the Paradise Theater and all the movies he and Sarah had seen together, how he'd used those memories to create good moments for the prisoners inside the camps and in the *Arisan Maru*'s hold. He told this to Qiu Jin and asked if it had all been predestined for him to work the projectors at the movie theater.

"Yes," she said. "It was. A mind is like a movie projector. You can turn on and off. You choose which movies to watch. If you don't like a movie, you shut it off. Show only the good ones. Watch them again and again."

Sam thought of how he and Sarah used to sit and watch the same movie multiple times over the course of its run, or use the time to neck. How they used to dream of a better life together. That's what he would try to remember. He wondered if she had waited for him, not knowing if he was alive or dead. He sipped his tea and again set down the cup. "You and your father are also lucky to be alive."

Qiu Jin lowered her cup. She spoke softly. "I did not think so. I wanted to be killed like my mother and my friends."

The comment saddened him, but Sam understood. He, too, had known that dark, desperate desire to die, and he did not ask Qiu Jin to explain. She did anyway.

"When Japanese soldiers came to our school, they raped and killed many girls for many hours."

Sam shifted in his chair. "I'm sorry."

"Rather than kill my father, the principal, they made him watch." Qiu Jin's voice turned bitter. "They raped student after student to dishonor him."

Sam recalled Yoshida's frequent belittling. How he had made Sam watch as he murdered nine blood brothers to dishonor him, then told Sam the only way to restore his honor was to take his own life.

Qiu Jin swallowed hard, then said, "After so much rape, the Japanese soldiers got tired. To shame my father more, they made him rape a student."

Sam shut his eyes and thought of the gentle fisherman.

"They brought him a sixteen-year-old girl, Wei, and ripped off her clothes. My father refused. He begged them to kill him. The Japanese killed Wei instead, stabbing her with bayonets."

Sam had no words to offer, stunned.

"They brought another naked girl, Yan," Qiu Jin said, voice soft. "Again, my father refused. He would not rape her. Again, he begged for the soldiers to kill him. They killed Yan too.

"When they brought the third girl, also sixteen, my father was a broken man. He cried and begged them to spare her."

What Sam had witnessed in the camps now seemed to pale in comparison with what the gentle fisherman had suffered.

"He . . ." Qiu Jin looked to be holding back tears. "To save the girl's life, he raped her while the soldiers laughed and jeered."

Sam said, "I'm so sorry."

"The soldiers got called away, and we escaped. For more than one year, we wandered. No food. No home. No money. Just begging." A lone tear rolled from her cheek to her chin.

"We came to Kitchioh village, and the people welcomed us. They wanted an English teacher, so I started to teach. After Nanjing, my father would never go inside a schoolhouse again. He helped on a fishing boat and worked very hard. In time, he got his own boat."

"And your boy, little Chen?" asked Sam.

"My brother," she said.

"You mean 'son,'" Sam said. "The correct English word is 'son.'"

Qiu Jin fell silent. She took a deep breath. Then she said, "My brother and my son."

The air thickened into a profound silence. Again, Sam couldn't find the words to speak. What could he possibly say after such a horrific story?

"Chen does not know," Qiu Jin said. "Only Father and I know what we were forced to do. And now you."

"That's why you're here, helping me, because of what happened in Nanjing. All you've been through. All your family has been through."

"That is why," Qiu Jin said. "We never fully heal from such deep wounds, but the deeper the wound, the further the light can enter our bodies and our souls." She managed a faint smile, then added, "I have much light inside."

"I don't know how."

"That day in Nanjing, when I was just sixteen, was the worst day of my life. Months later, when Chen was born, it could have been awful too, but I created a new story of my son, and his birth became the best day of my life. That day gave my life purpose," she said, making Sam think of his last conversation with Father Tom and the promise he'd made. "I would take care of Chen. I would educate children. I would fight for my country." Qiu Jin locked her gaze on Sam and placed a hand over her heart. "I grew. My relationships are deeper now, even with strangers, like you. I appreciate each moment of each day. Each person."

Sam's own trauma had certainly turned him into a different person, but he could not yet look at what he'd been through with the same perspective. He could not say he was a better person, and he did not know if he would ever become one.

Time would tell.

13

This Can't Happen

Guangdong Province, China
November 4, 1944

The following day, Sam and Qiu Jin traveled for miles in carriages towed behind bicycles. Sturdy porters pedaled across fertile green valleys dotted with walled villages. They passed through small towns with loud, tinny music, and the bustle of busy crowds. Given plenty of time to think, Sam processed the previous night's conversation. He knew the adage "Time heals all wounds," but he also knew Qiu Jin was telling him that was not true, not in and of itself. But if she could come to terms with her past, then perhaps Sam could also. Like Qiu Jin, Sam vowed to pick the best movies to remember.

If he survived.

By midafternoon they followed a fast-moving stream down a narrow mountain gorge. Thick trees and dense green brush bordering the trail provided protection from the sun; the wind gently whispered through the leaves and birds chirped. When the incline became too steep, Sam and Qiu Jin proceeded on foot while their porters carried the bicycles on their shoulders. Qiu Jin spoke to the porters in soft but sober tones. Everyone seemed to be on edge.

Minutes later, their hushed talk grew louder and more frequent.

"We're being watched," Qiu Jin explained to Sam, her voice stern.

Sam turned to look behind them, but Qiu Jin shook her head.

"Do not look. Just keep walking."

"How many?" Sam said. He listened for footsteps, but the rushing stream and the birds made it hard to hear anything else.

"Walk faster," she replied.

Qiu Jin and the porters sped up. A twig snapped in the woods to Sam's right. The group halted.

Qiu Jin gripped her sword handle, but she didn't draw the blade. Her eyes scanned the foliage. Moments later, she gestured Sam forward, setting an even faster pace. "Hurry," she urged. "They're coming."

Men's garbled voices came from directly behind them.

"Run!" Qiu Jin shouted.

The group broke into a sprint. Sam's scrawny legs and bandaged feet struggled to keep up. His chest heaved for air, but he concentrated on pumping his knees high and hard.

"Faster!" Qiu Jin cried. She grabbed Sam and half dragged him forward.

They scrambled another two hundred yards, past rock outcroppings and twisted tree roots, then rounded a sharp bend and came to a sudden halt. A dozen uniformed soldiers blocked their path, each armed with a rifle. Half the soldiers knelt, the rest stood, all of them with their fingers on the triggers of their weapons. Ammo clips and grenades hung from their belts and shoulders. What burned deepest in Sam's mind, though, were the soldiers' stonelike expressions. Men accustomed to war. Men willing to kill.

More soldiers approached from behind them, guns also pointed. More still came from the forest. A perfect ambush.

A stern-faced soldier stepped forward and leveled his pistol at Sam's forehead. Sam refused to raise his hands. He wouldn't be a prisoner again. His mind told him to surrender, but his heart and body refused.

Never again.

The squad commander stepped closer, grunted, then flashed a satisfied smile. Sam refused to break eye contact. They could kill him, but not without looking him in the eye.

The squad commander lowered his pistol. "We finally find you." His English was poor, but the meaning quite clear. He tipped Sam's hat back with the end of his pistol barrel for a better look. "American GI?"

Sam prepared for a hard slap, like so many slaps before, and suppressed a sudden urge to strike first.

"American GI?" the squad commander asked again in English.

Sam threw back his shoulders. "Damn right. *Amerika jin.*" Then he spat on the squad commander's boot. The others burst into laughter.

"Go ahead and celebrate, you sons of bitches," Sam said to the soldiers. "American planes are flying over Tokyo as we speak. You're all going to die right along with me."

14

A War Hero

Guangdong Province, China
November 4, 1944

The squad commander shouted something, and Sam realized from his recent experiences that the man spoke Cantonese, not Japanese. The soldiers relaxed.

"Sons of bitches," he said to Sam, still laughing.

Sam turned to Qiu Jin, who had placed a hand over her mouth to stifle her own laughter, though her eyes danced with it. "What the hell's going on?" he asked.

"I was wrong," she said. "Not Japanese soldiers. Chinese guerillas. They're on your side, Sam Carlson. They will escort us the rest of the way."

Sam looked at the commander, then at the others. The squad commander handed him a cigarette. "Not Japanese," he said. "Sons of bitches."

The others again laughed.

Sam joined in, but still didn't fully believe what had just happened. After having his hopes crushed so often, he couldn't fathom his good fortune. He wasn't yet out of the woods, not by a long shot, but at least he now had the ability to fight. He put the cigarette in his mouth, tentative, then leaned toward the man's lit match, and took a deep drag. He said the only thing possible, and he did it in perfect Chinese: *"Xie xie."*

Qiu Jin explained the local Chinese guerilla movement to Sam as the commander and his soldiers smoked and rested, their guns leaning against rocks. Sam had been too focused on the men's weapons to notice their simple uniforms lacked the buttoned shirts, high boots, and other attire of professional Japanese soldiers.

After a few minutes, the leader shouted something in Cantonese, then waved his hand in a circle. The soldiers quickly snuffed cigarettes but didn't leave butts on the ground. They slipped them into pouches, grabbed packs and rifles, rose, and formed a line. One of them obscured marks in the ground with a branch, leaving no trace they had been there.

"We go now," Qiu Jin said.

"Will they escort me all the way to Kunming?" Sam asked.

"No. They take you to Ag-farts."

That stopped him. "Ag-farts?"

"Ag-farts," the guerilla commander chimed. He flashed Sam a thumbs-up sign.

"Okay," Sam said. "Ag-farts it is."

The group wound its way up a switchback trail for more than a mile, crested a high ridge of pine forest, then stopped to survey a vast valley below and a city surrounded by a checkerboard of rice paddies. The squad leader pointed to the city. "Hingning." The group started their descent. The bicycle drivers rode the brakes hard to avoid careening down the mountainside. The group peeled off the main trail at the valley floor and turned along the tree line that bordered a series of rice paddies.

Three hundred yards later, they huddled in a shady grove to rest, and the guerillas made plans. Qiu Jin conversed in Cantonese as their escorts studied the city, presumably scanning for any trouble. After several minutes, the commander said, "Come." He guided Sam thirty feet to the tree line. Across the flat sea of seedling rice, on the city's edge, a compound emerged from the rice fields. The enclosure had tan walls fifteen feet high and a hundred feet long.

Moments later, the commander signaled for the group to move out. They stepped onto rice paddy embankments and worked their way through the maze of low dikes and fields. When they reached the compound, a heavy metal gate swung open and a man waved the entourage in, then quickly closed and locked the gate behind them. Three metal poles rose in the compound's center with a ring of white stones around the base. A flag billowed in the breeze from each pole—the center flag red, white, and blue, with stars and stripes.

The sight was so startling, Sam collapsed to his knees and gaped up at it. When the tears started, he was helpless to stop them.

Qiu Jin placed a hand on Sam's shoulder.

"Americans," the guerilla commander said, swinging a hand to indicate the compound. "Sons of bitches."

Half a dozen one- and two-story buildings lined the compound's interior. One structure had a fifteen-foot radio antenna mounted on its roof. The walled fortress had a garden area and a water well. Several jeeps and motorcycles sat parked nearby.

A tall man bounded down building steps and strode toward them in a crisp, khaki uniform, a gold oak leaf pinned on each shoulder—a US major. Other American soldiers exited the buildings as well.

Sam stood as the major greeted the guerilla commander. The guerilla leader gestured a thumb toward Sam. "American."

Sam stiffened to attention and gave a sharp salute. "Sergeant Sam Carlson. A Company, 194th Tank Battalion. Manila, the Philippines."

The major froze. He did not return the salute. "Did you say 194th Tank Battalion, Manila?"

"Yes, sir."

"Bataan?"

"Yes, sir."

"Put your hand down, Sergeant." The major shook his head. "As I live and breathe. A Battling Bastard of Bataan. Gentlemen!" he called out to the others in the compound. "Attention! We are in the presence of a goddamn war hero."

The major and the others in the compound, including the Chinese guerillas, snapped to attention and saluted Sam.

Sam didn't fully understand. He was just grateful to be there. "Thank you, sir. It's been a long time since I've seen Old Glory."

"No, Sergeant. Thank *you*." The major lowered his arm and extended his hand. "I'm Major Lucas Fletcher. And I am damn proud to welcome you." He shook Sam's hand. Then he pulled a small leather bag from his pants pocket and tossed it to Qiu Jin. The coins inside jingled. "The United States of America thanks you, ma'am."

"You are most welcome, Major." Qiu Jin slipped the payment into her shoulder bag.

"A hundred dollars," Fletcher said to Sam. "Standard rate for bringing us a downed pilot, though you're worth a lot more than that." He spoke to the Chinese commander and his soldiers. "Boys, help yourselves. You know where the candy store is." He gestured toward a nearby table with boxes. "We just got a new load. Guns. Ammo. Grenades. Cigarettes. The works."

"Got dynamite?" the guerilla commander asked while his men scrambled to the supply table.

"Enough to blow up half the bridges in Guangdong Province."

The squad commander gave the major a thumbs-up and turned to join his men.

"Sir, I don't understand," Sam said to Major Fletcher. "You're flying a US flag, have supplies for the guerillas, and pay bounties for returned Americans. What is this place?"

"We're a forward weather station," Fletcher replied, not trying to hide a sly grin. "We provide meteorological data to the Fourteenth Air Force. Our daily weather reports help American pilots from Kunming know what they're flying into." He cleared his throat and studied the sky as if checking the weather.

"Weather station?" Sam said.

Major Fletcher smiled. "It's complicated. I'll explain over dinner. I've been saving a good bottle of whiskey for Christmas, but I think we'll drink it tonight to celebrate your safe arrival."

"I'd like that," Sam said. "Can you tell me why the soldiers refer to this place as Ag-farts?"

Fletcher smiled. "We're a special unit of the Fourteenth Air Force out of Kunming, more than a thousand miles west of here," he explained. "They call us the Air and Ground Forces Resources and Technical Staff. The acronym is A-G-F-R-T-S, so . . . Ag-farts." Major Fletcher stared at Sam again, as if in disbelief. "A Battling Bastard of Bataan. As I live and breathe. People are going to want to know about you, son." He led Sam to a rustic room, where Sam shared a condensed version of his and the other POWs' ordeal. When he'd finished, the major sent an urgent radio message to Kunming.

Later in the evening, Fletcher told Sam that the top secret radio message had traveled halfway around the world to the Pentagon in Washington, DC. From there, it flew across the Potomac River to the White House, where a stunned President Roosevelt had ordered the tragic news of the POWs being put in the holds of unmarked freighters forwarded to Pearl Harbor, Hawaii. "FDR and Submarine Command now know we blew up a Japanese freighter carrying eighteen hundred POWs," Fletcher said.

Sam nodded. A tear rolled down his cheek. He'd done what he'd set out to do. He'd kept his word to Father Tom.

PART 6

1

Dreams Change

FRUPAC
Honolulu, Hawaii
November 4, 1944

Sarah spoke from the open doorway of Jasper Holmes's office in the FRUPAC building. "You wanted to see me, sir?"

"Yes, Ensign Haber. Come in. Close the door."

Closing Holmes's door was unusual. Sarah swung it shut and tried to read Holmes. He had been in a good mood lately. They all had been in a good mood, given the recent stunning progress of the war. In Europe, the Soviets were advancing through Eastern Prussia, and the Allies in Europe were fighting toward Germany. In the Pacific, General MacArthur controlled much of the Philippines, and would soon liberate Manila. B-29 bombers pounded the Japanese home islands, preparing for what felt certain to be the war's final chapter. Secret radio intercepts by Sarah and her colleagues helped the bombers avoid bombing POW camps in Osaka, Kyoto, Nagoya, and more than a dozen other cities. They also searched intercepted messages for any orders by Japanese command to retreating Japanese forces to execute the POWs.

"You're a damn fine cryptanalyst, Ensign Haber," Holmes said.

"Thank you, sir." Sarah went on high alert. Was she about to be fired?

"This cable arrived from Washington," Holmes said. "Straight from George Marshall's office at the Pentagon."

General George Marshall served as Army Chief of Staff and was FDR's top military commander. Sarah braced for devastating news as Holmes read the message out loud: "Be advised. Japanese freighter *Arisan Maru* sunk by torpedo October 24. Carried 1,800 American POWs. Only one survivor."

"They wanted us to know the ship carried POWs," Holmes said. "They apparently didn't think we did."

"Where did they get their information?"

"That survivor they mentioned."

"Just one?"

"Yes."

Perhaps to give her a moment to collect herself, Holmes lit his pipe and took a puff. "They'll call this an accident," he said at last, smoke escaping his lips. "No one will ever know otherwise."

"Accident?" Sarah said. "That was no accident. They ordered that submarine to fire upon that ship."

"They did," Holmes agreed.

"And I was a part of it."

"Don't flatter yourself, Ensign." Holmes's words had a bite. "You did your job, your sworn duty. The decision to fire on that ship was made way, way over your head, as well as mine. Clear your conscience. That's an order."

"I wish it was that simple," Sarah said.

Holmes came around the desk. "I've come to learn that secrecy is a double-edged sword," he said. "It sometimes inflicts deeper wounds on its wielder than upon the opponents. We don't get medals, Ensign Haber. Our work is secret, even within the military. But you and your colleagues turned the tide of this war. Your work saved thousands of lives, possibly hundreds of thousands."

Sarah didn't speak. She knew Holmes was right, but she didn't feel that way.

"You deserve a medal right now, Ensign Haber. A Purple Heart for gallantry, bravery, and deep devotion to your duty in the Pacific Theater, and for the invisible wounds you sustained while in service to your country."

Holmes was right. Sarah and her colleagues here in Hawaii and in Washington, DC, had helped to turn the war's tide and they'd saved thousands of lives. But there would be no medals, or any acknowledgment.

She also knew she had blamed herself for someone else's decision, and that person, not her, should bear the heavy burden of those eighteen hundred lives. She only wished she could have saved one more, that she could have saved Sam.

"Can I ask, sir, the name of the survivor?"

"It wasn't provided. I'm sorry. I can try and find out."

Sarah nodded, but the odds of Sam being that one survivor, or even still being alive at all, were minuscule, which was saying there was still a chance. And she steeled herself with the thought that she didn't even know if Sam was *on* the *Arisan Maru*.

What mattered was that, yes, he could still be alive.

And if Sam were dead, Sarah would grieve, but she would never forget. Sam would forever be her first love. She knew he would want her to carry on with her life. She would survive, as would Sam's parents and siblings, and all the other families in her small town who had lost brothers, husbands, fathers, and friends. Across America people would find a way to go on. They would hold each other up, support one another, and push each other forward.

Because, what else could they do?

Life would progress moment to moment, day to day, week to week, month to month, and year to year. They would rebuild their lives. The double-edged sword of secrecy of which Holmes spoke had indeed cut her badly, a deep wound that would take time to heal. Maybe years.

But it would heal.

"Are you okay, Ensign Haber?" Holmes asked. It didn't sound like a commanding officer speaking to an ensign. It sounded like a father concerned about his daughter's well-being.

"Yes, sir," Sarah said, though she wondered if her new insight would last. Only time would tell. Moment to moment.

"Something else, Ensign."

"Sir?"

"As you know, your commission expires six months after the war's end, but we are training more and more cryptanalysts every day, and can use them to provide our regular staff a break. I understand as well as anyone the pressure and the conflict this job inflicts. I also understand what you recently went through. As a result, I put in a request to allow you a two-week R&R."

"All the same, sir. I'd prefer to keep working."

"Paperwork is done, Ensign. You return stateside Monday, November 13. Go home. Spend the Thanksgiving holiday with your family. Recharge. Then get back here and we'll end this damn war together."

"I can't even think in those terms, sir."

"None of us can, but it will happen. Just as the Great War eventually came to an end. And when it does end, we'll have to get back to a new normal. Whatever that might be." He sighed. "One more thing I am obliged to impress upon you. While you are on leave you must maintain the confidentiality and secrecy of this operation. You cannot discuss anything about the work performed here. Not even the existence of this base."

"I understand, fully."

"That includes not discussing any message you deciphered—especially the message regarding the *Arisan Maru*. Word has come from the Pentagon that all messages will be classified. Brass up top intends to bury this bit of information."

"Until when?"

"I don't know," Holmes said. "But I suspect by the time they declassify our records, nearly an entire generation will have passed. No one will remember."

"May I ask why, sir?" Sarah suspected she knew, but she wanted to hear it.

"I don't know why, Ensign, not for certain. I can only deduce and suspect, like you. But I do know this, and I suspect you do too—the world has been forever changed, and none of us who experienced this war will ever be the same. Hopefully, we have learned from this horrific experience, and it is up to us, those who survived, to teach those who come after us, so this is never repeated. The world will always have its Adolf Hitlers, Benito Mussolinis, and Tojos. There will always be evil, and we must be prepared to prevent that evil from spreading, as you have done here. Does that help?"

"It does," Sarah said, though she doubted anyone in Washington ever said it so eloquently. She suspected the powers in Washington simply didn't want to answer to the American people for torpedoing a Japanese ship knowing it held eighteen hundred Allied POWs, though it was done with the intent to end the war and to save more lives, a rationale that now looked to have been realized. She understood their logic, but she knew it would be hard, if not impossible, for everyday Americans to stomach. It remained hard for her.

"Finally, you received a letter. Personal and confidential." He handed the letter to Sarah in an envelope marked only with a US Navy seal. No return address. Then he said, "Get home. Forget this war for a bit. Then get back here so we can finish it." He snapped to attention and offered Sarah a salute, which she returned.

Sarah left the commander's office stunned. She hadn't been home in so long. Now, the stark reality hit her like a sledgehammer. Could she go home, really? Could she go home to Eagle Grove and all the ghosts that would surely haunt her there? She couldn't imagine walking past the Paradise Theater without thinking of Sam, or past the Presbyterian church and not being reminded of the miracle of Eagle Grove. The thought of the white wedding dress in the storefront window brought her to tears. Maybe going home wasn't such a good idea. Maybe what she needed was a fresh start in a new place, where memories would not bombard and torment her.

She looked down at the letter and knew right away it was not from Grace. They had written to one another frequently. Grace had met a fella in DC and said things were getting serious. Sarah was happy for her and hoped something good came out of this war, for someone.

At her desk she used a letter opener to slice open the envelope and remove the letter. It was from Captain William Russell.

Dearest Sarah:

I hope this letter finds you well.

Forgive me for not writing earlier. Two reasons prevented it. One, my commission aboard the USS Alabama *did not allow time for letter writing, but that wasn't the primary reason. The primary reason was writing to you would have been too painful.*

I have thought of you often and of our time together in Washington, DC, which was, since my wife's death, the best year of my life. I have no doubt you have done a fantastic job at your new post in JICPOA. You are a cryptanalyst without peer.

You are also a woman without peer. I never thought I'd meet anyone, after my wife's death, who I could love again. But I have come to realize, through our many working dinners and our time spent at the Annex, I came to love you, with all my heart. I wanted you to know that, and to also know I still love you and likely always will.

But I also know you have someone else in your life, someone you love, and I wish with all my heart your soldier comes home to you and the two of you live a full life together as you clearly intended before this damn war got in the way.

I want you to also know that should that not happen, whatever the reason, or should your feelings and your dreams change, I am here for you. I can't promise you much, only that I will love you above all others, and hope that you can love me just as much.

I hope this war will soon come to an end.

My address and phone number following the war are above.

A man has to dream to live his life.

I dream of one day answering your call.

Bill

Sarah lowered the letter, then went back and read the last paragraphs. "Dreams change," she said out loud.

How very true.

2

OVER THE HUMP

Air and Ground Forces Resources and Technical Staff (Ag-farts)
Hingning, Guangdong Province, China
November 5, 1944

Early the following morning, the world seemed like a new place for Sam. A swirl of purple and orange stretched itself over tree-covered hills and pulled the sun behind it. Birds welcomed the new dawn. Sam made his way from the hut where he had slept to Major Fletcher, who was drinking coffee and sitting on a porch.

Fletcher told Sam news of his miraculous survival "will not be further disseminated until you are back home."

"Why can't they tell my family, my sweetheart?"

Fletcher shook his head. "We have to assume Jap forces are listening. There's been no mention of your name."

This sounded like military bull to Sam.

"Sorry to push you off so fast, given your weakened condition," Fletcher said, "but I'm told Jap forces are closing in and it's best to keep you on the move." He walked Sam to a large truck idling in the AGFRTS compound. "We've already lost a forward station near here. Ours might fall soon."

"But you'll be all right?"

"The guerillas will get us out of here if, and when, that time comes. We'll be fine."

"If you don't mind, sir, I'd like to say goodbye and thank Qiu Jin."

"I don't mind, Sergeant, but Qiu Jin left with the guerillas last night under the cover of darkness, after resupplying."

Sam had been asleep in his tent, passed out from too much whiskey. "Can I get a message to her somehow?" he asked, though he knew the answer.

"Negative, Sergeant. Too risky."

It was unlikely Sam would ever see the young woman again, like him, a survivor.

Sam looked around the compound, then gave a final, crisp salute to Major Fletcher and the American flag before he hopped into the truck and they departed the compound. His Chinese driver bounced the rickety contraption along steep, twisting roads. The vehicle spewed smoke, its engine burning camphor, a flammable oil made from local evergreen trees.

Each mile Sam progressed toward freedom, his fear of being captured increased.

So close now. He was so close.

Two hundred bumpy miles later, the truck rolled into a small village, where Sam spent the night. The next day, he and his driver covered another two hundred miles and reached a small base with an airstrip.

"Too many Japanese on roads," Sam's driver said in broken English. "You fly now." He gestured to the dirt runway.

Sam spent three nights waiting for a plane to arrive. During that time, he got new GI clothing from his American military hosts. He also enjoyed his first American food in years. At dinner, Sam caressed the crisp white tablecloth and gripped his silverware. The look and feel of it didn't seem real.

His third day, November 9, an American cargo plane tossed dust clouds as it skipped along the runway. As the plane refueled, the pilot stepped down from the cockpit.

"Are you Sergeant Sam Carlson?" he asked.

"I am."

The pilot snapped to attention and gave Sam a salute. "I am damn proud to have you on board my plane, Sergeant Carlson."

"And I am damn happy to be your passenger," Sam said.

They flew eight hundred miles over enemy-held territory to China's southwestern corner and landed at the large American air base in Kunming. Major General Claire L. Chennault, the commanding officer, gave Sam a personal welcome, then whisked him to a private office where his top staff waited. There, Sam shared more details about his story beyond what Major Fletcher's message had provided them. Afterward, Chennault sent an urgent update to Washington, DC, to confirm the former POW's arrival and his story.

Sam's hosts explained how the US Fourteenth Air Force had kept China in the war. As US bombers flew long-range missions over Japanese-held territories, planes carrying supplies flew to China over the Himalaya Mountains. Once in Kunming, the weapons, ammunition, and other supplies were distributed to Chinese military units.

On Sam's second night in Kunming, just as servers brought dessert, an air raid siren blasted. Soldiers leaped to their feet, knocking over chairs as they scurried to foxholes. After everything he'd been through, Sam figured the building was as safe as anywhere else, so he stayed behind and moved from table to table, eating the abandoned desserts. He'd pay for his gluttony later.

Sam's presence at Kunming was kept quiet and his stay short. He boarded a C-47 cargo plane with Major Homer Sanders. Major General Chennault told Sam he'd handpicked Sanders for the critical assignment of getting Sam home, and he had ordered Sanders to keep Sam from talking to anyone until the US Army could debrief him.

The first leg of the journey nearly killed them. Their airplane, nicknamed Double Trouble, dropped through treacherous narrow passes, several times losing thousands of feet in altitude in seconds. When it rose over the Himalayas, the world's tallest mountain range, many of its peaks hidden in clouds, two-hundred-mile-per-hour winds buffeted the plane. Freezing temperatures inside the aircraft added to Sam's misery, but it was a palace compared to his POW accommodations.

"Is that what I think it is?" Sam asked. He'd spotted a wrecked cargo plane out his window that looked like a duplicate of their own plane.

"It is," Sanders said in a solemn voice. "There are more than four hundred wrecks just like it spread across these mountains. The pilots call it 'the hump.' Try not to look."

"Too late," Sam said.

Three terrifying hours later, the plane landed safely in eastern India. Sam wobbled along the tarmac on weak legs. Major Sanders wasn't walking any more confidently. The pilot, however, strode over to the chief mechanic and received a five-dollar bill.

"What's that all about?" Sam asked Sanders.

Sanders smiled. "The pilot won the bet."

"The bet?"

"Whether Double Trouble would make it to Kunming and back. Welcome to Assam," Sanders said. "Home to the 490th Bombardment Squadron, Medium."

Sanders took Sam to the chief communications officer, Arnold Spielberg. "You won't stay long." The officer waved a piece of paper at Sam. "FDR ordered you home right away."

"FDR knows about me?"

"He does, Sergeant Carlson," Spielberg said.

"Can I let my family know I'm alive now?"

"Not just yet," Sanders said. "My job now is to get you on a plane to Washington, DC, leaving in two hours."

Spielberg studied Sam. "They made us bump all the other passengers from your flight," he said. "It seems you're a man with a lot of valuable information, Sergeant Carlson."

"Apparently," Sam said, including information that could be embarrassing to the United States military. After his hair-raising trip "over the hump," Sam dreaded getting back on a plane again, but he would have swum the ocean to get to American soil.

Another flight took him farther across India. The pilots realized they carried a valued passenger, even though they did not know any details and did not say much to Sam. They treated Sam to aerial views of the Taj Mahal and other sights. Two more flights took Sam to Karachi, then to the Iranian port city of Abadan. The plane lost one engine and a wheel shortly after departing Abadan and had to circle back. A rough landing back in Iran further damaged the aircraft.

When Sam stumbled from the plane, he saw the damage and said to the pilot, "You landed her on one wing, one wheel, and the nose."

The pilot smiled. "I'd call that a beautiful three-point landing," he said, like he did it every day.

When a new plane arrived, Sam eventually flew west toward Cairo. The pilot said, "I got firm orders not to ask you questions, but I reckon your being alive involves a miracle or two."

"More than a few, I'm realizing."

"I figured you might want to see some places famous for that kind of stuff." The pilot dropped low to give Sam close-up views of Jericho, Jerusalem, and Palestine.

When the pilot landed the plane safely on a Cairo runway, Sanders whisked Sam to a hotel to spend the night, but thirty minutes later, Sanders said a new message had arrived from Washington, DC. "They want you home 'yesterday.'"

Exhausted, but still eager to do anything that would get him home sooner, Sam left his Cairo hotel and boarded yet another plane, this one a cargo plane, and sat next to two large airplane engines headed to the United States for repairs.

In Casablanca, Sam was to switch to a chartered Pan American Airways military flight. The plane was waiting on the runway, but fully loaded with sixty senior officers, all of them ranked major or higher. Minutes before departure, the pilots got their new orders, and one by one, every officer exited the aircraft.

Sam's escort, Major Sanders, led him onto the empty Pan Am flight. From his window, Sam could see the angry and confused former passengers standing on the tarmac as their plane departed without them.

The flight from Casablanca took Sam across the Atlantic, first to the Azores, then Bermuda. He departed Bermuda at sunset, under a spectacular orange sky. Night came fast. Too excited to sleep, being this close to American soil, Sam stared out the airplane window at the vast, starry solitude and thought, as he always did, of Sarah.

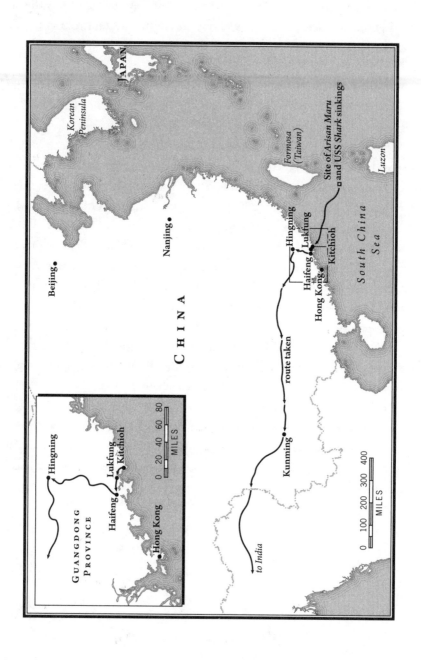

3

AMERICAN SOIL

New York City
November 13, 1944

As the plane approached New York City, Sam was alerted to the darkened Statue of Liberty, and he could barely make out her raised arm and torch seemingly reaching out to him.

"Welcome home," Major Sanders said.

Sam fought back tears. "Good to be home, sir."

In the terminal, a skeptical customs official delayed Sam's arrival, curious as to why Sam wore a plain, unmarked uniform, and why he didn't have any identification. Where exactly had he been?

Sam smiled. "How much time do you have?"

"Don't say another word," Major Sanders interrupted. "Wait here."

Sanders stepped away to make a phone call. Minutes later, the customs agent's phone rang. After a very brief exchange, the agent said, "Yes, *sir!*"

Sam was on his way again.

Major Sanders had more news. They had been ordered straight to Washington, DC, rather than stay overnight in New York City. Their tired pilots pulled the airplane back out of its hangar and refueled, and ninety minutes later, they landed in the nation's capital. A private car met Sam and the major. "The Statler Hotel," an exhausted Sanders said.

The driver replied, "Yes, sir. Right away, sir."

Sam leaned forward from the back seat to look at the driver. She wore a uniform. He settled back into his seat alongside Sanders. "A woman?" he asked. "In the Army?"

"Thousands of them in both the Army and the Navy," the major said. "They're doing an outstanding job." He paused, then added, "You'd be surprised what work they do."

When the car rolled to a stop, Sam climbed out and walked into the city's newest, fanciest hotel, just two blocks from the White House. The major checked his guest in while Sam admired the vast lobby, marble pillars, intricate throw rugs, and rich burgundy woodwork. Everything looked lush and comfortable, as if no war was going on, which made Sam angry and annoyed, but he summoned the spirit of Pete Chavez and plopped down onto a tall-backed velvet sofa, savoring the luxury.

After checking them in, Sanders took Sam to his room, which would have accommodated two dozen of his fellow POWs comfortably. "Order food, drinks, whatever you want, and charge it to the Army," the major said. He paused, then spoke in a stern tone. "Now, here is the hardest part. The phone in the room will not call out. You are still forbidden to call anyone or talk to anyone about your ordeal until you are fully debriefed."

Sam grew angry. "Why the hell not, Major? After everything I've been through, what my family and my sweetheart have been through, why can't I at least let them know I'm alive? My mother has no doubt worried herself sick, maybe even presumed me dead." He also feared Sarah had already moved on with her life, maybe had married someone else. "What's the difference if we at least let them know I'm alive?" he asked. "I'm not in any danger of being captured by the Japs in this hotel."

The major recited his next words slowly, as if each word was its own sentence. "I'm sorry, Sergeant. Those are my orders."

"Screw those orders. Can't an exception be made?"

"Not by me. But if I may? If your family presumes you're dead, do you really want to tell them differently over the phone, a disembodied voice?"

It was a good point. Sam was also taking out his anger and frustration on someone who could do nothing to solve the problem.

After Sanders left, Sam checked the bathroom. He flipped the light switch on, off, and on again, a convenience he had once taken for granted. He stroked the cold porcelain sink and mindlessly turned the water faucet on and off. He flushed the toilet. He put a rubber stopper in the white oval bathtub's drain, then turned on the hot water and left the room. While the bathtub filled, Sam wandered to the corner of his suite near the curtained window. A clothes valet stood beside a full-length mirror. He removed his clothes, draped them over the wooden stand, and stepped to the mirror. He had not seen himself in years, and truly did not recognize the person staring back at him. Dark rings circled his eyes. His Adam's apple stuck out like a spike below his chin. His ribs looked like a plowed field, curved in neat symmetrical rows. Hipbones jutted from his pelvis, and his legs looked like sticks. He had healed cuts, now a shade of purple, all over his body, remnants of the Japanese guards' bayonets.

The refreshing bath lasted an hour. Sam slipped into provided pajamas and marveled at the darkened city for a moment. He closed the curtains and prepared to get into the biggest bed he had ever seen, but the telephone on the nightstand drew his attention. He lifted the receiver and confirmed that while he could call for room service, he could not call out.

He debated finding a pay phone, then, thinking about what Major Sanders had said, he decided again that the major was right. Calling home would be a dirty trick. The shock of hearing his voice, without any preparation, without being able to see him in the flesh, might cause Sarah and his mother to faint, and give his father a heart attack. After so many years, they might not even recognize his voice, and think the call a prank. It would be cruel.

He decided he would walk into Eagle Grove so they could witness his resurrection from the dead and have no doubts.

A knock at the door startled Sam from his thoughts. When he opened it, skeletal versions of three friends he'd known in the Philippines stared back at him. Soldiers who'd been with him on Bataan. "We heard you survived," one said.

They hugged for a long minute, then Sam learned they, too, had been POWs and stuffed in the hold of a different Japanese hell ship out of Manila. Like Sam, they had barely survived the ship's sinking by an American submarine. They, too, were in Washington, DC, for debriefing. They, too, could tell no one of their ordeal, or that they remained alive.

They all laughed. "But we figured we could tell someone with the same secret and the same orders."

"How did you know I was here?" Sam asked.

"Interrogators told us where we could find you. But remember, we can't talk about the war."

Sam laughed with them. "That's fine with me. I'm tired of talking about this damned war."

He got back into uniform, and they headed downstairs to drink cold Ballantine beers, eat hamburgers, and catch up. Around 5:00 a.m., Sam crawled into his giant, soft bed. He tossed and turned, bewildered by such comfort, and finally pulled a blanket onto the floor, where he slept like a rock.

4

REENTRY SHOCK

Washington, DC
November 14, 1944

The next day, a car and driver arrived at precisely 14:00 hours to take Sam to the War Department headquarters in the massive new Pentagon. There, in a room with no windows, Sam spent hours explaining his mistreatment to five armed forces interrogators and a secretary. He recounted his final days on Bataan and the death march. He detailed the Japanese's refusal to honor the Geneva Convention in the POW camps, and the brutal physical and psychological treatment, including torture and starvation. He specifically noted Katsuo Yoshida and his "blood brothers" rule. He talked about burial duty and the mass graves outside Camp O'Donnell, providing their precise location and the estimated number of bodies buried there. He even listed the names of soldiers he could remember burying, and the names of the POWs Yoshida had personally killed.

He told them of the *Arisan Maru* hell ship, and its horrific conditions. Again, he specifically named Yoshida, and the crimes he had committed on the ship, how the prisoners had been locked in the hold with little food or water. He told of the many burials at sea. "Yoshida. If you get no one else, get that son of a bitch."

He discussed the torpedo attack, and the prisoners' escape from the hold. He told of how Major Paul Jones had promoted Father Thomas Scecina to captain for service to his fellow POWs in the face of death. He detailed each of Father Tom's extraordinary acts.

He told them of his voyage across the South China Sea to China, and he detailed Rudowski's acts of heroism—how he had shoved off the hold cover and saved the POWs from drowning, and how he had plucked Sam from the ocean. He said the big man had used his body to shield him from the deadly machine gun fire in the lifeboat and told them he believed Rudowski should be given the rank of corporal and be awarded medals for his heroism, posthumously.

"Rudowski," one of his interrogators said. "Do you know his first name?"

Sam still didn't recall Rudowski's first name, if he ever knew it. "Just Rudowski."

"We'll find him," the interrogator said, "and be sure his family knows."

The secretary wrote everything in shorthand, then typed it. After many revisions, the transcribed document captured things as well as possible. Sam signed the final paper, and an official stamped it "TOP SECRET" and whisked it away. His chief interrogator told him the interview would be used as the basis for a formal war crimes investigation against the Japanese POW guards and Katsuo Yoshida.

When he had finished, the car and driver brought Sam back to his hotel room, exhausted. He sat in a chair near the window, looked to the sky, and said, "I'm finished, Padre. I did as you asked. I bore witness for you all."

———

The following morning, an Army car picked Sam up at his hotel and took him to the Pentagon to meet with General George Marshall. The general stepped out from behind a giant desk, with an outstretched hand. "Welcome home, soldier. They told me your story."

Sam saluted the US Army's top official. "Thank you, sir. It's good to be back home." He shook the general's hand.

"I'm sorry we couldn't get you at Bataan or Corregidor back in forty-two," General Marshall said. "I'm sorry you had to be taken prisoner and suffered so much for so long. I'm damned sorry."

Marshall sounded sincere. "Thank you, sir," Sam said.

General Marshall reached into an open box his aide held and extracted a medal—the Purple Heart, for wounds sustained in service to one's country. A photographer stepped forward and snapped a picture as Marshall pinned the shiny medal on Sam's chest. Next, General Marshall pinned a Silver Star beside the Purple Heart and handed Sam a Presidential Commendation from Franklin Delano Roosevelt. Again, the experience seemed almost surreal. But Sam didn't feel any real sense of pride. He knew the medals were a photo opportunity for the Army more than for him. He wasn't even sure what he'd do with the medals. They wouldn't bring back Father Tom or Pete Chavez, who Sam assumed to be dead, or any of the others. Those were the POWs who deserved medals. They'd given their lives for their country.

Sam wanted to tell FDR face to face. He wanted to tell the president that "rendezvous with destiny" was just a bunch of words without action. He wanted to tell him that Americans, more now than maybe ever, needed their country's help to get back on their feet and to deal with the pain they experienced for the family members they had lost in the war. They needed jobs and a way to make a living to provide for their families. He thought of how ironic it would be if he'd made it home only to go hungry again, as he had when the Depression raged.

"Congratulations, soldier. You are a free man," General Marshall said, extending his hand.

"Thank you, sir." The word "free" rattled around inside Sam's head, but again, he was unsure what it meant. Was he free to leave the room? Free to go home? Free to speak of his experiences? He doubted all of them, especially the last. But he wasn't going to let his bitterness destroy what remained of his life. Like Qiu Jin, he would move on, as best he could.

"There's one more thing," the general said. "You are hereby ordered not to discuss your ordeal without the War Department's explicit permission. That order could change in the future, but for now, in the interests of national security, you may only say one thing to friends, family, the press, or anyone else: you were a prisoner of war held by the Japanese, and you escaped."

Sam had expected this order with the war still going on and Americans still in prison camps, but it still felt like the rug being pulled out from beneath his feet. Anger rose in his chest, but he thought again of the mission Father Tom had given him and which he had fulfilled. He'd done his duty. He didn't care about being on the news or in the newspapers. He didn't even care about the medals. All he cared about was fulfilling a promise to a friend.

He'd done that.

"Yes, sir," he said.

Now he just wanted to go home.

"Good. There's one more person who would very much like to meet you."

———

Sam stepped into the West Wing of the White House and awaited his final meeting, this one with President Franklin Delano Roosevelt. Again, it seemed surreal. He recalled how he had lain in his bed in Eagle Grove, hungry from skipping another meal, and imagined someday giving the president a piece of his mind. He couldn't believe that boyhood dream, born of anger, was about to become reality.

"Sergeant Carlson." Sam looked up at the young officer who had prepped him on meeting the president. "The president is ready for you, sir."

Sam followed the officer through a door into the Oval Office.

FDR remained seated behind his large maple-veneered desk. The president had hosted world leaders, signed landmark legislation, and held hundreds of press conferences from behind that desk. In awe, Sam stepped to the right of the desk as he'd been coached and shook FDR's hand, then assumed the parade rest position: hands clasped behind his back, feet twelve inches apart, head held still and facing forward.

The president looked as well dressed as ever in his suit jacket, bow tie, and wire-rimmed glasses. The Army made sure Sam also looked his best in a new formal olive drab uniform—shiny black shoes and belt, necktie, and a buttoned shirt. His suit jacket had brass buttons, various collar pins for military service, and a gold bar signifying his promotion to second lieutenant. His shiny medals dangled from his left breast pocket.

"Please sit." The president gestured to the elegant wooden chair with red velvet upholstery.

"Thank you, sir."

Sam had been instructed on this too. He moved to the chair in which ambassadors, cabinet members, and heads of state, including Winston Churchill, had sat. He took extra care not to knock anything off the president's famously cluttered desk. Its chaotic surface held a globe, pen holder, alarm clock, newspapers, books, drinking glass, small American flag, and wire inbox filled with papers. At its far corner, Sam spotted the legendary statuettes of a Republican elephant and Democratic donkey chained together as if forced to cooperate.

"They told me your story," the president said. "How you survived the Battle of Bataan, the death march, the POW camps. Then the Japanese hell ship and the torpedo attack. They told me you were adrift at sea for days, and of your long walk through occupied China." FDR paused as if trying to comprehend it all. "It is quite a story, soldier. I can't imagine what you must be feeling." FDR, too, looked and sounded sincere.

"Yes, sir. Thank you, sir. I'm glad to be home, sir."

FDR paused, then said, "It's just extraordinary. Miraculous, even."

Sam had been told to let the president lead the conversation. "I've been through hell, sir. But you're right. A lot of miracles got me here."

"I know they have, son. And on behalf of a grateful nation, I humbly and graciously thank you for your service."

"Thank you, sir," Sam said.

"I'm sorry we couldn't help you at Bataan," FDR said, his voice somber. "We had so few resources back then. We had to throw everything we had at Hitler."

"I understand, sir. The men fought with valor, sir. We lost a lot of good men."

"The Battling Bastards of Bataan," FDR said. "I know how hard you fought."

The president's voice sounded warm and confident, befitting a leader who, just a few weeks earlier, had been elected to an unprecedented fourth term in office. But, up close, Sam saw the toll those twelve hard years had taken on the president, just as the Depression had taken years from his parents. An economic depression and world war had left FDR old, thin, and frail.

"I only know a tiny fraction of what you've been through," FDR said. "But it's enough to know this: you should have a great sense of pride for what you have accomplished."

Inside, Sam smiled and thought of Pete Chavez, and he just couldn't resist keeping his good friend's memory alive. "It was my rendezvous with destiny, sir."

FDR smiled. "You listened to my fireside chat."

"Yes, sir. If I may, sir?"

"Please."

"Those are just words, sir. Back when I lived in Eagle Grove, I thought Americans needed jobs. They needed to earn an income to care for their families. They needed to get back the farms they lost to foreclosure. They needed to understand their lives had a purpose."

"I know, son, and we've tried to accomplish that with the Work Projects Administration under the New Deal, as well as the establishment of the Home Owners' Loan Corporation."

"Thank you, sir. Many people have also lost loved ones in this war and will be hurting. They're going to need help also."

"You're right, son. And we're working with the Red Cross and the USO to do just that. We've also established the Servicemen's Readjustment Act, better known as the GI Bill, to provide funds for returning veterans such as yourself, help you get back on your feet."

"I'd like to go to college, sir."

"Then you shall, son."

"I understand now, more than ever, that we all have a destiny, and none of us knows where our destiny will take us. I believe I fulfilled the first leg of my destiny, and I hope the rest of my destiny is yet to be written, sir."

"Thank you for your wisdom, Lieutenant. We're doing what we can to make that happen all across America." He smiled, weary. "And my destiny, I suspect, is coming to an end much sooner than yours."

"I hope not, sir. I hope you will remain in this office for many more years."

"I'm an old man," FDR said. "Time to give someone else the opportunity to rebuild this country into greatness."

"It already is great, sir. To me this is the greatest country on Earth, and if I had given my life to protect everything it stands for, I would have gladly done so, and with honor. But that wasn't my destiny."

"What was your destiny, soldier?"

"To make it home and be a witness for the many who didn't. To tell you and the War Department about the Japanese atrocities inflicted in the camps and on those hell ships, so all those men did not die for nothing. So we can bring home their bodies and give them a decent and honorable burial, for their families."

"We will do all we can to make that happen, as well, Lieutenant." FDR nodded. "I have to say, Lieutenant Carlson, I am quite inspired by you."

Sam smiled. "Thank you, sir. You have no idea how much that means to me. So many inspired me over these years and kept me alive. I owe them all, sir."

"I would love to meet those men someday."

"They didn't make it home, sir. But I will carry them with me here." Sam tapped his chest.

5

PARADISE

Eagle Grove, Minnesota
November 17, 1944

Friday night, Sarah left her parents' home, bundled up for the walk to downtown Eagle Grove. With the Depression behind them, residents had returned to the town, and some had reopened businesses. It seemed brighter, and the people Sarah now encountered on the streets seemed more alive. They smiled easier, and they asked her dozens of questions about what it was like to work as a WAVE in Washington, DC. She did her best to answer them, though often her heart wasn't in it.

The principal at the high school had asked Sarah to talk at a school assembly about her experiences working as a WAVE officer. Sarah did so, but the experience was bittersweet, not being able to tell the students, especially the girls, the importance of her job as a code breaker. She wanted them to aspire to be more than secretaries and receptionists, as she and so many women had.

The longer Sarah was home, the more she realized that she wouldn't stay in Eagle Grove after the war. That she couldn't stay. The old saying about not being able to go home again rang true. She wasn't the person she had been when she'd left. She had different dreams and ambitions. And Sam was not here. She would move on, to live somewhere else.

It wouldn't be Hawaii, and it wouldn't be Washington, DC. Those memories were also too fresh.

She'd written Captain Russell back. She told him he deserved an answer, that he was too good a man to spend his years waiting. She would always hold a warm place in her heart for him. He had made her years in the Navy not just tolerable, but enjoyable. She had enjoyed their weekly dinners and intelligent conversation, the USO dances, and his company. She suspected that's what he also felt.

But it wasn't love, though she didn't write that.

She also didn't tell him he was a memory she didn't wish to relive. She didn't want to relive the war or her career as a cryptanalyst. Commander Holmes had eased her guilt, but she would always remember the men who died aboard the *Arisan Maru* and the USS *Shark*. She also didn't tell Bill that, while she would always be fond of him, she loved Sam, and likely always would. Could she love again? Could she love another man as much as she had loved Sam? She didn't know, but she hoped in time she could. It just wouldn't be here in Eagle Grove.

She walked past the white Presbyterian church, but she no longer envisioned getting married there, if she married at all. She tried not to think in those terms.

She walked down Maple Street to Main. The ground was covered in snow and the temperature hovered somewhere below freezing, but it wasn't the arctic cold that winter would bring. She felt her cheeks flushing and wiped at her nose with a handkerchief as she continued past shops that had been repurposed. The pharmacy now had an ice cream and soda fountain counter. As she passed the window, students from the high school waved and smiled at her. She'd learned the kids met there before the movie to share a soda with their sweethearts.

Sarah returned their smiles and waves and walked on with a heavy heart, passing the department store window display. It had been changed some years ago, according to her mother, and now reflected a Christmas theme with a family of mannequins in various winter outfits with wrapped packages in bags on their arms.

When she reached the Paradise Theater, she stopped outside to study the movie poster. *Since You Went Away*, tonight's film, told the story of a young woman in the Midwest whose Army husband was presumed dead in the Pacific only to return home.

Sarah spoke the tagline printed on the poster. Beneath the poster, Mr. Larsen had put a handwritten note: *Filled with love and laughter, hopes and dreams.*

If only that were so.

It confirmed her decision to leave. This building held the most memories. She hoped in time they would be fond ones, but at present, they were just painful. She knew running the projectors would be the most painful of all, but when Mr. Larsen called to tell her the high school student who performed the job had called in sick, Sarah couldn't refuse the Larsens, who had done so much for her. The Larsens needed to work the counter on what was expected to be a busy Friday night. So, it was with reservations that Sarah had agreed to run the projectors, but she also knew she had to get past her memories so she could make new ones. She could not go through life scared.

Sarah caught her reflection in the window and marveled at how much she had changed. Seven years ago, she had been a high school senior wearing a skirt and sweater, her hair in a bow for her dates with Sam. That girl was long gone. The woman in the window had the start of worry lines at the corners of her eyes and mouth. Her hair fell in a gentle wave to her shoulders. She hadn't bothered to put on makeup, or dress up beneath her warm coat, scarf, and hat. She had no one to dress up for. She also carried a few extra pounds from eating too much chow in the Navy cafeterias and not getting enough exercise. She had developed a sweet tooth.

The theater lobby buzzed with excited customers. She nudged her way to the concession counter, where students at Eagle Grove greeted her and asked if she had come to watch the movie. They seemed glad to see her. She hadn't gone out much since she'd been home.

Mr. and Mrs. Larsen stood behind the counter, busy serving customers.

Sarah waved when Mr. Larsen started around the counter. "It's okay," she said. "I know my way."

"Your Coca-Cola and popcorn are already up there," Mr. Larsen said.

Sarah smiled through her tears.

"I think you'll find everything you need," Mrs. Larsen said. "And we threw in some chocolates."

"I'm going to be as big as a house if I keep eating sweets," she said. Sarah held out a dollar bill to pay, but Mrs. Larsen shook her head. "Don't be ridiculous."

Sarah climbed the staircase to the balcony, then continued to the projection booth. As she climbed the flight of stairs, she removed her gloves and her hat and slipped from her winter coat. The door to the projection room was ajar. She hit it with her shoulder and stepped in.

She dropped her hat, gloves, and coat on the floor and brought her hands to her mouth in a silent scream.

"Hi, sweetheart," Sam said softly. He raised a hand. "I'm sorry. I didn't mean to scare you. I know this is a shock."

Sarah hardly recognized him. Sam was painfully thin, his face narrow and angular, his hair cut nub short. His Army uniform hung from him as if he were made of wire; the left side of his chest was decorated with medals and ribbons, but they sagged on the fabric. He held his hat in scarred hands.

"Sam?" she whispered. "Oh my God, Sam? Is it really you?"

"It's me," he said. "I know I've looked better—"

She rushed across the booth and hugged him, then kissed him through her tears. He was so thin she felt his ribs through his uniform. When she pulled back, she said, "Sam Carlson, you've never looked better."

"You either, Sarah Haber."

"I hope we didn't spoil the surprise."

Sarah turned. Mr. and Mrs. Larsen stood crying at the door. "You knew?" she asked.

"I asked them to help me," Sam said. "I thought it better than just showing up at your front door."

"You two have a lot to talk about," Mr. Larsen said. "You go now. We can run the projectors."

"If you don't mind, Mr. Larsen," Sam said, "I think I'd like to watch this picture sitting right here. I understand the story has a happy ending."

The Larsens smiled, Mrs. Larsen through tears, and departed.

Sarah sat. It was as if she were seeing a ghost set up the first reel, then grab the second wooden chair and put it close to hers. The house lights dimmed— the Larsens' signal to begin. Sam turned the light switch off and flipped on the movie projector, just as he'd done so many lifetimes ago. The light shot ninety feet and exploded against the giant screen. With the darkness shattered, Sam eased back into his chair, and Sarah caught the glow reflecting on his cheeks, wet with tears, his and hers.

He handed her the bag of popcorn to share, then poured her half his Coke. They raised their cups, pretended they were glasses, and touched the rims.

"Ginger," Sam said.

"Fred," Sarah said. "When—?"

"Shh," Sam said gently, and Sarah did not persist. She leaned her head on his shoulder, and they watched the movie. Together again.

6

CATCHING UP

Eagle Grove, Minnesota
November 17, 1944

When the show ended, Sam and Sarah waited in the projection room for the crowd to disperse. If he left the booth now, Sam knew he would be inundated with questions, which would keep him from Sarah and the questions she had the right to ask him first.

Sarah put on her warm gear. Sam slid on his Army jacket. "Won't you be cold?" she asked.

"I'm sort of enjoying the cold."

Outside the building, Sarah took Sam's arm, and they started their walk at a leisurely pace, the memories flooding back to Sam, bringing tears to his eyes.

"Are you all right?" Sarah asked.

"Never better," he said.

"Do your parents know?"

"I got in this afternoon."

"On the train?"

"No. An Army car drove me to the house. I wanted to call them, and you, but the Army wouldn't let me make any phone calls until I made it home. I've been on planes for days, coming home from China."

"China?"

"It's a long story, sweetheart. They wanted to debrief me in Washington, DC, first, at the Pentagon. I met George Marshall, the Army Chief of Staff, and I met FDR himself in the Oval Office."

She stopped walking. "The president?"

He nodded.

"You must be important, Sam," she said, sounding concerned.

He thought about her statement. He wished he wasn't important. He would have been happy to have served his country and returned home anonymous to resume his life.

He had not told his parents any of it, and he wouldn't tell Sarah of the mistreatment either. He didn't want to relive it, and he didn't want them to know of his suffering. He sensed they had figured much out from his emaciated appearance. When the horrors came, and they did come, especially when he slept, he thought of Qiu Jin and replayed positive moments in his life, including the positive moments in the military with Pete Chavez and with Father Tom and Major Jones.

"I'm still just Sam. What happened to me is what was important, and I promised someone that I'd make it home and tell the Army all the things we went through in the prisoner of war camps and on freighters, what we called hell ships."

"Marus?" she asked.

He stopped walking and looked at her. "How do you know about marus?"

She sighed. "I have a lot to tell you too, Sam, but let's hold it for another time. This night is yours. Tell me about the Pentagon and the White House and meeting FDR."

As they walked, Sam filled her in on his experience meeting FDR in the Oval Office and what he'd said to him.

"You didn't," she said, smiling.

"I did. When this war is over, there's going to be a war tribunal, and they're going to go after those bastards who persecuted us."

"What did happen, Sam? Where have you been? I have so many questions."

He knew she did, and he struggled with where they could go to talk in private. They couldn't go to his parents' house or to Sarah's home. There would be too many people. They passed the stores on Main Street, all closed for the night, and turned left on Maple. "Let's go in there." Sam pointed to the Presbyterian church a block away.

The church doors were unlocked. They sat in a pew, silent for the moment. Sam didn't know where to begin. Candle flames flickered in crimson-red and forest-green glass along the sides of the pews, providing muted light and wavering shadows that danced on the walls.

Sarah squeezed his hand and waited. He told her of Pete Chavez and Father Tom, and soon the words flowed. Sam's stories about Pete made Sarah laugh, and it was the same warm, wonderful laugh he remembered. He told her more about how Father Tom always gave "that little extra" and how he had inspired the POWs, including Sam. He shook his head. "They all died when the *Arisan Maru* sank, Sarah. So many died."

Sarah wept.

Sam didn't press her.

"Are you all right, Sam? You're so thin."

She had no idea. He'd been eating since he'd climbed aboard the junk in China. He suspected the military didn't want the public to see photos of the emaciated POWs it had left behind in the Philippines. Army doctors had checked him out head to toe and listed all kinds of problems he'd deal with for a long time, maybe the rest of his life. "I'm all right," he said. Sarah suddenly looked pale, even in the flickering candlelight, and it worried him. "What is it, Sarah? Are *you* all right?"

"Everything is just happening so quickly. So all at once. You being home, like you've been dropped from the sky. All the lost years. I think . . . I think I'm just overwhelmed."

Sam could certainly relate. But he sensed something more, things *she* wasn't telling *him*. He'd give her time and space, as she was giving him.

Sam told her about the lifeboat and Rudowski. He told her of his escape through China and about Qiu Jin. "She and her village risked their lives to save me." He shook his head. "So many did. I feel guilty being alive."

"No, Sam," she said, again squeezing his hands. "It's like your priest told you. Being alive is your purpose."

"I know," he said. "Sometimes, it's just hard to accept."

"And you did it, Sam. You made it home for all those who didn't. And when this war ends, the people responsible for those crimes will be punished. You have to hold on to that."

He had assumed Sarah had taught at Eagle Grove these past years, but now he knew she hadn't. The person sitting in the pew beside him was his Sarah, but she was different. Older, certainly. More mature. Worldly. A worldliness she didn't get in Eagle Grove. She seemed stronger, wiser, and even more confident than the girl he had left.

"I've been talking too much," he said. "Tell me what you've been doing."

Sarah took a deep breath, then told Sam about how she had moved to Washington, DC, and eventually joined the WAVES. She told him she had worked at the Main Navy building, but she didn't provide all the details. She described Washington, DC, and her friend Grace and other friends she had made. Most of all, she praised her work girlfriends—what she called a sisterhood of intelligent, fun-loving, dedicated women.

Sam was stunned by it all, and yet, he thought she was toning down her recollections, again not telling him everything. Secrets now existed between them, and maybe always would.

And maybe that was okay.

She told him about the mountains of Colorado and the grueling Japanese Language School, and about applying to JICPOA in Hawaii, to be closer to where she knew he was being held prisoner.

"Why would they send a secretary to the Japanese Language School in Colorado?"

Sarah looked pale again, even in the flickering candlelight. "I can't tell you everything, Sam. When I can tell you, I will. I promise."

Again, he knew better than to push her. They had both been through so much. He could see that she was in the middle of sorting it all out, just like he was. They both needed time.

"Is there anyone else?" he asked. It was a question he'd wanted to ask and hadn't wanted to ask. Now it was out there. "I'd understand, Sarah. Three years is a long time to be away, without any word I was alive."

She smiled. "I received word you were taken prisoner. That was enough for me to hold on to. No, Sam, no one who meant as much to me as you. The war confirmed for me how much I love you and always will."

He smiled and thought of how his memories of her had sustained him and kept him alive. How her ring had literally brought him hope. "Before we go." Sam reached below the collar of his shirt and pulled out a string. At the end dangled Sarah's high school class ring.

She put her hands to her face. "My God, Sam. How?"

"I hid it from the Japs in the lining of a vest I made. I kept it there and squeezed it each time I wanted to give up and quit."

"All these years," she said. "You kept it all these years."

"All these years."

"Oh, Sam." She pulled him in and hugged him.

When they drew apart, he untied the ring from the string and held it out to her on his palm. Using both her hands, she folded his fingers around the ring, as she had once folded his fingers around his grandmother's engagement ring. "You keep it," she said. "It seems to have brought you some good luck. Maybe it will bring you more."

Sam didn't ask Sarah about her promise to marry him. She was right: This was all too sudden, and too much for either of them to take in. They both needed time.

Sarah bundled up and they left the church. Snow fell—large flakes floating gently and blanketing the ground, making a quiet night absolutely silent.

"How beautiful," Sarah said.

They walked past darkened windows.

"How long are you home?" he asked.

"I go back the Monday after Thanksgiving."

"Back where?"

"Hawaii."

"For how long?"

"My commission ends six months after the war ends. You?"

"Three-month furlough. After that, they haven't really said, though I'm certain it won't be overseas again. For the moment, I'm just happy to be here. Happy to be home."

They stopped and Sam turned to her. He wanted to kiss her. He hoped this war had not changed them both so much they could no longer live the life they had once dreamed of. But his dream now seemed a lifetime ago. In some ways it was. Sam wasn't the young, naive kid from Eagle Grove, and would never be again. He had traveled the world and experienced its incredible beauty, but also things no man should ever have to witness. Could he really just go on, choosing not to watch that film, as Qiu Jin had suggested? To watch only the positive reels? Could he ever again think of Fred and Ginger dancing on a ship and not think of bombs and torpedoes bearing down upon them? Could he travel to exotic places and not think of the searing heat and humidity that had baked his skin until it peeled from him like he was an overcooked turkey?

Was he still the Sam who loved Sarah, and was she still the girl who loved him?

Sarah rose onto her toes, paused for a smiling moment, then kissed him, her lips warm and gentle. It was the sweetest kiss, a kiss that told him things were going to be okay. Different, certainly, but okay.

When they opened their eyes, Sarah pointed to the sky. "Polaris," she said. "Do you remember?"

He laughed. He'd tell her the story of the lifeboat and finding Polaris another day. "How could I forget? I thought of you every time I saw it."

"Star light, star bright," Sarah whispered.

Sam held her close. He did not need to see the star to make his wish. His Sarah stood right beside him again. "I wish I may, I wish I might, have the wish I wish tonight," they said together.

When they finally said good night on her parents' front porch, Sam had trouble letting go of her. He waited until Sarah went inside, then started down the porch steps for the picket fence. Sarah called to him and ran back down the steps.

"I almost forgot." She reached into her coat pocket and removed her half-eaten bag of popcorn and the chocolates. "You can't go home empty handed," she said.

He didn't have the heart to tell her his sisters and Jacob were no longer children. Like the two of them, the years had aged them.

—

When he arrived at home, Sam tried to be quiet entering the house, but found his mother and father sitting at the kitchen table, drinking tea.

"You're awake," he said. "I hope you didn't wait up for me."

"We waited years for you, son," Sam's father said. "A few minutes more isn't anything."

Sam removed his hat and jacket, loosened his tie, and sat at the kitchen table.

"I'll make you a cup of tea," his mother said, getting up.

Sam reached out and touched her hand. "Hold on, Mom. I have something I want to discuss."

She returned to her seat looking uneasy. "What is it, son? We've both sensed something troubling you."

"No," he said. "Nothing like that. As you know, all too well, I've been missing for nearly three years. I have three years of back pay I haven't collected from the Army. Before I left Washington, I was told it would be sent here."

"It came, Sam," his mother said. "The envelope is on the desk in the other room."

"It isn't a fortune," Sam said, "but it's more money than any of us has likely ever had."

"It will be a good nest egg for you and Sarah," his father said.

Sam shook his head. "No. Sarah and I need some time to think over what it is we really want. If we both decide we want each other, we'll have the ability to use FDR's GI Bill for me to go to college, and to get a good loan. Tomorrow I'm going down to the bank. I'm going to buy back your farm and your house." His father stirred at this, as though to rise, but Sam held up his palm. "Hear me out. It's still in foreclosure, and nobody has been in any position to buy it with the Depression and a war going on. There will be enough money left over to buy some Holsteins and equipment—a tractor and such."

"I can't ask that of you, son," his father said, sitting back in his chair now and sounding stunned. "That money belongs to you. God knows you earned it."

"You didn't ask it of me, Dad. And I'm not a kid anymore. I'm a man, and I'm capable of making my own decisions, and I've decided to buy back the farm. But there's something else you should know."

His father reached across the table and gripped Sam's hands. "What is it, son?"

"I'm not going to be staying in Eagle Grove to work the place."

"Where are you going?" his mother asked.

"Well, first I have to go back to the Army to finish out my commitment. Likely at a base nearby. After that, I'm not sure. I just know this was my past. I have to find my future. I want to go to college."

"We understand," his father said.

"We do." His mother hugged him tight. "Of course we do." Though from the tears on his mother's cheeks, he knew she wasn't happy about losing her son, again.

"Sam?"

He looked up. His two sisters stood in the kitchen doorway, along with his cousin, Jacob.

"What are you all doing up?" their mother said.

"We heard Sam come home," his sister said. "We wanted to see him. Why is everyone crying?"

"We're just happy to all be together again," Sam said. He reached into his pocket and pulled out the popcorn bag.

"Popcorn!" the three of them said in unison.

Maybe they weren't as grown up as Sam thought. "And something else," he said, pulling out the chocolates.

Their eyes widened in delight.

"From now on," Sam said, "no one in this house goes to bed hungry."

7

No Peace

Eagle Grove, Minnesota
November 25, 1944

Sam and Sarah were together every day for the remainder of Sarah's leave. Each time they went to town they were besieged by Eagle Grove residents who wanted to know about the war, and asked when they thought it would end. The people meant well, and Sam and Sarah were always polite in answering their questions, but Sam didn't want to share her. On her last day he wanted her all to himself, and he suggested they leave town and go to Brainerd, someplace where they would not be recognized.

They stepped from the train and walked streets Sam had walked so long ago. "This is nice," Sarah said. "Peaceful."

Sam found himself broaching a difficult topic that had weighed on him since he'd arrived back in Eagle Grove: "Home really isn't home anymore, is it?"

She turned and looked at him. "What do you mean?"

"I'm different, Sarah. I'm not the same guy who lived there. And you've changed too."

"What about your dream of getting back the farm and all the cows? Of living and farming there?"

"I've done that, or at least I'm in the process of doing that. I used my back pay to get my parents' farm back, buy some cows, but that's my parents' dream. I want to go to college and then . . . I don't know what my dreams are anymore," he said. "I just know I can't achieve them in Eagle Grove. I want to start fresh. Someplace new."

Sarah processed this for a moment, then asked, "Where do you want to live?"

"I'm not sure yet," he said. "I think that's a decision best left until after the war. I'm sorry. I hope I haven't spoiled the day."

She smiled. "I was debating how to tell you I feel the same."

"You do?"

"You're right. There are too many ghosts in Eagle Grove. Not all bad, but like you, I want to move past them and start my own life. Our life."

Sam hadn't heard Sarah talk about a life with him, and now he wasn't sure what he felt. That was the problem. He remained confused about so many things. "What about your dream of teaching?"

"Dreams change," she said. "Would you want your life to include me?"

He smiled. "I love you, Sarah. I always have and I always will."

"But?"

He couldn't believe what he was about to say. For three years she had been all he'd thought about. But with time now to think, he realized his thoughts of Sarah represented his memories of home, of Eagle Grove, and the life he'd had there with his parents and his siblings. But he was no longer seventeen-year-old Sam, and he no longer knew what he wanted. They both still had much to process. War and an ocean no longer separated them, but something deeper did. Like a house blown away in a tornado, their past had vanished. Only the foundation remained. Sam hoped it was strong enough to support a new house they could live in together. But building it would take time.

"But . . . we both still have to finish our service," he said. A convenient excuse. "And we've had a lot to think about these past few days. I know your seeing me was a shock. And I don't want to hold you back from any of your dreams." He put his head in his hands. "I'm sorry, Sarah, everything has been one big blur. I'm still not sure this is real, that I'm not just dreaming. I'm afraid I'm going to wake up and be back in that POW camp, or in the hold of that hell ship."

She removed his hands and lifted his chin. "This is real, Sam. I'm real."

"I know. I just . . . I just need time to let things settle. We both need to think about what we really want. So that when that day comes, we can both be certain what we want is to spend the rest of our lives together."

"Is that a no, Sam Carlson?" she asked, with a hint of a smile that made him smile.

"It's a 'not yet,'" he said.

8

ONE MORE SURPRISE

FRUPAC
Honolulu, Hawaii
November 27, 1944

At the end of Sarah's two-week leave, she'd caught an Army transport plane to San Francisco, then another to Hawaii. The long return trip had given her time to digest everything that had happened. She'd stared out her airplane window for hours, thinking about Sam and what he had said. He was right. They were not those two high school sweethearts who had said goodbye on the train platform on a cold February night those many years ago. They were adults, who had been through so much, especially Sam. She wanted Sam to be certain he wanted to marry her. She wanted and hoped she would be his dream, as he remained hers. She still loved him, and this time if he asked, she wouldn't hesitate to marry him.

Monday morning, back at JICPOA, two Marine guards checked Sarah's badge, gave the naval officer a crisp salute, then let her enter. At her desk, she picked up where she had left off, though the tone and information in the messages she deciphered were now vastly different. The Japanese remained in retreat. The Allies were advancing rapidly, island by island. Sarah kept hoping to decode a message that the Japanese were preparing to surrender, but she knew they were a proud culture that considered surrender impossibly shameful. She feared the war would carry on for years, and she and Sam would remain in limbo.

Shortly after she'd begun work, her phone rang. The secretary said she had a phone call from a WAVE officer named Grace Moretti. Having been preconditioned from all the years she and her WAVES had answered difficult phone calls, Sarah immediately suspected bad news.

"Grace," she said when the secretary put her through.

"Honey, you are harder to reach than a five-star general."

"Is everything all right?"

"Everything is fine. Remember I talked about leverage? I used the WAVE card to get through and make this sound business related. I was just waiting for a decent time to call. What time is it in paradise?"

"A little after seven. What's going on?"

"I didn't want to put this in a letter. I'm getting married."

Sarah smiled, then thought of Sam, and wondered if she'd ever be calling Grace with such great news. While home, she had called Grace and told her about Sam's resurrection from the dead and his return to Eagle Grove, and about how they both needed time to decompress.

"Grace, that's wonderful. Congratulations. Is it Joe? The officer you've been dating?"

"It is, honey. He asked me in the snow near the reflecting pool in the National Mall. Got down on one knee and popped the question."

"I'm so happy for you, Grace."

"Well, I was hoping you would be, since you're going to be my maid of honor."

"I am? Oh, Grace, thank you."

"No one else even crossed my mind. We're getting married in the spring, here in Washington when the cherry blossoms are blooming. So, you and that guy of yours are coming back to Washington."

Sarah didn't immediately respond.

"Honey, you still there?"

"I'm here, Grace. Just . . . just so happy for you."

"Come on now. Don't shit a shitter. Everything okay with you and your man, Sam?"

Sarah didn't want to get emotional at work. "We both just need a bit of time, you know, like I told you before. We need to relax after all that's happened."

"Of course you do. You've both been to hell and back, what he went through, and you not knowing if he was dead or alive. Give it time for the dust to settle. You still love him, though?"

"I do."

"Well, he'd be a fool not to snap you up, honey. You remember when we first met? What I said?" Sarah didn't. "I said you are just one of those genuinely nice people, Sarah Haber. You recall that?"

"I do," she said and pressed a finger to the corner of her eye to catch a teardrop from falling.

"He knows that too. Couldn't miss it. Okay, I better let you get back to work. I'll write with the details soon."

Sarah said goodbye and hung up the phone. She'd no sooner done so than one of her colleagues approached and said, "Commander Holmes wants to see you. Says it's urgent."

Holmes had welcomed her back to JICPOA like a father welcoming back his daughter, and Sarah hadn't been the least bit offended. She walked down the hallway and rapped on his open door. "You wanted to see me, Commander?"

Holmes waved her in. "Shut the door."

Sarah did, immediately suspicious.

"Don't worry. I won't keep you in suspense," he said. "I wanted you to know that the story of an American sub sinking the *Arisan Maru* has gone public."

"What? How?" The news was like having a healing wound torn open. Sarah had come to terms with her part in the ship's sinking. Holmes had helped her understand she had only done her duty.

"A *Washington Post* newspaper reporter caught wind of the story and started asking questions. The War Department decided to release it to control the flow of information. It's running on the news wire and will be in all the major newspapers."

Holmes grabbed a paper from his desk and flipped it around for Sarah to see the banner headline.

U.S. Told 1,800 Americans Died in Sinking of Japanese Prison Ship

"How *much* of the story is out?" Sarah asked. "Do they know about us?"

"It's a sanitized version." Holmes handed her the newspaper. "They're calling it the deadliest accident in US military history. So as not to reveal our role in deciphering the Japanese messages."

Sarah got only a few lines into the article before she had to stop. "The whole world will know."

"Not the entire story, but a portion of it."

She forced herself back to the story, then said, "Those poor men."

"After the torpedo hit, the Japs locked them inside the ship's hold," Holmes said. "But the men managed to escape. Some got away from the ship before it went down. The lone survivor took refuge on a hatch cover before he found a lifeboat."

Sarah wanted to say, "I know." Sam had told her enough details for her to have realized he had been the lone survivor of the *Arisan Maru*, but she also knew he had been sworn not to tell anyone, and she didn't want to get him, or herself, in any trouble with the Army or the Navy.

"Apparently the Japs used the lifeboat to get off the sinking maru to a waiting destroyer, then cut it loose. The survivor played dead when a Jap destroyer came back to finish him off."

Sarah nodded but didn't speak.

"The survivor sailed two hundred and fifty miles to China, then traveled hundreds of miles to an American air base. It's hard to believe." Holmes traced a line in the article as he read it aloud, quoting the lone survivor: "'We felt absolutely no resentment for the Allied submarine that fired the torpedo. They could not have known the cargo was Allied POWs because the Japanese didn't put a red cross marking on the ship. As far as the Navy could have known, the ship could have been carrying Jap troops.'" Holmes looked up. "That one soldier just became a national hero."

"What do you mean?"

Holmes opened the paper to an interior page and turned it to Sarah. She scanned the headline.

Lone Survivor of 1,800 Lost on Jap Hell Ship

Below the headline was a picture of Sam receiving his medals.

"He's from Eagle Grove, Minnesota," Holmes said, giving Sarah a knowing look. "That's your hometown, too, isn't it?"

"Yes. Sam is . . ."

"I recall you telling me his name," Holmes said. "I am right, aren't I? Sergeant Sam Carlson?"

"Yes, sir. You are correct."

Holmes smiled. "I'm glad for you."

"Thank you, sir. I want you to know that I didn't say anything—"

Holmes raised his hand. "I have a spouse," he said. "And I will tell you, we don't keep secrets from one another. It isn't healthy. So, what you did and did not say is between you and your Sam."

Sarah nodded.

Holmes put the newspaper down. "Your sweetheart will be a household name as soon as his story is read in articles in papers all across America. And the War Department, at FDR's urging, is sending him on a nationwide speaking tour. He believes your Sam will be an inspiration to the country as it struggles to get back on its feet and we make a final push to end this war." He checked his wristwatch. "Ensign Haber, would you care to join me and Mrs. Holmes for dinner this evening? I know she'd enjoy having a woman to speak with, about anything other than this horrible war, and I sense you could use a friend tonight."

"I could, sir, yes."

"Then I will arrange it. Dismissed."

Sarah left the building and walked back to her office. She had no sooner reached it than her phone rang and the secretary said, "Phone call for you."

Sarah left her now-crowded office seeking privacy and picked up the phone in the unused conference room. She knew who it was before he said a word. Hawaii was five hours behind Minnesota, and Sam, like Grace, had likely been waiting for a decent time to call Sarah about the newspaper articles.

"Sarah? It's Sam. Listen, something has happened, and I wanted to be the one to tell you. It's a bit of a shock, but it looks like I'm going to be on the go again."

Sarah smiled. "What is it, Sam?" She wanted to let him tell her. "You sound excited."

9

FULL CIRCLE

Eagle Grove, Minnesota
February 10, 1946

After two devastating atomic bombs hit Hiroshima and Nagasaki on August 6 and August 9, 1945, the Japanese surrendered. Six months later, Sam returned to Eagle Grove. His national speaking tour had taken him by train to eight states, with one last stop scheduled for California in May. He'd used the tour to talk about all the men who'd served so bravely and told his audiences that he'd been kept alive and hopeful by Father Thomas Scecina's faith, Pete Chavez's sense of humor, Major Paul Jones's commitment to duty, and John Rudowski's bravery. He'd traveled to Indiana and spoken in person to Father Tom's family, his parents and his brothers, and told them all about Father Tom giving a little extra for all the POWs. In Tennessee, he met with Major Paul Jones's wife and his family. When he traveled to California, he'd stopped in Salinas and met with the Chavez family and told them of Pete's bravery, and how his humor had kept so many entertained. The Army had also found John Rudowski's family in Green Bay, Wisconsin, which was not a stop on Sam's tour, though Sam asked for and received a mailing address and sent the family a letter recounting Rudowski's heroism and bravery.

In between his stops, Sam had been stationed at the National Guard base in Brainerd. This trip home, before he left Eagle Grove again, he had something he needed to do.

He'd caught an early train, dressed in his olive drab wool service uniform the Army had given him to wear on his tour, including his medals. His father met him at the train station and drove him back to the family farm. Sam had not seen his father or mother look so proud since before the Depression first hit. His father's shoulders were square again, and the lines around his mother's eyes were laugh lines instead of worry lines.

"You got everything you need, son?" his dad asked.

"I think so."

"I'm so proud of you, son—and not just the medals and the commendations, though your mother's started a scrapbook."

Sam smiled. "It might be something to show the family one day."

"I don't need a scrapbook to remind me what a fine young man you've become. I'm proud of who you are, what you stand for. What you've been through makes me sick to my stomach. If I could change places with you, I'd do it in a heartbeat."

"I know you would, Dad."

"I'm going to pay you back the money you lent us."

"It's not a loan, Dad. I told you. It's yours."

"I appreciate it, but you know I can't take it. You let me pay you back. You know what that will mean to me."

"Okay, Dad."

They stood in an uncomfortable silence, then his father stepped forward and the two men embraced.

After stowing his gear at his parents' house, Sam marched downtown. His body had not yet fully recovered from his years in the camps, but he wanted to walk. Doctors said Sam might never be what he once was. His stomach still rebelled if he ate rich food, and he could not bring himself to eat even a single grain of rice. He was back to the weight he had been when the war started, but he wasn't nearly as strong. Mentally, he remained a work in progress. He still had debilitating migraines, and he didn't sleep through the night. Sometimes it wasn't more than a few hours before nightmares stalked him. He'd awaken from his dreams and believe he hadn't made it home, that he remained a prisoner of war. He'd see Yoshida's face-splitting grin and hear him laugh, then watch helplessly as he held his gun to another POW's head and pulled the trigger.

You are a selfish man, Sam Carlson. You have sacrificed the lives of these nine blood brothers.

"No!" Sam would yell, sometimes so loudly the hotel in which he stayed would call his room to make sure everything was all right.

In another dream, he remained in the ship's hold. Rudowski did not lift the hatch, and Sam did not have a pocketknife to cut the ropes. He, Father Tom, Rudowski, and Major Jones rode the ship to the ocean floor.

He hoped, in time, his mind and body would both heal.

Sam did not walk down Main Street. He walked along the edge of town, sticking to the path he had once walked every day he was in high school. He carried a bouquet of flowers through the building's double front doors and spun around to admire the school's motto engraved in the stone archway: "Enter to Learn, Go Forth to Serve."

Sarah had returned to Eagle Grove, though not to stay. She was waiting for Sam to finish his tour. In the interim, the high school needed a math teacher, and Sarah couldn't say no when asked to teach part time.

Sam made his way to the school office. The school administrator provided the number for the room in which Sarah taught. Sam walked down the hall with most of the office personnel, sensing something was about to happen, following him. As Sam and the group passed classrooms, teachers and students also took notice, exited their rooms, and joined the parade.

Sam put his finger to his lips and asked everyone in the hall behind him to be quiet. Then he pulled open the classroom's back door and stepped inside. Sarah stood at the chalkboard, her back to the class, intent on solving a mathematical equation. Several students turned in their seats, and then all of them did. Sam again put a finger to his lips and walked up an aisle between a row of desks.

"We are trying to solve for x," Sarah said. "Can anyone tell me how we might do that?"

The students didn't answer.

"I can," Sam said. "I'd ask the smartest girl in class, Sarah Haber."

She turned from the board. The chalk fell from her hand, striking the tile and shattering at her feet in a compact white starburst. "Sam," she said, then eyed the crowd filing into her classroom behind him.

Sam handed the flowers to a student to hold, then dropped to his knee and pulled the ring box from his pants pocket, a move he had rehearsed a dozen times. He held the box out and flipped it open. Inside, the diamond ring sparkled.

It was not his grandmother's ring. He wanted everything to be fresh and new. "Sarah Haber. Will you marry me?"

Sarah walked around her desk and down the aisle to where he knelt. She took the flowers from the student and held them to her nose, weeping. Then she said, "Sam Carlson, I've never loved anyone but you. Yes, I will marry you."

Sam slipped the ring on her finger and stood. Then he said, "If you don't mind, I've dreamed of this moment many times since seeing it in the movies, and I would like to see this dream come true."

He pulled her close, put one arm at her waist and the other behind her back, and dipped Sarah sideways.

She laughed out loud.

Sam pressed his lips against hers, and Sarah arched backward and lifted one foot off the ground, like the Hollywood movie star he'd always thought her to be.

When their lips parted, she said, "Fred."

Sam smiled down at her. "Ginger."

Afterword

The Hellships

From 1942 to 1945, an estimated 134 Japanese hellships transported roughly 50,000 Allied prisoners around the empire. A total of 21,039 POWs died during the voyages, making the phenomenon deadlier than well-known World War II events such as the Normandy campaign (16,000 Allied deaths) and the Battle of the Bulge (19,000 Allied deaths). It even surpasses the combined 20,000 Marines killed across the entire Pacific Theater at infamous locations like Iwo Jima, Saipan, Okinawa, and Guadalcanal.

The 40 percent POW death rate is staggering by any standard. American submariners, for example, suffered the highest death rates of any military branch during World War II, at 22 percent. In the bloodiest battle in Marine Corps history, the roughly 70,000 Marines at Iwo Jima suffered a 10 percent death rate. During the famous D-Day invasion at Normandy, less than 4 percent of American soldiers died.

Horrific conditions on the hellships led to shocking depravities. Prisoners drank urine, slashed their wrists to drink blood, and bit the throats of others. Relevant notes provide detailed examples and sources. Beatings, murders, suicides, and vampirism increased during the war's later stages as hellship conditions worsened. *Arisan Maru* survivors mention insanity and murder among POWs on their ship, but they do not cite vampirism, which we added from other hell-ships for illustrative purposes.

Despite the high death toll, the public knows little about the hellships compared to other World War II phenomena. Few movies and books have attempted to tell their story, perhaps because it defies the usual tropes of prisoner escape and heroism and is such a disturbing story to tell or hear.

A major cinematic attempt took place in 1989, with the release of the motion picture *Return from the River Kwai*. The British film focused on the sinking of the *Kachidoki Maru* and *Rakuyo Maru* hellships and the subsequent rescue of their Australian and British POWs by US submarines. But the CEO of Sony Pictures at the time—Akio Morita, a former Japanese naval officer in World War II—limited the film's global distribution and blocked it entirely from the US market.

The *Arisan Maru*

This Japanese freighter left Manila on October 11, 1944, with 1,800 Allied POWs crammed into its hold. It returned on October 20 for a few hours before departing again with the MATA-30 convoy shortly after midnight. The *Arisan Maru* sank on October 24, torpedoed by a US submarine. Several notes provide details.

The handful of survivors reported that conditions were so horrible, POWs literally prayed to die. The US War Crimes Office launched a formal investigation after the war that included several people but focused on Kiyoshi Yamaji, the Japanese second lieutenant in charge of prisoners on the *Arisan Maru*. We located defendants' written testimonies at the National Archives at College Park, in Maryland (hereafter cited as National Archives II). Relevant notes provide details.

By early 1945, sanitized versions of the *Arisan Maru* sinking ran in the *Washington Post* and other media outlets. A February 17, 1945, *New York Times* story, for example, was titled "U.S. Told 1,800 Americans Died in Japanese Prison Ship Sinking."

In late 2017, two men whose fathers died on the *Arisan Maru* visited Japan with eight other Americans as guests of the Japanese government. Part of the

US-Japan POW Friendship Program, the trip was the ninth such delegation to visit Japan in a spirit of remembrance and reconciliation.

While in Japan, the two men, Joe Brown and John Whitehurst, met with the *Arisan Maru*'s civilian radio operator, ninety-one-year-old Nobumi Ogawa. Then, in May 2018, Ogawa's son Mitsuhiro and grandson Takashi traveled to Albuquerque, New Mexico, where they participated in the annual convention organized by the American Defenders of Bataan and Corregidor Memorial Society. The nonprofit memorial society promotes education about the POW experience in the Pacific while also supporting reconciliation efforts.

The Survivors

Of the 1,800 POWs on the *Arisan Maru*, only nine survived the sinking. Japanese naval vessels recaptured four and took them to Formosa (Taiwan). One of them, Private Charles W. Hughes from Texas, died a few days later, on November 9, from exposure and poor treatment. Another recaptured POW, Corporal Glenn Oliver from Minnesota, was transferred to Japan, where he spent the rest of the war. The two others, Sergeant Philip Brodsky from New Jersey and Warrant Officer Martin Binder from Texas, stayed in various Formosa POW camps until the war ended.

The other five survivors miraculously found one another and an abandoned lifeboat: Sergeant Calvin R. Graef from New Mexico, Corporal Donald E. Meyer from California, Private Anton Cichy from Minnesota, Private Avery Wilber from Wisconsin, and Lieutenant Robert S. Overbeck from Maryland.

While the fivesome drifted at sea, a wooden mast built for that exact lifeboat floated to them. A keg of fresh water followed. Then a box containing just the right sail. With these resources, which some consider miraculous, the men sailed 250 miles to China.

Intelligence officers interrogated them as a group first, then split them into separate rooms, each with two interrogators and a secretary who typed notes. Later, the five survivors produced individual statements for the War Crimes Office. The five men signed a two-page joint statement immediately upon returning to the United States. Several notes cite their various written accounts.

The Characters

Many real people appear as *Hold Strong* characters. Important historical figures include Father Thomas J. Scecina, Major Paul M. Jones, Commander Edward N. Blakely, Lieutenant Commander John D. Harper, and Commander Wilfred "Jasper" Holmes. Dozens of notes provide details.

Most other characters are fictional composites. Sam, for example, represents the estimated 50,000 Allied prisoners carried on Japanese hellships, especially those on the *Arisan Maru*. Sam also reflects the experiences of the nine POWs who survived the *Arisan Maru* sinking, at least initially, including the five who returned home via China. Sam is not based on any one individual; he is truly a work of fiction.

Sarah represents thousands of WAVES who played a critical but little-known role in code breaking. She especially depicts the mysterious women selected to work in top secret code breaking at Pearl Harbor. Among 3,659 WAVES who served in Hawaii, only 72 worked at JICPOA: 61 enlisted women and 11 officers. Their names and stories remain unknown to the world.

Pete Chavez is a composite character representing the many Hispanic passengers on the *Arisan Maru*. His sense of humor was inspired by many examples documented among actual POWs, and by Sean Carmody, a friend who served in the Peace Corps with Chris and Jeff.

The fictitious Rudowski represents the many POWs who turned violent on hellships, including those who participated in vampirism and cannibalism. Several notes provide details.

On one level, Qiu Jin represents thousands of women raped during the Japanese attack on Nanjing (Nanking), including by forced incest and at an all-girls high school. On a higher level, she honors China's strong women, both past and present, known and unknown. She bears the name of a prominent women's rights activist who emphasized independence and education. China still celebrates the historical Qiu Jin as a national heroine more than a century after her martyrdom.

Katsuo Yoshida is a fictional character representing notorious Japanese soldiers detailed in various POW accounts. The real person in charge of prisoners on the *Arisan Maru* was Japanese second lieutenant Kiyoshi Yamaji. The former English professor at the University of Tokyo became the main focus of the war crimes investigation. Relevant notes provide details on Yamaji, as well as the real "Snookie," who *Arisan Maru* POWs killed with a hatch cover after escaping from the hold.

The Deadliest Accident in US Military History

Historians have called the *Arisan Maru* sinking the worst naval disaster in US history and the greatest loss of life at sea of Americans ever. We consider it not just the worst naval disaster but the deadliest accident in US military history. We define such incidents as those for which active-duty US military personnel were both the primary cause and victims of inadvertent mortality.

The definition includes military accidents such as the 1865 sinking of the steamboat *Sultana* but excludes nonmilitary incidents, such as when the civilian British ocean liner *Titanic* sank in 1912, killing 1,517 people. It also rules out prominent World War II sinkings such as the *Junyo Maru* and *Cap Arcona*, each of which resulted in more than 4,500 deaths by British military forces. Major hellship sinkings such as the *Tango Maru*, *Montevideo Maru*, *Koshu Maru*, and *Hofuku Maru* also involved other Allied nations as the main attackers, victims, or both.

Deadly US military accidents often take the form of "friendly fire." Examples abound from the Civil War (especially at the Battle of Antietam) to twentieth-century wars in Europe and Asia, to twenty-first-century wars in Iraq and Afghanistan. None match the *Arisan Maru* death toll.

The US government still considers the *Arisan Maru* sinking an unfortunate accident. Yet declassified military records, as presented in this story and documented in several notes, blur the line between accidental and intentional.

The USS *Shark II*

Various notes describe the real USS *Shark II* (SS-314) and her crew, including her final radio message to *Seadragon* on October 24, 1944. One note details an intercepted message from the Japanese destroyer *Harukaze*, in which it describes sinking a submarine that could have been the *Shark II*.

The US Navy credited the USS *Snook* with sinking the *Arisan Maru*, but ensuing research by John D. Alden and Craig R. McDonald raised doubts.

After careful examination of declassified radio intercepts, submarine war patrol reports, and related documents, we believe the USS *Shark II* sank the *Arisan Maru*. Vice Admiral Charles Lockwood, in his now declassified memo from November 27, 1944, about the *Shark's* demise, expressed his belief that the *Shark* sank the *Arisan Maru*. Perhaps this book can help create momentum to set the record straight.

Vice Admiral Charles Lockwood and Rear Admiral Richard Voge both wrote books after the war, in which they posit that the USS *Shark II* may have been sunk while attempting to rescue POW survivors from the *Arisan Maru*. Relevant notes provide details. We agree with them and wrote the story that way. We cannot help but wonder if the admirals knew something they could not say in public.

We spent time inside a Balao-class submarine, the USS *Pampanito*, to understand and describe the *Shark II* layout and function. Launched in early 1944, the *Pampanito* is nearly identical to the *Shark II*. It survived the war and now serves as a memorial and museum in San Francisco, California.

The Code Breaking

Cryptanalysts at FRUPAC/JICPOA in Hawaii broke the Japanese maru (freighter) code and used it with great efficacy to direct submarine and other operations. Several notes provide details and examples. By 1944, within minutes of a Japanese freighter reporting its daily noontime position to Tokyo, the United States had intercepted and decoded the message in Hawaii. Similar radio-spying units operated in Washington, DC, and at General MacArthur's headquarters in Australia.

Declassified radio intercepts that we reviewed included a space where analysts could specify a ship's "cargo." By regulation, Japanese freighters reported what they carried. This included, on occasion, the number of POWs. Freighters also informed Tokyo of their departures, destinations, daily noontime positions, and arrivals. FRUPAC/JICPOA radio spies intercepted this information around the clock.

The United States also received intelligence from spies in Manila. A vast network of double agents, expatriates, and friendly Filipinos provided a constant flow of information to Allied commands. One such spy, Josefina Guerrero, was a

Filipina who watched the Manila waterfront and shared details about ships and troop movements. She later received the US Medal of Freedom.

A group of 1,800 Allied POWs reaching Pier 7, then boarding the *Arisan Maru*, would have drawn considerable attention. A review of declassified records at the MacArthur Memorial museum in Norfolk, Virginia, for example, revealed a telling message sent from a Filipino guerilla unit to Allied headquarters in Australia. The October 11, 1944, message noted the loading of POWs onto Japanese freighters in Manila Harbor. Addressed to General MacArthur, the message starts, *11 OCTOBER APPROXIMATELY 2700 AMERICAN POWS WERE LOADED ON TRANSPORT AT PORT AREA, DESTINATION UNKNOWN.*

The *Arisan Maru* sailed from Manila Harbor that exact day with 1,800 POWs. Overall, it seems virtually certain that the Allies knew which convoys carried prisoners.

Ultra Secrecy

Of the 21,039 documented POW deaths aboard hellships, historians attribute only an estimated 1,540 to disease, starvation, thirst, suffocation, suicides, beatings, and murder. The overwhelming majority, more than 19,000, stemmed from Allied bombs, bullets, and torpedoes.

Even more shocking is the number of hellships sunk with full knowledge that Allied POWs were on board. Evidence strongly indicates that the Allies not only killed their own troops but often knew they were doing it. By 1944, every submarine in the Pacific was guided by secret Ultra intelligence. Submarine commanders had strict orders not to mention Ultra intelligence to their crews or in their official reports. Ultra messages did not disclose ships' cargoes to the submarine commanders, but FRUPAC/JICPOA knew. Submarine commanders received orders to attack convoys, not specific ships.

Submarine commanders' official war patrol reports document that they sank many Japanese ships at nighttime, including freighters in the same MATA-30 convoy as the *Arisan Maru*. Even if a ship displayed markings that indicated POWs were on board, such markings would not have been visible in the dark. Clearly, submarine commanders had orders to sink ships, regardless. Otherwise, they would have hunted only by day.

Shocking and heartless as it may seem now, the decision to sink ships carrying Allied POWs must be considered in context. Japan and the United States were locked in a bloody death struggle. Letting any ships pass unmolested, including those carrying Allied POWs, would enable Japan to do more harm in the future. It made strategic sense to sink everything that floated, then search afterward for any POWs.

Time Perspective Therapy for Mental Health

We are all time travelers. Each day, we recall our memories, experience our present, and anticipate our future. But how we move back and forth across time makes a big difference in how well our lives turn out. A large and growing body of scientific research shows that our "time perspective" can predict everything from educational and career success to general health and happiness to how well someone handles isolation during a pandemic.

Psychologists recommend striving for a healthy balance. Getting stuck in the past, living only for the moment, or being enslaved by ambitions for the future can undermine one's mental and physical health. Renowned Stanford University professor and psychologist Dr. Philip Zimbardo leads this effort. He created a rigorous questionnaire to assess one's "time perspective." Researchers and practitioners use the Zimbardo Time Perspective Inventory worldwide as a diagnostic and therapeutic tool. You can take the test at www.thetimeparadox .com and get your own score.

We are intrigued by recent applications of Time Perspective Therapy to post-traumatic stress disorder (PTSD). Initial studies have shown positive results among military veterans compared to other treatments. We heard Dr. Zimbardo describe it during a podcast interview with Tim Ferriss and decided to weave it into our story. We also list two relevant book titles in the selected bibliography.

One of the *Arisan Maru* survivors, the Minnesota tanker Anton Cichy, described the PTSD he still suffered into his nineties, more than sixty years after the war ended. Cichy noted PTSD's long-term physical and mental effects such as shakes and sleep disturbances. He also mentioned ongoing dysentery and its lasting impact on his health, leading to poor sleep and chronic fatigue.

In our story, Sam's path toward mental health gently reflects the "time perspective" approach without calling it by name. Three characters guide him toward a balanced time perspective: Qiu Jin (past), Pete Chavez (present), and Thomas Scecina (future). Perhaps these characters will inspire others to consider how they, too, think about time.

Of the eighteen hundred POWs on the Arisan Maru, *only nine survived. Japanese ships picked up four and took them to POW camps, where one died. The other five floated 250 miles in a lifeboat to China. The photo shows four of those five receiving medals from General George Marshall, US Army Chief of Staff, at the Pentagon on December 9, 1944. The fifth survivor received his medal eleven days later. While in Washington, DC, the five survivors also had a private White House meeting with President Franklin Delano Roosevelt. (Photo courtesy of the National Archives, Record Group 111-SCA, Book 3769, Photo 184798.)*

WANT MORE?

If you want to learn more about POWs in the Philippines, the brave men in the hold of the *Arisan Maru*, and other information, please visit Jeff's website: www.jefflangholz.com. You can access bonus materials:

- Historical photos
- Declassified military documents
- Interviews with the authors
- Discussion guide for book clubs
- Full list of 1,800 *Arisan Maru* POW passengers, organized by last name and by their 48 home states. ***Are you connected to this story through geography and/or ancestry?***
- Much more!

SELECTED BIBLIOGRAPHY

Dozens of books describe topics relevant to this story. We especially recommend the following:

Japanese Hellships

Blair, Joan, and Clay Blair. *Return from the River Kwai*. New York: Simon & Schuster, 1979.

Freeman, Sally Mott. *The Jersey Brothers: A Missing Naval Officer in the Pacific and His Family's Quest to Bring Him Home*. New York: Simon & Schuster, 2017.

Hubbard, Preston J. *Apocalypse Undone: My Survival of Japanese Imprisonment During World War II*. Nashville: Vanderbilt University Press, 1990.

Jones, Betty B. *The December Ship: A Story of Lt. Col. Arden R. Boellner's Capture in the Philippines, Imprisonment, and Death on a World War II Japanese Hellship*. Jefferson, NC: McFarland, 2011.

Kelly, Terence. *By Hellship to Hiroshima*. Barnsley, UK: Pen & Sword Books, 2006.

Michno, Gregory F. *Death on the Hellships: Prisoners at Sea in the Pacific War*. Annapolis, MD: Naval Institute Press, 2001.

Pearson, Judith. *Belly of the Beast: A POW's Inspiring True Story of Faith, Courage, and Survival Aboard the Infamous WWII Japanese Hell Ship* Oryoku Maru. New York: New American Library, 2001.

Sturma, Michael. *Hellships Down: Allied POWs and the Sinking of the* Rakuyo Maru *and* Kachidoki Maru. Jefferson, NC: McFarland, 2021.

The *Arisan Maru*

Champlin, Joanna M., Shawnee Brittan (dir.), and Drake Bingham. *Sleep My Sons: The Story of the* Arisan Maru. Oklahoma City: Westar Entertainment, 1996. Videocassette (VHS).

Masterson, Melissa. *Ride the Waves to Freedom: Calvin Graef's Survival Story of the Bataan Death March and His Escape from a Sinking Hellship*. Hobbs, NM: Southwest Freelance, 1999.

Wilber, Dale. *The Last Voyage of the* Arisan Maru. Baltimore: PublishAmerica, 2008.

Code Breaking During World War II

Holmes, Wilfred J. *Double-Edged Secrets: U.S. Naval Intelligence Operations in the Pacific During World War II*. Annapolis, MD: Naval Institute Press, 1978.

Mundy, Liza. *Code Girls: The Untold Story of the American Women Code Breakers of World War II*. New York: Hachette Books, 2017.

Smith, Michael. *The Emperor's Codes: The Thrilling Story of the Allied Code Breakers Who Turned the Tide of World War II*. New York: Arcade, 2011.

Winton, John. *Ultra in the Pacific: How Breaking Japanese Codes & Cyphers Affected Naval Operations against Japan, 1941–45*. Barnsley, UK: Pen & Sword Books, 1993.

Submarines in the Pacific Theater

Keith, Don. *In the Course of Duty: The Heroic Mission of the USS* Batfish. London: Penguin Books, 2005.

Lockwood, Charles A. *Sink 'Em All: Submarine Warfare in the Pacific.* New York: E. P. Dutton, 1951.

McCullough, Jonathan J. *A Tale of Two Subs: An Untold Story of World War II, Two Sister Ships, and Extraordinary Heroism.* New York: Grand Central, 2008.

Scott, James. *The War Below: The Story of Three Submarines That Battled Japan.* New York: Simon & Schuster, 2014.

The Philippines During World War II

Lawton, Manny. *Some Survived: An Eyewitness Account of the Bataan Death March and the Men Who Lived through It.* Chapel Hill, NC: Algonquin Books, 2004.

MacArthur, Brian. *Surviving the Sword: Prisoners of the Japanese in the Far East, 1942–45.* New York: Random House, 2005.

Thompson, Jan, dir. *Never the Same: The Prisoner-of-War Experience.* Carbondale, IL: Jan Thompson, 2013. www.nts-pow.com.

China During World War II

Chang, Iris. *The Rape of Nanking: The Forgotten Holocaust of World War II.* New York: Basic Books, 1997.

Peck, Graham. *Two Kinds of Time.* Seattle: University of Washington Press, 2008.

Pinck, Dan C. *Journey to Peking: A Secret Agent in Wartime China*. Annapolis, MD: Naval Institute Press, 2003.

Webster, Donovan. *The Burma Road: The Epic Story of the China-Burma-India Theater in World War II*. New York: HarperCollins, 2004.

Post-Traumatic Stress Disorder

Van der Kolk, Bessel. *The Body Keeps the Score: Brain, Mind, and Body in the Healing of Trauma*. New York: Penguin Books, 2015.

Williams, Mary Beth, and Soili Poijula. *The PTSD Workbook: Simple, Effective Techniques for Overcoming Traumatic Stress Symptoms*. 3rd ed. Oakland, CA: New Harbinger, 2016.

Zimbardo, Philip, and Rosemary K. M. Sword. *Living and Loving Better with Time Perspective Therapy: Healing from the Past, Embracing the Present, Creating an Ideal Future*. Jefferson, NC: Exposit Books, 2017.

Zimbardo, Philip, and Rosemary K. M. Sword. *Seeing Through the Grief: A Time Perspective Therapy Approach*. Jefferson, NC: Toplight Books, 2024.

NOTES

Writing about one of history's lesser-known tragic events was difficult for us on emotional and practical levels. Perhaps the most significant challenge, though, was the desire for accuracy. This is fiction, but we felt compelled to follow the true story as closely as possible, while also remaining faithful to the requirements of good storytelling. Doing so became a way to honor those who survived and those who did not. It is in that spirit that we include extensive research notes in the following pages. We thank the sources of these notes for their role in bringing this story to life.

The notes also serve another purpose: transparency. Like many fiction readers, we enjoy reading books that are "based on a true story" or "inspired by real events," yet find ourselves wondering, *How much of this is really true?* Authors often make such claims without backing them up in a meaningful way. The incredible true story behind *Hold Strong* deserves better. So do its readers.

Sources and Abbreviations

BLAIR and BLAIR: Blair, Joan, and Clay Blair. *Return from the River Kwai.* New York: Simon & Schuster, 1979.

BRITTAN: Champlin, Joanna M., Shawnee Brittan (dir.), and Drake Bingham. *Sleep My Sons: The Story of the* Arisan Maru. Oklahoma City: Westar Entertainment, 1996. Videocassette (VHS).

CALDWELL: Caldwell, Donald. *Thunder on Bataan: The First American Tank Battles of World War II*. Guilford, CT: Stackpole Books, 2019.

DAY: Day, Kenneth. *Forty-Nine Days in Hell: The Story of the* Oryoko [*sic*] Maru. Santa Fe: Bataan Veterans Organization, 1950.

GLUSMAN: Glusman, John A. *Conduct Under Fire: Four American Doctors and Their Fight for Life as Prisoners of the Japanese, 1941–1945*. New York: Viking Adult, 2005.

GRAEF: Graef, Calvin, and Harry T. Brundidge. "We Prayed to Die." *Cosmopolitan* 118, no. 4 (April 1945): 52–55, 177–80.

HOLMES: Holmes, Wilfred J. *Double-Edged Secrets: U.S. Naval Intelligence Operations in the Pacific During World War II*. Annapolis, MD: Naval Institute Press, 1978.

JOINT STATEMENT: "Joint Statement by Calvin R. Graef, Anthony E. Cichy, Donald E. Meyer, Avery E. Wilber, and Robert S. Overbeck." Located at the National Archives II under "Records of the Army Judge Advocate General, War Crimes Branch, Case Files 1944–1949," Record Group 153, Stack 270, Row 2, Compartment 8, Shelf 6, Box 1431.

LAWTON: Lawton, Manny. "Tragedy at Sea." In *Some Survived: An Eyewitness Account of the Bataan Death March and the Men Who Lived through It*. Chapel Hill, NC: Algonquin Books, 2004.

MASTERSON: Masterson, Melissa. *Ride the Waves to Freedom: Calvin Graef's Survival Story of the Bataan Death March and His Escape from a Sinking Hellship*. Hobbs, NM: Southwest Freelance, 1999.

MEYER: Meyer, Donald. "Five Came Back." Personal narrative. National American Defenders of Bataan and Corregidor (ADBC) Museum, Education and Research Center.

MICHNO: Michno, Gregory F. *Death on the Hellships: Prisoners at Sea in the Pacific War*. Annapolis, MD: Naval Institute Press, 2001.

MUNDY: Mundy, Liza. *Code Girls: The Untold Story of the American Women Code Breakers of World War II*. New York: Hachette Books, 2017.

OVERBECK: Overbeck, Robert S. "Voyage to China." Unpublished manuscript. Accessed April 12, 2024. https://overbeck.org/rso /VoyageToChina.md.

WILBER: Wilber, Dale. *The Last Voyage of the* Arisan Maru. Baltimore: PublishAmerica, 2008.

ZDON: Zdon, Al. "Survival Aboard a Japanese Hell Ship." Accessed May 22, 2024. http://picpimp.net/BestPosts/Cichy.htm.

Prologue

p. 1. *420-foot gray Japanese freighter, the* Arisan Maru: WILBER (p. 116) provides details about the *Arisan Maru's* history and technical specifications, including its 420-foot length, weight, depth, radios, radar, armaments, and sailing speed.

p. 1. *daily sightings of American warplanes over their prison camp*: GRAEF (p. 54) details the reactions by POWs and Japanese guards when carrier-based planes from Admiral William Halsey's Third Fleet flew over Cabanatuan POW camp on September 21. Prisoners in various degrees of undress celebrated the swarm of American planes overhead. Dumbfounded Japanese guards could do nothing to quiet the revelry. Even the sick and dying crawled out to witness the occasion.

p. 2. *The bell reminded Sam of a poem*: Sam's recollection refers to Rainer Maria Rilke's poem "Let This Darkness Be a Bell Tower," in *Sonnets to Orpheus* (II, 29).

p. 2. *Still, he figured anywhere would be better than the Philippines' oppressive heat and humidity*: MEYER [p. 8] notes the POWs' eagerness to leave the Philippines, but they harbored no misconceptions about the difficulty of such a journey.

p. 2. *Father Tom nodded to the ship's masts. "No Red Cross markings."*: WILBER (p. 140) notes that captains of this Japanese convoy's ships held a predeparture meeting that included discussion of whether or not to signal that the *Arisan Maru* carried POWs, as required by international law. The *Arisan Maru* captain testified during the ensuing war crimes investigation that he urged marking his ship, but the proposal was rejected as a security matter. The National Archives II holds the original copy of Minemaru Sugino's testimony under "Records of the Army Judge Advocate General, War Crimes Branch, Case Files 1944–1949," Record Group 153, Stack 270, Row 2, Compartment 8, Shelf 6, Box 1431.

p. 2. *Five armed Japanese guards roughly searched each prisoner*: MICHNO (p. 25) describes Japanese guards stealing prisoners' last few rings, watches, and other personal items as they boarded the *Fukkai Maru*. POWs on the *Arisan Maru* and many other hellships were allowed to bring certain items and managed to sneak on others. According to *Arisan Maru* survivors, "When the ship was loaded, the Japs had taken all Red Cross medical supplies, although they did not take what medicine we personally carried" (JOINT STATEMENT, p. 1).

p. 3. *Sam pinched the hem of the ragged vest*: Sam's ring in this story draws from the experience of Glenn Oliver, who boarded the *Arisan Maru* in a vest made from a tattered Army blanket. Sewn into the seam was a small knife and the class ring his girlfriend, Esther, had given him before he left home (Sally Macdonald, "He Survived—1,800 Fellow Prisoners Aboard Japanese 'Hell Ship' Died 50 Years Ago Today," *Seattle Times*, October 24, 1994).

p. 3. *The line's momentum stalled. POWs whispered and pointed at the upper deck*: This scene draws from actual events on the *Kachidoki Maru* when POWs boarding the hellship were shocked to see their sadistic former prison camp commandant, the notorious Lieutenant Tanaka (BLAIR and BLAIR, p. 69).

p. 3. *Katsuo Yoshida, their tormentor*: Yoshida is a composite fictional character. The real Japanese officer in charge of POWs on the *Arisan Maru* was Second Lieutenant Kiyoshi Yamaji. The actual commandant of Camp O'Donnell was Captain Yoshio Tsuneyoshi. The *Arisan Maru* ship captain mentioned Yamaji during the ensuing war crimes investigation: "In the afternoon of the same day, 1782 Americans were loaded onto the ship under the supervision of 2nd Lt. Kiyoshi Yamaji and forty Prisoner of War Guards under his command. By orders of the Manila TEIHAKUBA Headquarters, all the Prisoners were loaded into the upper half of the Number Two Hold." The National Archives II holds the original copy of Minemaru Sugino's testimony under "Records of the Army Judge Advocate General, War Crimes Branch, Case Files 1944–1949," Record Group 153, Stack 270, Row 2, Compartment 8, Shelf 6, Box 1431.

p. 4. *The former English professor had been educated in America*: GLUSMAN (p. 354) specifies that Kiyoshi Yamaji, the real Japanese second lieutenant in charge of POWs on the *Arisan Maru*, was a former English professor at the University of Tokyo.

p. 4. *"Must be a thousand men down there already"*: GRAEF (p. 55) notes the cramped situation in the No. 2 hold, suggesting that the Japanese packed 1,805 men in a space that could only fit 200.

p. 4. *Chavez took a deep breath, then bleated loudly, like a herded sheep. "Baa, baa."*: The sheep impersonation draws from William H. R. Emmett's eyewitness account on the *Rakuyo Maru*, where he heard the men *baaaaing* like sheep as they descended into the ship's hold (BLAIR and BLAIR, p. 68).

p. 5. *He gave a dramatic salute, quickly ducked under another bamboo strike, and descended the staircase*: GRAEF (p. 55) mentions the crude wooden steps leading into the hold and the raucous guards goading prisoners down the staircase.

p. 5. *Sam followed Chavez down into muggy, stifling heat and the familiar, horrific stench*: The description of the horrible smell draws from hellship survivor Tom Fagan's graphic account from the *Kenkon Maru*, where he describes the odor as a mix of sweat, urine, and feces (MICHNO, p. 61).

Part 1, Chapter 2: Dreams; Not Yet

p. 15. *promising Americans better economic times, what he called their "rendezvous with destiny."*: FDR said, "There is a mysterious cycle in human events. To some generations much is given. Of other generations much is expected. This generation of Americans has a rendezvous with destiny" (Franklin D. Roosevelt, "Acceptance Speech for the Renomination for the Presidency," Philadelphia, Pennsylvania, June 27, 1936. Available online via The American Presidency Project, www .presidency.ucsb.edu/documents/acceptance-speech-for-the-renomination -for-the-presidency-philadelphia-pa).

p. 16. *He walked barefoot, wearing shoes only to and from school, to church, and while playing sports*: Sam's lack of shoes draws from Lloyd Kilmer, a World War II veteran and son of a Minnesota dairy farmer, profiled in Tom Brokaw's book *The Greatest Generation* (New York: Random House, 1998, p. 61).

p. 17. *Sam's father ultimately accepted public assistance through the government's Works Progress Administration*: This example comes from World War II veteran Lloyd Kilmer, son of a Minnesota dairy farmer, who remembers the humiliation his father felt when he had to apply for government assistance to feed his family (Tom Brokaw, *The Greatest Generation* [New York: Random House, 1998], p. 61).

p. 18. *Sarah's scholarship to attend Mankato State Teachers College in Mankato, Minnesota, in the fall*: This university began as the Mankato Normal School in 1868, then changed to Mankato State Teachers College in 1921, then changed names twice more before becoming today's Minnesota State University, Mankato.

p. 21. *Sam had taken a ninety-foot strand of wire scrounged from his family's abandoned dairy farm, scaled the church roof, and connected the wire to the bell*: This apocryphal prank mirrors one committed by Louis Zamperini as described in Laura Hillenbrand's book *Unbroken: A World War II Story of Survival, Resilience, and Redemption* (New York: Random House, 2010, p. 7).

Part 1, Chapter 3: Rendezvous with Destiny

p. 24. *"The chief 'product' of women, in case you hadn't noticed, is men."*: Sarah's words pay tribute to early feminist Anna Howard Shaw (https://sos .oregon.gov/archives/exhibits/suffrage/Pages/bio/shaw.aspx).

p. 28. *"The first member of our family to finish high school."*: This is based on World War II veteran Lloyd Kilmer, son of a Minnesota dairy farmer, whose high school graduation provided a sense of satisfaction since he was the first in his family to earn a diploma (Tom Brokaw, *The Greatest Generation* [New York: Random House, 1998], p. 62).

p. 28. *"And I have nothing for you."*: This scene draws from World War II veteran Bud Lomell's memory of the night he graduated from high school. His father wept for providing no more than a dish of ice cream for the accomplishment. Bud's father lamented that he could not afford to send his son to college. It was the first time Bud saw his father cry (Tom Brokaw, *The Greatest Generation* [New York: Random House, 1998], p. 127).

Part 1, Chapter 4: Committed

p. 34. *The company commander drilled them to perfection*: CALDWELL (p.
18) describes the historical figure, company commander Captain Ernest
Miller, whose service record includes his enlistment in the Minnesota
National Guard at age fourteen and deployment to France in World War
I. Captain Miller later became a civil engineer and was credited with
designing Camp Ripley.

p. 34. *Sam completed basic training and was assigned to the National Guard's
34th Tank Company*: Like our fictitious Sam, one of the real recruits
at the National Guard's 34th Tank Company in Brainerd, Minnesota,
Sergeant Milan E. Anderson, listed his occupation as assistant manager
at a movie theater (https://bataanproject.com/provisional-tank-group
/anderson-sgt-milan-e).

p. 34. *Considered a "light" tank, the M2A2 had strong armor*: CALDWELL
(pp. 24–28) provides detailed descriptions of tanks used in the National
Guard units before and during the war.

Part 1, Chapter 6: A Change of Plans

p. 48. *"President Roosevelt just federalized our unit."*: CALDWELL (p. 20)
details the transition of National Guard units. Europe was on the brink
of war in 1939, and the United States started to increase its military
preparedness. The ratification of the Selective Service Act in September
1940 resulted in an expansion of all Guard units, including the 34th
Tank Company from Brainerd. Unlike the 192nd GHQ Reserve Tank
Battalion, which was mobilized immediately, the 34th Tank Company
wasn't called up right away, possibly due to insufficient space at the
military bases. Eventually, the company received orders to depart for Fort
Lewis, Washington.

p. 50. *February 20, Sam and eighty-one khaki-clad men gathered on the Northern Pacific Railway station's snowy platform for a warm send-off from friends and family*: CALDWELL (p. 20) details the frigid weather and warm send-off. Around midnight on February 20, 1941, eighty-two officers and enlisted men congregated at the Northern Pacific Railway station in snowy subzero weather for the departure.

p. 51. *the Brainerd Ladies' Drum and Bugle Corps struggled in the cold to play patriotic music to keep the mood upbeat*: CALDWELL (p. 20) notes the band and optimism as the newspaper reported that a significant portion of the town braved the cold to bid farewell to the men. They stomped their feet to maintain warmth while a local band filled the air with patriotic tunes. The atmosphere was positive, with everyone anticipating the men's return within a year.

Part 1, Chapter 7: Rain, Rain, and More Rain

p. 54. *Washington's warmer weather appealed to Sam*: The Bataan Project profile for Minnesota tanker and *Arisan Maru* passenger Glenn Oliver mentions that it was constantly raining, putting many men in the base hospital to halt the spread of colds (https://bataanproject.com /provisional-tank-group/oliver-cpl-glenn-s).

p. 54. *Sam's day began at 06:00*: The Bataan Project profile for Minnesota tanker and *Arisan Maru* passenger Glenn Oliver details life at Fort Lewis (https://bataanproject.com/provisional-tank-group/oliver-cpl-glenn-s).

p. 54. *Wouldn't that be something, Sam, if I taught a president?*: Sarah's thought about teaching future leaders pays tribute to distinguished educator Ivan Welton Fitzwater, who wrote the poem "Only a Teacher?" (www.tnonline .com/20170110/the-future-of-the-world-is-in-my-classroom-today).

p. 55. *The Army promoted Sam again*: Sam's leadership skills and promotions follow the actual trajectory of Salinas, California, tanker

Ben Saccone, whose leadership skills were noteworthy as he rose to the rank of first sergeant, the company's highest enlisted position (CALDWELL, pp. 22–23).

p. 56. *"My family used to pick sugar beets alongside a local guy named John Steinbeck."*: Steinbeck stopped working in Salinas Valley farm fields after the 1935 commercial success of *Tortilla Flat*, but he continued to write about the valley's land and people in books such as *Of Mice and Men*, *East of Eden*, and *The Red Pony*.

p. 57. *Sam, his new tank driver, Pete Chavez, and the rest of their detachment drove their twenty tanks and various support vehicles through the Kentucky countryside*: The Bataan Project profile for tanker Benjamin R. Morin details this trip. The ninety vehicles included twenty tanks, twenty motorcycles, seven armored scout cars, seventeen jeeps, twenty large two-and-a-half-ton trucks, five one-and-a-half-ton trucks, and one ambulance (https://bataanproject.com/provisional-tank-group/morin -2nd-lt-benjamin-r).

p. 60. *"They're sending me to the Philippines."*: The Bataan Project profile for Minnesota tanker and *Arisan Maru* passenger Glenn Oliver notes that the 194th Tank Battalion received orders on August 15, 1941, in Fort Knox, Kentucky, for duty in the Philippines. It also details the train trip across the US to San Francisco, where the men boarded the USAT *President Coolidge* on September 8 and sailed for the Philippine Islands (https:// bataanproject.com/provisional-tank-group/oliver-cpl-glenn-s).

Part 1, Chapter 8: Fred, Ocean Liners, but No Ginger

p. 61. *The USAT* President Coolidge *set sail at 21:00 for the Philippine Islands*: CALDWELL (pp. 47–49) describes the luxury ocean liner *President Coolidge* and its passengers departing San Francisco on September 8, carrying three military units: the 194th GHQ Reserve Tank Battalion,

the 2nd Battalion of the 200th Coast Artillery Regiment, and the 17th
Ordnance Company.

p. 62. *When word spread that the ship's chaplain needed an assistant—someone to
organize entertainment—Chavez nabbed the job*: This position and its perks
draw from the real experience of Private Lester Tenney of B Company
(CALDWELL, p. 52).

p. 64. *palm trees and a turquoise ocean served as a gloriously cinematic backdrop*:
Arisan Maru passengers made memorable stops in Hawaii during their
initial deployment to the Philippines. Calvin Graef notes dreaming
of tropical beaches and hula girls. Graef and friends started their
exploration at Waikiki Beach, then branched out to the rest of the island
(MASTERSON, pp. 8–9).

Part 1, Chapter 9: A Few Good Women

p. 72. *"I can tell you this, though: they picked girls from a variety of colleges and
majors"*: Who were these special women who went into code breaking?
MUNDY (p. 16) describes them as intelligent and resourceful. They
had made every effort to pursue as much education as their situation
allowed during an era when women were seldom motivated or recognized
for such endeavors. They possessed skills in mathematics, science, or
foreign languages or, frequently, in all three areas. They were committed,
patriotic, and prepared to do covert work without any expectations for
public accolades.

p. 73. *"You will say you perform menial tasks, like filing and typing and
emptying trash cans and sharpening pencils"*: MUNDY (p. 17) details
their cover stories by indicating that the women were instructed to say
they performed menial tasks when asked about their work in public.
Some humorously claimed to be ornaments for their superiors. Their
assertions were easily believed, reinforcing the stereotype of women in
subservient roles.

p. 73. *"to tell anyone will be considered an act of treason, punishable by death. The fact that you are women will not be considered toward leniency"*: MUNDY (p. 17) describes the potential death penalty, and how being female did not mean the women would be spared the wartime consequences of treason.

Part 1, Chapter 10: A Day of Infamy

p. 77. *Sam's platoon of five tanks sat parked in a patch of bushes and tall cogon grass next to Clark Field's main runway*: As Minnesota tanker and *Arisan Maru* passenger Glenn Oliver awaited the attack, his tank sat directly across from the control tower in some tall cogon grass and brush. He was ordered to hold fire unless he spotted paratroopers or transport planes landed (https://bataanproject.com/provisional-tank-group /oliver-cpl-glenn-s).

p. 77. *Major Paul Jones came out and climbed atop one of the tanks*: Nicknamed Red by his West Point classmates, the highly respected major Paul M. Jones was a passenger on the *Arisan Maru*. His West Point biography provides more details: www.westpointaog.org/memorial-article?id=c64dd248-cfbd-4043-89f9-2a966518195a. We adjusted Major Jones's role on Bataan and in the POW camps for narrative purposes.

p. 79. *"Bombs! Bombs! Take cover! Get down, goddammit. Get down!"*: Minnesota tanker and *Arisan Maru* passenger Glenn Oliver described the day of the attack, Monday, December 8, 1941, from where he stood in front of his tank counting what he thought were American planes approaching Clark Field: two formations with twenty-seven planes in each group, for a total of fifty-four planes. Then Oliver heard a strange whistling noise, and bombs began to explode to the north and then on the buildings and runway (https://bataanproject.com/provisional-tank-group /oliver-cpl-glenn-s).

p. 80. *he sprinted and dove headfirst into a trench*: Sam's actions parallel those of Minnesota tanker and *Arisan Maru* passenger Anton Cichy, who noted in ZDON that he ran toward a trench, only to find it already full. Cichy dove under a tank to avoid the bullets [p. 3].

p. 81. *Something struck Sam in the back of the head*: Sam's wound parallels that of Minnesota tanker and *Arisan Maru* passenger Glenn Oliver, who was hit by shrapnel during the attack. Oliver was hospitalized, and later received the Purple Heart (https://bataanproject.com /provisional-tank-group/oliver-cpl-glenn-s).

p. 82. *The Zero sped past him so fast it was almost a blur, but so low Sam spotted the pilot's eyes*: Minnesota tanker and *Arisan Maru* passenger Anton Cichy describes seeing the whites of the pilot's eyes in ZDON [p. 3], as the bombs exploded in front of and behind him.

p. 83. *He passed where his barracks once stood but only saw a crater*: Minnesota tanker and *Arisan Maru* passenger Anton Cichy describes the destroyed housing in ZDON [p. 3]. After the attack finally ended, he went back to his barracks, but it had been obliterated by a direct hit.

Part 1, Chapter 11: Poking the Bear

p. 86. *Seconds later, a bridge behind Sam—the one his tank had just crossed— erupted in a ball of fire*: This bridge was near a town called Calumpit and marked the Allies' last major defensive stand before entering the Bataan Peninsula. The order to blow the bridge came at 6:15 a.m. on New Year's Day, to allow a few more groups of stragglers to cross (CALDWELL, p. 115).

p. 86. *Time after time, Sam's tank platoon and others sped forward to engage and delay superior Japanese forces*: Minnesota tanker and *Arisan Maru* passenger

Anton Cichy mentions this losing battle in ZDON [p. 3]. He described the tough fighting and the ultimate retreat to Bataan.

p. 86. *called suicide missions by many. The tank crews had orders to "hold at all costs"*: CALDWELL (p. 109) details the tankers' instructions and how the commanding officer told the men to hold their ground until ordered to withdraw.

p. 86. *a Japanese shell had decapitated one of Sam's bow gunners*: The decapitated soldier was Private Henry Deckert, a company cook who had begged his way onto a tank crew and died on December 22 near Lingayen Gulf. CALDWELL (p. 93) graphically describes the decapitation and blood spraying throughout the compartment.

p. 88. *"What are you doing, Padre?"*: As a separate note details, Father Tom's commanding officer wrote in a medal citation that Father Scecina could normally be found on the front lines and showed little regard for his own life and safety (Fred W. Fries, "New Indianapolis High School to be Named for Fr. Scecina: Hoosier Priest Killed as POW during War II," *The Indiana Catholic and Record*, Vol. XLIII, No. 45, November 7, 1952, p. 3).

p. 88. A little extra. *That's how he'd heard one soldier in his unit characterize what Father Tom gave in these worst moments*: During Tom's early career as a priest, one of his parishioners noted that Tom always "gives that little extra." The line later became the motto of Scecina Memorial High School, which still celebrates him on October 24 each year with a Father Tom Mass. An article for the school's fiftieth anniversary detailed Tom's life and death, noting that Scecina Memorial High School opened to continue Tom's legacy of striving to "give that little extra" (Brandon A. Evans, "Scecina High School Remembers Its Founder on Milestone Day," *The Criterion*, October 17, 2003, p. 7).

p. 90. *"We have twenty-four thousand sick and wounded troops in the open-air hospital"*: Several sources document the desperate condition of troops on Bataan. CALDWELL (p. 161), for example, notes that the open-air hospital at Cabcaben housed 24,000 infirm soldiers who would be slaughtered in the next wave of attacks.

p. 91. *they would have to make a last, desperate attack on dug-in Japanese forces*: CALDWELL (p. 162) describes this last-ditch attack as a suicide mission without support of artillery units or infantrymen.

p. 91. *Sam received a command over his radio: "Blast. And we have one hour to comply."*: CALDWELL (p. 162) describes the tankers getting the "Blast" order at 5:35 a.m. on April 9. The order compelled the men to return to battalion headquarters to destroy their tanks and prepare to surrender.

p. 92. *Sam knew his men wanted to fight. He did too*: Tankers from two companies, C/192TB and C/194TB, wanted to keep fighting, but after the threat of court-martial, they, too, surrendered (CALDWELL, pp. 162–63).

p. 92. *Japanese forces would almost certainly overrun them in the morning and, in the absence of a surrender, kill them all*: Arisan Maru passenger and Minnesota tanker Anton Cichy described the need to surrender or die in ZDON [p. 3].

p. 92. *In a nearby field, they destroyed their equipment and their tanks*: GLUSMAN (p. 159) details the destruction of antiaircraft guns and rifles; trucks and ammunition dumps were set ablaze.

p. 93. *This time, the shell exploded in the clogged barrel, destroying it*: CALDWELL (p. 162) describes how the men destroyed their tanks, including pulling on long lanyards to fire the plugged guns.

Part 1, Chapter 12: The Hike

p. 96. *"Going on a hike, boys," Chavez called out*: Many Bataan Death March survivors euphemistically called it "the hike." The term even appears in the title of Bataan survivor Bernard T. FitzPatrick's book, *The Hike into the Sun: Memoir of an American Soldier Captured on Bataan in 1942 and Imprisoned by the Japanese until 1945* (Jefferson, NC: McFarland, 2012). Dozens of books describe the Bataan Death March. CALDWELL (pp. 166–73) dedicates several pages to tankers' experiences during the march.

p. 96. *Already starved, sick, and exhausted, the POWs were forced on an exodus from Bataan at the hottest, driest time of year*: Minnesota tanker and *Arisan Maru* passenger Anton Cichy described his weakened state in ZDON [p. 3]. He lamented that the only meal prepared on the march ended up in the dirt when the cook missed Cichy's mess kit while spooning the food out.

p. 96. *On his right arm was an American flag tattoo*: CALDWELL (p. 169) describes how the Japanese amputated a sailor's arm that bore an American flag tattoo. American medics applied a torniquet and saved the man.

p. 97. *Other prisoners, fearing they would be next, died by suicide, bolting into nearby fields*: In ZDON [p. 3], Minnesota tanker and *Arisan Maru* passenger Anton Cichy describes men cut down by machine gun fire for breaking ranks. MASTERSON (p. 40) adds that most men who broke ranks to rush toward a water source did not make it back.

p. 97. *Fallen men held out their canteens, desperate for water*: MASTERSON (p. 41) describes Calvin Graef's desperate effort to fill his canteen from a roadside fountain where some POWs received lifesaving water and others were bayoneted to death.

p. 97. *"The buzzard squad is coming," Sam would say*: CALDWELL (p. 172) describes what became known as "buzzard squads" of Japanese soldiers with bayonets that finished off those soldiers who collapsed from exhaustion.

p. 98. *"Stand up, Father Tom," Sam said. "Fall in. There's nothing you can do."*: The dying soldier who Father Tom assisted was forty-five-year-old John E. Duffy. From Ohio, Duffy served as chaplain for General Douglas MacArthur's First Philippines Corps. Japanese guards bayoneted Duffy on the Bataan Death March, as depicted here, then left him for dead (Donald R. McClarey, "The Other Father Duffy," www.the-american-catholic.com /2008/10/23/the-other-father-duffy).

p. 98. *"Through this holy anointing"*: Local Filipinos rescued Duffy from the roadside after Father Tom anointed him and departed. They nursed Duffy back to health, then helped him reach a guerilla unit. Duffy was recaptured in 1943, survived a journey on a hellship, and spent the remainder of the war as a POW in Manchuria before returning home. A 1945 letter from Duffy mentioned Father Thomas Scecina anointing him on the Bataan Death March (unpublished letter from John E. Duffy to Joseph E. Ritter, September 10, 1945, available at the Archdiocesan Archives in Indianapolis).

p. 99. *The guards packed the men into the cars until they couldn't sit*: After walking twenty-six miles, the POWs traveled the final six miles inside hot railroad cars, what many considered to be the worst part of the journey. Minnesota tanker and *Arisan Maru* passenger Anton Cichy describes in ZDON [p. 4] that many men died in the boxcars due to the heat, and they were packed in so tightly the dead could not fall to the floor.

Part 1, Chapter 13: Finding Her Purpose

p. 103. *"Not dead. No. No, not dead. But he's missing, Sarah."*: In May 1942, the military sent letters to family members whose loved ones' status was unknown at the time of surrender. Two months later, in July, the military sent letters to families of those soldiers considered missing in action. The Bataan Project includes many examples of these letters, including those sent to the family of *Arisan Maru* passenger and Minnesota tanker Anton Cichy (https://bataanproject.com/provisional-tank-group/cichy -pvt-anton-e).

p. 105. *"Yes. We can presume that you are good at crossword puzzles?"*: MUNDY (p. 4) mentions that interviewers asked women code-breaking candidates if they were good at crossword puzzles. MUNDY (p. 93) also notes that at least one senior military official considered it an inappropriate question because crossword puzzles are meant to be solved, while codes and ciphers are not.

p. 105. *"Are you married, or engaged to be married?"*: Recruiters also asked this question of women code-breaking candidates (MUNDY, p. 4). The rationale for the question is unclear but seems based on a belief that single women represented a better long-term investment, i.e., that they would likely stay with the military longer than women who would soon marry and start a family.

Part 1, Chapter 14: Home, Unsweet Home

p. 109. *"You are enemies of the Empire of Japan, captives, not prisoners of war."*: Minnesota tanker and *Arisan Maru* passenger Anton Cichy in ZDON [p. 4] described the welcome talk given to prisoners in perfect English by the Japanese officer in charge. The officer, Captain Tsuneyoshi, received a life sentence for war crimes (CALDWELL, p. 178). We have replaced Tsuneyoshi with the fictional Katsuo Yoshida for dramatic purposes.

p. 111. *To supplement their diets, the men scoured the camp for grasshoppers, rats, snakes, dogs, and just about anything else edible*: Minnesota tanker and *Arisan Maru* passenger Anton Cichy details his desperate quest for food in ZDON [p. 4]. He ate grass and leaves but gained strength in the rainy season when he found night crawlers.

p. 111. *Chavez soon learned through the grapevine that smuggling rings, or underground markets, sometimes emerged in POW camps*: Smuggling rings, work assignments, and certain other details borrow from POWs' real experiences at Cabanatuan and other camps where the men relocated and spent most of their time in captivity. We consolidated those details into Camp O'Donnell for dramatic purposes.

p. 115. *The sickest POWs were taken to Zero Ward*: CALDWELL (p. 176) notes that one of the barracks was converted into a makeshift hospital with no medicines and soon named St. Peter's Ward because men carried there rarely left alive. The men were laid on the floor elbow to elbow until they died.

p. 117. *Sam hated the burial detail more than any of the others*: Minnesota tanker and *Arisan Maru* passenger Anton Cichy notes in ZDON [p. 4] that so many men died, it was hard to find enough men healthy enough to bury them. Cichy also describes a time when he was forced to carry a bloated dead soldier on a plywood plank for two miles before digging the grave. He tried to avoid burial details after that but often had no choice due to the cruelty of his captors.

p. 117. *by the following morning the dead would rise to greet them, either from water pressure, or having been dug up and partially eaten by wild dogs*: Minnesota tanker and *Arisan Maru* passenger Sergeant Ted Cook describes the horrors of burial duty and the cemetery. Due to the high water table, the men had to hold the fallen soldiers down with a pole while covering the body with dirt. Sometimes the bodies were dug up by wild dogs or would sit up during the night (https://bataanproject.com /cook-sgt-ted).

Part 1, Chapter 15: Rudowski

p. 120. *Sam had survived malaria, dysentery, dengue fever, and other diseases*: Minnesota tanker and *Arisan Maru* passenger Anton Cichy describes a feverish bout with malaria in ZDON [p. 4]. Cichy ultimately traded a few cigarette butts he found, tossed by the Japanese guards, for some quinine that helped him recover.

p. 120. *but beriberi crushed him*: We chose to give Sam beriberi because two *Arisan Maru* passengers, both Minnesota tankers, described being afflicted by it. Anton Cichy notes in ZDON [p. 5] that he contracted beriberi, which caused his legs to swell so much the skin broke open. Glenn Oliver also developed beriberi shortly after arriving (https://bataanproject.com /provisional-tank-group/oliver-cpl-glenn-s).

p. 120. *"Maybe you'll get a good work assignment today."*: CALDWELL (p. 190) describes the work details, noting that all POWs had to perform tasks or risk cuts to their food rations. Jobs inside the camp included burial detail, cleaning buildings, cooking, and KP. Outside of the camp, some POWs were forced to build airstrips and bridges.

p. 120. *Men often did not return; they dropped dead from beatings or exhaustion, or their guards killed them for sport*: In ZDON [p. 4], Minnesota tanker and *Arisan Maru* passenger Anton Cichy mentions that the guards' primary weapon in the camp was a pick handle, a four-foot-long piece of lumber used to beat prisoners.

p. 120. *"You're staying here to rest. I'll take your place on whatever work detail you pull."*: Fellow POW and Army chaplain John E. Duffy describes Scecina helping other prisoners. He notes that Father Tom set himself apart by accepting details for POWs who were too sick to work (unpublished letter from John E. Duffy to Joseph E. Ritter, September 10, 1945, available at the Archdiocesan Archives in Indianapolis).

Part 1, Chapter 16: Into the Unknown

p. 131. *"Other girls are 'hot bedding.'"*: The hot bedding and other details come from MUNDY (p. 24). The phrase describes how women who worked alternating shifts shared expenses by sleeping in the same bed.

Part 1, Chapter 17: The Long Walk Home

p. 135. *The group paused for a wild dog to cross their path, a human arm in its mouth*: In the documentary film about the *Arisan Maru*, survivor Anton Cichy notes how dogs lugged human limbs around the mass graveyard (BRITTAN).

Part 1, Chapter 18: Leverage

p. 144. *She and other recent recruits had to overturn metal trash cans to use as seats*: MUNDY (p. 16) notes that the Washington, DC, code-breaking headquarters soon became so crowded that some recruits sat on wastebaskets turned upside down.

p. 144. *Many of the women were also ex-schoolteachers*: MUNDY (p. 52) lists several reasons why the Army and Navy both preferred to hire schoolteachers as code breakers. The women were youthful yet mature, intelligent and educated, familiar with difficult work, unaccustomed to high pay, and not distracted with husbands or children.

Part 1, Chapter 19: Blood Brothers

p. 149. *"Your blood brothers," Yoshida said*: Many sources document the "blood brothers" rule. *Blood Brothers* by Colonel Eugene C. Jacobs provides an especially detailed and credible description by a senior Army officer who was a POW in the Philippines. If one man escaped, the other nine might be used for bayonet practice until dead, or a Japanese officer would behead them all with his samurai sword (Eugene C. Jacobs, *Blood Brothers: A Medic's Sketch Book* [Otbebookpublishing, 2018], p. 7).

p. 149. *"You chose to put yourself ahead of your fellow prisoners, your blood brothers"*: *Arisan Maru* passenger Calvin Graef mentions that "blood brothers" were also called Ten Men Squads. If one POW escaped, the other nine would be shot (MASTERSON, p. 51). Graef notes how the presence of Ten Men Squads at Davao Penal Colony discouraged escape attempts (MASTERSON, p. 54).

p. 151. *"Some say I went a little crazy," he whispered*: Historians have documented how Japanese POW camp commanders and guards were widely regarded as the dregs of Japanese society, men too emotionally or physically unfit for important military service on the front lines. Laura Hillenbrand detailed one such guard in *Unbroken*: Mutsuhiro Watanabe. Nicknamed "the Bird," Watanabe was unstable, venomous, violent, and a sexual sadist. He openly disclosed that beating on POWs brought him to climax (New York: Random House, 2010, p. 236).

p. 151. *"A man can die but once"*: Yoshida's line comes verbatim from William Shakespeare's *Henry IV, Part 2*. Yoshida's ensuing quote, "Off with his head!" appears in two Shakespeare plays: *Henry VI, Part 3* and *Richard III*.

Part 2, Chapter 2: The WAVES

p. 171. *When President Roosevelt signed a bill into law creating a Women's Naval Reserve, Sarah, at Captain Russell's urging, accepted a commission to the WAVES*: FDR created the WAVES on July 30, 1942, as a new Naval Reserve corps. We adjusted the date by a few months for dramatic purposes.

Part 2, Chapter 3: The Safest Secret

pp. 177–78. *They went out together and protected one another:* MUNDY (p. 25) details how the women looked out for one another at USO dances and bars. Among one group, if someone ordered a vodka Collins, that signaled a stranger was getting too curious about their work. The women would go to the ladies' room, then exit the bar.

p. 178. *The women were often tormented by what they knew, and always utterly powerless to do anything about it:* MUNDY (p. 20) mentions that a number of women broke coded messages relevant to ships and units of their loved ones.

p. 178. *"It's about Sam. He's alive.":* Families of POWs in the Philippines received official letters in early June 1943 informing them that their loved ones were alive. We adjusted the date by several weeks for dramatic purposes. The two-sentence letters read: "REPORT JUST RECEIVED THROUGH THE INTERNATIONAL RED CROSS STATES THAT YOUR SON [INSERT RANK AND NAME] IS A PRISONER OF WAR OF THE JAPANESE GOVERNMENT IN THE PHILIPPINE ISLANDS. LETTER OF INFORMATION FOLLOWS FROM THE PROVOST GENERAL." The Bataan Project lists several such letters for tankers, for example, at https://bataanproject.com /provisional-tank-group/babb-pvt-john-b.

Part 2, Chapter 5: Dreaming in Japanese

p. 188. *Unlike the Army, the Navy had refused to allow female code breakers to serve in Hawaii, let alone overseas:* The Navy did not permit women to serve overseas until 1944. The first WAVES arrived at Pearl Harbor in mid-1944, led by Winifred Quick Collins. Her autobiography provides a compelling account of the groundbreaking work she did in Hawaii and beyond: *More than a Uniform: A Navy Woman in a Navy Man's World* (Denton: University of North Texas Press, 1997).

p. 189. *"I spent thirteen years as a commissioned officer and commanded the submarine S-30"*: HOLMES and several sources document Holmes's professional background, including his time as a submarine skipper. Chronic back pain led to his initial retirement and secret life as popular fiction writer Alec Hudson.

p. 190. *A Marine provided Sarah a red badge identifying her as assigned to FRUPAC*: JICPOA staff wore yellow-banded identification cards, but Sarah's top secret "traffic analysis" work likely occurred in the adjacent FRUPAC building. Staff there wore red-banded identification cards that signaled an even higher security level. For a detailed description of strict security in the two buildings, and the importance of the yellow and red identification cards, see Bill Amos, "Pacific Duty—Part II," *North Star Monthly*, December 4, 2010, www.northstarmonthly.com/features/pacific -duty---part-ii/article_93e33564-5684-559d-996b-d5d281230d87.html.

Part 3, Chapter 1: New World

p. 195. *"Speedo! Speedo!"*: MICHNO (p. 94) and other sources note how Japanese guards often shouted, "Speedo! Speedo!" as they herded POWs onto hellships.

p. 196. *"No more room," another yelled*: *Arisan Maru* POWs reported, "We were all forced into the No. 2 hold. The crowding was such that it was almost impossible to move" (JOINT STATEMENT, p. 1).

p. 196. *"Sardines get more space in the can than this"*: Chavez comparing the men to sardines packed in a can is inspired by Roy M. Offerle, survivor of the *Dainichi Maru* (MICHNO, p. 62).

p. 196. *Each time the crowd stopped, the guards used rifle butts and bayonets to prod the POWs farther forward*: The process of creating more room by jabbing rifle butts and bayonets at POWs draws from the *Dainichi Maru* (MICHNO, p. 62).

p. 196. *soldiers in front of Sam raised their arms to pass an unconscious body overhead*: Passing unconscious POWs overhead and then laying them on the deck draws from actual events and eyewitness accounts from the *Kachidoki Maru* (BLAIR and BLAIR, p. 70) and the *Noto Maru* (MICHNO, p. 192).

p. 196. *"We're in the belly of a whale."*: Survivors of multiple hellships, including the *Nagato Maru*, compared their ship to a whale that had swallowed them. Timbers lining the sides of the hold reminded them of ribs (MICHNO, p. 80).

p. 197. *Chavez pointed to tiered bamboo shelves running along the side of the ship*: GRAEF (p. 55), WILBER (p. 134), and OVERBECK all provide descriptions of the bamboo tiers inside the *Arisan Maru* hold, as do the survivors in their JOINT STATEMENT (p. 1): "Around the two sides of the hold benches were constructed on three levels. Twenty-two men were assigned to each space, 14 x 7 and about three feet high. On the other two sides of the hold there were two levels."

p. 197. *"It's a slave ship," Father Tom said*: Several hellship survivors compared their vessels to slave ships. MICHNO quotes four men from the *Argentina Maru* (p. 3), *Nagato Maru* (p. 80), *Lima Maru* (p. 38), and *Yashu Maru* (p. 173).

p. 197. *All up and down the racks, prone men kicked and shoved for space*: DAY (p. 3) provides a grim, detailed description of men crammed into bamboo tiers on the *Oryoku Maru*. Fistfights broke out, and some of the older officers quickly fainted. Men realized that only those near the front of each bay would get sufficient air.

p. 198. *Sam guessed the hold might be seventy or eighty feet long*: Precise measurements of the *Arisan Maru*'s holds do not exist. WILBER (p. 133) estimates the No. 2 hold was ten feet high, forty to fifty feet wide, and fifty feet long.

Part 3, Chapter 2: Setting Sail

p. 201. *By the time the* Arisan Maru *was ready to sail, its human cargo of eighteen hundred POWs had descended into chaos*: Who were the 1,800 passengers? GLUSMAN (p. 354) details the composition. The men represented all ranks and service branches, and came from POW camps across the Philippines. The hundred or so civilians were British, Dutch, and American.

p. 201. *"Sit down. Please sit down now," he said to the POWs*: Yoshida ordering the POWs to sit draws from events on the *Oryoku Maru*, where men were ordered to sit, despite it requiring more room than standing (DAY, p. 3). GRAEF (p. 55) notes that men on the *Arisan Maru* lacked enough room to sit on the floor, let alone lie down.

p. 202. *The ship's horn emitted a sudden high-pitched blast that ripped through the hold*: MEYER [p. 9] and other eyewitness accounts mention that the sound of air raid sirens hastened the *Arisan Maru*'s departure.

p. 202. *"Formosa?" Sam said*: The modern island nation of Taiwan was formerly called Formosa.

p. 203. *The ship's movement brought much-needed fresh air sweeping into the hold*: Survivors from the *Yoshida Maru* and other hellships described how the ship's movement channeled cooler air into the suffocating hold (MICHNO, p. 69). OVERBECK mentions that after the *Arisan Maru* set sail, Japanese guards eventually agreed to remove hatch covers and let some fresh air enter.

p. 203. *"Our bodies can't take this," Sam said. "Not after Bilibid.":* The food situation at Bilibid Prison had become unbearable by this time and would only worsen for the next several months. A US military report found that the average POW weight dropped to less than 120 pounds, and one to four men died per day. Bilibid's POWs ate twice daily, at 8:00 a.m. and 8:00 p.m., but it totaled less than two hundred grams, nearly all of it rice gruel. For details on conditions in Bilibid and other camps, see the November 1945 *Report on American Prisoners of War Interned by the Japanese in the Philippines*, prepared by the US Office of the Provost Marshal General.

p. 203. *A rumor started in the hold, speculation that the prisoners were part of an exchange:* The Red Cross prisoner exchange and ship-to-freedom rumors draw from the *Toko Maru* detailed in MICHNO (p. 36). In reality, at least six hundred of the *Arisan Maru* POWs were destined for the Kwantung Army in Manchuria, China (MICHNO, p. 250).

p. 203. *"More likely we're being taken deeper into the Japanese Empire to work in the mines":* MICHNO (pp. 38, 68) describes POWs speculating where they were going, as well as Japan's potential advantages such as more medicine, fewer diseases, and kinder guards.

p. 203. *When the POWs sat, Jones and a few other officers disconnected the buckets of cooked rice from the ropes, then distributed them in different directions:* The food distribution system comes from the account of a British POW who was on the *Yoshida Maru*. Officers organized the sharing of food so that each man got at least one mouthful. Starving men became more patient when they knew food was coming (MICHNO, p. 69).

p. 204. *The soldier scooped out a handful of rice, about the size and shape of an orange, then plopped it into Sam's cupped hands:* Minnesota tanker and

Arisan Maru passenger Anton Cichy describes the food in ZDON [p. 5], noting that the men each got two small balls of rice.

p. 204. *The giant propellers churned the sea and the ship settled into a gentle rocking motion*: Listening to the giant propellers draws from a *Kenkon Maru* survivor's account in MICHNO (p. 61).

p. 204. *He wondered where this hell ship was taking them*: The earliest documented example of World War II POWs using the term "hellship" or "hell ship" might be Bob Davis aboard the *Nagato Maru* in November 1942 (MICHNO, p. 80). The term could date back to the American Revolutionary War, when an estimated ten thousand men died on British ships used to hold American prisoners of war.

Part 3, Chapter 3: First Full Day at Sea

p. 205. *"Wonder how many guys suffocated in there."*: Suffocation was a major problem on hellships. Although accurate numbers do not exist for the *Arisan Maru*, DAY (p. 4) estimates that fifty men suffocated the first night on the *Oryoku Maru*.

p. 206. *In the early afternoon, a merciful downpour cooled the ship*: OVERBECK mentions capturing rainwater in the *Arisan Maru* hold. When heavy rains arrived, the men used strength and teamwork to fill their stomachs and collect extra water in containers.

p. 206. *Men below the hatchway opened their mouths to catch the drops*: POWs standing under open hatchways with mouths open to catch rainwater are mentioned in accounts from various hellships, including the *Amagi Maru* (MICHNO, p. 107).

p. 206. *Desperate for any distraction, Sam and others around him swapped memories of loved ones and favorite foods*: Several sources describe hellship passengers' discussions of food and other future pleasures. Gushing mountain springs, waterfalls, and other water themes were popular (MICHNO, p. 61). They also discussed desserts, salads, and future plans to own restaurants and farms (DAY, p. 14).

p. 206. *"Could be anchoring for the night," Jones said*: WILBER (p. 135) suggests that the *Arisan Maru* anchored on this night near Culion Island in Coron Bay, at the northern part of the larger Palawan Islands complex. The bay's tight access and shallow waters would have helped protect the freighter from submarines.

p. 207. *a soldier threw an empty canteen and hit the priest in the head*: MICHNO (p. 249) notes how canteens became weapons inside hellship holds. POWs on the *Hokusen Maru*, for example, killed men by clubbing them on the head with a full canteen.

p. 207. *Ordained in June 1935 at age twenty-four*: Details about Father Tom's professional career path come from multiple sources, especially "New Indianapolis High School to be Named for Fr. Scecina: Hoosier Priest Killed as POW during War II," by Fred W. Fries (*The Indiana Catholic and Record*, Vol. XLIII, No. 45, November 7, 1952, p. 3).

p. 208. *He had even married a young soldier to an Army nurse on the front lines as enemy shells exploded all around them*: The line about Tom's performing a wedding during a battle comes from a letter written from a US Army captain and former POW to a Catholic priest in Leopold, Indiana, informing him of Scecina's death (Edward Saalman, letter to Father John Herold, January 2, 1946).

p. 208. *"Let us pray"*: Prayer services occurred on many hellships, for example, the *Oryoku Maru*, where an evening prayer was part of the routine (DAY, p. 16).

p. 208. *"we are eighteen hundred Jonahs in the dank black belly of this whale."*: Scecina comparing the POWs to Jonah in the dark belly of hell comes from a *Nagato Maru* survivor (MICHNO, p. 82).

p. 208. *"Let us offer each other the kiss of peace."*: The "kiss of peace" or "Pax," the Bible-based practice of mutual greetings, dates to the second century, a fact Father Thomas Scecina would have known. We include it here, acknowledging that the modern Catholic form began after the 1960s Second Vatican Council and that many non-Catholics practice it today.

p. 209. *"More fine dining aboard the* Stinko Maru.*"*: Chavez's term comes from POWs who called the *Nagara Maru* the *Stinko Maru* (MICHNO, p. 34).

Part 3, Chapter 4: The Beast

p. 211. *Sam helped Father Tom pin down a POW who had gone berserk*: MEYER [p. 9] describes pinning berserk POWs on the *Arisan Maru*. While being held down during fits of insanity, the men continued to yell and scream, which further panicked other POWs.

p. 211. *"Sanity. Civilization. It's all fading away."*: Several hellship sources document men drinking urine, pinning violent soldiers to the ground, and other things mentioned in this chapter. *Arisan Maru* passengers noted that men went mad (GRAEF, p. 177) and stark crazy in MEYER [p. 9]. Sergeant Avery E. Wilber estimated that hundreds went insane (GLUSMAN, p. 355).

p. 211. *"a gang, led by Rudowski, is biting throats and sucking blood. Murdering men."*: The vampirism and murders draw from multiple eyewitness accounts on various Japanese hellships. DAY (p. 6), for example, notes that small groups of men lacking water committed cold-blooded murder to drink blood. Sergeant James D. Gautier Jr. on the *Canadian Inventor* hellship describes crazed POWs slashing at others to drink their blood

(MICHNO, p. 180). Andy Carson on the *Nissyo Maru* noted seeing men whose throats had been torn open during the darkness of night, realizing that someone drank the dead man's blood to save his own life (MICHNO, p. 188). Corporal George Burlage on the *Hokusen Maru* described men crazed by thirst who bit throats to get blood (MICHNO, p. 248). MICHNO (p. 260) compares the men to vampires.

p. 212. *The fourth day at sea, three POWs managed to restore power to two large electric blowers*: Arisan Maru passenger Calvin Graef describes the POWs finding and fixing the blowers. The men enjoyed two days of fresh, circulating air, until Japanese guards realized the situation and cut off electrical power to the hold (GRAEF, p. 177).

Part 3, Chapter 5: Burial at Sea

p. 216. *"We are not in Geneva."*: Yoshida's reference to not being in Geneva draws from an eyewitness account on the *Arisan Maru* (WILBER, p. 99).

p. 217. *"Island by island, Japan is freeing its neighbors from the rule of Western colonial powers."*: Yoshida describes a concept known as the Greater East Asia Co-Prosperity Sphere. Propagated by Japanese nationalists and militarists, the idea was to create a pan-Asian bloc free of Western dominance. In reality, Japan used the concept to occupy countries and install puppet governments that served Japan's economic and ethnic goals, i.e., to have Japan replace the old colonial powers.

p. 217. *"letting us bury our dead at sea tonight."*: Men died throughout the *Arisan Maru*'s trip, but burials only happened two or three times, at night ("Perpetuation of Testimony of Calvin Robert Graef," Judge Advocate General's Department—War Department. April 27, 1946. Located at the National Archives II under "Records of the Army Judge Advocate General, War Crimes Branch, Case Files 1944–1949," Record Group 153, Stack 270, Row 2, Compartment 8, Shelf 6, Box 1431).

p. 217. *"The heat in here keeps the bodies warm."*: MEYER [p. 9] compares the blistering heat inside the *Arisan Maru* to being trapped in an oven.

p. 218. *"Take whatever clothes they have"*: POWs removing and repurposing clothing from corpses draws from real events on the *Oryoku Maru* (DAY, p. 14).

p. 218. *"These were American soldiers."*: The horrific, ankle-first removal of corpses from the hold draws from actual events on the *Oryoku Maru* detailed by DAY (p. 13). The heartrending sight of human remains being hoisted feet first to the deck affected even the most hardened POWs. Men worried they would meet a similar fate.

p. 218. *Robert Lothrop, whom they'd all first met when transferred to Camp Cabanatuan*: For details on the historical Major Robert Blake Lothrop, a passenger on the *Arisan Maru*, see his West Point memorial: https://alumni.westpointaog.org/memorial-article?id=83a870b5-e625 -4b8a-ab6e-106f81fa7562.

p. 219. *where the naked corpses had been stacked like firewood*: The comparison to stacking bodies like firewood draws from an eyewitness account on the *Oryoku Maru* (DAY, p. 4).

p. 219. *"Not exactly the most civilized burial."*: GRAEF (p. 177) describes the informal burials on the *Arisan Maru*. The deceased received sad, silent salutes from burial detail members, but the ceremony lacked common elements such as flags, weights, slabs, rifle shots, and the playing of taps.

Part 3, Chapter 6: Escape

p. 223. *Lothrop gripped the ship's railing and, before Sam could react, vaulted over the side*: Versions vary regarding how and why Major Lothrop went overboard. This portion of our account follows that of *Arisan Maru* passenger Robert Overbeck, who said the major leaped overboard and tried to swim toward shore (OVERBECK). GLUSMAN (p. 355) relates a popular version whereby Lothrop squeezed out of a porthole and dropped into the water.

p. 224. *He fired four shots*: GLUSMAN (p. 356) specifies that when a sentry raised the alarm, Lothrop was killed by four direct hits as he swam away from the *Arisan Maru*. While researching this story, we spoke with Major Lothrop's daughter, Joanne, by phone in Arizona, and she confirmed the lack of details surrounding her father's passing. We have used the likely timing, location, and means of Major Lothrop's death but adjusted how and why he entered the water.

p. 224. *"Shot while trying to escape"*: MEYER [p. 9] mentions that crazy men were taken on deck, where they jumped off the ship and were shot. This suggests that Lothrop might not have been the only prisoner shot after leaping overboard.

Part 3, Chapter 7: Breaking Point

p. 230. *They descended through another hatch*: Japanese soldiers in charge of prisoner transport ships faced pressure to deliver POWs capable of doing slave labor. One prison camp commander in Japan complained that he requested able-bodied workers, not walking corpses (MICHNO, p. 75).

p. 230. *"We've rearranged the rats," Yoshida said to Sam*: Yoshida's line draws from statements of real Japanese officers who compared their hellship cargo to rats on the *Lisbon Maru* (MICHNO, p. 45) and the *Junyo Maru* (*"Juno Mayru* [sic]: Torpedoed By British Submarine HMS *Tradewind*," HistoryNet.com, June 12, 2006, www.historynet.com /juno-mayru-torpedoed-by-british-submarine-hms-tradewind).

p. 230. *"it looks to me like the captain ordered some of the men to the forward hold."*: In his testimony during the ensuing war crimes investigation, the *Arisan Maru* captain, Minemaru Sugino, detailed this decision to transfer prisoners to another hold: "I myself think that the Prisoners were very crowded by having so many put into so small an area. Three days after that ship left Manila, 1st Lt. Toshio FUNAZU, the Transportation Officer on the ARISAN MARU, and Lt. Yamaji consulted with me on the bridge; it was there decided that some 500 of the Prisoners would be moved out of the upper Number Two Hold and into the Number One Hold." The National Archives II holds the original copy of Minemaru Sugino's testimony under "Records of the Army Judge Advocate General, War Crimes Branch, Case Files 1944–1949," Record Group 153, Stack 270, Row 2, Compartment 8, Shelf 6, Box 1431.

p. 230. *"It will at least give everyone here more elbow room,"* Chavez said. *"But I'm gonna be upset if I hear they have a bowling alley up front."*: In reality, the hundreds of POWs who moved to the *Arisan Maru*'s forward hold suffered greatly. MEYER [p. 9] describes oil and coal dust smeared over the men's bodies and causing infection. With no room to lie down, and coal dust working deeper into their painful lesions, many sick men cried and prayed to die. GRAEF (p. 177) details how the six hundred men had to sleep on coal, and each time the ship rolled in rough seas, the coal buried them.

p. 230. *A short while later, a POW bolted up the staircase*: The desperate POW climbing out of the hold draws from a *Toko Maru* incident described in MICHNO (p. 38). The POW reached the top of the ladder, and a guard opened the hatch cover. But when the POW raised his head up to deck level, the guard bayoneted him in the neck.

p. 234. *"It's a big city, for sure"*: The *Arisan Maru* approached this port city on October 19, 1944, after nine days at sea.

Part 4, Chapter 1: Back in the Hunt

p. 239. *Though she was the only woman, Sarah knew her work was generally on par with or ahead of the other code breakers, and she had quickly gained their respect*: Treatment of women code breakers is a complex topic that deserves detailed, nuanced discussion like that provided in MUNDY (pp. 77, 79, 137, 160, 181, 237, 278). One of the Navy's top female officers of the time adds that every gain women made required a lengthy battle to overcome barriers such as military tradition, male chauvinism, ignorance, and entrenched interests (Winifred Quick Collins, *More than a Uniform: A Navy Woman in a Navy Man's World* [Denton: University of North Texas Press, 1997], p. 94).

Part 4, Chapter 2: Cruel Twists

p. 241. *"The whole goddamn trip was one big circle"*: MEYER [p. 9] describes the *Arisan Maru* returning to Manila and learning from cooks on deck that the harbor was strewn with bombed ships.

p. 242. *"Shore got hit too."*: Our description of bomb craters, overturned vehicles, burning buildings, and strewn bodies in Manila Harbor draws from eyewitness accounts seven weeks later as POWs boarded the *Oryoku Maru* (DAY, p. 2).

p. 243. *"They're loading supplies again?"*: WILBER (p. 141) specifies that the *Arisan Maru* loaded papayas, rice, and bananas during its brief return to Manila. MASTERSON (p. 72) adds sugar and water to the list.

p. 243. *"We're setting sail."*: LAWTON (p. 113) and WILBER (p. 138) specify the *Arisan Maru*'s October 20 departure date—the same day the Allied invasion force landed two hundred miles to the south, at Leyte.

p. 243. *Sam wished the Allied planes would return and bomb them again*: MEYER [p. 9] describes POWs straining to listen for the sound of Allied planes, hoping and praying the *Arisan Maru* would be bombed where it sat in Manila Harbor.

p. 244. *For three days, the convoy sailed north in stormy seas*: When the *Arisan Maru* left Manila Bay on October 20, the ship sailed into a typhoon. Heavy seas caused such misery inside the ship's hold that many POWs prayed for a bomb or torpedo to end their suffering (LAWTON, p. 114).

Part 4, Chapter 3: FRUPAC

p. 247. *converting the five-digit numerical strings into Japanese characters*: MUNDY (pp. 244–48) details the complex process of converting a coded message into usable information, with emphasis on the Japanese maru (freighter) code group.

p. 248. *Sarah placed the decoded message in her "Urgent" box above the one labeled "Routine."*: MUNDY (p. 153) details the three message categories: routine, urgent, and frantic.

p. 248. *Sarah had yet to receive a "Frantic" message*: Intelligence officer Bill Amos detailed the heady experience of working in such a top secret, high-stakes setting. Only the atomic bomb Manhattan Project was guarded more closely. Action ebbed and flowed, depending on the quality of the intercepts (Bill Amos, "Pacific Duty—Part II," *North Star Monthly*, December 4, 2010, www.northstarmonthly.com/features/pacific-duty ---part-ii/article_93e33564-5684-559d-996b-d5d281230d87.html).

p. 248. *It was now a race to reach the prison camps before the thousands of POWs could be executed*: A mass execution did indeed occur seven weeks later, in what historians call the Palawan Massacre. On December 14, 1944, on the Philippine island of Palawan, Japanese guards, fearing imminent

Allied attack, put 150 POWs into trenches, doused them with gasoline, set them on fire, then shot those attempting to escape. Only eleven POWs survived. For details, see Bob Wilbanks, *Last Man Out: Glenn McDole, USMC, Survivor of the Palawan Massacre in World War II* (Jefferson, NC: McFarland, 2004).

pp. 248–49. *At the other nine desks, her colleagues had also forgone sleep and were frantically processing stacks of intercepts, clacking typewriter keys, and studying a large wall map*: The description of the room draws from an article written by a former analyst long after the code-breaking operations' presence had been declassified. See Bill Amos, "Pacific Duty—Part II," *North Star Monthly*, December 4, 2010, www.northstarmonthly.com /features/pacific-duty---part-ii/article_93e33564-5684-559d-996b -d5d281230d87.html.

p. 249. *The room was a giant brain, singularly focused*: The wording here draws from MUNDY (p. 22). Code breaking was a team effort. The women collaborated, sharing pieces of information in ways that produced positive outcomes.

p. 249. *Thirty-five soldiers on the* Awa Maru *have fallen sick from food poisoning*: US cryptanalysts cracked Japanese code 6789, among others, which included health updates such as how many Japanese soldiers suffered from various diseases (MUNDY, p. 227).

p. 249. *She didn't want to be the person taking it to Commander Holmes*: Wilfred "Jasper" Holmes played a key leadership role in the intelligence operations at Pearl Harbor. Thirty years after the war ended, when the US government declassified many military secrets, Holmes wrote a book detailing his experience: *Double-Edged Secrets: U.S. Naval Intelligence Operations in the Pacific During World War II.*

p. 249. *Commander Holmes had chosen her from among four hundred candidates*: Holmes was instrumental in convincing Admiral Nimitz to allow women into JICPOA. He described the female staff as dependable, hard working, and proficient. Holmes believed JICPOA would have operated better in its early days if women had been permitted to work there (HOLMES, p. 211).

p. 250. *Called A-Day, the massive amphibious landing involved more Allied ships and troops than the D-Day operation four months earlier*: A-Day was the official name of the amphibious assault on Leyte Island to begin retaking the Philippines. For details on the entire operation, we recommend John Prados, *Storm over Leyte* (New York: Penguin Random House, 2016).

p. 250. *"I have returned. By the grace of Almighty God, our forces stand again on Philippine soil."*: Numerous sources document MacArthur uttering these exact words to a large, anxious radio audience. For the full text of MacArthur's proclamation, see M. Hamlin Cannon's *Leyte: The Return to the Philippines* (Washington, DC: Office of the Chief of Military History, Department of the Army, 1954, p. 154).

p. 250. *"The MATA-30 convoy has twelve freighters."*: MUNDY (p. 227) notes how cracking the Japanese code 2468 delivered one of the most important breakthroughs of the war. The code routed nearly every single maru (freighter) making its way around the Pacific to supply the Japanese army. Like most Japanese naval vessels, merchant marine ships sent a daily message giving their exact location and where they would be at noon. Radio spies in Hawaii and Washington, DC, deciphered and translated the messages within minutes, then forwarded the details to Submarine Command.

p. 251. *"Harukaze," the former submarine skipper said, puffing on his pipe, the sweet aroma of tobacco filling the room. "She's a tough old SOB."*: Built in 1922, the *Harukaze* was twenty-two years old at this time and had seen action around the Pacific. The destroyer escorted convoys like the MATA-30 for most of 1944. Heavily armed and with a crew of 148, the *Harukaze* suffered some damage from a November 4, 1944, submarine attack but survived the war. For details, see Hansgeorg Jentschura, Dieter Jung, and Peter Mickel, *Warships of the Imperial Japanese Navy, 1869–1945* (Annapolis, MD: Naval Institute Press, 1977).

p. 251. *Every morning the vice admiral from Submarine Command updated submarine positions*: HOLMES (p. 161) mentions that Rear Admiral Richard "Dick" Voge arrived each morning to receive the daily book showing detailed routes of Japanese convoys and suggested targets.

p. 251. *"No requests for safe passage."*: BLAIR and BLAIR (p. 87) state that the vice admiral in charge of Pacific submarines, Charles Lockwood, always honored Japanese requests for safe passage, even though he might have suspected many were a ruse. Lockwood certainly would have granted permission for a Japanese ship carrying Allied POWs. As noted earlier, WILBER (p. 140) mentions a meeting of the MATA-30 convoy ship captains during which the *Arisan Maru* captain proposed marking his ship, but the suggestion was vetoed.

p. 252. *"The* Arisan Maru *is also reported to be carrying fifteen tons of aluminum and nickel, and thirty-six boxes of airplane parts"*: In his testimony for the war crimes investigation, the *Arisan Maru* captain noted there was military cargo on board, in addition to the POWs. That cargo, which US radio spies likely knew about, would make it illegal for the Japanese to request safe passage. The cargo included 124 Army troops and prisoner of war guards, ingots of aluminum and nickel (15 tons), and 36 boxes of airplane parts (3 tons). The National Archives II holds the original copy of Minemaru Sugino's testimony under "Records of the Army Judge Advocate General, War Crimes Branch, Case Files 1944–1949," Record Group 153, Stack 270, Row 2, Compartment 8, Shelf 6, Box 1431.

p. 252. *"We're choking off enemy supply lines one torpedo at a time."*: The title of Vice Admiral Charles Lockwood's postwar book, *Sink 'Em All*, reflects Submarine Command's sink-anything-that-floats view toward unrestricted submarine warfare on Japanese ships. Written in 1951, it does not mention the use of code breaking and Ultra messages, knowledge of which would remain classified for decades to come.

p. 252. *"They'll change it, and it could take us months to break it again, possibly years. How many more men will die?"*: On June 7, 1942, the *Chicago Tribune* ran an article indicating that the Americans had cracked the Japanese naval code, then used it to win the Battle of Midway. Security tightened around Ultra after that alarming press leak. The Japanese tweaked their naval code several times during the war but never changed the main, basic code structure. For details about the *Chicago Tribune* blunder, see Elliot Carlson's 2017 book, *Stanley Johnston's Blunder: The Reporter Who Spilled the Secret Behind the U.S. Navy's Victory at Midway* (Annapolis, MD: Naval Institute Press).

p. 253. *"I chose you for the position anyway, because he also told me of your strong sense of duty and commitment, and of your integrity."*: Integrity was the most desired quality for the women entering code breaking. It was even more important for the select few going to JICPOA in Pearl Harbor. Cryptography and other skills could be learned, but integrity was a matter of character (Jennifer Wilcox, *Sharing the Burden: Women in Cryptology during World War II* [Fort George G. Meade, MD: Center for Cryptologic History, National Security Agency, 1998], p. 3).

p. 253. *"A one-in-four chance he's on that freighter, give or take."*: We based Sarah's estimate on a detailed 1945 US government assessment of POWs in the Philippines, while acknowledging that precise numbers do not exist (US Office of the Provost Marshal General, *Report on American Prisoners of War Interned by the Japanese in the Philippines*, November 1945,

www.mansell.com/pow_resources/camplists/philippines/pows_in_pi
-OPMG_report.html).

p. 253. *"I'll show this to Admiral Nimitz right away."*: Jasper Holmes moved
seamlessly across topics, locations, and levels of hierarchy—including
direct contact with Admiral Chester Nimitz. For details about Holmes
and his key role, see Bill Amos, "Pacific Duty—Part II," December 4,
2010, *North Star Monthly*, www.northstarmonthly.com/features/pacific
-duty---part-ii/article_93e33564-5684-559d-996b-d5d281230d87.html.

Part 4, Chapter 4: War Patrol

p. 255. *The USS* Shark: The USS *Shark II* (SS-314) is the actual submarine
involved with this historical event. Constructed by the Electric Boat
Company in Groton, Connecticut, it was commissioned on February 14,
1944. The submarine was 311 feet long with a surface cruising range of
11,000 miles at 10 knots. For details and photos, see www.navsource.org
/archives/08/08314.htm.

p. 255. *Submarine commander Edward Blakely received the coded message from
his ensign*: Edward Noe Blakely commanded the USS *Shark II* from its
christening as his first submarine command. After completing trials and
initial training, Blakely took the submarine through the Panama Canal
and to Pearl Harbor, arriving April 24, 1944, with his new ship and crew
ready for action. Various online resources provide details, including the
Naval History and Heritage Command website: www.history.navy.mil
/research/library/research-guides/modern-biographical-files-ndl/modern
-bios-b/blakely-edward-n.html.

p. 255. *Only the submarine commander had the authorization to decode an
Ultra Secret message*: The process we describe here, including the skipper
reading and burning the message, draws from a thorough description in
BLAIR and BLAIR (pp. 88–89). The code-breaking secret was so carefully

guarded that only the submarine commander had authorization to decipher Ultra messages.

p. 255. *He entered the Navy upon the sudden death of his father at forty-seven*: We know little about Edward Noe Blakely's real father, Dillwyn Parrish Blakely, except that he died on May 8, 1927, at the age of forty-seven (www.findagrave.com/memorial/60757763/dillwyn_p_blakely).

p. 255. *after reading Alec Hudson's adventure stories about submariners in the* Saturday Evening Post: Wilfred "Jasper" Holmes divulges his secret life as popular fiction writer Alec Hudson in HOLMES (p. 9). Holmes wrote for the *Saturday Evening Post* under the pen name Alec Hudson. Once Holmes rejoined the Navy in 1941, the Navy had to approve his stories in advance of publication.

p. 256. *his executive officer, John D. Harper*: Several online sources provide details about the real John Dott Harper, second-in-command on the *Shark*, among them www.oneternalpatrol.com/harper-j-d.htm. Details were also provided through personal communications with Nestor Sanguinetti, whose wife, Barbara Arntz, is the former spouse of Harper's son, John Scott Harper.

p. 256. *They'd largely been on "lifeguard duty," picking up downed American pilots*: The *Shark* rescued downed American aviator Bill Emerson, who later wrote a rare firsthand account of life aboard the *Shark* submarine (Bill Emerson and Kathy Emerson, *The Voices of Bombing Nineteen*, 1993, p. 53, www.emersonguys.com/bill/vb19.htm).

p. 256. *Four weeks into the* Shark's *third patrol, their drought was continuing*: In his now declassified memorandum about the *Shark*'s sinking, Vice Admiral Charles Lockwood, commander of Submarine Force, Pacific Fleet, noted on page 1 that the *Shark* reported to Submarine Command on October 22 that "she still had her full load of twenty-four torpedoes, so up until that time she had made no torpedo attacks." See "Loss of USS *Shark*: Narrative Report of Last Known Events During Third War Patrol of *Shark*. Memorandum from Commander Submarine Force, Pacific Fleet to Commander in Chief, United States Fleet," Serial 00963, November 27, 1944. Located at the National Archives II under "Action Reports," Record Group 38, Stack Area 370, Row 44, Compartment 20, Shelf 7+, Record ID A1-351, Box 98.

p. 257. *"Drum sank a cargo vessel twenty-four hours ago."*: Several primary sources document US submarines' successful attack on the MATA-30 convoy, which sank eight ships totaling over 40,000 tons. We consulted the US Navy's declassified summaries of this engagement for specifics, which are available at the National Archives II under "Action Reports," Record Group 38, Stack Area 370, Row 44, Compartment 20, Shelf 7+, Record ID A1-351, Box 98. Intercepted Japanese radio communications from the *Harukaze* on October 24, October 25, and October 26, 1944, also specify sinkings.

p. 257. *Nor could he tell his executive officer the last words his mother said to him*: We know little about Edward Noe Blakely's mother, Florence Noe Blakely. She was born February 28, 1884, to Edward T. Noe and Mary A. R. Noe, and died January 29, 1956, at the age of seventy-one. She appears to have been an only child. Her sole child had the same first name as her father, Edward. See www.findagrave.com/memorial/60757771/florence-blakely.

p. 258. *"We need to let this convoy and its ships come to us."*: MICHNO (p. 251) describes other submarines sinking MATA-30 ships while Edward Blakely and the *Shark* struggled to get into proper position.

p. 258. *"We'll sink ships, Harp"*: Lieutenant Commander John D. Harper had two nicknames: "Harp" and "Johnnie." The 1939 Naval Academy yearbook (*Lucky Bag*, p. 125) mentions these and other details, including

Harper's optimism and love of tennis and fishing in Colorado (https://archive.org/details/luckybag1939unse).

p. 258. *This freighter had to be the* Arisan Maru, *given its position so far behind the other ships in the convoy*: WILBER (p. 144) details the *Arisan Maru*'s position at the convoy's rear, noting that the ship could only do six knots and might have been taking on water. Radio spies in Pearl Harbor undoubtedly intercepted the ship's daily message to Tokyo, reporting its exact location.

p. 261. *"Enoe," Harper said, using Blakely's nickname at Annapolis*: Blakely had two other nicknames at Annapolis: "Eddie" and "Blake." His profile in the 1934 Naval Academy yearbook (*Lucky Bag*, p. 131) provides these and other personal details used in this chapter (https://archive.org/details/luckybag1934unse/page/130).

p. 261. *"Radio* Seadragon," *Blakely finally said*: The USS *Seadragon* commander wrote in his war patrol report that at 06:45 on October 24, he "received message from Shark that she had radar contact on a single freighter." This was the last message received from the submarine, and all subsequent attempts to contact *Shark* failed (see "USS *Seadragon*, SS194—Report of Eleventh War Patrol," Record Group 38, Records of the Office of the Chief of Naval Operations, National Archives II).

p. 261. *"Rev her up, Willie," Blakely said to his chief motor machinist*: Willie E. Hawthorn from Vallejo, California, served as the *Shark*'s chief motor machinist's mate. For a complete list of *Shark* crew names, ranks, and roles, see www.oneternalpatrol.com/uss-shark-314.htm.

p. 262. *"Missed her off the stern"*: *Arisan Maru* survivor Calvin Graef describes the first torpedo in MASTERSON (p. 72). Graef was on deck with the cooking detail when he noticed the Japanese crew running toward the ship's front. He looked toward the water and watched as the torpedo sped toward the freighter, then barely missed.

p. 263. *"She missed off the bow"*: *Arisan Maru* survivor Calvin Graef describes the second torpedo in MASTERSON (p. 73), noting that it, too, barely missed.

Part 4, Chapter 5: Blasted

p. 265. *"sounds like the Jap crew's running."*: GRAEF (p. 178) compares the Japanese crew to a track team racing toward the stern.

p. 265. *"The ship's under attack."*: *Arisan Maru* survivor Calvin Graef said the attack began around 5:00 p.m., and the ship's sirens blared loudly (GRAEF, p. 178).

p. 266. *"Hit us, Navy!"*: The words POWs yelled at this point, hoping to be sunk by a Navy torpedo, draw from the eyewitness account in GRAEF (p. 178). Men shouted until their voices gave out.

p. 266. *The POWs around him fell quiet, an eerie silence*: MEYER [p. 9] describes a strange, unearthly stillness settling over the crouched men as they held their breath and waited.

p. 266. *"Deck gun," Sam shouted*: GRAEF (p. 178) notes that the five-inch gun on deck began blasting in an attempt to explode the incoming torpedo. Japanese ships often fired at incoming torpedoes but rarely succeeded in hitting such a fast-moving object. The only exception we found occurred on the *Lisbon Maru*. See www.britain-at-war.org.uk/WW2/Hong_Kong /html/body_lisbon_maru.htm#AlfHunt.

p. 266. *"They're firing the cannon."*: WILBER (p. 116) provides extensive details on the *Arisan Maru*'s size, history, and armaments, including the freighter's short-barreled 200-millimeter cannon.

p. 266. *"Sounds like a boat engine coming our way"*: Comparing an incoming torpedo to a boat engine draws from an eyewitness account on the *Hokusen Maru* (MICHNO, p. 247).

p. 266. *The freighter lurched with the violent explosion, then shuddered and heaved out from under the POWs' feet, tossing them like rag dolls*: *Arisan Maru* survivors give different accounts of the attack. One says a single torpedo hit, another says two, and a third says three. One survivor says the ship broke in half; others imply it stayed in a single piece. One survivor says the stern started sinking first, but another says the bow. They all seem to agree the ship took at least three hours to sink.

p. 267. *Sam scanned the devastation inside the hold*: *Arisan Maru* survivors give graphic accounts of the devastation. Calvin Graef in MASTERSON (p. 73), for example, notes that the torpedo instantly killed a few hundred men and spread tiny pieces of flesh, bones, and blood everywhere.

p. 267. *A second loud explosion again jolted the ship*: Survivors' accounts differ regarding the number of torpedoes that hit the *Arisan Maru*, as noted earlier. Our careful review of eyewitness accounts, declassified documents related to the sinking, and comparable torpedo attacks lead us to conclude that one torpedo hit on the starboard side, followed by secondary explosions of the freighter's boilers or depth charges. WILBER (p. 146) agrees that one torpedo hit, effectively splitting the *Arisan Maru* in half. GRAEF (p. 178) mentions the first two torpedoes missing, as well as the ship's boilers exploding. On a separate hellship, a torpedo explosion caused the deck gun ammunition to explode in a loud bang, which might also have happened on the *Arisan Maru*. Finally, eyewitnesses agree that the *Arisan Maru* stayed afloat for three hours before sinking, which further suggests a single torpedo strike instead of three.

p. 267. *Father Tom and Sam scrambled to their feet and made their way toward the hatch*: Calvin Graef vividly details the horrific scene near the hatchway in MASTERSON (p. 74), comparing the blood and flesh to a slaughterhouse. Bodies closest to the torpedo blast had been reduced to dime-sized pieces. Others, farther away, were cut in half.

p. 267. *Major Jones tumbled down the stairs*: *Arisan Maru* survivor Calvin Graef and a few others were on deck cooking rice for POWs when the torpedo attack began. This scene borrows from their forced reentry into the No. 2 hold, as described in GRAEF (p. 178).

Part 4, Chapter 6: Careful What You Wish For

p. 271. Click-boom! *A second explosion knocked more men to the floor*: MICHNO (p. 253) details the Japanese destroyer *Harukaze* locating the *Shark* with sonar, dropping seventeen depth charges, and joining the destroyer *Take*. This event occurred in the Luzon Strait between Hainan Island and Bashi Channel, 177 nautical miles northwest of Cape Bojeador, Luzon (20°41' N, 118°27' E).

p. 271. *Blakely's crew had survived three different depth charge attacks during their first war patrol*: For a gripping description of previous depth charge attacks on the *Shark*, including the skipper's detailed war patrol reports, see "History of Ships Named *Shark*" by the Navy Department, Division of Naval History, Ship's History Section, https://navsource.org /archives/08/pdf/0831411.pdf.

Part 4, Chapter 7: Trapped

p. 273. *"Water's rising fast"*: OVERBECK details that *Arisan Maru* POWs were anxious to exit the hold, afraid they might get caught beneath the deck of a sinking ship. While captive in a Luzon POW camp, they had met British and Dutch survivors of a torpedoed hellship that sank so fast that most prisoners remained trapped below deck.

p. 273. *"I'm gonna have a look. Japs or no Japs. Someone's gotta check."*: POWs who tried to exit the hold faced significant risk. After the war, an *Arisan Maru* guard, Lieutenant Funazu, testified that the man in charge of the prisoners, Lieutenant Yamaji, said, "Try and keep the prisoners quiet. However, if panic occurs and they riot, I have grenades ready" (WILBER, p. 145).

p. 274. *Sam swiveled to check the view, then froze*: Japanese guards ordered the *Arisan Maru* POWs to stay in the hold after the torpedo hit. The POWs' commanding officer stuck his head out the hatchway to protest, but guards threatened to shoot him, then sealed the hatches ("Perpetuation of Testimony of Calvin Robert Graef," Judge Advocate General's Department—War Department. April 27, 1946. Located at the National Archives II under "Records of the Army Judge Advocate General, War Crimes Branch, Case Files 1944–1949," Record Group 153, Stack 270, Row 2, Compartment 8, Shelf 6, Box 1431). The deck machine gun draws from a real one on the torpedoed *Noto Maru*, where nervous Japanese guards brandished the machine gun at POWs as if daring them to come on deck.

p. 274. *"Wait a bit," Father Tom said*: MEYER [p. 10] notes that the chaplain attempted to calm the men, assuring them they would escape the hold.

p. 274. *Snookie lowered the six-by-six-foot cover across the opening*: *Arisan Maru* survivors reported that the Japanese guards battened down the No. 2 hold hatch, so there was no chance of escape (MASTERSON, p. 73). They also closed the hatch on the forward hold after cutting the rope ladder (letter from Martin Binder, p. 2, located at the National Archives II under "Records of the Army Judge Advocate General, War Crimes Branch, Case Files 1944–1949," Record Group 153, Stack 270, Row 2, Compartment 8, Shelf 6, Box 1431). In the BRITTAN documentary film, *Arisan Maru* survivor Donald Meyer also mentions guards sealing the hatchways before abandoning ship. Other versions suggest the hatches were not sealed firmly, if at all.

p. 275. *"Saved themselves but left us to die."*: *Arisan Maru* survivors noted in their official statement that Japanese guards immediately closed hatches, then evacuated the ship "within five or ten minutes, using the life boats" (JOINT STATEMENT, p. 2).

p. 275. *POWs shouted throughout the hold. Hysteria and panic set in*: WILBER (p. 147) describes the POWs lapsing into a pandemonium that bordered on mass hysteria.

p. 275. *"Stop!" A shout rang out. "Stop, dammit." The POWs gradually silenced*: GRAEF (p. 178) describes a red-haired major, whom we believe to be Paul M. Jones, rising to address the men. WILBER (pp. 147–48), too, states that this was likely Major Paul M. Jones of the 26th Cavalry Regiment.

pp. 275–76. *"We're in a hell of a jam."*: Major Jones's rousing speech is inspired by the eyewitness account in GRAEF (p. 178). Jones likely used the word "American" because nearly all the prisoners came from the United States. The ten exceptions were seven Brits, two Dutchmen, and one Irishman.

p. 276. *hundreds of POWs cheered*: GRAEF (p. 178) notes that the major's inspiring words elicited cheering by the men.

p. 276. *"Men, I've asked Father Tom to say a few words."*: WILBER (p. 148) mentions that Father Thomas Scecina played a vital role during these critical moments.

p. 276. *"Please, Lord," Father Tom said, his voice strong and confident, "if it be Thy plan to call us now, give us the courage to go as men."*: Father Tom's words here are inspired by the eyewitness account described in GRAEF (p. 178).

p. 276. *"Let's get the hell out of this shithole."*: The wording here is inspired by that of an unnamed POW cited in GRAEF (p. 178).

p. 277. *Rudowski sprang up with a loud grunt and pushed the hatch so hard it popped into the air*: Accounts vary regarding how the POWs escaped from the holds. Our version follows the one in GRAEF (p. 178), where POWs mustered their last bit of strength to force the hatch cover open. The survivors' JOINT STATEMENT (p. 2) notes, "Some men in the No. 1 hold shinnied up the stanchions, thirty or forty feet. They dropped rope ladders down and all the men got out." CALDWELL (p. 216) describes a gruesome version in which men made pyramids of dead bodies, then climbed atop them to open the hatches.

p. 277. *"Japs are gone."*: MEYER [p. 10] states that by the time the prisoners reached the deck, all Japanese had departed. The *Arisan Maru* POWs later realized "a few merchant marine Japs were left on board" (JOINT STATEMENT, p. 2).

p. 277. *Father Tom refused to go up, staying at the bottom to push soldiers too weak to climb, ignoring the rising water*: MEYER [p. 10] describes the chaplain keeping the men calm and reducing panic as men escaped the hold.

p. 277. *Others, animated skeletons, looked like walking dead, swatting at the bright light*: This scene draws from an eyewitness description from the *Nagato Maru*, where squinting men emerged on deck (MICHNO, p. 82).

p. 278. *Sam picked up a jacket from the pile*: *Arisan Maru* survivor Philip Brodsky mentions in LAWTON (p. 116) that he saw a stack of life preservers on deck. GRAEF (p. 178) specifies about 1,000 life preservers, made of kapok and capable of keeping a person afloat for about two hours.

p. 278. *As the men got their life jackets, some jumped over the railing, saying they feared the suction when the ship sank*: Various survivor accounts describe men jumping overboard right away, including Philip Brodsky in LAWTON (p. 116).

p. 278. *At the ship's bow more POWs were staggering from the forward hold, covered in coal dust, soot from burning fuel and oil, and blood*: A previous note already described the miserable conditions in the forward hold. When the torpedo hit that hold nearly head on, it instantly killed hundreds of men.

p. 278. *Behind them, waves lashed at a hole in the bow. When the waves receded, they took lifeless floating bodies*: Calvin Graef describes the scene near the forward hold in LAWTON (p. 121), highlighting his anger as lifeless bodies were flushed out of the wrecked hull, including the mangled corpses of his close friends. Graef lamented that the carnage could have been avoided if the ship had been marked as carrying prisoners.

p. 279. *Sam didn't know much about ships*: *Arisan Maru* passenger Philip Brodsky describes the dilemma in LAWTON (p. 117). Would the freighter sink in a few minutes or a few days? Would another ship come collect them, perhaps even an American one?

p. 279. *He looked to the Japanese destroyer, where dozens of desperate American soldiers had swum*: LAWTON (p. 122) describes Calvin Graef and nearly two hundred other POWs swimming toward the nearby Japanese destroyer. The men did not want to be taken prisoner again, but with no land in sight, that bad option seemed better than drowning.

p. 279. *Japanese sailors lined the railing, using long poles to force the struggling swimmers away from the boat*: Three *Arisan Maru* survivors described swimming toward the Japanese destroyer only to be forced away. GRAEF (p. 178) provides extensive details, including the use of long poles to pin Americans underwater until they drowned. MEYER [p. 10], too, describes being jabbed with long poles. OVERBECK says he was clubbed in the head with a bucket. *Arisan Maru* survivors noted in their official statement, "Some of the American prisoners immediately went into the water and headed for two Japanese destroyers who were picking up Jap survivors. We saw no large ships, only the two destroyers. Those who reached the Japanese destroyers [Graef and thirty-five or forty others] were beaten off with poles and long sticks" (JOINT STATEMENT, p. 2).

p. 279. *"Depth charges," he said to Father Tom*: GRAEF (p. 178) witnessed the Japanese destroyer launching depth charges every few feet. MEYER [p. 10] confirms that a Japanese destroyer arrived and began attacking the submarine with depth charges.

p. 279. *"I'm going to see if there's any chow or fresh water left."*: MEYER [p. 10] says men searched the ship for food.

p. 279. *In the ship's galley, a surreal orgy of eating had begun*: The orgy of eating in the galley draws from the account in LAWTON (pp. 116–17), which compares POWs in the galley to wild animals.

p. 279. *Others poured vegetable oil, ketchup, or sugar down their throats*: Minnesota tanker and *Arisan Maru* passenger Anton Cichy details gorging himself on rice, fish, and brown sugar until he vomited in ZDON [p. 5]. Swigging ketchup straight from bottles comes from *Arisan Maru* survivor Philip Brodsky's account in LAWTON (p. 117).

p. 279. *stacks of shoebox-sized Red Cross packages*: The presence of stolen Red Cross packages comes from the survivors' official postwar statements and was a major topic of the ensuing war crimes investigation. Calvin Graef said in his official statement (p. 5) that "we occasionally saw Nips on the boat eating chocolate out of emergency wrappers which indicated they were Red Cross supplies." Martin Binder confirmed that "supplies from the Red Cross were loaded aboard the ship before we sailed, we were not given them at all." See "Perpetuation of Testimony of Calvin Robert Graef," Judge Advocate General's Department—War Department. April 27, 1946, and "Testimony of Martin Binder, November 8, 1946" (p. 2). Both original documents are stored at the National Archives II under "Records of the Army Judge Advocate General, War Crimes Branch, Case Files 1944–1949," Record Group 153, Stack 270, Row 2, Compartment 8, Shelf 6, Box 1431.

Part 4, Chapter 8: Run Silent. Run Deep.

p. 281. *This explosion felt closer than the first dozen*: Vice Admiral Charles Lockwood noted in his postwar account of this incident that seventeen depth charges were dropped (Lockwood, *Sink 'Em All*, p. 211).

Part 4, Chapter 9: Give That Little Extra

p. 285. *Give That Little Extra*: The motto of Scecina Memorial High School in Indianapolis is "Give That Little Extra" (www.scecina.org/about).

p. 286. *One by one, they hauled the dying men up onto the deck and to the stern*: GRAEF (p. 178) mentions carrying sick and dying men out of the hold and onto the deck.

p. 287. *"Thank you," he said. "I didn't want to die alone down there.":* The bloody POW reaching deck only to die while clutching his guts draws from a real death on the *Nichimei Maru* (MICHNO, p. 97).

p. 287. *Father Tom moved to the next soldier in line:* WILBER (p. 148) and other sources note that Scecina opted to stay on the *Arisan Maru* and hear confessions for three hours rather than save himself.

p. 287. *"I'll absolve the entire group—a general absolution.":* Historical accounts suggest that Scecina might have performed the general absolution first, before hearing individual confessions, but we reversed the order for dramatic purposes. The profile for his 2016 induction into the Indiana Military Veterans Hall of Fame, for example, says that Scecina gave general absolution first, then spent three hours hearing individual confessions until the ship sank (https://imvhof.com/2016-class).

p. 288. *Sam moved to where Major Jones lay on the deck:* Major Paul M. Jones was posthumously awarded the Silver Star and Purple Heart for his actions in the Philippines. His West Point biography states that he "died as he lived—with never a blemish on his record. His selflessness will never be forgotten by those who served with him in training, in combat, in prison, or in death." Jones was "survived by his widow, Helen Bickerstaff Jones of Brookline, Massachusetts." For details, see www.westpointaog .org/memorial-article?id=c64dd248-cfbd-4043-89f9-2a966518195a.

p. 288. *"US military regulations authorize me to make battlefield promotions.":* Battlefield promotions have a two-century tradition in the US military, including more than 25,000 made during World War II. The US Army posthumously promoted Thomas J. Scecina to the rank of captain, but we hastened that promotion for dramatic purposes. The US military also awarded Scecina the Silver Star with one oak leaf cluster, the Bronze Star, the Purple Heart, Prisoner of War Medal, American Defense Service Medal, the American Campaign Medal, and the Combat Action Ribbon

(Stephen Peterson, *There's a New Kat at Scecina* [Bloomington, IN: Booktrail Agency, 2016, p. 3]).

p. 288. *"The Japanese excused chaplains. Tom volunteered to stay with the men."*: A 1952 article details how Father Scecina suggested that chaplains accompany their men on the transport ships, even though the Japanese did not require them to do so. The chaplains drew lots at Bilibid Prison, and Scecina was designated to go with the *Arisan Maru* group (Fred W. Fries, "New Indianapolis High School to be Named for Fr. Scecina: Hoosier Priest Killed as POW during War II," *The Indiana Catholic and Record*, Vol. XLIII, No. 45, November 7, 1952, p. 3).

Part 4, Chapter 10: Baptism

p. 291. *Thanks to the life jacket, he shot upward and breached the surface*: Calvin Graef mentions his long drop into the ocean in MASTERSON (p. 74).

p. 291. *Father Tom at the railing, a shadow backlit by the fading sun*: *Arisan Maru* survivor Glenn Oliver described the silhouetted figures in his official war crimes investigation testimony: "There were still many men aboard her when she went down. I could see them silhouetted against the sky." See page 3 of "Perpetuation of Testimony of Glenn S. Oliver, In the Matter of Acts Committed against Survivors of the SS *Arisan Maru*," Judge Advocate General's Department—War Department. December 3, 1946. Located at the National Archives II under "Records of the Army Judge Advocate General, War Crimes Branch, Case Files 1944–1949," Record Group 153, Stack 270, Row 2, Compartment 8, Shelf 6, Box 1431.

p. 291. *The priest raised his arms, one holding his crucifix, high above his head in what was no doubt one final blessing*: Floating in the ocean, Donald Meyer watched the chaplain comfort the men and administer last rites during the final moments before the *Arisan Maru* sank (BRITTAN).

p. 292. *A strong current pulled Sam from the wounded freighter.* OVERBECK details how a stiff wind and strong waves carried floating POWs away from the sinking ship.

p. 292. *He spotted another group of perhaps two dozen men gripping a cluster of boxes, poles, crates, oilcans, boards, and other items lashed together.* GRAEF (p. 179) describes helping a group of floating POWs join pieces of wreckage into a makeshift raft.

p. 292. *Doubt crept in and he turned back to the raft, but the current, wind, and waves had pushed it too far away. Sam would never catch it.* Sam's swimming to get debris, then being unable to return to his larger group, comes from Calvin Graef's actual experience as detailed in BRITTAN.

p. 292. *He grabbed it, caught his breath, then dragged his upper body from the water.* MEYER [p. 10] describes using an *Arisan Maru* hatch cover for flotation.

Part 5, Chapter 1: Letting Go

p. 295. *As night fell, a strong wind had picked up, chilling Sam to the bone. Distant shouts in the darkness had floated across the water.* OVERBECK mentions a strong breeze, waves ten to twelve feet tall, and how voices of the nearby men eventually faded away.

p. 295. *"Sharks!":* MASTERSON (p. 26) reveals that the men knew sharks were abundant there and wondered how the other POWs were faring against them. *Arisan Maru* survivor Martin Binder detailed seeing several sharks and trying to scare them away (letter from Martin Binder, located at the National Archives II under "Records of the Army Judge Advocate General, War Crimes Branch, Case Files 1944–1949," Record Group 153, Stack 270, Row 2, Compartment 8, Shelf 6, Box 1431). Other survivors, floating in separate locations, mention the fear of being eaten by sharks but do not report seeing any (MASTERSON, p. 26, and LAWTON, pp. 125, 127).

p. 295. *Was he delirious?*: Hallucinations about lifeboats and other things in the dark night draw from MEYER [p. 11]. LAWTON (p. 123), too, details the men believing they had spotted a lifeboat only to realize it was not real.

p. 295. *A white lifeboat*: LAWTON (p. 124) details two *Arisan Maru* survivors spotting a white lifeboat at dawn, deciding it was real rather than an illusion, then swimming toward it.

p. 296. *Closer. He drove himself toward it*: MASTERSON (p. 20) notes the lifeboat was an estimated 100 to 150 yards away, and the men swam roughly thirty minutes to reach it. Our story matches that, with Sam pausing halfway to rest and get his bearings.

p. 297. *As he descended beneath the surface a third time, he knew it would be for one final push*: Sam's three attempts to enter the lifeboat draw from Anton Cichy's three failed attempts described in the documentary film about the *Arisan Maru* (BRITTAN).

p. 297. *This time something, or someone, clasped his wrists*: LAWTON (p. 124) details how two *Arisan Maru* survivors, Calvin Graef and Donald Meyer, swam to the lifeboat but lacked the strength needed to scale its four-foot sides. Three men already on the lifeboat—Cichy, Wilber, and Overbeck—noticed the exhausted swimmers and helped them aboard.

p. 297. *He balled into a fetal position, violently coughing, gagging, and spitting up seawater*: Anton Cichy describes feeling a hand grab his and pull him upward, but then he passed out. Cichy woke up later inside the lifeboat (BRITTAN). The description in ZDON [p. 6] confirms the sequence of events.

Part 5, Chapter 2: More Bad News

p. 299. *At sea, the Imperial Japanese Navy had arrived for a final, all-or-nothing battle between hundreds of ships*: Jasper Holmes, head of the Estimate Section, and his radio spies kept constant real-time track of Japanese forces at Leyte and around the Pacific. His declassified memoranda provide details and are available at National Archives II, under Joint Intelligence Center, Pacific Ocean Area, Summary of Ultra Traffic, 0000/20–2400/20 Oct 1944, in JICPOA, Summary of Ultra Traffic, 11 September–December 1944. Record Group 457, SRMD-007, pt. 1, p. 120.

p. 300. *the Japanese called these "kamikaze" raids, which meant "divine wind."*: The Battle of Leyte Gulf was the first time the Japanese used organized kamikaze raids. John Prados details the Japanese decision to send kamikaze groups in *Storm over Leyte*, pp. 192–94.

p. 300. *"The Japanese destroyer* Harukaze *reports sinking a sub."*: While researching this book, we reviewed several messages that FRUPAC/JICPOA staff intercepted and decoded from MATA-30 ships during the convoy's trip from Manila to Formosa. In an October 24 message, the *Harukaze* describes attacking a submarine and concluding that it was sunk. Jasper Holmes treated such messages with skepticism, believing that 90 percent of these claims were probably inaccurate (HOLMES, p. 148). Declassified intercepts relevant to this story are available at National Archives II, "Intercepted Radio Traffic and Related Documentation," under Record Group 38, Record Identification A1 344, Stack Area 370, Row 01, Compartment 01, Shelf 01+, Boxes 1152, 1371, 1372, 1749, 1750, and 1752.

p. 300. *"*Harukaze *dropped seventeen depth charges. Bubbles, heavy oil, clothing, cork rose to surface"*: In his 1951 book, *Sink 'Em All: Submarine Warfare in the Pacific*, Vice Admiral Lockwood describes the *Shark*'s October 24 sinking, based on a report from the Japanese received after the close of the war. The unnamed report details the Japanese counterattack, when escorts dropped depth charges seventeen times and saw debris float to the surface. Vice Admiral Lockwood likely based his statement on top secret Ultra intercepts that would remain classified for decades to come, rather than on the unnamed postwar report from the Japanese. For example, we reviewed a declassified October 24, 1944, intercept from the *Harukaze*, noting, "We saw [a] column of water 20 meters high and heard a large explosion. In the vicinity heavy oil and flotsam came to the surface." The radio message mentions seeing "papers," "cork," and other debris. Located at National Archives II, "Intercepted Radio Traffic and Related Documentation," under Record Group 38, Record Identification A1 344, Stack Area 370, Row 01, Compartment 01, Shelf 01+.

p. 300 *"Gekichin."*: HOLMES (p. 73) describes FRUPAC/JICPOA staff closely monitoring Japanese radio traffic during battles, watching for key words such as *gekichin* (destruction of an enemy ship) and *chimbotsu* (sinking of a Japanese ship).

p. 300. *"Said they were commencing to attack."*: We reviewed three declassified military documents that mention the USS *Shark*'s final radio communication, including the detailed one by Vice Admiral Lockwood: "However, the patrol report of the U.S.S. SEADRAGON states that at 1615 on 24 October 1944, she received a message from the SHARK stating that she had made radar contact with a single freighter. This is the last known message from the SHARK. At 1858 on 24 October the SEADRAGON attempted to contact the SHARK by radio but was unable to raise her and neither the SEADRAGON nor the BLACKFISH was able to raise the SHARK after that time." Cited in "Loss of USS *Shark*: Narrative Report of Last Known Events During Third War Patrol of *Shark*. Memorandum from Commander Submarine Force, Pacific Fleet to Commander in Chief, United States Fleet," Serial 00963, November 27, 1944. Located at the National Archives II under "Action Reports," Record

Group 38, Stack Area 370, Row 44, Compartment 20, Shelf 7+, Record ID A1-351, Box 98.

p. 301. *Holmes had explained official procedure to Sarah in the event of a submarine sinking after the USS* Seawolf *went down:* The USS *Seawolf* was lost on October 4, 1944. Of note, two other submarines, the USS *Darter* and the USS *Tang,* both were sunk within twenty-four hours of the October 24 sinking of the USS *Shark.*

p. 301. *Next, the Navy would send telegrams to the families of the* Shark's *eighty-seven men:* The standard telegram wording appears in many published sources, including James Scott's 2014 book *The War Below: The Story of Three Submarines That Battled Japan* (New York: Simon & Schuster, p. 278).

p. 301. *The crew and the sub were not "missing.":* Vice Admiral Lockwood reflected this hard truth in a personal letter he wrote after the USS *Wahoo* failed to return. Any submarine reported as overdue was likely never coming back (cited in James Scott, *The War Below: The Story of Three Submarines That Battled Japan* [New York: Simon & Schuster, 2014], pp. 278–79).

Part 5, Chapter 3: Survivors

p. 304. *"We're damn lucky to be alive.":* Nearby submarine commanders assumed the *Shark* crew were all dead at this point. George H. Browne, commander of the USS *Snook* (SS-279), wrote in his official war patrol report that he could not reach the *Shark* by radio late on October 24. Hours later, his 2:00 a.m., October 25 entry reads: "Joined Blakely's Pack. Sent orders to BLACKFISH to take charge of pack because he knows patrol plan being followed" (see *USS* Snook, *Report of Seventh War Patrol* by G. H. Browne, Office of Naval Records and History, Ship's Histories Section, US Department of Defense).

p. 304. *"We don't have room for a bunch of Jap prisoners"*: Space and supplies were carefully calibrated on submarines. Having left Pearl Harbor on September 23 with orders to depart for home on November 3, the *Shark* had completed more than half her scheduled war patrol at this point. We base this calculation on "Loss of USS *Shark*: Narrative Report of Last Known Events During Third War Patrol of *Shark*. Memorandum from Commander Submarine Force, Pacific Fleet to Commander in Chief, United States Fleet," Serial 00963, November 27, 1944. Located at the National Archives II under "Action Reports," Record Group 38, Stack Area 370, Row 44, Compartment 20, Shelf 7+, Record ID A1-351, Box 98.

p. 305. *"Could be a trap."*: The concern draws from BLAIR and BLAIR (p. 227), who note that although submariners lacked official proof of Japanese lure attacks, they exercised great caution around all debris and lifeboats.

p. 305. *As the sub cruised near the debris field, lookouts called out a mix of planks, timbers, and other debris tied together as makeshift rafts*: BLAIR and BLAIR (p. 228) describe the USS *Pampanito* submarine warily sweeping past a POW-strewn debris field to get a close inspection before committing.

p. 305. *If it were a trap, they'd fight back*: The shotgun, machine gun, and other weaponry here match what the USS *Pampanito* crewmen carried as they approached floating POWs from the *Rakuyo Maru* (BLAIR and BLAIR, p. 228).

p. 305. *"Ready for some target practice?"*: BLAIR and BLAIR (p. 228) detail how submariners often shot Japanese survivors and how the US Navy did not officially condone or disapprove of such measures. Referring to the USS *Pampanito* submarine as it approached floating *Rakuyo Maru* survivors, they state the boarding party was preparing to kill the men on the debris. MICHNO (p. 212) confirms this, citing direct quotes from USS *Pampanito* sailors. For a detailed analysis of how US submarine crews treated Japanese captives in ways both good and bad, see Michael Sturma's book *Surface and Destroy: The Submarine Gun War in the Pacific* (Lexington: University Press of Kentucky, 2011) and his 2016 article "The Limits of Hate: Japanese Prisoners on US Submarines during the Second World War" (*Journal of Contemporary History* 51, no. 4: 738–759).

p. 305. *"First you bastards sink us. Now you're gonna shoot us?"*: This dialogue draws from words that an Australian or British *Rakuyo Maru* survivor spoke as the USS *Pampanito* submarine drew near (BLAIR and BLAIR, p. 229).

p. 306. *"Only one man."*: Lieutenant Commander Harper's insistence that only one man grab the rope draws from comments made by boarding party leader Tony Hauptman as the USS *Pampanito* rescued POW survivors (BLAIR and BLAIR, p. 229).

p. 306. *Harper yelled at them to stay on the raft*: Harper's order draws from one issued by crewman Tony Hauptman as desperate POWs swam toward the USS *Pampanito*, while a shipmate prepared to fire a machine gun (BLAIR and BLAIR, p. 229).

p. 308. *Seeing the emaciated POWs brought some to tears*: BLAIR and BLAIR (p. 231) describe the USS *Pampanito* submarine crewmen's shocked response to the condition of the survivors. Some crewmen were so upset they could no longer perform their duties.

p. 308. *"Two per bunk"*: Harper's two-per-bunk order draws from the rescue of *Rakuyo Maru* survivors by the USS *Pampanito*. The survivors were deemed skinny enough to fit two per bed (BLAIR and BLAIR, p. 235).

p. 308. *He found the chief pharmacist's mate. Subs did not carry doctors on board*: Twenty-seven-year-old Leon M. Brown from Princeton, Indiana, served as the USS *Shark*'s chief pharmacist's mate (www.oneternalpatrol.com /brown-l-m.htm).

p. 308. *"Sit those in the worst shape over here. I'll give them morphine shots to knock back their pain."*: BLAIR and BLAIR (p. 235) provide a vivid eyewitness description of *Rakuyo Maru* survivors picked up by the USS *Pampanito*: The survivors were in shock and barely able to speak. Fifteen received morphine shots.

p. 308. *"Take the healthiest ones to the rear and give them a water-soaked rag and two slices of bread"*: The conversion of tough submariners into tender nurses, their eager volunteerism, and the specific food items they fed to hellship survivors all draw from the actual performance of the USS *Pampanito* crew, detailed in BLAIR and BLAIR (p. 236).

p. 309. *"Some of our boys are so upset they can't even look at the POWs."*: The crew's emotional distress draws from the USS *Sealion* submarine crew, who joined the USS *Pampanito* in rescuing *Rakuyo Maru* survivors: the submariners felt awkward facing the survivors, knowing that their own torpedoes had caused such pain and suffering (BLAIR and BLAIR, p. 237).

Part 5, Chapter 4: Resurrection

p. 311. *Rudowski bit a piece of firm, dry biscuit in half, then extended the rest toward Sam*: *Arisan Maru* survivors managed to open a sealed storage compartment in their lifeboat that contained about a gallon to a gallon and a half of a dry biscuit known as hardtack (BRITTAN).

p. 311. *He shoved the food into his mouth and chewed hard*: *Arisan Maru* survivor Anton Cichy described the stiff hardtack in ZDON [p. 7], noting that it nearly broke his teeth.

p. 312. *He drank a swig, then spewed salt water onto the floor*: The *Arisan Maru* survivors' JOINT STATEMENT (p. 2) describes them finding water contaminated with salt water: "Just at dark Overbeck was the first man to find a half submerged life boat. It had been stripped of equipment and supplies. The water kegs had been filled, we believe by the Japs, with salt water." LAWTON (p. 124) details one of the men swigging the water only to find it contaminated with salt. BRITTAN notes the men finding two wooden kegs of water but does not mention salt contamination.

p. 312. *"Japs used them to row over to the destroyer."*: *Arisan Maru* survivors all agree their lifeboat came from the *Arisan Maru*. MEYER [p. 12] speculates that the lifeboat broke loose from where the Japanese had tied it. LAWTON (p. 125) suggests that Japanese officers from the sinking *Arisan Maru* cut the lifeboat adrift after using it to reach their nearby destroyer. GRAEF (p. 180) notes that the lifeboat's sails and oars had been removed.

p. 313. *"Right there. Looks like another pole."*: LAWTON (p. 125) details the men finding and retrieving the floating pole, a strenuous endeavor that drained their energy.

Part 5, Chapter 5: Quick Descent

p. 316. *"Negative, sir. Still no radio or radar."*: It was not uncommon for submarines to lose radio communications after a depth charge attack. When the USS *Pampanito* was overdue, for example, Vice Admiral Lockwood expressed hope that it was just a matter of the submarine's radio being damaged (HOLMES, p. 155).

p. 316. *"You're a free man. You're on board a United States Navy submarine"*: Blakely's words echo those of Yeoman Charles McGuire on the USS *Pampanito* after a rescued hellship survivor introduced himself as a prisoner of the Japanese (MICHNO, p. 215).

p. 317. *"Thank you, sir," Chavez said*: Chavez's feelings reflect those documented among hellship survivors picked up by the USS *Pampanito*, as described in BLAIR and BLAIR (p. 255). The survivors were still traumatized by their ordeal but thrilled to be free, saved by what seemed to be a miracle.

Part 5, Chapter 6: Life and Death at Sea

p. 320. *"Damned if it ain't the mast built for this style lifeboat"*: LAWTON (p. 126) describes the men recovering a mast that fit their lifeboat perfectly.

p. 320. *"Let's make a pact," Sam said*: This cannibalism conversation draws from a real one among *Arisan Maru* survivors Philip Brodsky and Glenn Oliver, detailed in LAWTON (p. 128). While floating at sea, the men made an agreement not to kill and eat each other.

p. 320. *As night deepened, the temperature dropped, the air frigid*: LAWTON (pp. 128–29) describes the harsh conditions on the lifeboat, including relentless heat by day and freezing temperatures at night, made worse by desperate thirst.

p. 321. *A hundred feet away, Sam spotted a floating corpse*: LAWTON (p. 128) details the *Arisan Maru* survivors spotting a corpse, then one of them swimming about 150 yards to search the body for a canteen of water.

p. 323. *if they found another corpse, they'd have to eat it*: LAWTON (p. 128) describes Philip Brodsky and Glenn Oliver hoping to find a second floating corpse. The starving men knew they were desperate enough to eat it.

p. 323. *Instead of a dead body, Sam picked up a small fish that flopped into the lifeboat at midday*: Philip Brodsky describes this minnow in LAWTON (p. 128). He and Glenn Oliver split the tiny minnow in half and spent a full hour eating it.

p. 324. *A large wooden box bobbed next to their vessel*: Three *Arisan Maru* survivors mention the wooden box that bumped into the lifeboat. OVERBECK offers the most detailed account, including the men's delight to find a sail inside the box.

p. 324. *Rudowski helped him hoist the heavy box from the shifting sea*: Hauling the box into the lifeboat draws from LAWTON (p. 126), who also details the wooden box's dimensions and how it was sealed with screws.

p. 324. *"Not a sail. A God-given miracle."*: GRAEF (p. 180) notes that the sail was the exact type for this particular lifeboat.

p. 324. *Sam pulled ropes and pulleys from the box*: LAWTON (p. 125) mentions that the box contained ropes, pulleys, and a sail.

p. 325. *"Which way's China?"*: The question here is inspired by GRAEF (p. 180). After the men opened the floating box containing a sail, rope, and pulleys, one of them asked which direction would take them to China.

p. 325. *For the next hour the men rigged the two poles and then ran a rope through the mast's tip*: Hoisting the sail proved to be a long, complicated task. Calvin Graef notes in GRAEF (p. 180) that it required five hours of difficult labor. OVERBECK mentions that the men's weak condition and the boat rolling in the waves added to the difficulty.

p. 325. *They rested often but never for long*: BRITTAN details a complication the men encountered while rigging the sail. They forgot to put the rope through the pulley on top of the mast, making it impossible to raise the sail. Ninety-eight-pound Calvin Graef fixed the problem by climbing to the top of the mast and feeding the rope through the pulley's throat.

p. 325. *An enemy destroyer, and it appeared to be headed right at them*: All five *Arisan Maru* survivors on the lifeboat describe spotting the destroyer, causing them to lower the sail and play dead. Their JOINT STATEMENT (p. 2) states "Five of us climbed aboard it [the lifeboat] at different times during the night. A Jap destroyer then came in the morning. We laid in the bottom of the boat in the water without moving. There was no effort to pick us up. We saw no Americans on the deck of the destroyer, only Japanese."

p. 326. *"You saw what they did to those POWs who swam to that destroyer."*: LAWTON (p. 125) notes that the men believed this destroyer was one they had seen the previous night, when the *Arisan Maru* was sunk. Based on an intercepted Japanese radio message we found at the National Archives II, this destroyer could have been the *Harukaze*, whose captain radioed that he was still in the area "mopping up" at this time.

p. 326. *"Play dead."*: Three survivor accounts detail the men playing dead. Calvin Graef, for example, notes in BRITTAN that he urged everyone to spread out and play dead. As the men did so, they could see the destroyer's forward guns aimed straight at the lifeboat.

p. 326. *He pushed Sam onto the sail and sprawled his big body across him, pinning him to the floor*: LAWTON (p. 125) details the five *Arisan Maru* survivors strewn across each other playing dead, making it pointless for the Japanese to pick up the Americans or shoot them.

p. 326. *"It's circling, about two hundred yards away."*: MEYER [p. 12] states that the destroyer circled the lifeboat three times. LAWTON (p. 125) specifies the distance as roughly two hundred yards.

p. 326. *Machine gun fire erupted*: LAWTON (p. 125) notes that the terrified *Arisan Maru* survivors saw machine guns aimed at them and were convinced they would die at any moment. In reality, machine guns never fired. We added machine gun bursts for dramatic purposes.

p. 326. *More chatter came from the ship, Japanese gibberish*: MEYER [p. 12] and LAWTON (p. 125) both mention *Arisan Maru* survivors being able to see the Japanese officers on board the destroyer, examining the lifeboat through binoculars.

p. 326. *The destroyer departed*: MEYER [p. 12] notes that the destroyer left suddenly, perhaps convinced the lifeboat passengers were dead. LAWTON (p. 125) confirms that the destroyer's departure was quick. OVERBECK's account suggests the *Harukaze* might have received an urgent order to relocate, given the destroyer's abrupt sounding of bells, activity on deck, and swift speed toward the horizon.

p. 327. *"They're gone," he said, sighing*: MEYER [p. 12] notes the men's sense of relief after the Japanese destroyer departed and how it was fortunate that they had not yet rigged the sail when the destroyer first arrived. LAWTON (p. 125) confirms this good fortune, adding that the destroyer would have fired upon and killed the men if their lifeboat had been under sail.

Part 5, Chapter 7: Revelations

p. 330. *"Hell, us skippers are so spoiled now, we complain if a convoy shows up ten minutes late."*: Various sources quip that submarine commanders were disappointed if a convoy did not arrive within minutes of its predicted time and at the expected location. See, for example, www.microworks.net /pacific/intelligence/submarines.htm.

p. 331. *"So our code breakers told you the* Arisan Maru *was carrying American POWs?"*: Code-breaking units and Submarine Command knew which ships carried Allied POWs, but they probably did not provide specifics to submarine commanders. They ordered submarine skippers to attack convoys, not individual ships. Like other skippers, Commander Blakely likely knew that any given torpedo could kill hundreds of Allied POWs, but he lacked specifics. We adjusted this for dramatic purposes.

p. 331. *"Seven-five-zero," the helmsman said, the last words Blakely or his men in the control room would ever hear*: No one knows the exact circumstances of the USS *Shark*'s demise. Our scenario involves the *Shark* being sunk after surfacing to search for Allied POWs. We based this on Vice Admiral Charles Lockwood's direct assertion after the war that the *Shark* might have been sunk while trying to rescue American prisoners of war (Lockwood, *Sink 'Em All*, p. 211).

Part 5, Chapter 8: New Mission

p. 334. *Rudowski's survival-of-the-fittest, law-of-the-jungle choices*: OVERBECK and others mention the law of the jungle and how it slowly consumed POWs trapped inside the *Arisan Maru*.

p. 335. *he knew he needed to sail west*: WILBER (p. 151) notes that the Americans had a general idea which direction would lead them toward China.

p. 336. *He thought of Sarah and the North Star*: OVERBECK mentions navigating the lifeboat by the North Star. The star's location helped him maintain a westward course toward the China coast. WILBER (p. 151) also mentions the men using the North Star to navigate on the lifeboat, a technique he learned from his father.

p. 336. *He took catnaps now and then, and fatigue and hunger played tricks with his mind*: OVERBECK describes mental strain during this stretch. He saw lights and heard the voices of his dying friends on the *Arisan Maru* as they screamed for help and called his name.

p. 336. *Two squalls nearly sunk the boat, but also dropped gallons of fresh rainwater into it*: In reality, the five men in the lifeboat had enough food and water to reach China if they rationed it carefully. LAWTON (p. 124) describes them finding a five-gallon wooden keg of fresh water that bumped against their boat. BRITTAN comments on this lucky find and says it was two kegs of fresh water, not one. Anton Cichy mentions in BRITTAN that Calvin Graef was put in charge of rationing the water.

p. 337. *an explosion of red, green, and blue lights danced in the water around the lifeboat's hull*: Our description here expands on the colorful phosphorescence mentioned in OVERBECK.

p. 337. *On the morning of the third day, as Sam sliced through the sea with a full sail*: LAWTON (p. 126) states that although the storm was slackening, the typhoon's winds were still strong enough to make sailing dangerous.

p. 337. *a dark speck appeared on the western horizon*: OVERBECK notes that they did not see any other vessels before this moment, although they did spot a single plane passing high above them. The mood was upbeat as the Americans planned for their arrival on shore.

p. 337. *Ten minutes later, Sam determined the specks were boats*: The Chinese fishing junks came into view around dusk on October 26 (WILBER,

p. 151). For dramatic purposes, we slightly adjusted dates here and for the remainder of the story.

p. 337. *"Let this be the China coast and let those be Chinese fishing junks."*: MEYER [p. 12] estimates the Americans had a fifty-fifty chance that the fishermen were Chinese, not Japanese. Even if they were Chinese, the fishermen might turn the Americans over to the Japanese military for a bounty. OVERBECK mentions that the Americans discussed their options then voted to approach one of the junks.

p. 337. *He picked a fishing boat at random and sailed straight for it*: Eyewitness accounts vary regarding the number of fishing vessels. GRAEF (p. 180) says two, and MEYER [p. 12] suggests more than two. OVERBECK implies multiple junks.

p. 337. *calling out when he reached the boat's side, his voice hoarse and weak. "Hello?"*: MEYER [p. 12] describes making initial contact with the fishing boat. When the Americans drew near and yelled, several Chinese men, women, and children emerged from the large junk's cabin to stare.

p. 338. *"Thank you," Sam said when two young men helped him climb aboard*: MEYER [p. 12] describes quickly being helped aboard. WILBER (p. 152) adds that a rope was tossed to the lifeboat, then used to pull the Americans on board.

p. 338. *He counted eight men*: Ninety-six-year-old *Arisan Maru* survivor Anton Cichy specified in a 2010 interview in ZDON [p. 7] that the Chinese fishermen were big, sturdy, and eight in number.

p. 338. *An imposing six-foot-tall man emerged from below deck*: OVERBECK details meeting the junk captain, including the man's mustache, large build, and look of authority.

Part 5, Chapter 9: American GI

p. 339. *British or American?*: The captain's written question about nationality comes from WILBER (p. 152).

p. 339. *He extended both arms straight in front of him and slowly pointed his thumbs up*: The thumbs-up comes from MEYER [p. 12], who notes that upon hearing the Americans mention Chiang Kai-shek, the junk captain put his two thumbs up in a victory sign.

p. 339. *"Japan no good."*: OVERBECK richly details the junk captain and the Americans' efforts to communicate through drawings, gestures, and words to signal they were allies, not enemies. Overbeck drew a Japanese flag and spat on it, and the Chinese crew responded with smiles and comments. When the junk captain also spat on the Japanese flag, the Americans felt confident they were among friends.

p. 340. *After the workers sank what was left of Sam's boat*: MEYER [p. 12] details how the fishermen stripped the boat of anything valuable, chopped the wood to use as fuel, then sank what remained. OVERBECK adds that when only the lifeboat's steel shell was left, the fishermen poked a hole in it, and the vessel quickly sank.

p. 340. *The junk set sail, and the crew moved Sam below deck*: OVERBECK mentions that the passageways and rooms below deck were so low the Americans could not stand upright.

p. 340. *Women brought Sam clothing and fish, a paste-like rice, and stale bread, which he moistened with warm tea*: MASTERSON (p. 76) details how the Americans were in such poor condition that their Chinese hosts started them on watery rice gruel, served about every hour, to avoid shocking their weakened bodies.

p. 340. *They brought out a towel and a bucket of heated water, and some of the men, including Sam, bathed*: WILBER (p. 152) mentions that the men received water and towels for bathing, then Chinese clothing, blankets, and spots on the deck where they could sleep.

p. 340. *Sam slept in the crew quarters beneath warm blankets for the first time in years*: MEYER [p. 12] says the seas were so rough the men held on to one another to keep from rolling overboard. WILBER (p. 153) adds that rain began to fall, so the Chinese crew ushered the Americans back below deck.

p. 340. *A broad bay stretched along a coastline of white sand*: The five Americans sighted the China coast on the morning of October 27 (WILBER, p. 153). MEYER [p. 12] estimates they were anchored roughly two miles from shore. *Arisan Maru* survivors noted in their official statement that the fishing junk had picked them up about fifty miles off the China coast (JOINT STATEMENT, p. 2).

p. 340. *"Zung Gwok," the captain said. China*: Our translation here draws not from modern, generic Cantonese but rather from a traditional dialect believed to have been spoken in this specific region when the events took place.

p. 340. *another Chinese junk pulled alongside, its crew passing them a bunch of bananas but talking animatedly*: MEYER [p. 12] details this meeting during which the Americans received delicious bananas and a warning to move before the Japanese military arrived.

p. 340. *"Jat Bun gwai," came the captain's reply. Then he added in English, "Japanese."*: The exact translation is "the Japanese ghost," a historical way of referring to the Japanese at that time, reflecting a disapproving attitude toward Japan.

p. 341. *"We go to China to day."*: According to WILBER (p. 152), the Americans weren't sure if the captain's words meant today or in two days.

p. 341. *The captain climbed in*: MEYER [p. 12] mentions a small rowboat being brought from another junk, and the large captain boarding it with the Americans.

p. 341. *When they neared the coast, Sam split his focus between the outpost and the shore*: WILBER (p. 153) indicates that a Japanese military outpost sat just three miles from where the Americans came ashore.

p. 341. *Instead of landing, the captain slipped through a narrow gap into a shallow estuary, the sandy bottom only three feet below. Japanese ships could not follow them*: WILBER (p. 153) explains that the shallow estuary entrance would require dredging if the Japanese wanted warships to enter.

p. 341. *"Japanese there."*: WILBER (p. 153) describes this as the only spot on the China coast that the Japanese did not occupy. LAWTON (p. 126) confirms the Americans' fortuitous landing on a rare stretch of China coast not occupied by Japanese forces, perhaps due to its isolation. We found a declassified memorandum dated November 1, 1944, in which senior military officials in Washington, DC, urgently discuss which parts of the Chinese coast were still unoccupied. Perhaps they had potential *Arisan Maru* survivors in mind.

p. 341. *The silent countryside of rice paddies, low hills, and lush forests passed by for the next two hours*: WILBER (p. 153) notes the sampan journey took roughly two hours.

p. 341. *"Kitchioh," he said*: WILBER (p. 153) specifies the village name as Kitchioh, with these coordinates: latitude 22.8167, longitude 115.8000 (22°49' N, 115°47'60" E). OVERBECK confirms the village name and puts its location halfway between Swatow and Hong Kong.

p. 341. *He took a step and waved for Sam to follow*: Accounts vary, but Calvin Graef states that all five Americans entered the village stark naked (MASTERSON, p. 77). WILBER (p. 153) suggests that the men wore Chinese clothing received on the fishing boat.

p. 341. *He followed him along a dirt road past rustic homes, some made of cement with tin roofs. Others had mud walls and thatched roofs*: Arisan Maru survivors' estimates of Kitchioh's size vary. GRAEF (p. 180) calls it a tiny village. OVERBECK refers to it as a good-sized village. Calvin Graef states in MASTERSON (p. 77) that Kitchioh was a fairly good-sized city.

p. 342. *He gripped the fisherman's thick thumb and said, "Ah ba.":* *Ah ba* means "Father" in traditional Cantonese.

p. 342. *The little boy first to approach Sam gently stroked the hair on Sam's leathery arm*: OVERBECK describes numerous local boys' fascination with the hair on the Americans' legs, including pulling the hairs out as mementos.

p. 342. *Sam thought of this man as the village mayor or elder and bowed deep and long to show respect*: MEYER [p. 13] mentions that the mayor soon appeared.

p. 343. *He excused himself several times to throw up, but always returned and slowly ate more*: Calvin Graef details this food binge in MASTERSON (p. 78), including the constant eating and throwing up. The starving men hoped to retain the nutrients needed to build strength for their upcoming journey.

p. 343. *Late in the afternoon, Sam got a warm bucket to bathe with and a clean set of Chinese clothes*: GRAEF (p. 180) mentions the Americans being entertained like royalty, including gifts of Chinese clothing and enjoying an eight-course dinner.

p. 343. *Evening came, and he enjoyed another meal seated at a large, round table in the mayor's wooden house*: OVERBECK details the first-night banquet, including numerous toasts with rice wine.

p. 343. *Their words flew past Sam, but their expressions of friendship reassured him*: Calvin Graef details how well Chinese hosts treated the Americans. The villagers displayed many acts of kindness, including giving Graef medicine for his vomiting and sores (MASTERSON, p. 79).

p. 343. *The drinking and feasting did not end until late in the evening*: OVERBECK describes the banquet winding down and the men sleeping in a school, using blocks of wood as pillows.

p. 343. *"Japanese soldiers coming," he explained*: BRITTAN describes the Americans' desire to rest and regain strength, only to learn in the middle of the night that a Japanese garrison had sent troops to capture them. OVERBECK provides similar details, adding that the Japanese soldiers would come from an offshore island nearby. Other accounts indicate the men waited until morning to depart and also met an American soldier (spy) in the village.

Part 5, Chapter 10: Qiu Jin

p. 345. *Sam stumbled from bed, fumbled with his borrowed clothes, and staggered outside*: MEYER [p. 13] states the Americans returned the borrowed clothing before departing because the pants and sweaters were too valuable to their owners. The men left town wearing underwear the junk captain gave them.

p. 346. *"He says he is sorry," Qiu Jin said. "Many spies here. A Japanese military outpost learned you are here. They are sending troops."*: WILBER (p. 155) states that a local official explained the possible presence of Japanese spies in the village. LAWTON (p. 126) details how the Chinese hosts were friendly but worried about Japanese punishment. They insisted that the Americans move on.

p. 346. *Sam tailed Qiu Jin along narrow dirt trails*: WILBER (p. 155) speculates that one reason Japanese forces bypassed Kitchioh was due to its lack of roads.

p. 346. *She kept a fast pace*: MASTERSON (pp. 79–80) describes the expected pursuit. The Chinese hosts learned that the Japanese military knew about the Americans and would arrive in the morning.

p. 347. *"Nanjing?" Sam said*: In December 1937, the Japanese army swept into the ancient Chinese city of Nanking (Nanjing), then proceeded to loot and burn the defenseless city. The army systematically raped, tortured, and murdered more than 300,000 Chinese civilians. Several books, documentaries, and movies detail Japanese atrocities in Nanjing, including Iris Chang's *The Rape of Nanking: The Forgotten Holocaust of World War II* (New York: Basic Books, 1997).

p. 347. *"Will the Japanese hurt your father for helping me escape?"*: LAWTON (p. 126) mentions the Kitchioh villagers were welcoming, but afraid of punishment if caught sheltering Americans. Ample documentation describes Japanese brutality toward Chinese civilians during World War II. The cruelty increased after locals assisted American aircraft crews from the Doolittle Raid. We do not know what happened, if anything, to the Kitchioh villagers after the *Arisan Maru* survivors departed. Did Japanese troops really arrive the next morning? If yes, did they punish villagers for assisting the Americans?

p. 347. *Qiu Jin climbed atop it and scanned the landscape behind them for pursuers*: OVERBECK details the walk, noting the hot sun, people working in farm fields, and how concerns about Japanese pursuers motivated the Americans to walk quickly.

Part 5, Chapter 11: Blistered Steps

p. 349. *Sam dangled his feet in the water.* Anton Cichy describes blistered feet and the painful thirty-mile walk in ZDON [p. 8], made worse by their lack of shoes. Calvin Graef adds in BRITTAN that the men walked all night and the next day with little rest.

p. 350. *The ferryman pulled on a thick rope stretched across the river.* The ferry pulled by ropes comes from Anton Cichy's account in ZDON [p. 8].

p. 350. *Every three miles or so, they stopped at a stone gatehouse with an elaborate archway stretched over the road:* OVERBECK describes the men stopping at a stone gatehouse every three miles to gorge themselves on eggs, rice cakes, fish, fruit, and other food items bought from local vendors.

p. 350. *They went into the villages to purchase more rice cakes, hard-boiled eggs, tea, and other items from vendors' stalls:* OVERBECK describes using tea to quench thirst rather than untreated water. Because the tea was served in tiny porcelain cups and was so hot the men could only sip it, they ordered ten at a time.

p. 350. *"Japanese attacking this region now. Major offensive."*: The Japanese military waged a major offensive called Operation *Ichi-Go* (Operation Number One) from April to December of 1944. The ambitious campaign involved an estimated 450,000 troops in a series of major battles intended to create a land route to French Indochina and knock out American air bases in southwestern China. For details, see Stanley Sandler, ed., *World War II in the Pacific: An Encyclopedia* (New York: Routledge, 2000). For a personal account of the American retreat, see Theodore White's 1958 book *The Mountain Road* and its 1960 movie adaptation starring Jimmy Stewart.

p. 351. *"This city is Lukfung. We sleep here."*: Most modern maps spell this city as Lufeng, but we use its historical spelling, Lukfung, per US military maps from that time and WILBER (p. 155).

p. 351. *"He wants to know if you're a downed pilot"*: A loose network of Chinese guerillas, civilians, and US intelligence agents collaborated to recover and return downed American crews, mostly bombers from the Fourteenth Air Force in Kunming (Dan C. Pinck, *Journey to Peking: A Secret Agent in Wartime China* [Annapolis, MD: Naval Institute Press, 2003]).

p. 351. *Sam did his best to eat the food, until his stomach rebelled*: The stomach issue comes from OVERBECK, who describes one of the Americans being unable to hold his meals along the road but always willing to eat again at their next stop.

p. 351. *She slid back a chair and urged Sam to sit, then removed the covers of various dishes and named them in Cantonese*: We have Sam sleep in and eat a big breakfast per WILBER (p. 155), who notes the POWs ate well on the morning of October 30 before departing.

p. 352. *She laughed, reached into a bag, and pulled out a pair of traditional Chinese shoes*: Anton Cichy mentions in ZDON [p. 8] that a Chinese government official gave the Americans cash, which they quickly used to have shoes made. MEYER [p. 13] confirms this, adding that the men also had clothing made.

p. 352. *Outside, two men stood next to an oversized wood-and-wicker chair strapped atop two horizontal poles*: Anton Cichy mentions in ZDON [p. 8] that on this day, the men were carried farther inland by way of sedan chairs.

p. 352. *"You ride today"*: OVERBECK provides details on the sedan chairs, their strong porters, and the experience of riding in one.

p. 352. *"When shopping, I hear in market the Japanese search hard for you."*: Anton Cichy mentions in ZDON [p. 8] that the Americans learned the Japanese were searching diligently for them.

p. 352. *A plane with a large red circle painted under each wing flew over the hill, low and slow*: Calvin Graef mentions the search planes in BRITTAN, noting that the planes dropped low to inspect the men. Graef also describes how the Americans' Chinese attire helped them blend in with other people on the road, concealing them from the low-flying search planes (MASTERSON, p. 80).

Part 5, Chapter 12: A Prisoner Within

p. 355. *the city of Haifeng*: WILBER (p. 155) specifies the city name as Hoifung, but spellings vary.

p. 355. *"Xie xie,"* Sam said to the departing men: Anton Cichy appreciates the porters in ZDON [p. 8], marveling that they covered thirty miles in just half a day.

p. 355. *Copper-colored brassware hung on storefront pegs*: The description of Haifeng draws from a local US intelligence agent's evocative portrayal of nearby Hingning (Dan C. Pinck, *Journey to Peking: A Secret Agent in Wartime China* [Annapolis, MD: Naval Institute Press, 2003], p. 4).

p. 356. *"The Japanese came like a swarm of locusts and destroyed everything, looking for the pilots. They burned entire villages."*: Japanese forces killed at least 10,000 Chinese civilians in retaliation for helping the Doolittle Raid aircraft crew members, and up to a quarter million people as part of the larger Zhejiang-Jiangxi campaign. The Japanese commander Shunroku

Hata was sentenced in 1948 as a war criminal for failing to prevent the massacre of 250,000 Chinese civilians.

p. 356. *Afterward, Qiu Jin arranged a traditional massage*: Details for Sam's massage, agonizing but effective, were inspired by a real massage described in OVERBECK.

p. 357. *They named her after a famous educator and activist who fought for women's rights*: Several sources document the historical Qiu Jin, an eloquent orator who spoke out for Chinese women's rights such as the freedom to marry, freedom of education, and abolishment of the practice of foot binding.

p. 358. *"When Japanese soldiers came to our school, they raped and killed many girls for many hours."*: As noted earlier, numerous books, movies, and other media document the Japanese attack on Nanjing (Nanking). Japanese soldiers raped tens of thousands of women and girls, including ones hiding at Ginling Women's College and other educational institutions. See, for example, Sheng-Ping Guo, "The Living Goddess of Mercy at the Rape of Nanking: Minnie Vautrin and the Ginling Refugee Camp in World War II (1937–1938)," *Religions* 7, no. 12 (December 17, 2016): 150, https://doi.org/10.3390/rel7120150.

p. 359. *"Only Father and I know what we were forced to do. And now you."*: The incestual rape draws from author Iris Chang's bestselling book on the Nanjing massacre, in which she describes sadistic Japanese soldiers forcing Chinese men to commit incest with their daughters, sisters, and mothers (*The Rape of Nanking: The Forgotten Holocaust of World War II* [New York: Basic Books, 1997], p. 95).

p. 360. *Sam's own trauma had certainly turned him into a different person, but he could not yet look at what he'd been through with the same perspective*: The concept of converting trauma into something positive is called "posttraumatic growth." Since the 1990s, hundreds of scientific studies have examined posttraumatic growth in a variety of subjects and settings. For a 2020 *Harvard Business Review* article about the concept, written by its founding practitioner, Richard G. Tedeschi, see "Growth after Trauma" at https://hbr.org/2020/07/growth-after-trauma.

Part 5, Chapter 13: This Can't Happen

p. 361. *The following day, Sam and Qiu Jin traveled for miles in carriages towed behind bicycles*: OVERBECK describes the bicycles, including how fast and uncomfortable they were compared to the sedan chairs.

p. 361. *Sturdy porters pedaled across fertile green valleys dotted with walled villages*: The description of local scenery draws from OVERBECK, who provides vivid details on the exotic sights and sounds.

p. 361. *When the incline became too steep, Sam and Qiu Jin proceeded on foot while their porters carried the bicycles on their shoulders*: OVERBECK mentions steep mountain passes where the porters carried the bicycles while the former prisoners walked. MEYER [p. 13] confirms the bicycles had to be carried at times due to steep hills.

p. 362. *A dozen uniformed soldiers blocked their path*: Our description of the soldiers draws from American intelligence agent Daniel Pinck, who lived in this area at the time and describes guns and grenades carried by local Chinese guerillas. Pinck notes that although the guerillas appeared malnourished, they carried heavy rifles of Balkan manufacture, cartridge belts, and Czechoslovakian hand grenades (Dan C. Pinck, *Journey to Peking: A Secret Agent in Wartime China* [Annapolis, MD: Naval Institute Press, 2003], p. 22).

Part 5, Chapter 14: A War Hero

p. 365. *"Not Japanese soldiers. Chinese guerillas."*: This case of mistaken identity loosely draws from a real incident mentioned in MEYER [p. 13], where the Americans were nearly shot by a Chinese guard. The Americans communicated their identity just in time.

p. 365. *"They will escort us the rest of the way."*: WILBER (pp. 154–55) mentions a Chinese leader, General Yu, who assisted the five escapees directly and indirectly during their walk to freedom, working with an American intelligence agent, Ed Baron. On their second day in China, General Yu sent a security detail to accompany the Americans and the interpreter who was already with them. For dramatic purposes, we have the security detail meet Sam on the road rather than in Lukfung. We also have Sam meet his first fellow American in Hingning, not earlier.

p. 366. *Sam had been too focused on the men's weapons to notice their simple uniforms lacked the buttoned shirts, high boots, and other attire of professional Japanese soldiers*: Japanese soldiers' uniforms varied across time and theater and were particularly ragtag by this stage of the China campaign. An untrained and stressed person like Sam could mistake Chinese guerillas— which he would never have seen before and might not have known existed—for poorly supplied Japanese soldiers.

p. 366. *a city surrounded by a checkerboard of rice paddies*: American intelligence agent Daniel Pinck lived in this area at the time and describes this city, Hingning, as sitting amid a valley of rice paddy fields (Dan C. Pinck, *Journey to Peking: A Secret Agent in Wartime China* [Annapolis, MD: Naval Institute Press, 2003], p. 8).

p. 367. *A flag billowed in the breeze from each pole—the center flag red, white, and blue, with stars and stripes*: *Arisan Maru* survivor Avery Wilber describes seeing a US flag and how wonderful a sight it was after two and a half long years. ("On Corregidor, 1941," unpublished manuscript by Avery Wilber, https://cdn.townweb.com/townofnavarino.org/wp-content/uploads/2019/02/AverysStory.pdf).

p. 367. *When the tears started, he was helpless to stop them*: GRAEF (p. 180) describes the men breaking down upon seeing an American flag, crying like babies. Graef provides additional, vivid details and powerful emotions in MASTERSON (p. 86).

p. 367. *"I'm Major Lucas Fletcher. And I am damn proud to welcome you."*: Major Lucas Fletcher was in charge of this station and oversaw US intelligence operations in southeastern China. Before the war, Fletcher worked as a sales agent in China for the British and American Tobacco Company (Dan C. Pinck, *Journey to Peking: A Secret Agent in Wartime China* [Annapolis, MD: Naval Institute Press, 2003], p. 4).

p. 367. *"The United States of America thanks you, ma'am."*: At this stage of the war, the American government paid a going rate of one hundred dollars in gold to Chinese fishermen and others for each American they safely delivered, usually downed pilots (WILBER, p. 155).

p. 368. *"We provide meteorological data to the Fourteenth Air Force"*: Established in March 1943 in Kunming, the Fourteenth Air Force played a crucial role in supporting the Chinese military and attacking Japanese forces. From the early Flying Tigers to the latter units, the Fourteenth Air Force waged a long and difficult campaign that hampered the Japanese war effort. Several histories discuss the Fourteenth Air Force, for example, Carl Molesworth, *Wing to Wing: Air Combat in China, 1943–45* (New York: Orion Books, 1990).

p. 368. *"I've been saving a good bottle of whiskey for Christmas"*: GRAEF (p. 180) mentions the commanding officer opening a special bottle of whiskey he had been saving for Christmas. The whiskey was probably Four Roses, based on a description of Major Fletcher by one of his colleagues (*Journey to Peking: A Secret Agent in Wartime China* [Annapolis, MD: Naval Institute Press, 2003], p. 8).

p. 368. *"The acronym is A-G-F-R-T-S, so . . . Ag-farts."*: Humorously called "Ag-farts," the 5329th Air and Ground Forces Resources and Technical Staff (AGFRTS) housed intelligence agents from the Office of Strategic Services (OSS), predecessor to the modern Central Intelligence Agency (CIA). Richard Harris Smith notes in his detailed history that most AGFRTS intelligence officers had lived in China before the war and could navigate the language, food, and customs (Richard Harris Smith, *OSS: The Secret History of America's First Central Intelligence Agency* [Guilford, CT: Lyons Press, 1972], p. 240).

Part 6, Chapter 1: Dreams Change

p. 374. *"Only one survivor."*: The US government learned after the war ended that a total of nine POWs survived the *Arisan Maru* sinking. In addition to the five men who sailed a lifeboat to China, four prisoners were plucked from the sea by Japanese warships and taken back into captivity. One died there. The afterword provides more details.

p. 374. *"I've come to learn that secrecy is a double-edged sword," he said*: The wording here is inspired by HOLMES (p. 215), where secrecy is compared to a weapon that can cause deeper wounds on its bearer than upon adversaries.

p. 374. *"We don't get medals, Ensign Haber. Our work is secret, even within the military."*: HOLMES (p. 62) mentions that the secret nature of his work slowed his career advancement compared to peers. MUNDY (p. 16) adds that women in code breaking had no expectation of public recognition for the secret work they did. MUNDY (p. 19) also notes that the female code breakers took their secrecy oath seriously, belonging to a generation of women who neither expected nor received acclaim for their civic accomplishments.

Part 6, Chapter 2: Over the Hump

p. 380. *His Chinese driver bounced the rickety contraption along steep, twisting roads*: In MASTERSON (p. 83), Calvin Graef quips that the decrepit truck seemed to be held together by baling wire and prayers. But each time the truck broke down the driver was able to repair it.

p. 380. *The next day, he and his driver covered another two hundred miles and reached a small base with an airstrip*: *Arisan Maru* survivor Avery Wilber describes this leg of the journey ("On Corregidor, 1941," unpublished manuscript by Avery Wilber, https://cdn.townweb.com/townofnavarino .org/wp-content/uploads/2019/02/AverysStory.pdf).

p. 380. *He also enjoyed his first American food in years*: MEYER [p. 13] describes spending three comfortable days at this landing strip, savoring American food served on white tablecloths with real silverware, not chopsticks.

p. 381. *They flew eight hundred miles over enemy-held territory to China's southwestern corner*: *Arisan Maru* survivor Avery Wilber mentions the flight over enemy-held territory, noting that the survivors waited two days until a plane could come fly them out ("On Corregidor, 1941," unpublished manuscript by Avery Wilber, https://cdn.townweb.com /townofnavarino.org/wp-content/uploads/2019/02/AverysStory.pdf).

p. 381. *Sam shared more details about his story beyond what Major Fletcher's message had provided them*: WILBER (p. 156) notes that the escapees received a personal welcome from General Chennault and told their story with a rapt audience. Claire Lee Chennault led the Flying Tigers and the Republic of China Air Force in World War II. For details, see his memoir, *Way of a Fighter: The Memoirs of Claire Lee Chennault* (New York: G. P. Putnam's Sons, 1949).

p. 381. *Sam figured the building was as safe as anywhere else, so he stayed behind and moved from table to table, eating the abandoned desserts*: Sam's opportunistic gorging on chocolate desserts during a bombing raid draws from real events described in MASTERSON (p. 88).

p. 381. *Sam's presence at Kunming was kept quiet*: WILBER (p. 156) specifies the departure date as November 28. The five *Arisan Maru* survivors spent roughly four weeks traveling and recovering in China, but we condensed that period.

p. 381. *Major General Chennault told Sam he'd handpicked Sanders for the critical assignment of getting Sam home, and he had ordered Sanders to keep Sam from talking to anyone until the US Army could debrief him*: WILBER (p. 157) mentions their escort officer, Major Sanders. Calvin Graef notes in MASTERSON (p. 87) that Chennault (misidentified in MASTERSON as "Chaevis") gave the assignment to Major Sanders, with orders from Washington that the survivors were not to speak to anyone except Major Sanders during their trip home.

p. 381. *Their airplane, nicknamed Double Trouble*: Calvin Graef mentions the airplane's nose art in MASTERSON (p. 91).

p. 381. *When it rose over the Himalayas, the world's tallest mountain range, many of its peaks hidden in clouds, two-hundred-mile-per-hour winds buffeted the plane*: Calvin Graef provides a riveting account of this flight in MASTERSON (p. 90), including sudden drops caused by strong winds.

p. 381. *Freezing temperatures inside the aircraft added to Sam's misery*: *Arisan Maru* survivor Avery Wilber mentions that the flight over the Himalayas was cold because the plane lacked a functioning heater ("On Corregidor, 1941," unpublished manuscript by Avery Wilber, https://cdn.townweb .com/townofnavarino.org/wp-content/uploads/2019/02/AverysStory.pdf).

p. 381. *"There are more than four hundred wrecks just like it spread across these mountains. The pilots call it 'the hump.'"*: Calvin Graef describes the dangerous crossing in MASTERSON (p. 90), noting the large percentage of planes that crashed during the attempt.

p. 382. *Sam wobbled along the tarmac on weak legs*: Calvin Graef notes in MASTERSON (p. 91) that he shook so badly, it probably appeared he was having a malaria attack.

p. 382. *The pilot, however, strode over to the chief mechanic and received a five-dollar bill*: The five-dollar bet comes from Calvin Graef's account in MASTERSON (p. 91). The chief mechanic had wagered that the airplane could not fly to Kunming and back.

p. 382. *"Home to the 490th Bombardment Squadron, Medium."*: Detailed in many books and documentaries, the 490th Bomb Squadron was nicknamed Burma Bridge Busters. The pilots developed a special bombing technique that helped them destroy more than two hundred bridges, slowing the Japanese advance.

p. 382. *"You won't stay long." The officer waved a piece of paper at Sam*: This communications chief may have been Arnold Spielberg, father of Hollywood filmmaker Steven Spielberg. Master Sergeant Arnold Spielberg completed his duty around this time, then sailed by ship back to the USA in December. For a 2006 interview in which Arnold Spielberg details his time in India, see Arnold Spielberg, "An Interview

with Arnold Spielberg for the Rutgers Oral History Archives," by Sandra
Stewart Holyoak and Shaun Illingworth, Rutgers Oral History Archives,
May 12, 2006, https://oralhistory.rutgers.edu/alphabetical-index
/interviewees/30-interview-html-text/146-spielberg-arnold.

p. 382. *"FDR ordered you home right away."*: BRITTAN mentions that FDR
issued a direct order for the five men to be returned to Washington, DC.
Calvin Graef confirms FDR's order in MASTERSON (p. 87), citing
Major General Chennault (misidentified in MASTERSON as "Chaevis").

p. 382. *"They made us bump all the other passengers from your flight"*: The *Arisan
Maru* survivors departed after just three or four hours on the ground.
When they saw passengers bumped off their next plane, they realized
that the higher-ups were tightening the level of security around them
(MASTERSON, p. 92).

p. 382. *They treated Sam to aerial views of the Taj Mahal and other sights*:
MASTERSON (p. 92) details the cargo plane buzzing the Taj Mahal,
chasing camels over Egyptian sand dunes, and other unauthorized side
trips. Calvin Graef quipped that their daring pilot nearly flew them
through the Taj Mahal's front door.

p. 382. *The plane lost one engine and a wheel shortly after departing*: Arisan
Maru survivor Avery Wilber mentions the plane's mechanical problems
at Abadan, noting that they had to turn back because of engine trouble
("On Corregidor, 1941," unpublished manuscript by Avery Wilber,
https://cdn.townweb.com/townofnavarino.org/wp-content/uploads
/2019/02/AverysStory.pdf).

p. 382. *"You landed her on one wing, one wheel, and the nose."*: Sam's
commentary on the pilot's daring landing draws from that of *Arisan Maru*
survivor Calvin Graef in MASTERSON (p. 92).

p. 383. *"I got firm orders not to ask you questions, but I reckon your being alive involves a miracle or two."*: Calvin Graef details the unnamed pilot's words in MASTERSON (p. 93).

p. 383. *The pilot dropped low to give Sam close-up views of Jericho, Jerusalem, and Palestine*: The list of locations comes from *Arisan Maru* survivor Avery Wilber, who mentions that the pilot flew low over these places ("On Corregidor, 1941," unpublished manuscript by Avery Wilber, https://cdn .townweb.com/townofnavarino.org/wp-content/uploads/2019/02 /AverysStory.pdf).

p. 383. *"They want you home 'yesterday.'"*: MASTERSON (pp. 93–94) details landing in Cairo, then checking into a hotel for the night, only to learn that the Washington, DC, higher-ups wanted the survivors in the nation's capital immediately. The exhausted men dressed, returned to the airport, and boarded another plane.

p. 383. *sat next to two large airplane engines headed to the United States for repairs*: *Arisan Maru* survivor Avery Wilber describes the two large airplane engines and how each time the plane hit turbulence, he feared the engines might break loose and crush him ("On Corregidor, 1941," unpublished manuscript by Avery Wilber, https://cdn.townweb.com /townofnavarino.org/wp-content/uploads/2019/02/AverysStory.pdf).

p. 383. *In Casablanca, Sam was to switch to a chartered Pan American Airways military flight*: After sixty officers were kicked off the airplane and the five *Arisan Maru* passengers boarded, one survivor quipped that those officers probably assumed the newcomers were criminals on their way to spend a lifetime in prison (MASTERSON, p. 94).

p. 383. *Sam stared out the airplane window at the vast, starry solitude*: Sam's moment of reverie comes from Calvin Graef's description in

MASTERSON (p. 95). As Graef stared out the window, he felt a divine presence and a sense of oneness with the galaxy.

Part 6, Chapter 3: American Soil

p. 385. *As the plane approached New York City, Sam was alerted to the darkened Statue of Liberty*: Sam's description and emotion draws from Calvin Graef's in MASTERSON (pp. 95–96). MEYER [p. 13] mentions shouting out loud as he spotted New York City lights and realized he was finally home.

p. 385. *In the terminal, a skeptical customs official delayed Sam's arrival*: Sam's delay at customs closely follows real events detailed in WILBER (p. 157).

p. 385. *Sanders stepped away to make a phone call*: We have few details on Major Sanders, except that he joined the five survivors in Kunming, escorted them all the way home, stayed with them in Washington, DC, and enforced the explicit order that the men speak to no one. Our best guess is that this was Homer L. Sanders.

p. 385. *Major Sanders had more news. They had been ordered straight to Washington, DC*: MASTERSON (p. 96) details the last-minute order to proceed straight to Washington, DC, as well as the flight there.

p. 386. *"Thousands of them in both the Army and the Navy," the major said*: While being driven to the Statler Hotel, the *Arisan Maru* survivors were surprised to learn that women now served in the military, including their driver. Their escort mentioned the excellent work the women were doing (MASTERSON, p. 104).

p. 386. *"Order food, drinks, whatever you want, and charge it to the Army"*: The offer to order food and other items, billed to the Army, comes from Calvin Graef's description in MASTERSON (p. 97).

p. 386. *"After everything I've been through, what my family and my sweetheart have been through, why can't I at least let them know I'm alive?"*: Upon reaching his Statler Hotel room, *Arisan Maru* survivor Calvin Graef phoned several family members, including his wife, Bobbie (MASTERSON, p. 97).

p. 387. *When he opened it, skeletal versions of three friends he'd known in the Philippines stared back at him*: Sam's reunion with three old friends draws from actual events detailed in MASTERSON (p. 97). Sally Mott Freeman also describes this meeting in *The Jersey Brothers: A Missing Naval Officer in the Pacific and His Family's Quest to Bring Him Home* (New York: Simon & Schuster, 2017, p. 386).

p. 388. *He tossed and turned, bewildered by such comfort, and finally pulled a blanket onto the floor, where he slept like a rock*: Calvin Graef describes his inability to sleep on the hotel bed, then sleeping for ten hours straight after he relocated to the floor (MASTERSON, p. 98).

Part 6, Chapter 4: Reentry Shock

p. 389. *Sam spent hours explaining his mistreatment to five armed forces interrogators and a secretary*: Calvin Graef notes that this initial debriefing focused on the recent past, from the *Arisan Maru* sinking to the survivors' arrival in Washington, DC (MASTERSON, p. 99).

p. 390. *Sam signed the final paper, and an official stamped it "TOP SECRET" and whisked it away*: All five *Arisan Maru* survivors in Washington, DC, signed a single joint statement. We reviewed the original copy at the National Archives II. Several of our notes reference JOINT STATEMENT. Each survivor also produced a detailed individual statement for the ensuing war crimes investigation, available in the same National Archives location as their joint statement.

p. 390. *His chief interrogator told him the interview would be used as the basis for a formal war crimes investigation against the Japanese POW guards and Katsuo Yoshida*: WILBER (pp. 173–74) summarizes the results of the investigation and includes a verbatim transcript of the March 12, 1948, final conclusions by the Army's lead prosecutor for the Philippines Area, Frank G. O'Neill. The prosecutor recommended that File #479 be closed because the two responsible parties, both senior Japanese military leaders in the Philippines, had already been tried, sentenced, and hung for similar war crimes. The *Arisan Maru* captain was found, questioned, and interned, then released on the grounds that he was not the person in charge of the prisoners. The report makes no mention of Kiyoshi Yamaji, the second lieutenant in charge of POWs on the *Arisan Maru*. We suspect he died during the war's final months or shortly thereafter.

p. 390. *"Welcome home, soldier. They told me your story."*: Graef describes the meeting with Marshall in MASTERSON (p. 99). Sally Mott Freeman also details the private meeting with General Marshall, noting that the quiet and dignified Marshall apologized to the former prisoners for not being able to help them on Bataan and Corregidor. The *Arisan Maru* survivors thanked Marshall for his candor (Sally Mott Freeman, *The Jersey Brothers: A Missing Naval Officer in the Pacific and His Family's Quest to Bring Him Home* [New York: Simon & Schuster, 2017], p. 386).

p. 391. *Next, General Marshall pinned a Silver Star beside the Purple Heart and handed Sam a Presidential Commendation from Franklin Delano Roosevelt*: Calvin Graef details this emotional medal ceremony in MASTERSON (p. 100).

p. 391. *"You are hereby ordered not to discuss your ordeal without the War Department's explicit permission."*: WILBER (p. 160) notes that the survivors received orders not to speak about their ordeal without Pentagon permission. Calvin Graef attributes this directive to General

Marshall, who explained the need to keep their ordeal top secret (MASTERSON, p. 99).

p. 393. *"And on behalf of a grateful nation, I humbly and graciously thank you for your service.":* Arisan Maru survivors provide few details about their meeting with President Roosevelt. Calvin Graef explains in MASTERSON (p. 100) that the moment was too personal to be discussed publicly. Sally Mott Freeman describes Roosevelt as warm and sympathetic during the meeting (Sally Mott Freeman, *The Jersey Brothers: A Missing Naval Officer in the Pacific and His Family's Quest to Bring Him Home* [New York: Simon & Schuster, 2017], p. 386).

p. 393. *"you should have a great sense of pride for what you have accomplished.":* FDR urging Sam to feel proud of his efforts comes from *Arisan Maru* survivor Calvin Graef's brief account of the meeting (MASTERSON, p. 100).

Part 6, Chapter 5: Paradise

p. 397. *The old saying about not being able to go home again rang true:* Sarah's realization draws from that of *Arisan Maru* survivor Calvin Graef, who returned home to Silver City, New Mexico, and quickly realized he could never fully fit into that community again (MASTERSON, p. 107).

Part 6, Chapter 6: Catching Up

p. 407. *Sam reached below the collar of his shirt and pulled out a string. At the end dangled Sarah's high school class ring:* Sam's ring follows the path of *Arisan Maru* survivor Glenn Oliver, who successfully hid his wife Esther's high school class ring for his entire two-and-a-half-year ordeal (Sally Macdonald, "He Survived—1,800 Fellow Prisoners Aboard Japanese 'Hell Ship' Died 50 Years Ago Today," *Seattle Times*, October 24, 1994).

Part 6, Chapter 8: One More Surprise

p. 417. *"A* Washington Post *newspaper reporter caught wind of the story and started asking questions."*: The enterprising reporter who broke the story was Len C. Schubert, Wisconsin manager for the United Press Association, based in Milwaukee. WILBER (pp. 160–63) details how Schubert discovered the secret story. When Schubert confronted military officials, the Army quickly released a sanitized version of the story to control how the event was portrayed.

p. 417. *U.S. Told 1,800 Americans Died in Sinking of Japanese Prison Ship*: A *New York Times* article with this exact title ran February 17, 1945, on page 3. The subtitle was "One of Five Survivors Describes Torpedoing Last October—Washington, without Confirmation, Asks Foe for Names."

Part 6, Chapter 9: Full Circle

p. 421. *His national speaking tour had taken him by train to eight states*: Sam's national speaking tour draws from the real experience of *Arisan Maru* survivor Calvin Graef, detailed in MASTERSON (pp. 106–7). Graef mostly met with relatives of POWs who were still imprisoned at the time and of those POWs who had died. Graef later acknowledged that he had no idea how painful the speaking tour would be.

p. 423. *spun around to admire the school's motto engraved in the stone archway: "Enter to Learn, Go Forth to Serve."*: This inspiring motto carved above a school entrance draws from the real experience of a prominent WAVE in World War II, Claudine "Scottie" Scott (Tom Brokaw, *The Greatest Generation* [New York: Random House, 1998], p. 152).

Afterword

p. 425. *From 1942 to 1945, an estimated 134 Japanese hellships*: MICHNO (e.g., p. 282) provides extensive details on hellships, including the names and dates they sailed, number of passengers, and number of POW deaths.

p. 425. *The 40 percent POW death rate is staggering by any standard*: The detailed comparisons of death rates come from MICHNO (p. 298).

p. 425. *Horrific conditions on the hellships led to shocking depravities*: Several sources describe murder, vampirism, and other shocking behaviors on hellships. See the relevant notes for details. MICHNO (p. 289) documents how the behaviors increased over time as conditions on ships worsened.

p. 426. *Few movies and books have attempted to tell their story*: The claim that Sony executive Akio Morita blocked distribution of *Return from the River Kwai* appears in MICHNO (p. 305), and is based on documentation from an ensuing lawsuit.

p. 427. *While in Japan, the two men, Joe Brown and John Whitehurst, met with the* Arisan Maru*'s civilian radio operator, ninety-one-year-old Nobumi Ogawa*: Ollie Reed Jr. details the reconciliation visits related to the *Arisan Maru* in "WWII Hell Ships: Loss and a Search for Forgiveness," *Albuquerque Journal*, May 6, 2018. For the Defenders of Bataan and Corregidor Memorial Society, see www.adbcmemorialsociety.org.

p. 428. *Among 3,659 WAVES who served in Hawaii, only 72 worked at JICPOA*: The total number of WAVES who served in Hawaii comes from one of their senior officers, Joy Bright Hancock, in her book *Lady in the Navy: A Personal Reminiscence* (Annapolis, MD: Naval Institute Press, 2014, p. 206). The number of women at JICPOA was harder to find, perhaps due to the secretive nature of their work. The topic receives brief mention in the definitive history of US naval intelligence, on page 235 in *A Century of U.S. Naval Intelligence* by Captain Wyman H. Packard (Washington, DC: Office of Naval Intelligence and the Naval Historical Center, 1996).

p. 430. *The United States also received intelligence from spies in Manila*: MICHNO (p. 294) details Josefina Guerrero and other spies based in Manila, concluding that the Allies certainly knew which convoys carried POWs. We thank Jim Zobel at the MacArthur Memorial for locating the declassified message from a Filipino guerilla unit to Allied headquarters in Australia, noting the October 11, 1944, loading of Allied POWs onto a Japanese freighter in Manila Harbor.

p. 431. *Of the 21,039 documented POW deaths aboard hellships*: The specific numbers and causes of POW deaths on hellships come from MICHNO (p. 292).

p. 431. *Even more shocking is the number of hellships sunk with full knowledge that Allied POWs were on board*: The role of secret Ultra intelligence in sinking hellships comes from MICHNO (pp. 211, 293).

p. 432. *Cichy noted PTSD's long-term physical and mental effects: Arisan Maru* survivor Anton Cichy's description of his PTSD appears in ZDON [p. 10].

ACKNOWLEDGMENTS

First, we thank all who have served and sacrificed. This entire twelve-year project is for you.

Special thanks to the World War II soldiers and sailors. Heroes. Every one of them.

For assistance with historical documents, we thank the National Archives and Records Administration staff, especially Nathaniel Patch. At the Archdiocese of Indianapolis, archivist Julie K. Motyka located vital records. We thank archivist James Zobel at the MacArthur Memorial in Norfolk, Virginia, who found the proverbial needle in a haystack: a Philippine guerilla unit's message informing General MacArthur's command that a Japanese ship full of POWs departed Manila Harbor on October 11, 1944.

We thank more than thirty friends, family members, and others who reviewed early versions of the manuscript. Special shoutout to Mike Kelleher, who served in the Peace Corps with Chris and Jeff in Sierra Leone, West Africa. Mike reviewed rough drafts of the manuscript, provided strategic advice, and gave steady encouragement throughout. Mike even spent hours sifting through boxes of declassified documents at the National Archives and Records Administration, where he made important finds. We are blessed and grateful for his friendship.

Chris especially thanks his wife, Vera Naranjo Segura, whose belief in him surpasses his own. Her love and patience created the space to commit to this project. He also wishes to recognize all of the classroom teachers who foster wonder and empathy through the power of storytelling.

Jeff thanks his wife, Karen Lowell; father, Keith; and late mother and "Army brat," Lynne Langholz. He also thanks his children, Elsie and Jakob, for their kindness and patience during their dad's obsession. Special thanks to Patrick Collins for his support throughout.

Bob thanks his mother, Patty Dugoni, who gave him a love of reading and writing, and his wife, Cristina, daughter, Catherine, and son, Joe, for always understanding when a writer says, "I'm almost done." He isn't. Bob also thanks Chris and Jeff for trusting him with their incredible, decade-long project. He's said many times, how amazed he is at the volume of research that has gone into the re-creation of these events to ensure accuracy and authenticity. He is pleased to have played a part in bringing to life these characters and this story of World War II's atrocities, but also of the enduring and triumphant power of love and of human resilience. May this book serve as a reminder to all of the horror of war, so we are not doomed to repeat it.

A deep, grateful bow to Rebecca Scherer, Logan Harper, Jane Berkey, and the rest of the team at the Jane Rotrosen Agency for their guidance and support, and to Mark Sullivan for his early encouragement and assistance. Special thanks to Meg Ruley, who believed in this project from the outset and shepherded it to completion with her infinite wisdom, patience, and humor. We are lucky to have Meg in our corner.

Thanks to our incredible editor at Lake Union, Danielle Marshall, for championing the novel and insisting on nothing but our best. Thank you to everyone else at Lake Union who supported *Hold Strong*, especially Chantelle Aimée Osman, Jen Bentham, Abi Pollokoff, Valerie Paquin, Michael Schuler, Phyllis DeBlanche, and Karen Parkin. It's quite a team, and we are humbled to be part of it. Special shoutout to developmental editor David Downing for his keen eye and many insightful suggestions. Special thanks also to our copyeditors, Valerie and Michael, who fine-tuned the manuscript and helped to make it sing.

Most important, our sincere thanks to you, our readers. We hope you enjoyed this story and will recommend it to your friends, family members, and colleagues.

ABOUT THE AUTHORS

Photo © Douglas Sonders

Robert Dugoni is the *New York Times, Wall Street Journal, Washington Post*, and Amazon Charts bestselling author of the Tracy Crosswhite series; the Charles Jenkins series; the David Sloane series; several standalone novels, including *A Killing on the Hill, The World Played Chess*, and *The Extraordinary Life of Sam Hell*; and coauthor of the nonfiction exposé *The Cyanide Canary*, a *Washington Post* Best Book of the Year. Dugoni is the recipient of the Nancy Pearl Book Award for fiction, a multi-time winner of the Friends of Mystery Spotted Owl Award for best novel set in the Pacific Northwest, and a finalist for many other awards. His books are sold in more than twenty-five countries, have been translated into more than thirty languages, and have reached millions of readers worldwide. For more information, visit robertdugonibooks.com.

Jeff Langholz, PhD, is an award-winning teacher, researcher, entrepreneur, and writer whose work has appeared in more than 250 media outlets, including the *Wall Street Journal*, the *New York Times*, *National Geographic*, and the *Economist*. His adventures span five continents and include stints as a rice farmer in West Africa with the Peace Corps, a Fulbright Scholar in South Africa, a salmon fisherman in Alaska, a tree farmer in Central America, and a mediator in New York. He is a professor at the Middlebury Institute of International Studies in Monterey, California.

Photo © CarlosCharpentier_live images®

Chris Crabtree teaches middle and high school English language arts and literature at Costa Rica International Academy in Guanacaste, Costa Rica. Chris and his wife, Vera, live in a rustic, rural town on the outskirts of Santa Cruz, Costa Rica, with their dogs Bety and Bruno.